PRAISE FOR ELIZABETH ESSEX
and *Almost a Scandal*

"Elizabeth Essex will dazzle you with her sophisticated blend of vivid historical detail, exquisite characterization, and delicious sexual tension. *Almost a Scandal* is a breathtaking tale of rapturous romance and awe-inspiring adventure!"

> —*USA Today* bestselling author Julianne MacLean

"The perfect blend of fast-paced adventure and deliciously sexy romance. I couldn't put this book down! *Almost a Scandal* gets a place on my keeper shelf—I will read anything Elizabeth Essex writes!"

> —*New York Times* bestselling author Celeste Bradley

"Witty and entertaining, Elizabeth Essex is not to be missed!"

> —Lorraine Heath, *New York Times* bestselling author

"With a lyrical style and a sexy twist, Elizabeth Essex is an author to watch!"

> —Jenna Peterson

Almost a Scandal

ELIZABETH ESSEX

St. Martin's Paperbacks

FIC
ESSEX

ALMOST A SCANDAL

Copyright © 2012 by Elizabeth Essex.
Excerpt from *A Breath of Scandal* copyright © 2012 Elizabeth Essex.

All rights reserved.

For information address St. Martin's Press, 175 Fifth Avenue, New York, NY 10010.

ISBN: 978-1-250-00379-9

Printed in the United States of America

St. Martin's Paperbacks edition / August 2012

St. Martin's Paperbacks are published by St. Martin's Press, 175 Fifth Avenue, New York, NY 10010.

10 9 8 7 6 5 4 3 2 1

To the Essex gentlemen:
To the daring and darling youngest Essex spring, for drum barrages to give the proper feeling for battle, and for all things within the realm of twelve-year-old boys;
and to the indispensable and deeply loved Mr. Essex, who held firm in his belief that this book should be called "Love Amidst the Cannonballs," for saying, all those years ago, "Stick with me, kid."

Chapter One

It wasn't the first time Sally Kent had donned a worn, hand-me-down uniform from one of her brothers' sea chests, but it was the first time it had felt so completely, perfectly right. She had always been tall and spare, strong for a girl, but dressed in the uniform of His Majesty's Royal Navy, she felt more than strong. She felt powerful.

Powerful enough to ignore the voice of conscience thundering in her ear, telling her she needed to stay quietly on land and learn to be a young lady. Powerful enough to face down the potential scandal. Powerful enough to abandon her younger brother to his chosen fate.

Because Richard had rejected all claims to duty and honor. He had forsaken his family. He wasn't coming back.

That morning, the very morning he was to have worn his uniform and boarded His Majesty's Ship *Audacious* with all the other candidates for midshipmen, he had disappeared, gone as if he had been swallowed whole by the heavy, obliterating rain.

Richard had left her, quite literally, holding his bag.

And she was going to use it. Sally closed her mind to the insistent guilt whispering in her ear, wrapped her breasts in cotton strapping, and put on every single piece of that uniform, from the faded blue midshipman's coat and white breeches, down to the black buckled shoes. She ignored the hard pounding of her heart in her chest, jammed the dark beaver hat low over her eyes, and walked down the stairs and out of the inn. She swallowed her fear, crossed the wet cobbles, and took her brother's place at the sally port on Portsmouth's rain-drenched quay.

"Richard Kent?"

A lieutenant glared at her from under the dripping brim of his cocked hat. An irate lieutenant. He stood in the stern of a ship's boat, impervious to the filthy weather and the rise and fall of the vessel tossing fitfully beneath him. The sharp vertical lines of the scowl between his dark brows could have scraped barnacles off a hull, but his low voice was incongruously smooth. "This is His Majesty's Royal Navy, Kent. Not a damned church fete. We're not going to issue you a bloody invitation."

Sally pushed her voice downward. "Aye, sir," she answered. "I'm Richard Kent."

"I know," he rumbled. "Now get in the bloody boat."

Sally jerked her chin into her collar to hide beneath the dark brim of her hat. She would have known that deep, laconic voice anywhere, even over the pounding din of the rain.

David St. Vincent Colyear.

But would he know her?

He had been eighteen years old and on the verge of taking his lieutenant's exam the last time she had seen him, the summer her brother Matthew had brought him home to Falmouth. Col, they had called him. Six years ago, he had been long and lean, but by God, clad in the endless fall of his gray sea cloak, he was a leviathan now. A great oaken mast of a man looming up from the waist of the small boat.

A man grown. A man whose jaw looked as sharp as an axe blade and whose piercing eyes, the color of green chalcedony stone, were just as hard and impenetrable.

"Well, Kent?" Col's voice was low and dangerously soft—disconcerting in such a hard-looking man. "What's it to be?"

There was no question. There hadn't been any question

since the very moment she had made her decision to tie the black silk stock around her neck and shrug herself into the loose folds of the blue coat.

She wasn't going to waste another moment living quietly and learning to act like a decorous young lady. She wasn't going to be left ashore like some half-pay junior officer. Useless.

She was going to act.

Sally looked beyond Col, to the ship riding low at anchor some half a mile beyond. His Majesty's Ship *Audacious,* her thirty-six cannons hidden behind the closed gunports, called to Sally, even in the dirty weather of Portsmouth Harbor. She was a perfectly balanced frigate of war, trim, elegant, and sleek, her masts and spars soaring high above the deck—a vision of leashed, lethal power.

Unlike Richard, Sally would give anything to experience that power.

Here was her chance. And why shouldn't she take Richard's place?

"Aye, sir. I'll come directly."

"'At's the way of it, Mr. Colyear." The windburned tar at the gig's oars knuckled his forehead to Col in approval as he reached to secure Richard's sea chest—her sea chest—in the bow of the boat. "Them young gentlemen need firm talkin' to, if they're to become anythin' more than loose cargo."

"Thank you for your insight, Davies." Col's tone was the only thing in the boat that remained dry. "Get that dunnage stowed, and cast off as soon as may be. There's more important work to be done this day than ferrying sniveling boys to their duty."

Having divested himself of that cold piece of shrapnel, Lieutenant Colyear did not deign to speak to her again for the remainder of the time it took to row out to the frigate. He took his stance in the stern of the vessel and retreated into stony silence beneath the gray wall of his cloak, as if she were as inanimate and unimportant a piece of cargo as the sea chest.

Even standing with quiet balance in the stern, David Colyear was the farthest thing from inanimate she could conceive. His hands moved decisively on the tiller, and his body adjusted with an easy, innate grace to the haphazard perturbations of the boat beneath him.

And his eyes. Those glittering stony green eyes never stopped moving, never stopped roving over the harbor, evaluating the lay of a vessel's waterline, calculating the weight of a gun, assessing the work left to be done.

Those sharp eyes cut to hers and caught her looking.

Sally shrank into herself like a startled turtle, hunching her shoulders to cover the embarrassed flush sneaking its way over her collar. She would give herself away faster than a sinking cannonball looking at him like that. Better to look forward, toward *Audacious*.

The frigate grew slowly in the gray murk of the downpour, until they were dwarfed by the loom of the hull and the complicated, orderly cobweb of spars and rigging dawning above them. Above toward heaven.

Her foolish, pounding heart tangled in her chest just at the sight of her. Infatuated, that's what she was, the way any other nineteen-year-old girl would have been at the sight of a handsome man, instead of a warship.

But she wasn't like other girls. She was a Kent, and to her this frigate, this warship, was more terribly beautiful than any man could ever be.

Because Kents were made for the sea. Almost from their birth, they had been marked for duty and devotion to the senior service. One after another, the men of her family, her four older brothers and countless cousins, had been formed, educated, and prepared for the navy. One after another, they had learned that devotion to honor, duty, and sacrifice were what made a Kent. One after another, they had left the rambling house overlooking Falmouth Bay and had made their way down to the harbor and to their destinies.

All but her.

And Richard. Stubborn, insistent, pious Richard. Richard who would rather read sermons and watch from his lofty, safe pulpit while other mortals sinned and fought and loved and truly lived.

Sally couldn't help but twist back to look at the stone quay receding slowly in the distance, for one last attempt to make out his form.

There was no one. He simply had not come.

She swallowed the bitter heat of disappointment and disillusionment. So be it. She would not look back again. Sally blinked the rain out of her eyes and fixed her gaze forward, toward the future.

With every oar stroke that brought them nearer, the ragged pounding of her heart rose higher and higher, until the roar filled her ears. Until her pulse matched the incessant drumming of the rain against the surface of the water. Until it grew to a thunderous cascade of sound and sensation that obliterated all else, burning with a single euphoric flame.

She was going to do it. She was going to take Richard's place. She was going aboard.

First Lieutenant David Colyear hauled himself onto the streaming deck to await the damned dithering boy's appearance. And to cool the hot end of his normally slow temper, now burnt to a cinder by the dirty weather and the relentless responsibilities of fitting out the ship to his captain's orders.

Luckily for them both, the boy managed to follow him with alacrity, clambering quickly through the port open at the waist of the ship, despite his too-big-looking shoes making his feet as awkward and ungainly as a seal's flippers.

God help the sodden boy because he wouldn't. Col's friends and former shipmates, Owen and Matthew Kent, had written him to expect reticence and indifference from their weedy youngest brother, but not the near disobedience that had prompted Col, for their sakes alone, to fetch the boy from shore when he had finally shown up hours later than expected. He owed the Kents that much—to save the boy from himself—because they had done as much for him. They had been steadfast friends, and Col knew it had been through Captain Kent's good offices that he had been recommended for and received his post on *Audacious*.

There was nothing, absolutely nothing, he might not do

for such friends. Except further mollycoddle their reticent, recalcitrant baby brother.

"Let me advise you on two points, Mr. Kent." He kept his tone low and his eyes on Kent's face, to make damn sure the boy understood. "I discommoded myself to fetch you from the quay for your brothers' and family's sake, not yours, and now have served my debt to them. I will not do so again. Do not think to trade on your brothers' or your father's reputations with me. You will have to do the work of two men to ever equal one of your brothers in my eyes. And do not *ever* keep your captain, or your ship, waiting on you again. Do I make myself perfectly clear?"

Young Kent unfolded himself into something approaching straight and tall—straighter and taller than Col had expected given such an unpromising beginning.

"Aye, Mr. Colyear. My apologies, sir. It won't happen again."

The frank, ready admission was another surprise. Funny, he had remembered Richard Kent as pale and bookish, his sullenness a cold contrast to the burning flame of his hair. But this boy had changed in the years since he had last seen him. His face had become more puckish, more like Matthew's, with its broad cheekbones and wide gray eyes that ought to have looked sober, but somehow managed to appear mischievous.

This boy's eyes were alight, if not with his brothers' mischief, then with bright intelligence as he took in his surroundings. Perhaps there was more Kent in the boy than his brothers suspected after all.

It was cautiously promising. And it took much of the bluster out of his sails. "I'm glad we understand each other. See to it that it doesn't. I will show you to the captain now."

"No need to discommode yourself, sir. I know my way."

"Do you? Pray precede me there immediately."

The lad knuckled his dripping hat, and in a trice scrambled deftly down the aft ladder and across the main deck to the captain's stern cabin.

Their captain, Sir Hugh McAlden, was an exacting leader, expecting diligence and strict adherence to his orders. Yet he never pushed his officers or men as hard as he pushed himself, and in doing so, had made a name for himself as an audacious and successful frigate captain at a relatively young age. Col knew he was lucky to serve under such a man, despite the heavy burden of his high expectations.

The scarlet-coated marine sentry, standing guard outside the bulkhead door, announced their entry. "Mr. Colyear and"—his gaze barely flicked over young Kent. All the marine saw was the midshipman's uniform, telling him the boy was beneath his notice—"a young gentleman."

Captain McAlden was working at his table in the gray light from the wide bow of the stern gallery windows. He wore the less formal, undress uniform of a post captain with seniority, his blue coat practical and unadorned by gold braid. Yet the lack of finery did not equate with a lack of ambition or acuity. Just the opposite. The man was as sharp and instinctively incisive as a shark.

Col came smartly to attention. "Compliments of the deck, sir, the new staysail jib has been bent on, and we now carry a full company of men, including our last young gentleman, just arrived."

With his cool blue eyes and reserved demeanor, Captain McAlden had a reputation for being a cold man. But Col knew it was his decisive self-control, and steely determination that daunted lesser, less perceptive men.

The captain's gaze cut quickly from Col to Kent, and then away and back, to hold for a long moment of consideration, as if he had just come to understand who the young gentleman was. He chipped the ice from his voice. "Was there some problem?"

The captain's gaze stayed with Kent, and Col could hear the boy's long inhalation, steadying himself to explain why he had been so damnably late to report for his duty.

Col spoke before Kent could answer. Though he had sworn not to, Col took pity on him. For his family's sake. "No, sir."

He heard the words come out of his mouth with his usual calm, measured deliberation, though he felt anything but sure of what he was doing.

"Very good, Mr. Colyear. And the powder?"

"I've made the signal, and the barge is due to be alongside by six bells in the afternoon watch. I've also had tarpaulins rigged in anticipation, to keep the powder as dry as possible in this weather."

"Well done. Let us hope the rain will abate. Thank you." The captain returned his cool, probing gaze to the boy. "Mr. Kent, is it?"

The boy was smart enough to keep his answer brief and his eyes on the deck beams overhead. He nodded sharply in acknowledgment. "Captain, sir."

Captain McAlden eyed young Kent closely, the way a cook might look at a fish lying on a bed of ice, searching out the whiff of rot. "You've the look of your father, all right. But a bit old for volunteer midshipman, aren't you?"

The boy brought his gaze level with his captain. No shrinking, no flinching. Good. "Fifteen, sir."

"Most of my young gentlemen come aboard when they're twelve or thirteen. Your father's left it a bit late. Not like him."

"He wanted me to finish my studies, sir."

Actually, Col knew from Matthew Kent's letter that Captain Kent and Richard had been arguing for years about the boy taking his place, ever since Richard had first declared his ambition to take holy orders. The whole family had taken sides, and needless to say, family opinion had not erred on the side of the church. Matthew, Owen, and Dominic Kent had been scathing in their description of what they saw as their youngest brother's shocking lack of enthusiasm for the navy. Richard had been the one to insist upon his precious schooling.

The captain considered Kent for another long moment before he checked his gaze over to Col, to see if he had anything pertinent to add. Col gave the captain a small shake of his head in negation. He wasn't going to be the one to spill any Kent family secrets.

"I'm sure book learning has its place—and you'll get plenty of schooling and study here as well," Captain McAlden continued. "But what a young man needs in order to undertake this profession is experience. And that's what you'll get, and plenty of it."

The captain looked down at the papers on his desk for a moment before he spoke again. "I had the honor of being asked by your father to put your name on my ships' books to reserve a place for you some time ago. What, if I may ask, made you finally resign your ambitions to the sea, Mr. Kent?"

"Family tradition, sir. I expect I'll come to like it."

"Like it?" Captain McAlden's voice subsided into an amused growl. "A man who will go to sea for his pleasure will go to hell for his pastime! We none of us have to like it, Mr. Kent, we just have to endure it."

The boy managed to reef down his smile, but he made no sound, although his intelligent gray eyes were dancing with laughter.

"Family tradition and service aside," the captain continued in a more serious vein, "I'll warn you, you'll get no special treatment here. In fact, as the son of Captain Alexander Kent, more will be expected of you. Your father is held in great esteem by all who know him—everyone from me and the Lords of the Admiralty, down to the larboard gunners. He's a damn useful man with a frigate. One of the best." He pinned Kent with a slow, penetrating stare. "I'll expect you to be useful as well. On a frigate of war every man must have several stations, and I will expect you to learn them all. I'll make you a credit to your father, whether you will it or not. No easy task, as you look a pretty, soft sort of boy."

Col nearly smiled. As it was, he was obliged to look out the stern gallery at the rain, and swallow hard to keep down the laugh that threatened to rise in his throat. His memories of the youngest Kent, along with Matthew's letters, had put him in expectation of a reedy, whining sort of boy. The specimen in front of them was lean, straight, and unflinching in comparison to what Col had expected. But, he had to admit, with his mischievous urchin's face, he *was* a pretty sort of boy.

Captain McAlden leveled his last instruction at Kent. "I advise you to put any thought but that of the strictest obedience from your brain, and turn yourself diligently to this profession. Your father has entrusted your training into my care, and I mean to make both a sailor and a man out of you."

Something that could not possibly dare be a smile floated across the boy's wide mouth.

"I will apply myself with all diligence, sir."

Chapter Two

Well. It was lucky Captain Sir Hugh McAlden hadn't actually gotten Richard, wasn't it? If the captain thought Sally "a soft sort of boy," what on earth would he have made of Richard, for Sal was easily twice as hard as her missing younger brother?

Perhaps she ought to be worried about what might have become of Richard, of where he might have gone to hide, or if he were safe and well, but the cold fact of the matter was that she was now far too busy trying to keep her own head above water to worry about where Richard might have chosen to swim.

"Follow me, Mr. Kent."

At that moment, Sally was actually rather glad Richard had so perversely refused to accept his responsibilities, for if he had not, she would not be following such a man as David St. Vincent Colyear down the companionway to the orlop berth. Following Mr. Colyear—and she must endeavor to always think of him as *Mister* Colyear and not Col, though he *was* taking up more of his valuable time to escort her to her berth—was infinitely preferable to any of the useless activities she had been supposed to be doing at home.

She had no talent for the sort of decorative idleness that passed for accomplishment in a female. She had a talent for sailing. And by God, she was finally free to use it.

Free to follow David St. Vincent Colyear below, to the gun deck. *Audacious* was a well-kept ship, and as they descended into the hull, the dense, oily smells of tar and oakum enveloped her. To Sally, the pungent scent was headier than any perfume. It was a balm to the disquiet in her soul.

Below, the pummeling quiet of the gray, streaming top deck gave way to boisterous celebration. On the gun deck, where the majority of the ship's crew messed and hung their hammocks, was a riot of blue jackets, red kerchiefs, and tar-smeared, wide trousers. The low space rang with a cacophony of song and fiddle playing, card gaming, and catcalling, as the men made the most of their last day in port. Sally could only assume most of the men had been confined to the ship for fear they would desert once ashore, or render themselves stupefied with drink.

Although there seemed to be plenty of that on board as well. Loose behavior seemed to be the order of the day, and Sally was surprised, and more than a little curious, to note the presence of more than a few rowdy-looking women of the sort who frequented the waterfront taverns. Her father had never allowed such women on his ship while Sally and Richard had lived aboard with him—at least as far as Sally knew—but on *Audacious,* tarts seemed to be everywhere, their garish clothes and painted faces filling up the dim spaces like gaudy lanterns.

Mr. Colyear appeared entirely unperturbed by the hurly-burly atmosphere. He passed easily through the men without breaking into their pleasures, acknowledging their knuckled salutes by name, speaking with a short nod as he passed. "Wharton. Hayes."

Though he was second in command of the ship only to the captain, Col's authority seemed to come all from who he was, and not from his rank. There was admiration and respect on both sides. Mr. Colyear was well-liked.

What an interesting man David St. Vincent Colyear had become.

A man still very much on duty. "Unlike other frigates, on *Audacious* you'll be housed in the orlop deck cockpit with the other midshipmen." Mr. Colyear's low voice rumbled back to her as he moved down another companionway ladder with the rolling, well-coordinated speed of one long accustomed to shipboard life. "The senior warrant officers share the gunroom with the commissioned officers. And here the warrants with wives—the bo'sun and the gunner—take the space normally alloted to midshipmen."

His voice was rough and warm all at the same time; it sounded as if it came from somewhere deep in his throat but was softened by the journey to his mouth. Like a cannonball loaded with cotton batting, tamped down and ready.

Ready for anything. Especially masquerading midshipmen. Sally shrugged her loose coat up around her ears.

Mr. Colyear and his battered but well-fitted coat were far too outsized for the low clearance belowdecks. He took up the entire breadth and depth of the cramped companionway as he led the way below, forced to stoop to make his way, his lean shoulders blotting out what little light filtered down between the deck timbers. He did as Sally had been taught from childhood to do, and trailed a hand along the posts and braces, or the deckhead, the underside of the deck beams overhead, to feel his way along. Counting the wooden frames, so even in the intermittent light of the lower deck, he might know at any moment exactly where in the architectural map of the hull he stood. His long fingers brushed across a knee timber with the same sort of offhand, instinctive caress a sailor gave to the living ship he loved.

The strangeness of the thought made her skin feel warm and tight, as if her coat and shirt were no longer falling in loose drapes, but pressing tenaciously to her body beneath their folds. Devil take her. Her face was sure to be flaming with telltale heat.

She batted all thoughts of *Mister* Colyear and his long, capable fingers roughly aside. If she was to survive aboard *Audacious,* she had to guard against such ridiculously weak, girlish thoughts.

"Tell me what you know of my ship, Mr. Kent."

My ship. Mr. Colyear's choice of words revealed a very

great deal about him, and his ambitions. The manning of *his* ship, the calling of watches, and the way the men performed their assigned tasks were all the responsibility of the first lieutenant. The tall, implacable, ambitious first lieutenant.

But while her mind was busy canvassing Mr. Colyear's ambitions, Sally recited her reply by rote, pulling the answer to his question easily out of the seemingly fathomless supply of naval facts she had accumulated in her brain since childhood.

"Apollo class frigate of thirty-six guns, built at Buckler's Hard by Henry Adams in 1803. Runs one hundred forty-five feet, two inches at the gun deck and one hundred twenty-one feet, eleven and three-quarters inches in keel. Thirty-eight feet, two and one-quarter inches in beam. The guns are comprised of twenty-six eighteen-pounders on the upper deck, with a further two nine-pounders and ten thirty-two-pounders on the quarterdeck, while the forecastle is armed with two nine-pounders and four thirty-two-pounder carronades. She carries a full complement of two hundred sixty-four men."

And just one girl.

And one tall, ambitious, handsome, stony-eyed first lieutenant, who paused and turned to regard her with wry, penetrating amusement during her recitation. The stern set of his mouth never varied, but his eyes—those glittering eyes that made the backs of her knees wobble like loose canvas sails—glinted like beacons in the dark. Mr. Colyear's sharp eyes raked her meticulously, making note, she was sure, of every telltale mistake of her obvious imposture.

In the passageway between decks he was so close—too close—that she could smell the rain evaporating off the heat of his body. A jangle of warning shook through her, but she wanted to back away and step closer all at the same time. She wanted to draw that rainy scent of him deep into her lungs and hold it there, even as her head told her feet to move away, to stop leaning toward him, to preserve her own ambitions from discovery. But neither her feet nor her lungs were functioning properly. She couldn't draw a proper breath, as if Mr. Colyear had sucked all the air out of the passageway and left her nothing but the curious pressure building in her chest.

No. It was only that she had drawn the bindings around her breasts too tight. But whatever it was that made her heart tumble within her chest, it was heady. It was dangerous and reckless, unnerving and undoubtedly rash.

And in that moment, with Lieutenant Colyear looking at her with those cooly penetrating eyes, it was exciting. It was exciting to think that she might fool him, and fool them all.

She had not felt this alive, this happy, in years.

Devil take her. Sally clamped her mouth down to keep from grinning like a bottle-nosed porpoise. She had to allay his suspicions. She had to be Richard. Or at least a better version of him. "Mr. Colyear"—she firmed her voice—"I know what you must be thinking, sir. I—"

"Do you?" His expression didn't change, but his eyes seemed to grow brighter and more glittering, as if she had awakened instead of dampened his curiosity. "I think not."

"I know you're displeased—"

"At the moment . . . I'm not." That laconic, almost-soft voice pushed up hard against the solid weight of the pause he took between the words. "You're a dark one, Mr. Kent. But I think you might just do."

Oh, but *he* was the dark one, because then he smiled and the corners of his mouth tipped down just enough to press dimples deep into the sculpted planes of his cheeks. It was a begrudging smile, but a smile nonetheless. She felt it unfurl slowly within her. The jangle of warning melted into a burst of pleasure that she felt all the way down to the tips of her sodden toes.

It made her want to say more, to tell him the number of sails and the square footage of canvas, to share her unbridled enthusiasm for the glorious thing that was this ship. Just so he might be impressed. Just so he might be tempted to let his mouth stretch open across his white teeth in one of the rare wide smiles she remembered, but had yet to see. Just so he might let loose with the booming cannon of his laugh she had heard that long-ago summer.

But he wasn't going to be impressed.

Mr. Colyear had not gotten to the elevated rank of first lieutenant at the young age of four and twenty, under such a man as Captain McAlden, by being the kind of man who would be impressed with a dizzy, jabbering midshipman. A man as ambitious and careful with his career as Col would not let himself be taken in by such an obvious attempt to win his admiration. He would look beyond the extraneous recitation of facts and want to know the reason behind it. He would look at her more closely, more carefully, the next time, and he would not be so easy to fool when the light was better, or his vision was not obscured by the pouring rain.

If she were to carry this imposture off, she needed to steer clear of his admiration. She would have to curb every last impulse to attract his notice. She would have to remember duty, service, and family honor came before all else. She would have to keep her distance from the admirable, handsome, ambitious Mr. Colyear.

Her lovely, idiotic euphoria had certainly been checked by the cold grip of reality now.

"Your berth, Mr. Kent." Mr. Colyear shouldered a short bulkhead door open. "Do make yourself as comfortable as you can."

This time, Sally could hear the wry humor warming his tone. Comfort would not be an option. The cockpit was the mean, dark area set off at the sternmost portion of the lower deck, below the waterline, for the midshipmen to mess and hang their hammocks. The room Mr. Colyear showed her was as cramped and low as she had expected in a frigate, the space allocated to midshipmen being commensurate to their rank—nonexistent.

Two lone boys currently inhabited the small space. One was splayed in a hammock in the deep, openmouthed sleep of the young and completely exhausted, while the other sprang up from the narrow table in the center of the room, where he appeared to have been reading in the low wash of light afforded by the lantern hanging from the beam overhead. As her eyes adjusted to the dimness, Sally could discern Richard's sea chest taking up space just inside the passageway, efficiently delivered by some unseen hand while Mr. Colyear had taken her to see the captain.

"Your fellow inmates include Mr. Jellicoe here." Mr. Colyear gestured to the blond boy in the bright new blue coat—clearly his was not a hand-me-down—who was standing to attention at the table. "And Mr. Worth, I should think." Mr. Colyear hooked a thumb in the hammock's direction. "There are sure to be a few more young gentlemen, if the rats haven't eaten them. Introduce yourselves. You've missed mealtime, Mr. Kent. As have I." The emphasis in his quietly ironclad tone told her his trip to fetch her from the quay had been the reason. "But I'll expect you to come on duty with the larboard division at eight bells of the afternoon watch. Understood?"

It was remarkable how a voice so even and disconcertingly calm could convey such implacable warning. "Aye, Mr. Colyear, sir. I'll be on duty for the dog watch."

There was a flicker of movement from his straight, dark brow that was all the reward and acknowledgment she was going to get for making it clear she was conversant with the watch and time-telling system. "Good. Because now, if you young gentlemen don't mind, I've got a full load of powder to take on board."

And with a final wry, glittering look that was still not quite a full smile, he backed out, shutting the bulkhead door behind him.

Sally wasn't sure if it was relief or disappointment that sagged through her quavering innards at his departure. Whatever it was, it allowed her to turn her mind to what came next. The dog watch didn't commence until early evening, so Sally reckoned she could remain at leisure for at least an hour more before going on duty for the first time. It was more than enough time for her to get settled in and get the lay of things.

But the blond boy's face contained nothing of her certainty. Poor lad. At least she knew what could be expected aboard ship. This must all be utterly new and confusing to him. She extended her hand. "Richard Kent. How do you do?"

Her greeting was met with only a tentative, wavering sort of smile. "William Jellicoe. Will. So you're the missing Mr. Kent. I recognize you from the inn."

Devil take Richard. Devil take him. Sally had thought he had kept to their room at the George Inn, preferring to retreat into his sad tome full of dreary sermons while she and Jenkins, the manservant her father had sent along to accompany them to Portsmouth, had completed the last of the necessary purchases for Richard's dunnage, but who knew what her brother had gotten himself up to. Perhaps Will Jellicoe had even seen Richard as he made his escape, crawling out a window, or sneaking off on the post chaise. It was a small world, the navy.

"I'm sorry." Sally waded in with vague politeness. "There were so many fellows there . . . I don't quite recall . . ."

"I'm sorry I never got a chance to introduce myself. There were a lot of other boys there. It seems to have been a popular inn for naval officers." His hand fiddled with the edge of his coat. "I was just afraid I might have offended you, when I offered to stand you a pint."

Oh, the devil and all his nasty minions could take Richard. She could only imagine that Richard had informed Will Jellicoe trenchantly that he did not drink spirits. Or that twelve-year-olds ought not to be buying heavy drink in public houses.

"No, not at all. I hope you will forgive *my* manners. I had . . . something else weighing on my mind at the time. I'd be honored to call you Will. And you must call me Richard."

God forfend anyone should call her Dickie. That would be too ironic even for her admittedly unrefined tastes.

"Thank you." Will Jellicoe sank back down to the table with what she hoped was more equanimity than before. "I had no idea it was going to be like this." He gestured to the cramped space with scattered, disorganized sea chests littering the floor. "It's not at all as I imagined."

The poor boy looked completely at sea, in more ways than one. While she might have her own concerns about what the devil she was going to do if she were caught impersonating her brother, at least she wasn't so completely out of her element as Will Jellicoe seemed to be.

"Not to worry. I'm sure there will be a servant along presently, but we can set it all to rights in no time. How many of us are there?"

"Six, I think," her new friend informed her. "That's Ian Worth there, sleeping. Mr. Beecham is on deck with the watch and Mr. Dance is . . . something to do with signals, Mr. Colyear said. I think."

"Are we all new?" What a raveled cat's-paw that would be, with six midshipmen who didn't know the way of things.

"No. Just the three of us, here. Mr. Lawrence—I think he is the third lieutenant—said Mr. Beecham and Mr. Dance joined *Audacious* on her last cruise, but I don't know when that was. And then there's Mr. Gamage." Everything about Will Jellicoe's heavy, resigned tone held a warning.

"And Mr. Gamage is . . . ?" Sally prompted.

"Damien Gamage. He's older than the rest of us. Older than even Mr. Colyear, and Mr. Horner and Mr. Lawrence, who are both third lieutenants, I think. Mr. Gamage has made it clear he's very much senior here, and we're to do his bidding."

"What does he mean, his bidding? Does he mean to play the bully boy?" Already Sally could feel her blood rise against the indignity and injustice, though her stomach knotted in dread.

Her father had never tolerated such behavior aboard his ships, but Sally had heard enough talk from her brothers to know Mr. Gamage's type—a man who had been midshipman for far longer than the allotted six years, and who had probably failed to pass for lieutenant. That made him in all likelihood stupid, and potentially mean. While she was sure that such an active and intelligent commander as Captain

McAlden would put paid to such behavior, in the meantime she would watch her step with Gamage, and caution and advise Jellicoe on how to do the same.

"He's starboard watch?"

Will shrugged with hopeless confusion. "Don't know, but he's up there now, with the others. And he didn't sit to classes with the schoolmaster with the rest of us this forenoon— which is what they called the morning, which seems to have been what they called the night—although no one remarked upon it."

"You'll grow accustomed to it," she assured him, "and I'll help." But there was another offense for Mr. Colyear to add to the list of her sins—she had missed the day's mathematics and navigation lessons whilst waiting in vain for Richard.

But one problem at a time. "Right. Where's Mr. Gamage's dunnage?" At Will's blank, uncomprehending look, Sally amended her question. "Where does he like to hang his hammock and store his sea chest? There?"

There was one sea chest stowed apart from all the others, taking up easily twice as much space as the others.

"I would guess that was his, though he did not say so," was Jellicoe's best answer. "Worth and I came in just as he was going on deck, and he did not introduce himself beyond shoving my face against the wall, when I made the intemperate mistake of looking at him."

"Good Lord. Are you all right?" Sally was appalled. And for the first time, even a little afraid. The tangle in her stomach knotted up tighter. The threat of physical violence from a shipmate had never occurred to her. But Will Jellicoe and Ian Worth were both smaller than she was. They would be even more vulnerable. They needed protection.

It seemed she was going to have to swallow both her fear and her new-made vow to steer clear of Mr. Colyear to appeal to him on their behalf. He was sure to see to their defense. "Devil take the man. But the first thing we need to do is give this Mr. Gamage plenty of room and little to complain about."

Sally fell to the piles of dunnage with her usual single-minded zeal. "The first thing you need to know about naval life is that it never pays to be idle."

Will Jellicoe fell right in with her. He was an energetic helper, and made logical suggestions while they sorted out the sea chests and various storage boxes. What was more, he kept a good humor throughout the exercise, even while young Ian Worth, who looked to be a very young twelve, slept on, oblivious to their exertions.

"I'd rather shift his lot," Will said with matter-of-fact cheerfulness, "than have him wake up and start heaving again."

Sally took another look at the boy asleep in the gently swaying hammock. On closer examination, he did look a bit fishy around the gills. "He's been sick?"

"Since the moment he set foot in the boat at the sally port this morning."

Poor lad. Sally herself had never had occasion to suffer from seasickness. Perhaps it was because she had gone to sea aboard her father's ships as a youngster and had gotten her sea legs under her before she'd had time to worry about being ill. Or maybe some people were just built that way.

"It's nothing to be ashamed of, though. It is said that Admiral Nelson himself, a man my father esteems very highly, suffers terribly whenever he goes on board his ships. How about you? How have you fared?"

Will shook his head. "So far so good. Although I must say, when he first started at it"—he hooked his thumb at the sleeping boy in unwitting imitation of Mr. Colyear—"the stench was foul enough to fair turn my stomach."

"Please." Sally was about to hold up a hand to stop him. Just because she had never felt seasick before was no reason to tempt fate to be unkind. "I can imagine."

But Jellicoe rambled happily on with the fascination for disgusting things peculiar to young boys—a fascination she needed to share if she were to be taken for one of them. "All over his clothes, it was, but Lieutenant Colyear, he took one look at him when we came on board, asked him if he could swim, and then pitched him straight back over the side, into the harbor."

"No!" Sally felt her eyes grow round as a porthole. "Mr. Colyear threw him into the drink? That's famous!"

Will nodded, his own blue eyes dancing with the terrible, ghoulish amusement boys seemed to get at the pain and suffering of their compatriots. "Pitched him right off the deck, by the seat of his pants, he did, and told the boatswain—"

"Say 'bo'sun,' " Sally broke in to instruct.

"He told the bo'sun to 'fish him out,' cool as you please. But he was all right, Worth was, only cold and dripping wet. But it stopped him pitching up. And stinking, anyway," Jellicoe finished with a satisfied sigh. "It *was* absolutely famous."

Sally couldn't keep herself from laughing out loud. Mr. Colyear—no, Col; in this instance she really could only think of him as Col—had repeated a trick she had heard her brothers talk of, any number of times. A good swim was often the best cure for a bout of the queasies. But pitching a boy like a mackerel over the side of a frigate, fifteen feet above the water, was a spectacle well worth admiring. Sally was more than sorry she had missed it.

There she went again, letting her admiration for Col get the better of her brain. Mr. Colyear was too sharp and decisive by half. Better to turn her brain to figuring out how to deal with the problem of Mr. Gamage without attracting any more of that steely awareness.

Above their heads, where the preferred object of her thoughts was presumably directing the stowing of powder without pitching anyone else into the drink, seven bells rang out. Only a half hour left until the end of the watch.

"Has it gone as late as that?" She wanted to get on deck, to get on with the business of being twice as useful as anyone else, and becoming acquainted with the crew before Mr. Colyear had need to look for her, but she couldn't just abandon Jellicoe and young Worth. Someone needed to wake the boy up and set him to rights.

Just when she had set herself to performing the job, a nut-brown old seaman wove his uneven way into the room—the mess attendant, carrying a posset in his gnarled, arthritic hands. "I've got just the thing for the young sir, here."

The devil and Saint Elmo. Fate was certainly playing dice with her today. Here was another person who knew her. And knew Richard. Angus Pinkerton, the former personal steward of her father.

To be sure, he looked a vast deal older and more careworn than the last time she had seen him, when she had lived aboard her father's ship. He resembled nothing so much as an old apple, his cheeks polished red by the wind, and what was left of his hair rose in white tufts from his pate, as if the years of exposure to Atlantic gales had blown all the color out of it.

She could not hope to pass unnoticed under the attention of this man, who for years had been like a mother to her, shepherding her and Richard under his care. Angus Pinkerton may not have been the brightest star in the constellations, but he had an uncanny ear for knowing what went on in a ship. It was a devilishly small world, the navy.

But whether he recognized her or not, she ought to be safe with Angus Pinkerton. He was an honest man, through and through, but loyal down to his creaking bones. She had only to keep him from blurting out the truth to anyone else.

"Pinky?" Sally ventured. "Is that you?"

"Young sir?" The old tar swung around. "Why, bless my heart, it's—"

"Richard," she broke in with what she hoped was a confident smile. "Richard Kent. Captain Kent's son, from *Adamant,* back in the year one. Do you remember?"

Pinky squinted up his cloudy blue eyes and laughed. "Of course I remember. Is that *you* then, young sir? Well, I never would have recognized you, so tall and grown you've gotten. But my eyes aren't what they used to be. How kind you are to remember your old Pinky."

Sally breathed out her relief. "Good to see you, as well. But Pinky, what in heaven's name are you doing aboard *Audacious*? And as servant to the orlop? I thought you were meant to be comfortably pensioned off, at your sister's farm, somewhere in Dorset. Or was it Devon?"

"How good you are to remember. But my Jeanie—that was my sister, you see—well, she died." He heaved a sigh of lament out of his chest. "And her husband, well, he weren't what could be called a *comfortable* man. And I got to missing the sea. And good Captain McAlden found me this easy berth, looking after you young gentlemen."

"My father will be glad to know you're safely tucked up here."

"Good of you to say so, and you'll be sure to send my compliments to your father, Cap'n Kent. But *you* won't be needing no looking after at all, if I know you, young sir. Sharp as a brass needle, you always were." He cast his rheumy eyes around the cabin. "And you've put this all to rights, I shouldn't guess."

"Just so," Sally answered, even as she swallowed down the cold lump of apprehension clogging her throat. Richard had not been as sharp as anything. He had been miserable aboard their father's ship, often ill, and always out of sorts. It was she who had followed Pinky around like a remora and learned all the tricks of the old salt's trade. But if she and Richard seemed to have melded themselves together in Pinky's mind's eye, so much the better. "How long have you been aboard, Pinky, and what can you tell me about Mr. Gamage?"

Pinky's eyebrows rose in proportion to his wariness, while he lowered his head and his voice to a soft growl. "I only been with Captain McAlden's young gentlemen for this last cruise, when young Mr. Beecham came aboard. I don't mess for Mr. Gamage. He's got his own creature, Tunney, as his servant, and doesn't share with anyone else. Likes to have his own way, Mr. Gamage does. An' he knows how to make it so. You didn't hear it from me"—he cupped his hand over his mouth to speak confidentially—"but you young gentlemen be sure to lock up your valuables, and your foodstuffs—whatever you brought with you—or he'll have 'em for his own in a trice."

"Do you mean he would steal them?" Sally couldn't keep her voice down. She wouldn't. She was appalled at the very idea. She was quite sure such a thing, no matter how trivial, would never have been allowed on her father's ships. "You're joking. Please tell me you're joking. Stealing is a flogging, if not a hanging, offense. Captain McAlden doesn't strike me as the sort of man who would put up with anything of the sort. He knows as well as any—probably better than any—that a man who would steal, especially food, from his shipmates will do just about anything . . ." It was beyond Sally's comprehension—too much of an abomination of all codes of conduct to which she had been raised.

"That's just low," she sputtered. "The lowest."

"Now, young sir, that's just the way things are, more often than not. He's too canny to let it look like thievery, but it'll be gone all the same. But you didn't hear it from me." Pinky was shaking his jowly head like a wary bulldog. "I don't want no more troubles."

Pinky's tepid plea couldn't hope to soothe the hot indignity rising in her chest. "Has Mr. Gamage made trouble for you, Pinky?"

The old man began to look even more uncomfortable. His already glowing face flushed a darker shade of crimson. "Now, nothing out of the way of things." He rubbed his nose to hide his discomfort at her scrutiny while he relocated his glance down to his feet. "I'll say no more."

"Come now, Pinky. You know you can trust me. I give you my word as Captain Alexander Kent's son that no mention of what you say will pass beyond this berth." She shot an instructing glance at Jellicoe. "And I'm sure Mr. Jellicoe will give you his word, as well."

"Indeed, Pinkerton. I pledge you my word as Earl Sanderson's son to keep your confidence."

Good Lord. No wonder the accommodations on board were not what Will Jellicoe had expected, or been accustomed to. And he'd never breathed a word of it, not even when she was ordering him about like a dockyard stevedore. Sally liked him all the more for it.

But Pinky didn't seem much impressed by titles. Sally supposed that at his age, he had earned the right to never judge a man on anything less than his own character. He screwed up his face sideways, as if he were trying to chew on his dilemma a moment longer before he decided what to tell them.

"Is it gambling?" Sally prompted. "You always did like to throw the bones, Pinky. Did you get into debt to him?"

"No, no. It weren't the money, just the deed. It were just a few of us, you understand—Edwards, he's steward, and Coggins, who's purser. Just a few friendly throws. But Cap'n McAlden, he don't stand for no gambling on board while at sea."

"Mmm." Sally tried to make a sound of comforting commiseration. "Not even card games in the wardroom?"

"Well, them's gentlemen's games, 'int they? Mr. Colyear sees to it the officers play only for penny points."

"And you weren't playing for pennies?"

Old Pinky canted his head sideways and closed his eyes with a wry smile, as if to ask, What had she expected? "Ah, well, young sir. A man's got to look after himself."

"So he does, Pinky. I can't disagree." But it was certainly a damned pickle, if this Gamage had both the purser and the captain's steward in his obeisancy. "Tell you what—I'll put my brain to it for a spell, and see what I can think up for you."

"That's right good of you, young Kent. You were always a good 'un. Don't know how I can thank you enough."

"Yes, well, you might begin to thank me by getting young Mr. Worth here up and presentable before eight bells. I'd like to get us all on deck before Mr. Colyear has even begun to think of us."

"Right you are, young sir. But don't you worry about Mr. Colyear. He's another good 'un. Knows his business. Fair and hardworking, he is."

"I'm glad to hear it. I'm counting on you to help us get on, and stay on, the good side of the man."

"Right you are, young sir. For you surely don't want to get yourself caught out by him on the other side."

Chapter Three

There was something about young Mr. Kent that had already gotten under Col's skin. Something . . . not exactly wrong, but certainly not quite right.

But Col would damn himself before he gave any more time over to pondering the prickling unease that wandered down the back of his neck whenever he thought of the boy. He had already missed his dinner by working through the watches, and still there was more work yet to be done.

"See to it that tarpaulin's stowed," Col directed the third lieutenant, Jack Horner. God only knew what the man's proper Christian name was, for they had rechristened him Jack years ago. "And get some men of the afterguard to take the slack out of that mainsail brace."

"Aye, sir." Horner was already calling to the men idling in the waist. "You there—"

There was always something more to be done, some task, or piece of equipment, or tackle no one else managed to see. Excepting, of course, the captain, who saw everything. And Col would be thrice damned before he would let his captain down by failing to notice even something so mundane as a slack rope. More lives were lost through carelessness than ever were to cannonballs.

But Col was clearly the only one who could see something wrong with Kent. No one else, even the captain, seemed to share his confounded unease—or was it distrust?—of the boy.

Col found his hand migrating to rub the pent-up, pinching tension out of his neck. Perhaps he was still on his guard from overseeing the careful stowage of so many tons of volatile black powder in the hold. In such an endeavor there was no room for error. And certainly no room for niggling thoughts about inconvenient midshipmen.

Perhaps he had let himself become predisposed to disliking the boy after reading the letters Matthew and Owen Kent had sent. Or perhaps he was simply annoyed at the sopping waste of time and daylight it had taken to collect the little sod from the quay.

But he hadn't exactly been a little sod, had he? It would have been easier if Richard Kent had remained the recalcitrant laggard of the sally port, or the hesitant parson of his brother's letters. Col would have known how to deal with such a boy—tossed him in the drink the way he had Ian Worth. But once young Kent had seemed to snap out of his dithering at the sally port and come aboard ship, he had been nothing but bright and pleasing. Too pleasing.

Something was wrong.

Yet, here was Kent, ushering Will Jellicoe and a still groggy, though slightly less green, Ian Worth up the quarterdeck ladder, before the quartermaster had even rung the eight bells signaling the changing of the watch.

Kent was instructing the others in a low tone, but with the aplomb of a twenty-year veteran, gesturing here and there, confident, knowledgeable, and professional, and with a connoisseur's interest in the work. His wide, urchin's face was as bright and shiny as a new penny—an open canvas of his obvious enthusiasm.

Why had Matthew warned him the boy wouldn't know a halyard from a handspike when there he was, pointing out the various masts, and shepherding the others to the correct corner of the quarterdeck where they could observe without being in the way of the running of the ship? The boy was more than just pleasing, he was downright useful.

It didn't tally up. Something, damn his clenching gut, was definitely off.

Though the rain had abated, Col was still as wet as the painted wooden figurehead at the bow of the ship, and in no mood for inconvenient midshipmen who had somehow already gotten underneath his skin. There was work to be done.

"Gentlemen," he addressed all three of them, careful to keep both his tone and his gaze neutral, to mitigate this strange awareness of young Kent.

"Mr. Colyear, sir." Kent answered for all three with a neat tug on the brim of his hat, which he had pulled down low over his eyes, almost as if he hoped to avoid Col's notice.

No chance of that.

"I make you known to Lieutenant Horner. Mr. Horner is the officer of the deck for the dog watch." He indicated each in turn. "Mr. Jellicoe, Mr. Worth, and Mr. Kent, midshipmen."

Kent repeated his obeisance to the lieutenant, and, with a subtle elbow to Jellicoe, encouraged the younger boys to follow suit. Already the leader.

Contrary to Matthew Kent's assertions. The fist of unease in Col's gut punched higher. Perhaps a test was in order.

"Normally," he addressed the three boys, "your education will be left to Mr. Charlton, the sailing master, but as he is at this moment busy with the captain, your training falls temporarily to me. And as we remain safe at anchor in port, and you three have yet to learn enough to make yourselves particularly useful, you young gentlemen can spend an hour or so climbing the mizzen shrouds to fetch me down that pennant." Col pointed upward to the signal flags that had been raised earlier to communicate with the dockyard powder barge. "However long it takes."

Up, up, up their eyes went, to the faraway-looking flags flapping lightly in the damp evening breeze. All but Kent, whose quick, perceptive gaze danced from Col to the signal chest, and from there to the running line from whence the flags would normally be hauled down, as if he knew well and good that Col could have taken the pennant down from the safety of the quarterdeck if he so chose. As if he knew Col had ten such tasks to hand, ready to be assigned at a moment's notice, to keep the men and boys employed and away from idleness. Within the space of a second, the boy had seen all.

Perhaps the knot in Col's gut was merely the unpleasant and highly inconvenient result of having been so quickly found transparent. There was definitely more Kent in this boy than any of them suspected.

It only left to be discovered if the boy would have the infernal impudence to say so.

But, "Aye aye, sir," was all the youth said as he ducked his head in obedience. Yet even with his eyes downcast, Col could detect the telltale trace of all-too-familiar Kentish mischief gamboling at the corners of his lips.

In contrast, both Will Jellicoe and Ian Worth, who was now a rather extraordinary shade of dead-fish white, looked openly terrified at the prospect of scaling the rigging. Col knew he did them a kindness, though they would never see it as such. The midshipmen needed to learn sooner rather than later to manage their fear and their footfalls upon the shrouds and horses aloft, because if they couldn't do it whilst they were safely in harbor, in weather that was merely damp, they would never manage it on the heaving, open sea or in one of the howling gales of the unforgiving Atlantic.

Young Kent showed no such trepidation. Indeed, quite the opposite. He was all swift decision, already moving toward the starboard rail, as if the prospect filled him with eager anticipation, and signaling by an encouraging toss of his head for Worth and Jellicoe to follow.

There was another thing to tax Matthew about—contrary to Matthew's opinion, his younger brother was clearly a natural leader. Within a handful of hours, the two younger midshipmen were already looking to him for guidance. Richard Kent was only the son of a mere, although distinguished, sea captain, but he had quite literally assumed command over his little band of midshipmen, two boys who were the sons of important noblemen. Jellicoe was the second son of the Earl Sanderson while young Worth was the "spare" of the Viscount Rainesford. But such behavior was entirely in keeping with the Kent family's forthright character. Standing and lineage mattered little to them—the only things that counted were loyalty and usefulness.

In all, young Kent was exactly as Col might have wished. So why wasn't he pleased? Why did his skin prick when he looked at the boy? What was this slow roiling tension deep in his gut?

Such unease was normally reserved for men like Damien Gamage, whose habitual ineptitude and malice had earned him Col's oversight, not an eager, almost gamin boy with a wide-open, guileless face that showed his every thought.

And right now Kent's thoughts and concerns were all for his friends. The slight offshore breeze brought Kent's quiet instruction to Col's ears.

"Right," Kent was asking Worth and Jellicoe, "have you ever done this before?"

"No." Will Jellicoe strove to mask his fear with grim determination.

Ian Worth, on the other hand, looked not only terrified but miserably so.

Kent gave him a gentle pat of encouragement on the shoulder. "You'll do just fine. It's like climbing a tree, only a bit wigglier. Just follow me and place your feet as I do." Kent swung himself over the rail onto the chains, and started up the lower set of shrouds easily, with the sort of natural animal grace of the young and fearless. "It's like shinning up a rope, not climbing a ladder. Stay centered on the shroud, and place your feet on the ratlines to either side, like this." He demonstrated the most stable position. "And don't look down."

Jellicoe followed at a slower but steady pace, with some of the same easy coordination. Young Worth did well enough, though he moved very slowly, and soon began to lag behind.

"That's it, lads," Kent called encouragement down to them. "Steady on. Nearly there." Though they were only a fraction of the way up the mizzen masthead, and had a full other set of shrouds to the mast top above them. But Kent kept them at it, coaxing them at the parting of the futtock shrouds and coaching them onto the masthead over the tricky weather edge, instead of through the easier lubber's hole.

It was all something Col had seen a hundred, if not five hundred, times before. So why was he wasting his valuable, short leisure time watching three midshipmen go aloft for the first time? He had already remained on duty, making the final preparation to sail and taking on the powder, through three changes of the watch. By all rights he ought to be snug in the gunroom with a good glass of claret, washing the taste of the rain from his gullet, not watching three adolescent boys go through their paces. Their education was not his job.

But still he stayed, unable, or unwilling, to turn his eyes from the problem that was Richard Kent. Because, despite the encroaching dark, the height, the danger, and the trivial nature of the task, the lad's young, freckled face was split with an impish grin that beamed with happiness, and even though the flaming Kent hair was hidden beneath the dark beaver round hat, the boy all but glowed with an aura of delight and vitality. There was so much of a boyish, single-minded sense of fun in the lad that turned the mundane task into a game.

Richard Kent looked ridiculously happy.

Col remembered that feeling, of being alone, yes, and away from his family for the first time, but also being on his own and ready to prove himself, of wanting to show what he could do. Of liking the physical exertion and inevitable exhaustion that followed. Of being hungry enough to eat anything that was put in front of him, no matter where it came from, or what species it had once been. Of being not just satisfied with the work, and ambitious for what was to come, but happy with each new skill acquired or new situation conquered. Happy discovering the man he was meant to be.

"Mr. Colyear, sir?" Lieutenant Horner asked cautiously. "Are you . . . remaining on duty, or leaving the deck?"

Col craned his neck upward to the rigging above, growing darker in the purpling evening twilight, searching his head for an excuse, any excuse, to stay. The boys were at the second set of shrouds, working their way up to the cross-trees of the mizzenmast top. In another moment, Kent would clear the lines and take in the signal pennant. Then all they had to do was climb themselves back down, and he would be shed of them.

Aloft, Kent made short work of untying the offending pennant, furling it carefully and stowing it safely inside his waistcoat. And then, in the long moment while Kent waited for the other two midshipmen, Col swore he saw the boy close his eyes and lean into the wind, like a carved figurehead at the bow of a ship, all heedless delight.

The air in Col's lungs grew still like the atmosphere before a storm, pent up and watchful. Warning him to pay attention.

His feet were already moving, carrying him to the rail, giving him a better vantage point.

But there was nothing else to see. The boy was in no danger. He gripped the lines surely, though his hands did look too small, his slender, articulate fingers and almost fragile wrists too delicate to be so capable. But he *was* capable and sure aloft. There was no need for alarm. No need for the feeling that clawed at his chest like a maddened bear straining to get loose.

In another moment all three boys were collected at the crosstree, and then Kent directed them back down before slinging himself out into the standing rigging to come sliding hand over hand down a backstay like an experienced topman, looking like he had enjoyed the ride all too much. Col remembered that euphoria well from his own first conquering of the mastheads.

But Kent took Col's watchful demeanor as disapproval. "I'm sorry, sir." The boy bit his grin into obedience.

"It's no sin to enjoy yourself, Mr. Kent. There is a great deal of pleasure in a job well done, and in a fear conquered, as long as it never interferes with duty."

A wary relief spread itself across the boy's animated face. "Aye, sir. Thank you, Mr. Colyear. But I wasn't afraid. I like being aloft." And then, as if he thought he had said too much, the boy ducked his head to hide beneath the brim of his hat. A long sweep of his Kent-red hair escaped his queue to slide down around the curve of his cheek. Kent fished it back over his ear with a quick, economical flick of his fingers.

The gesture, and the strange grace of the boy's hands, sent another shot of alarm firing into his gut, demanding attention.

Damn his eyes. It was only hair, however vibrant a ginger, pulled back in a short queue, much like his own. The other two boys, the scions of Society, had had theirs cut shorter in deference to fashion. But young Kent just looked like a naval man through and through, like his brothers, or like Mr. Horner and Col himself. There was nothing strange about that.

Yet try as he might, his head could not convince his gut. What was he missing?

Kent fished the signal flag out of his waistcoat, folded and rolled improbably precisely, and ready to be stowed. "The signal flag, sir."

"Thank you, Mr. Kent." Col acknowledged the task with a nod. "Mr. Horner, you have the deck. When the watch is done, you can show these three"—he cast a look up to include Jellicoe and Worth, still picking their way down— "and make a thorough tour of the lower decks to see that all the lights are put out. Then send them to bed, so they'll be ready for the sailing master to make a mash out of their brains with the mathematics of navigation in the morning."

Col left the quarterdeck to Mr. Horner, and headed down for the sanctuary of his small cabin in the gunroom. All his gut needed was a decent claret to chase away any lingering thoughts of the inconvenient strangeness of Richard Kent.

"Will you be wanting to set a kedge, sir, before the storm comes?"

Col was halfway down the quarterdeck ladder when Kent's words made the hairs at the back of his neck stand to attention. He had turned back, retracing his steps to Kent before he could stop himself.

"What storm?" Horner was asking, full of a junior officer's perturbation for a midshipman. "The rain has stopped."

Kent said nothing, but Col could see one eyebrow arching up into the brim of his hat. In answer he turned to look over the larboard rail to the southwest, toward the Channel, his nose tipping up to the light breeze.

Col followed his gaze, but saw nothing particularly ominous. It was as it had been all afternoon—the worst of the rain had passed and the leaden sky was dripping its slow way into evening. But his brain still held the image of the way the lad had put his nose into the breeze above, and Col had shipped with enough Kents to not discount the boy. "What makes you think so, Mr. Kent?"

The boy winced his eyes closed for the briefest moment at finding Col near. His answer was so reluctant and low Col had to bend his head down to hear it. "I suppose I can smell it, sir."

Jack Horner looked to Col. For himself, he could smell nothing out of the ordinary. *Audacious* smelt of salt and air, and tar and hemp, and the funk of two hundred and sixty-odd men living cheek by ruddy jowl. "And what does a storm smell like, Mr. Kent?"

The boy's shoulders shifted in an uncomfortable shrug. "Like storm."

Col chose to be patient. He made a simple spinning motion with his finger to draw the response out of the reluctant lad.

"It smells like heat over cold, or today, like cold over heat. The air, I think, felt colder when I was above and it was moving. Maybe slightly faster, or in a slightly different direction, than below?" He scrunched up his nose. "And it smelled heavy, like . . ." He tossed up his hands in exasperation. "Like there was a great bloody blow coming out of the western Channel."

Kent seemed to think better of continuing, but Col could hear what he reckoned was the ring of truth in Kent's tone. The boy believed he could smell it. And the boy was, for all his alleged faults, a Kent.

"Then we had best ready a kedge, should the need arise. Mr. Horner, if you would? Take Mr. Worth and Mr. Jellicoe, so they may learn the benefit of the kind of preparedness young Mr. Kent here so presciently advises. And as for you,

Mr. Kent." Col swung the fullness of his regard back to Kent, who ducked his head again, still vainly trying to hide beneath the brim of his beaver hat. "If there's as heavy a blow as you predict, then we had best clear out the lower decks of all visitors. And women."

A careful stillness fell over the boy as his eyes met Col's. "Women, sir?"

"Yes, women. Surely you noticed them belowdecks earlier? I must say I found it hard not to."

The look Kent gave him in answer was hard to classify. His face turned an interesting shade of crimson, and his gaze faltered, as if he hardly knew where to look, he was so discomposed. When he answered, his voice was cracked with the uneven anxiety of adolescence. "Yes. I saw them."

Here at last was something of the parson. "Well, we had best get them off while they can still be got off. It will be a hell of a thing to try and shift them out of here in a gale. Mr. Larkin." Col moved to the quarterdeck rail and called to the bo'sun's mate on duty below in the waist. "Pipe all visitors ashore."

"Aye, aye, sir."

"Very good." Col turned back to young Kent, who was twitching uncomfortably inside a blue, hand-me-down midshipman's coat that had to have once been Matthew's, judging from the carefully repaired tear along one sleeve. Col remembered that night. And he could never forget that fight. "Well, Mr. Kent? Are you ready to brave the bawdy?"

There it was again, that twitch of his lips that didn't dare to be a smile—a familiar though more reserved cousin, perhaps, to Matthew's mischievous grins. "Aye, sir. I suppose this is the portion of my training that falls under the heading of becoming a man."

The tone was so angelically bland that Col could all but see the mischievous imp sitting on Kent's shoulder. Damn, but there was *much* more Kent to this boy than anyone could have thought.

"That it does, Mr. Kent, that it does."

The bo'sun's shrill whistle rent the air as Col descended

the companionway ladders from the quarterdeck down two
flights to gun deck level. It always amused Col that the gun
deck on a frigate was an arcane naval misnomer, as the guns
were all housed on the main deck above, and the so-called
gun deck was instead fitted out for the accommodation of the
crew. Forward of the mainmast was a large open area where
the men hung the hammocks, messed, and stowed their dunnage. And occasionally, when in port, entertained.

Although "entertainment" was probably not the best word
to describe the frantic action on display. Indeed, the first sight
that greeted Col as he stepped off the companionway ladder
was the bare naked arse of a sailor oscillating away like a
bilge pump. The fellow—Griggs, one of the quarter gunners,
he thought, from this view—was pumping away into a woman
who had backed up to a deck post for better leverage.

In the middle of this affectionate display of commerce,
the cheerful doxie looked over the quarter gunner's shoulder, and tossed Col a wink. "Wanting a turn, love?"

However much he admired her cheek and her entrepre-
neurial spirit, the thought was not to be borne. But before he
could speak, the mischievously angelic voice breezed into
his ear.

"Is she talking to you or me?" Young Kent had stopped on
one of the higher steps and was peering over Col's shoulder
at the spectacle.

Col tried to curb the impulse—and he had never before, or
at least since becoming first lieutenant, been a man subject to
the whims of impulse—to laugh. Because Kent was already
laughing. At himself. It was . . . "disarming" was the only
word Col could think of.

"Me. You're too damn young, even if you are a Kent." Col
redirected his voice at the doxy. "Alas, madam, I must decline
your charming offer. All visitors ashore. Hove to, Griggs."

"Aye, sir, but if you'd just give us a minute to finish our
business wif' Long Peg, I'd be much obliged, Mr. Colyear."
The gunner didn't even turn around, but kept his mind on
the task, quite literally, at hand. And already, Col guessed,
paid for.

Griggs's huffing and puffing continued, oblivious to all bystanders, until he at last began to reach his noisy crescendo.

Col half expected the stammering return of the crimson embarrassment, but instead of prigging up like a parson, behind Col, young Kent removed his hat and laid it solemnly across his chest.

"Devil take me if I don't feel like I ought to take my hat off for such a biblically instructive display."

There was nothing Col could do but laugh out loud and listen as the boom of his mirth echoed off the curved interior of the hull. It carried over the din and caused more than one sailor to turn and stare. "Bloody hell. You surprise me, Mr. Kent."

"Do I?" The imp seemed to like the notion. To be sure, the lad's face was flaming like a radish, but his eyes were dancing with familiar Kentish mischief. "I fancy I surprise myself."

"Not like I would, dearie." The well-endowed piece of crumpet that was Long Peg began a leisurely tucking in of her assets. She sent a wide-toothed smile at the boy behind him. "Have a go then, ginger? I could do a little tidbit like you in a heartbeat."

Kent's smile widened across a flash of teeth. "I very much doubt that, madam," he countered with a small, elegant bow. "Though I thank you for your generous offer."

"'E's too young for you, Peg," someone called. "But you could do 'im for a wet nurse!"

The deck exploded into ribald laughter, and the boy seemed happy to laugh along with them. He wasn't shocked or disapproving of the men at all. He was, instead, laughing so with such jovial humor that his warm gray eyes began to water.

"Mr. Colyear, I beg you will preserve me from such a fate. She's as like to smother me as anything." The boy backhanded a tear of laughter out of his eyes with the cuff of his coat. "Oh, devil take me. You have no idea. It's all so marvelously ridiculous."

Col couldn't stop the laughter that was rumbling out of his own chest. And he didn't want to. He wanted to laugh, the way he always did with the Kents. Damn his eyes, but it was going to be good to have a Kent on board. Clearly the boy had untapped depths.

"Visitors ashore, visitors ashore," Larkin was bawling from aft.

Col could hear the steady fall of the cane as Larkin beat against posts and deck beams to make himself heard and get attention.

"Perhaps, sir," Kent suggested when he regained his composure, "you might like me to see that the marines are mustered at the rail to prevent the men from trying to join their . . . companions, sir?"

Col liked the boy more and more. Bright and pleasing, with a self-deprecating sense of humor. And something more—the ability to look ahead and see what remained to be done. It seemed like such a simple thing, but in Col's experience, it was rare indeed.

For the first time in a long time, Col felt some of the weight of responsibility he carried around on his shoulders ease. Remarkable. After an unpromising start to their association, the tide in the boy had indeed changed. With luck, this was going to be one hell of a cruise.

Chapter Four

"Out and down, lads. Out and down. Show a leg." The shrill call from the bo'sun's whistle, and the bawling of his mate, pierced the darkness of the orlop deck. "All hands. All hands to weigh anchor."

Sally was already out and down and up and out, and had been since five bells. She had lain awake most of the night, listening to the storm, and waiting for the marine on sentry duty to hail a coming boat, or the sound of Jenkins, or even Richard himself coming aboard. And then there had been the riot of snoring from some of her fellow inmates in their cockpit asylum that had risen over the howl of the wind and lashing rain. She wasn't exactly sure who the worst offenders were, as they had all been asleep in their hammocks by the time she had quite deliberately turned in very late last night, and she hadn't wanted to light a lamp. In the deep of the night the bloody confounded racket had made her reconsider the wisdom of her plan. But this morning had dawned fine, and despite the lack of sleep, she was anxious to be out the door with her coat on, before any of the other midshipmen had stirred to life.

And getting up before any of the others provided her with time to change in the dark. She had also quite deliberately chosen to hang her hammock closest to the backside of the cockpit's canvas door, so the corner might provide some small measure of privacy. And in its proximity to the door, she had the shortest route up and out.

As she made for the companionway, Pinky, God bless his tousled head, bustled toward her with a steaming mug of something dark and bitter and aromatic that resembled neither coffee nor tea, but something in between. Whatever it was, it was welcome.

"Take you up one, young sir," he advised.

Sally took a scalding gulp before she gasped out, "Ahh, God love us. Thank you, Pinky."

"I'll have a breakfast ready for you after all the hammocks are piped up and we've weighed for the Channel. But I can get you a bit of bread and cheese if you're hungry. You didn't get no supper last night. You've only to ask an' I'll keep a good supper back for you."

"I thank you, Pinky, no. I had much rather arrive on deck and get the lay of things before Mr. Colyear's exacting eye can find me." Before the man had any reason to cast his meticulous gaze her way for a second or third look at her. Devil take him, but he had watched her closely last night. But then again, he watched everything with that raking eye of his. Why should she be any different?

"Don't you worry about Mr. Colyear, now. He's a fair man, he is, as is the captain."

"Speaking of fair, and mindful of what you told me, my sea chest is *full* of dried herbs and sundry things to give over to your keeping. For the whole mess, mind you, not just me. I'm sure you can use them to make all our mouths water."

Pinky's rheumy eyes lit up. "Oh, aye. Just so, young Mr. Kent, just so."

She had packed those herbs for Richard herself, harvesting most of them from the kitchen garden and wrapping them carefully in paper packets with injunctions to use their contents for the betterment of his fellow midshipmen. She had also thought it would be a good way for Richard, who tended to be a rather solitary young fellow, to make friends. Anyone who could improve the quality of the food aboard ship was bound to be well liked. She had fussed at Richard, instructing him and telling him how to go about it. How unnecessary it had all been.

"They're fresh—just days old."

"Ah, you've as good a nose as ever." The pleased contentment at the thought of bringing their mess proper food brought the apples back into Pinky's cheeks. "I only tell you so's you know—I'll always keep as good a meal for you as I can, no matter the hour."

"Excellent, Pinky. My thanks. I know I can rely on you. And so can you rely on me. We'll have a good mess of it. Now, wish me luck." She took one last gulp of the still scalding, but strengthening brew.

"Good luck, young sir."

It only occurred to her, as Pinky disappeared down the deckway, that she did have as good a nose as ever. But Richard never had.

Was the old man, though he never said it out loud, trying to tell her he knew that it was she and not Richard under his care? Or was it just that old age was mixing the memories up in his mind? And how could she ask without giving herself away?

It was going to be devilishly difficult, this balance, this being Richard and also necessarily being herself. Mentally, she could be herself, but physically she would just have to become more like Richard. Or more like a better version of him, like Matthew or Owen. Or, even better, more like the boys of the orlop cockpit, with their swiped sleeves and unrestricted, bounding walks. She would make a study of them, the same way she had made a study of navigation and sails and spars—she would observe them until it became second nature.

If only she had long enough.

On deck she headed aft, toward the taffrail, where she might have a better view of the town, and could draw a long breath of damp sea air into her lungs. Devil take her, but she loved the heavy, salty smell of it. A proper lungful she could get here, much more so than in Falmouth, where even the breeze off the sea quickly became laden with the scents of the land. But out on the water there was nothing but the wind. The close smell of belowdecks, or even the oak, hemp, and tar of the deck, disappeared. It was nothing but possibility, that smell. It was freedom. And it was home.

At the taffrail, she could still recognize a whiff of the dank mustiness of Portsmouth less than a mile inshore, hulked down at the edge of the water. The square, gray town wavered over the dark slate-colored water of the harbor. Portsmouth, where Richard might still be. Where he might have changed his mind and be trying to right his wrong.

Devil and Saint Elmo, if only he didn't. If only they were away and downchannel before anyone could find her and put her off.

"See anything of interest, Mr. Kent?"

She jumped—literally started back like a scalded cat—at the low rumble of Mr. Colyear's voice, rough and somehow liquid, like the water of the surf being churned into the sand. Devil take her. Clearly, she was already too late to escape Mr. Colyear's notice. He was already there, standing to larboard of the mizzen with the same solid immutability as the mast.

He shifted his eyes her way only momentarily before looking ahead, down the length of the ship, and spoke without changing his stance. "Nice and early, I see."

"Good morning, Mr. Colyear." It was a pretty dawn, with a warm yellow light to the east. A fine day to put to sea. A marvelous day for a fresh start. Provided Richard didn't come.

Sally glanced over the rail, back across the harbor. It looked quiet enough. Boats were working closer in to the quay, but none looked to be venturing out to *Audacious*.

"Mr. Kent?"

"No, sir." She lied automatically in answer to his first question, even though *everything* was of interest to her. Especially the inscrutable Mr. Colyear.

He had come up close behind her. So close, she had to look up to see him. With his lean ranginess, he loomed over her like a cliff, with a craggy handsomeness that appealed even as it daunted. There was something about Mr. Colyear that was irrefutably direct. His well-worn uniform spoke of utility, as if he cared nothing for appearances, only for results. His face had a squareness to it, a spare quality, as if the years of life at sea had honed him down to the essentials, so that his outer appearance matched his character exactly. There was nothing extraneous or purely decorative. His dark eyebrows were straight across the tops of his eyes. His nose was straight, exactly the right size for his face. The only part of him that was unnecessary was the slight dimple that bisected his chin. It was the only suggestion of softness or excess on the man.

Not that she was interested in his handsomeness. Or his approval. Not at all. She was far more concerned about the possibility of boats coming out from the town.

She was about to say so when Mr. Colyear's attention shifted away from her to the instruments—the compass and barometric glass, which had risen as the worst of the wet weather had abated, leaving them a high, clear morning. Then his eye moved beyond, to the mainmast stays, and then beyond again, his eyes roving in their constant catalogue of the ship. Constantly assessing and making instantaneous judgments. Before he turned back to her.

And now he frowned at her in that minutely considering way of his. Sally saw an almost imperceptible flicker of his dark straight eyebrows before he made that wry downward cant of his lips that was somehow still a smile. "Hell of a storm last night, Mr. Kent. Regretting your impulse toward family tradition already?"

"No, it's not that, sir." She didn't regret it at all. The impulse, as he called it, to family tradition was the only thing she was sure of. She was not afraid of the voyage or the service. She was absolutely sure she could do the work.

Mr. Colyear was still waiting, with all the inescapable patience of the sea itself.

"I just wondered if the watermen—though it seems strange to call them watermen, don't you think, when they are all women?" In Portsmouth harbor the rowers from the quay were all women, the men having been pressed into service by the navy's insatiable appetite for men to fill out her crews. But she was nearly babbling, sounding like a complete looby. Mr. Colyear's intense, meticulous regard still managed to discompose her even when she had screwed her courage down fast. Every time he looked at her in that particular, silently measuring way of his, her insides went all a-jumble, as topsy-turvy and out of tune as a broken fiddle.

Because any moment he was going to look at her and his face would lighten, and then darken with recognition. It would have been so much easier if he had simply looked at her and known. If he had hauled her up by her lapels the way she expected, and declared her a fraud, and tossed her into the drink.

Yet he did none of that. He just stared at her for the longest, most uncomfortable minute, while she waited for him to *see* her. To recognize *her*.

When he finally reacted, he leaned in close, close enough to speak quietly, so no one else might overhear. With his dark head tipped down close to hers, she could smell the scent of ocean, of heat and salt rising from the wool of his worn blue coat, and soap, and something else, something that had to be entirely Mr. Colyear. Something entirely, dangerously alluring.

"You are a member of this ship's company now, Mr. Kent. You'll be lucky to leave this ship at the end of two years' time, and only then at your captain's pleasure." His voice itself was an elegant fog, disconcertingly soft. Patient even, as if the words rolled around in his throat, taking their time before gathering themselves into something weighty enough to be spoken. "And certainly not this morning."

"No, of course not, sir. I had no thought of *leaving*." That at least was entirely the truth. "Only of . . . others coming."

Mr. Colyear's head tipped back slowly as he weighed her words for another very long moment before he spoke in the same low, patient tone. "What are you up to, Mr. Kent?"

"Nothing, sir." She lied more easily with every passing remark, even as she hated herself for the hypocrisy of her deceit. But the truth was that she wanted to stay. And she would stay. If only they would let her. If only Richard stayed away. If only she could appease Mr. Colyear's damnable curiosity.

This time he smiled full out, his lips riding open to show the gleaming row of strong, white teeth. "Mr. Kent, you are an abominable liar."

The desperation of wanting something so uncertain was a physical thing, a pain that added to the cat's-paw of misery coiled deep in her gut. She could only answer with the truth. "Thank you, sir. For I have no wish to be a good one. I only wanted to make sure we're to sail immediately."

"Outrunning creditors, are you, Mr. Kent? Or some young lady's family?"

Sally would have laughed if she hadn't suddenly felt so near tears. She was definitely outrunning some lady's family—her own. But he must be teasing her—the cool green of his eyes had warmed to a luminous jade. "No, sir," she assured him as firmly as she could. "Nothing of the kind."

Mr. Colyear took another very long moment of consideration, with his green eyes probing more gently, but no less relentlessly, before he spoke. "Do you see *that* flag, Mr. Kent?"

Sally followed the long length of his arm to see the pennant flying from the mainmast. "The Blue Peter, sir?"

"Do you know what it means?"

"All persons should report on board as the vessel is about to proceed to sea."

"Correct. We will up anchor and sail within the hour. So think no more of the shore."

"Aye, sir." She tried to order her face to show him she was content with that, but her mind wasn't accustomed to sitting still. She wasn't very good at waiting. Still she worried. Richard could come, or be brought by force, until the moment *Audacious* shipped its anchor and left the shore behind. Until they cleared Spithead, she would not be safe.

And even then, Lieutenant David Colyear would not be done with his looking.

Until there was nothing left for him to see. Nothing but a

competent officer. Someone who was useful. "I am entirely at your disposal, Mr. Colyear."

"And so you are, Mr. Kent, so you are." He mulled that smile of his around his lips for a while to make sure he was ready to be openly pleased. "I think this morning we shall rate you midshipman, as you seem to know your business well enough."

In truth, she was a little taken aback. Sally had assumed she was rated as a midshipman, not just a gentleman volunteer. She had forgotten that she could be rated or disrated aboard ship entirely at the first lieutenant's or the captain's pleasure. But perhaps Mr. Colyear was merely amusing himself at her expense.

Yes. She saw the almost infinitesimal turndown at the very corner of his lips and knew he was amused. Just as he had been last night, when she had made her joke about the gun deck's potential for biblical instruction, to cover her embarrassment at having to witness bare-breasted women being tupped by bare-arsed men while standing next to the unperturbable Mr. Colyear. Who with his eagle eyes, she was sure, saw every nipple and nolly in the place.

Her face still felt hot with the infernal embarrassment. But it was no wonder nobody saw her as a woman, if ripe old tarts of Long Peg's variety were their measure of femininity. "I am most obliged, sir."

"And I am obliged by the fact that I shan't have to explain things to you in the same way I might with Mr. Jellicoe or Mr. Worth, for you seem to have retained a great deal of knowledge from your time aboard your father's ships. More than your brothers expected."

Ah. So he had had letters from at least one of her brothers. Matthew, she suspected. He was always the most loquacious of the Kent brothers. And particularly vocal in his disapproval of Richard's ambitions for the church. If Mr. Colyear had been expecting Matthew's version of Richard, it was no wonder why he was not disappointed in *her*.

The thought amused her enough to say, "And how shall I be most useful to you this morning, Mr. Colyear?"

There it was again, that long, considering stare, this time aided by the smallest pleating of his brow as he narrowed his gaze upon her. Let him look. If he was searching for a trace of the parson, he would never find it in her.

Finally, he inclined his ridiculously perfect, imperfect chin in another almost imperceptible gesture of approval. "You've changed, Mr. Kent." There was that bright eye again, raking her over, turning over every loose piece of her in his mind. Weighing her up like a short charge of powder. It was all she could do to keep from fidgeting with her coat, pulling the lapels tighter over her chest. "I didn't recall you being so . . . athletic. Nor did your brothers."

"I'm older since they saw me last, sir."

"Yes, perhaps you have grown up." He let up his probing stare momentarily to cast his glance over the barometer and, from there, back up to the set of the sails. "I'm assigning you to keep the first watch of the officers, with Mr. Horner as the officer of the deck. You and Mr. Gamage will be the midshipmen attending him, as well as Mr. Northam, the master's mate."

She was unlucky to have drawn duty with the still unseen Mr. Gamage, but from what she understood of his character, she was glad neither Jellicoe nor Worth had been put with him. They were both too green to be able to handle him.

"As you seem to know enough that you won't make a poor example to *Audacious*'s people, in sail drill and in weighing anchor, you'll be with the division of the foretop."

"Aye, sir." She touched her hat to hide the thrill of elation that jangled under her skin and propelled her forward, toward the foremast.

"Not just yet, if you please, Kent. The captain will want the ship mustered first and to address the people. Stand at ease."

It was a trial to do so when she was so filled with happy fidgets at the thought of going aloft. But the interim proved instructive. It was something of a revelation to watch Mr. Colyear at work. Just as she had seen yesterday, he knew every man by name, and was quick to note which of *Audacious*'s people, perhaps more professional or ambitious than others, came on deck and fell to their work before the rest of their divisions. Mr. Colyear was a man who openly respected the men without being overly familiar, and from what little she had seen, the feeling was mutual. Pinky had been open in his own admiration of the first lieutenant, and she knew Pinky judged a man on character alone.

Speaking of judging on character—Jellicoe and Worth followed on the heels of two other midshipmen she had not yet met.

"Richard Kent." She introduced herself quietly to the two older boys.

"Charles Dance." Dance was a serious young man who looked to be her age of nineteen or perhaps twenty. He was tall, and had sandy brown hair and hound-dog-sad blue eyes. He shook her hand gravely and said no more.

"Beecham, Marcus." The dark-haired boy with beautiful almond eyes greeted her with a sideways grin, and shook her hand as well. "So you're the famous Mr. Kent. Pleased to meet you. We missed each other yesterday. It's often thus, when we're on opposite watches."

"Yes, but famous? How so?" Sally was worried her late arrival at the sally port would mark her as a laggard.

"Hasn't everyone heard of the Kents?" Beecham answered.

Everyone in the navy had, and she had always been proud of it, always wanted to be counted as one of them. But now she felt all the burden of that heavy expectation rather more personally. "I'll do my best not to disappoint."

Beecham laughed. "Better you than me, man!"

"If you're through there, Mr. Beecham." Mr. Colyear's quietly wry tone made its way to them, calling them back to attention without any trace of the screeching anxiety often employed by others of his profession. Mr. Colyear's way was to correct instead of intimidate.

Speaking of intimidation, last of all the officers to scale the quarterdeck ladder was an older midshipman, identified as such by the white patches on the collar and cuffs of his too-small blue coat. He was nearly thirty years old by her eyes, older than all her brothers, and despite the weathered tan of his skin, and his weight, which showed him to be a man fond of his grub, he looked pinched, as if he were habitually displeased. This had to be Damien Gamage.

He wasn't excessively tall—in fact, Sally guessed that she was taller, though he outweighed her by at least five stone—but he was easily tall enough to intimidate both Worth or Jellicoe. As soon as he ascended the quarterdeck, Mr. Gamage simply claimed the spot where poor Ian Worth had been standing, by abruptly elbowing the boy aside, as if Gamage had a right to whatever spot he wanted despite his lateness.

So he was a blaggard as well as a bully. It only remained to see if he was a blockhead as well. Sally glanced back at Mr. Colyear to see what he made of such antics, but his eyes were all for the men gathering in the waist, and not the officers.

Sally kept her eyes on Gamage, and decided his air of intimidation was more an effect of his bulk than his stature. The man had a largeness of person that was somehow slack, as if in the approach to his middle years, he had given up all pretense of rigor, and was beginning to run to fat. But there was still enough meat on him to make her mindful not to dismiss him out of hand. Ian Worth easily gave way, and moved around to shelter beside her. Everyone, she noticed, from the ship's boys to the professional tradesmen like the carpenter and his mates, all the way up to the officers themselves, gave Gamage as wide a berth as possible, as if they none of them wanted to be in any way associated with him. Or meet with his sulky wrath.

How was such behavior allowed under either Captain McAlden or the all-seeing Mr. Colyear? How could they not see what Gamage was? But she had no time to ponder such imponderables when Captain McAlden came smartly up the quarterdeck ladder and the crew fell instantly silent.

Before the captain even spoke, Sally had to force herself to stand still, to quell the excitement building within her bound-up chest. Even without the added distinction of formal uniforms, the expanse of blue coats was the most exhilarating thing she had ever seen. There was the splash of scarlet as well from the commander of the marines, Major

Lesley, that was echoed in the straight line of the seagoing soldiers lined up to one side of the quarterdeck.

It was a sight to behold, and this time, for the first time, she was a real part of it, not just a bystander. She was one of them, arrayed in her smart blue coat just like the rest.

Below them, in the waist, two hundred fifty-odd men and boys were gathered in a colorful hodgepodge of blue coats and red waistcoats, calico shirts and kerchiefs, straw hats and knit caps. No two men looked alike, although to her eyes it was easy to pick out the foretopmen, who were known to traditionally dress with more fineness, by their smarter kerchiefs and gold earrings, which superstition said gave them keener eyesight. These would be the men with whom she was to work.

Captain McAlden spoke from the quarterdeck rail.

"*Audacious* will join the Channel Fleet in blockade duty, proceeding to the station off Brest. We are ordered to find the enemy wherever he may be. The combined French and Spanish fleet under Villeneuve and Gravina are still at large and must at all cost be kept from joining with the Corsican's invasion fleet in Boulogne. We will patrol the Channel in search of any portion of that fleet trying to enter these waters, harry all French shipping we might encounter, but also keep a fresh eye upon the harbor at Brest to make ourselves eminently useful to His Majesty and the Lords of the Admiralty." The captain leaned both arms down on the quarterdeck rail. "But we will also take every conceivable prize that we can. There will be a guinea to the man who first sights a ship taken as a prize."

A cry went instantly up from the topmen. "Huzzah!"

"And there'll be more of the same opportunities for those of you not in the tops. *Audacious,* see to your stations."

"Hip, hip," the call came from the waist.

"Hurrah!" came the answering cheer.

As soon as the cheer had been repeated the requisite three times, the captain turned to the sailing master. "Mr. Charlton, you may weigh the anchor."

And so it began, with the orders echoing from the officers

of each division. Sally dove forward, down the deck to her station in the foremast.

"Man the capstan. Up anchor. Heave away."

All over the ship, men clambered to their stations—topmen scrambled aloft and waisters hove to the braces and halyards in anticipation.

"Lively there, men," she called as she climbed onto the starboard chains and the foretopmen scampered by up the shrouds.

Her heart sped up, pounding against her chest like white-caps with the thrill of the moment. It was happening. Richard hadn't come, and she was beyond glad. She was going to sea.

Chapter Five

She was half afraid her hands would be clumsy and fumbling in her excitement. But experience and elation buoyed her, and in no time she was above, at the masthead. Around her, the wiry, agile topmen climbed to their stations with a minimum of instruction from their captain of the foretop, a long, lanky, earringed fellow named Willis.

"Lay out." She ordered them out along the yards. "That's it. Steady now, lads."

They arrayed themselves across the rope horses of the forecourse sail yard, and above, on the foretopsail yard, and even gallant and royal yards in anticipation of the order to unfurl. Clearly *Audacious*'s people wanted to see her out of port in the style of their namesake—boldly.

"Up and down," came the cry from the bow as the ship was warped over the bower anchor.

Below in the waist, the capstan was manned by idlers and marines, who lent their discipline as well as their strength to the endeavor. Above, as she looked out from the foretop, the barely bowed line of the horizon stretched out before her in an infinite arc. It was nothing and everything all at once—it was infinite possibility.

Elation was like an opiate blossoming through her veins. She had never been so happy.

At the capstan, one of the older crew members scraped

an old, worn-out fiddle into a lively song to set a rhythm for the effort of turning the great winch, and for hauling sheets and tacks. Sally recognized the old tune—a favorite of her family, but not one usually employed in the navy, where "Heart of Oak" was the preferred tune—and from the sheer exhilaration of the moment, she began to sing.

> *Dance to your daddy, my little laddie.*
> *Dance to your daddy, my little man.*

She broke off when she found the men staring at her, but a wiry young sailor encouraged her. "Go on then, young sir. You've a fine voice for it."

The compliment couldn't help but warm her. Her voice was perhaps average, certainly not the kind of female voice that was characterized as "accomplished" in a drawing room, but it was strong and clear, and well suited to the buoyant tunes of the navy.

> *Ye shall have a fish and ye shall have a fin.*
> *Ye shall have a herring when the boat comes in.*
> *Ye shall have a codling boiled in a pan.*
> *Dance to your daddy, my little man.*

At the chorus, more of the men of her division joined in. The singing didn't stop her vigilant attention to the task at hand. "Mind the lifts, there." She watched for fingers and feet placed correctly so as not to get wrenched up by running lines. "Hold ready."

The predictable easy motion of the ship at anchor began to give way as *Audacious* began to respond to her helm and Mr. Colyear's booming baritone brought the orders for the loosening and setting of the sails. "Let fall the forecourse. Haul away there."

"Forecourse away," she called at the top of her lungs.

Below her, canvas cracked and began to swell with the wind.

"Sheet home," came the call as the foresail caught the breeze and billowed out.

Elation poured over her, leaving her drenched and breathless, sputtering to draw air into her lungs as she felt the ship beneath her feet respond to the helm. The hempen stay she clutched grew taut and alive in her hand, vibrating with the power of the wind rushing over her, washing her clean. She felt free, and empty of expectations.

And conversely full of possibilities.

She turned her gaze farther aloft, to the next course of sails. Any second now, Mr. Colyear would call out, and she wanted to be ready. She wanted the men of her division to be ready so that she might show Mr. Colyear she knew her business twice as well as anyone else. She would make a fine example to *Audacious*'s people.

"Cast off your foregallant gaskets and stand ready." And just as the men complied, she could hear Mr. Colyear's voice calling the next order.

"Away t'gallants," she called out the moment his commanding voice reached her straining ears.

It was an added thrill, this give and take, the anticipation and completion of his orders. It was heady to know she played an integral part in the great choreography of making sail. It made her daring and full of herself and her own importance. It made her almost want to tell him that it was *she*—it was Sally Kent and not Richard who so capably leapt to do his bidding almost before he told her. It was she who was useful enough to earn his admiration.

When ye are a man and ye shall want a wife
Ye shall wed a maid and love her all your life
She shall be your lassie, ye shall be her man
Dance to your daddy, my little man.

Up in the rigging she was useful. She was happy. She could sing with all her joy and elation and let the wind take it away wherever it would.

It broke over Col suddenly and swiftly, the knowledge. So swiftly that he pushed it away, for once distrusting his finely honed instinct. He had no time to ponder imponderables. He had a crew to run, heading out of the Portsmouth roadstead, with the eyes of the rest of the bloody fleet upon them.

"Let go the main'sle," he ordered. "Take in that starboard tack. Mizzencourse away."

He raised his brass speaking trumpet to make sure he was heard over the singing from the foretop. The damned singing, pounding and nagging at his brain like an alarm bell.

Normally he never minded singing. He actually preferred to have a fiddle at the capstan to give the men a lift, set the pace and help them along. It was tedious, backbreaking work raising two anchors, and every help was welcome. And the topmen were known for their daring and élan, and often sang when hauling away and setting or reefing sails.

But that song. He heard it now, just as he heard it in his head every time he thought of that summer he had spent with the Kents at Cliff House in Falmouth. It had only been a six-week, taken for the purpose of studying for the lieutenancy exams while the *Fortune* had been laid up for repairs, but the memories had stayed strong with him.

A vivid mental image of the sister, the only girl, dropped into his mind like a miniature discovered in his pocket—all burnished red-gold hair and sun-kissed cheeks. Sarah Alice— Sally. She had been everywhere with them that summer, a constant shadow, sailing, fishing, laughing. Everything he and the Kent boys had done, she had done, too. And she had been good company—the best. Always game and laughing. She had been the first girl whom he thought it a pleasure to be with. Her brothers had accepted her company without question or bother, in a way that they never had with Richard, who had been felt to be too young, too unathletic, and too uninteresting to be included in their games and adventures. And so Col had accepted her, too. And she had sung.

In the evenings, as the light leached out of the day and darkness had fallen, they had taken out their instruments and played. And she had laughed and sung with such cheerful sweetness that he had never forgotten it. Or her.

The boy singing in the foretop could not be Richard Kent. He could not be the diffident, solemn boy of Matthew's letters, who preferred his own company and the reading of Fordyce's sermons to adventure and games. The Richard Kent who had hidden from his brothers' rough teasing would not have climbed the ratlines with such eagerness, not to mention skill and grace. The Richard Kent who had preferred the indoors would never have grabbed a handful of rope and leaned his face into the bright, blowing wind.

Col rounded the quarterdeck and strode forward, heedless of his duty, heedless of his captain's surprise. Heedless to everything but the need to see. To make sure.

Col tipped up his head and shaded his eyes, and looked again at Kent. At the urchin face turned almost gamin with delight. At the red-gold hair streaming from his queue in the wind. At the unbridled smile widening his mouth. Without his hat to shield and darken his features, Kent looked, as the captain had said with such accuracy the first day he arrived, a soft, pretty sort of boy.

Because he wasn't a boy at all. Because now, in the clear morning light, Col could see nothing but the sister. Sally Kent. Damn her.

Now that his brain had finally caught up with his gut, recognition roared through his body like a wayward cannon shot. Awareness scorched every fiber of his being. He should have known. He should have recognized her immediately.

But part of him had. The part that had lain awake nights, in the dark, cramped confines of his cabin, thinking of tall, laughing, ginger-haired girls. Thinking about the supple, natural grace of her body. And wondering what her lips might have tasted like.

Sally Kent. Damn her eyes.

"Mr. Colyear?" The sailing master was recalling him to his forgotten duty.

"Royals away," Col ordered through his teeth. The

command, he noted, was immediately carried out in the foretop, as if she had anticipated his order. Damn her laughing gray eyes.

He wanted to haul her down from the crosstrees by her coat and shake the truth from her. He wanted to cast her over the side like so much jetsam. He wanted to examine every last inch of her to make sure, to prove beyond a shadow of a doubt that he had not dreamt her up to assuage his unanswered longings. To make sure that it really was she and not Richard Kent. That he had not imagined it to be her just to satisfy this unnerving, unholy attraction.

God help him. What he wanted wasn't bloody important. He was an officer of His Majesty's Royal Navy and his thoughts and actions were not his alone—they were his ship's. Somewhere off the blasted larboard rail Napoleon had gathered his bloody army not ten miles from the English coast. And he needed every able man he could get. Even if they weren't a man.

But he had to be bloody damn sure.

Sally Kent. Damn, damn, damn her fine gray eyes.

When Col regained his place on the quarterdeck, his captain approached. "Mr. Colyear." His tone was bemused. "You seem preoccupied. That's not like you, sir."

"I beg your pardon, sir." Col recalled himself and checked his instruments. Despite his momentary lapse in judgment, the ship was still making good sea way, sailing west by south on the larboard tack with the wind out of the east, six points large on the quarter.

The forenoon was stretching fair and bright before them. And he was in hell.

Consumed by his thoughts. By her.

Her. Her. Her.

It ought to be a comfort to know he wasn't going mad. Not entirely. He ought to feel vindicated. He had been right. Something had been wrong. Terribly wrong. And terribly right.

He had to tell his captain. The sooner the better. In fact,

every mile of ocean that slipped under *Audacious*'s stern would make it more and more difficult to see her put ashore. If he were to speak, he had to do it now.

And yet, he found himself hesitating. Finding other tasks that demanded his immediate attention. "Take the slack out of the mizzen topcourse brace." Gathering his thoughts and mustering his arguments, while he tried to find equally compelling reasons not to do so.

The list that ran in his head was short, uninspiring, and insufficient. Because the Kent family would suffer if he allowed her to be called down now, disgraced before the entire ship's company. Because there was work to be done and *Audacious* needed all the able seamen it could carry, and as long as she did the work, he could choose the time and way to tell Captain McAlden without embarrassing the Kents, or endangering his ship. And because he still wasn't entirely sure.

Because he had to be sure he wasn't making excuses for the bloody unwarranted fascination he seemed to have developed for a young boy.

Damn his own eyes. Either way, he was in hell.

"I expect we will have a most rewarding cruise," his captain was saying to Mr. Charlton, "blockade duty notwithstanding."

Normally, Col would have welcomed such conversations and discussions amongst such men. Despite the vast difference in their ages, the captain and the sailing master had always honored him with the distinction of being treated like a colleague and not merely a subordinate. Mr. Charlton was the most senior of all the officers—warrant or commissioned—at the age of fifty-eight, while Captain McAlden was a seasoned thirty-six. Col's years only numbered four and twenty, yet he was never made to feel inferior in the presence of the two men, who had a great deal more experience than Col. Their principled treatment of him gave him his own model to follow in his interactions with the officers and men beneath him, from the grizzled, veteran bo'sun to the youngest, greenest midshipman.

Well, apart from throwing green young boys covered with vomit into the harbor, he treated all of his brother officers with the respect he himself had been so decently given. And he would have to give Kent that same respect, that same benefit of the doubt, until he was sure.

"Blockade duty is good only for two things." Captain McAlden's words on their duty mirrored Col's opinion. "Gun drill and sail drill. After a month, we shall be well practiced and out of patience with both."

"If we were to take prizes, the men would put up with any number of hours of gun drill," added Mr. Charlton.

"We *will* take prizes, wherever we can find them," the captain asserted. "And we will do more than that to harry the French. We will take the fight to them, if they will not bring it to us."

Col could hear the relish, the unbridled enthusiasm and determination behind his captain's words. "Sir?" he prompted.

"We are victims of our own success. If we blockade the ports too well, the French won't venture out, so we have fewer chances of taking prizes. We will need to be bold, Mr. Colyear, and think beyond our normal horizons." The captain gave Col one of his wry half-smiles before he asked, "When was the last time you were on land, Mr. Colyear?"

Col's gut clenched up at the mere thought. "You know I never go ashore if I can help it."

"Did you even set foot upon the quay in Portsmouth?"

"A guinea says he didn't," Mr. Charlton answered.

"No bets, Mr. Charlton. And only a fool would take it. Well, Mr. Colyear?" The captain was making sport of him.

"No, sir. I haven't set foot on land since Gibraltar, last spring. And only then for less than ten minutes. I'm not fond of the way the land reacts underfoot."

Their smiles were all at their expense.

"Not even the ladies can tempt our Mr. Colyear ashore," Captain McAlden observed. "But I tell you, man, you shall think very differently of the land when you have got a wife."

He did not bother to repeat that he should not want a wife for the very reason that it would require him to go ashore.

They had heard his objections to marriage before and would only be more amused, for Captain McAlden was of a different opinion entirely. Indeed, on their last cruise—chasing Villeneuve's French fleet across the Atlantic—the captain had ordered a diversion in their course to the island of New Providence, ostensibly to reprovision the ship for their swift passage back to England with Admiral Nelson's dispatches for the Admiralty, but in reality so the captain could spend a long day and night with his wife, Lady McAlden, who lived there.

"Well, I should like you to reconsider, Mr. Colyear," his captain advised. "Not about the wife, for such things are the province of a man's own discretion, but about the land. For what I have in mind, I should very much like to send you ashore."

Col forced himself not to react like a puling midshipman. Not to let his damned fear and hesitation show. "Ashore, sir, or merely inshore for a mission, like a cutting-out expedition, for example?"

"Very much like a cutting-out expedition, Mr. Colyear. Such acuity confirms my opinion that you are one of the finest young officers I have ever had the privilege of having serve under me. And, much as it would pain me to part with you, I should like to see you in your own command. But to accomplish that we will need to be truly audacious."

The warm praise burned away Col's misgivings. "I thank you for your confidence, sir. But how exactly is that to be accomplished?"

McAlden's devilish, one-sided smile was out in full force. "By being lucky, of course."

"I thought you did not believe in luck, sir?"

"I don't," his captain answered, still smiling his secret, ironic smile. "I believe in preparation. Luck is merely when preparation meets opportunity. And I want you to be prepared for every opportunity, Mr. Colyear, including those ashore. But it is early days yet. On another tack entirely, I should like your opinion as to the current state of the crew."

Col was thoroughly prepared for such a discussion. In his

head, he had already divided the whole of *Audacious*'s people in different watches and divisions based on what he already knew of their abilities and temperaments. "We've retained most all of our crew from the last cruise. Only two invalided out in Portsmouth. So the topmen and the gun crews should be well manned with veterans. We've taken on five new landsmen, but I'm sure you'll want daily sail and gun drill—perhaps alternating days while we work new hands in."

"Admirable. Mr. Charlton, have you any recommendations?"

"Mr. Davies has put forward William Moffatt's name for gunners mate. Good man, steady. Been in seven years."

"Mr. Colyear?"

"Excellent choice, sir." And so they went through the ranks. While the captain never interfered with his sailing master or his first lieutenant's prerogatives, he liked to know everything that went on aboard his ship, including all matters of the crew's division, which were Col's to decide.

"Quite satisfactory," Captain McAlden remarked. "And what of the officers? What do you make of the boys so far?"

Here was his chance to speak. Now. With England still off the starboard rail.

"Dance and Beecham continue to come along well." Col eased into the dangerous topic. "Mr. Dance especially is maturing in his abilities."

"Excellent. And Mr. Gamage?"

Col was sensible, as were they all, of their failures with Mr. Gamage. The navy liked to see something come of its investment in a man's training, and Col took it personally, as a mark against his professionalism, that Mr. Gamage did not improve. He strove to push the resignation from his voice. "He continues to be Gamage."

"Not much you can do for him if he can't learn his mathematics enough to pass the exams. Mr. Charlton? Any thoughts about putting him up as a master's mate?"

"I've broached the idea, sir, only to be told by Mr. Gamage that he considers the position to be below that of a gentleman."

"Well, damn his impudence. And without the mathematics there is nothing to be done. And the new boys? I have high hopes for young Kent. A bright, eager lad. He certainly seemed to know his business in the foretop. His father will be pleased to hear of it."

"Have you written to Captain Kent?" Col wished the impulsive question back even as he asked. While Captain McAlden rarely interfered with his lieutenant's disposition of the men, he would be taken aback by Col's inquiry after his personal correspondence, even if he did not hear the urgency in Col's normally level voice.

"Have you some objection, sir? Do you not share my good opinion of the boy? Come, Mr. Colyear, if you know something to the boy's detriment, let me hear what you have to say, for I would not give such a man as Captain Kent false hopes."

Now was the time, the perfect time, to disclose his misgivings about Kent. Now, while she could be put off discreetly and quietly, while they were still within sight of the English coast. Now.

But what if his misgivings were wrong? What if his much-vaunted instinct was wrong? The insult to Richard Kent, and by extension to his family, would be monumental. Not to mention utterly humiliating for Col himself.

He had to be sure.

"No, sir." The words felt dry and tight in his throat. "None at all."

"Good. It is for you to decide, of course, but I should recommend putting our able young Mr. Kent with Mr. Gamage. That pairing seems likely to cause the least amount of trouble."

"Agreed, sir. Young Mr. Worth is with Mr. Dance, and Mr. Jellicoe with Mr. Beecham. I've already seen to it."

"Excellent." The captain smiled. "That is why I count on you, Mr. Colyear. You always see what needs to be done."

"Yes, sir." Col swallowed his misgivings down like a dose of bitter medicine. "I hope to God I have."

Chapter Six

"A word, Mr. Kent, when you are done with your lessons."

Sally blinked to adjust her eyes to the full brightness of the sunlight after having her eye to the sextant, and found Mr. Colyear standing directly in front of her. He had not been on the quarterdeck earlier, when they had begun the lesson, for she had found herself looking for him, seeking out his tall form even before she realized what she was doing.

The forenoon had been spent in the company of the rest of the midshipmen—minus Mr. Gamage, who had disappeared below the moment Mr. Charlton had called them to attend him—at lessons on the mathematics of navigation. They had just finished learning to take the noon reading of the zenith of the sun, a skill she had acquired years before, when Mr. Colyear had materialized before her, like a shark rising out of the water, grim, silent, and intent.

But that just seemed to be his way, his method for keeping the officers and men on their toes. Sally was glad she was already on her toes, for that was undoubtedly why he wanted to speak to her. He must have noticed that Mr. Charlton had singled her out for praise in the quick and accurate accomplishment of her calculations. Perhaps Mr. Colyear wanted to add his own praise for the efficiency with which she had seen his orders followed that morning. "Certainly, Mr. Colyear. I am at your disposal."

"Walk with me, if you please."

She turned to follow him down the gangway toward the bowsprit. In his usual manner, his eyes never stopped roaming, never stopped canvassing the ship for work to be done. Or work to be done better.

"Lincoln," he said to one of the forecastle men, "see that sheet is coiled properly. Higgins, report that split in the chain wale to the carpenter. I don't want that giving way at the wrong moment."

Sally merely followed in his wake, conscious of her appearance, striving to walk as she had been observing Jellicoe and Beecham doing. Trying her best to appear to be boyish. To be her better version of Richard.

Now that Mr. Colyear wasn't bending his thorny, unrelenting gaze upon her, she could appreciate his vigilance, and appreciate his qualities—as a professional man, of course. He saw everything that needed to be seen, everything that needed to be done. In the setting of the sails that morning, the moment she had noticed a correction that needed to be made, he was already there, calling out his orders before she even got the words out of her mouth.

He was quite remarkable. And he wasn't at all like her brothers, who were voluble and impulsive. Mr. Colyear was even-keeled, keeping his emotions in check behind his formidable intelligence and self-control. It had been a great pleasure to listen for his well-tempered, precise commands.

"Young Mr. Kent," he began slowly, giving each word the full measure of its weight. "I hardly know what to do with you."

He sounded baffled, and just a little put out. But Sally had heard such tones before. How many times had her father or one of her brothers sounded the same, when she had exasperated them with her tomboy, hoydenish antics?

She gave Mr. Colyear the same answer she had always given them. "Put me to work, sir. Anywhere you please, though I like the foremast, and especially the captain of the foretop, Willis. Excellent man. Knows his business. But if it please you, I can do almost any duty you should need or desire."

"I have no doubt you can." Mr. Colyear shook his head ruefully and looked out over the rail at the sea, reading its ebb and flow the way most people read a book—all its secrets were open to him. "You're an odd one, Kent."

Sally was buffeted back by that, as if by a stiff headwind. Odd was not helpful or admiring. Odd was certainly not promising. Odd was not good.

"Last night I was happy to find that your brothers had gotten you wrong. They never thought there would be any making a sailor out of you. Best left to your books and dour sermons was Matthew and Dominic's theory. But you don't seem the sort for books. Not at all."

Her stomach began to knot up like a cat's-paw. This was very definitely not good. "Have I done something wrong, sir?"

"If you've done what I think you have, it's the wrongest thing I can think of. Damnation, but I'm not sure of you, Kent. Not sure at all." Mr. Colyear swiped his hat off his head and ran his fingers through his black hair in a gesture of utter frustration, making him look disheveled. And thoroughly appealing. "Ever since you came on board you've captured my attention in a way that has"—he searched for a word—"unsettled me."

"I'm sorry, sir. I didn't mean to—" She could hear the sharp edge of panic fraying her voice, but her heart seemed to be rising into her throat. She seized upon the first excuse. "I know I was tardy coming aboard but—"

"And why was that, Kent?" He turned to look at her, his gaze raking across her, searching her face, looking at her as if the answer he sought might be written across her skin. Up close, his voice sounded throaty and ashen, as if it had been dragged through a fire. Everything about him looked that way, dark and saturated with charcoal—the sooty black of his rumpled hair, the liquid depths of his eyes that darkened now that all the light had gone out of them, and the shadowed dark of his skin, burned and bronzed by the years of exposure to sun and wind and rain. Up close, everything about him seemed dark and relentless. "Why were you tardy coming aboard?"

She would have to lie despite the heat that raced under her skin, scorching her. Despite the fact that he had said only this morning that she was an abominable liar. She would have to lie because not to do so would be to give in. To give up her dream.

So she cleaved as closely to the truth as possible, desperate to make him believe her. "I was unsure, sir. Unsure if I should take my place."

A frown pleated three identical vertical marks between his eyebrows as he continued to watch her. "You still felt that perhaps the church was your true calling?"

She should have known that her brothers' letters would be frank and revealing. She should have been better prepared for Mr. Colyear's probing inquisition. "Yes," was the only thing she could answer. It was the truth—or at least it was Richard's truth.

"And what, may I ask, do you think now?"

Sally put every ounce of terrified conviction into her answer. "That it was absolutely the right decision to come aboard."

"Absolutely?"

"Yes, sir. I was meant for the sea." This was undoubtedly the truest thing she had ever said. She knew it to the bottom of her soul. "Mr. Colyear, can you doubt my commitment? I have tried—I am trying—very hard to prove my worth. To prove my usefulness, just as Captain McAlden instructed. Have I not done so?"

"You have." He looked her in the eye and she felt again the strength of that look, the singleness of focus. It made a person feel as if they were the only thing in the world he could see, when she knew that wasn't true—he saw *everything*. He always had. "But you ought to know as well as I, Kent, that sometimes, even that is not enough."

He knew. The knowledge was there in the quiet resignation of his voice, in the pained way he closed his eyes so he might no longer have to look at her. She told herself it was inevitable that he should know her. But even that cold knowledge could not alleviate the searing knot of pain radiating from her chest.

She turned away so he might not see the hot wash of tears rising in her eyes. She would not cry. Devil take her, she was a Kent.

"It's funny. All day I've been thinking of that summer. The summer I spent with your family at Cliff House, there in Falmouth. I recall it was a very fine house, with a great prospect down to the sea."

"Oh, yes." She could hear the bleak, frustrated attempt at humor in her voice, as she attempted to follow his improbable segue. "I don't think my father could abide in any house for longer than a day, if it did not have a view of the sea."

"It was your brother Matthew's idea to use the time to study for our lieutenancy examinations. Ambitious, Matthew Kent was. Still is, I'm sure. Do you remember?"

"I do." She remembered as if it were yesterday. She had been old enough to envy them their careers, had hung on their every word, Col and Matthew. But especially Col. "Everyone was home for the same fortnight. Matthew, Dominic, Owen, Daniel, and Father. It was the last time we were all there, together."

"I recall it particularly. The way you were then, how you sat together in the evenings and sang songs and— One of you played the mandolin."

It had been she who played the mandolin. Richard played the violin. The damn instrument was still taking up space at the bottom of her sea chest.

"You used to play that same song as Punch did this morning. 'Dance to Your Daddy.'"

The damn song. She should have known. She should have anticipated that he *heard* everything with the same focus, the same acute attention that he *saw*. But still, she could not give in. "It's a very old tune."

"Yes," he agreed calmly. "All the men seemed to know the words. It was a proper rousing send-off this morning."

It was killing her, the waiting. The waiting for his condemnation. Knowing it was coming. Knowing she deserved it. The heat piling up in the back of her throat kept her from answering.

"I remembered the song." He looked at her briefly then, and she could see the truth, the full understanding deep in his green eyes. "Do you remember that evening, when we caught fireflies in your orchard? The phosphorescent insects lighting up as the late twilight gave way to dark. Do you remember?"

"Yes." The word tasted like misery, cold and ashen in her mouth.

He had instantly, with a few precise words, conjured up the soft magic of that evening. She could smell the pungent green of the long grass they crushed beneath their feet, tromping about the overgrown orchard to capture the glowing insects in an empty jam jar.

"And one landed in your hair, and I was obliged to brush it off, though it looked charming there, lighting up your ginger hair. The green against the orange glow."

The heat behind her eyes felt blinding. It was worse, this slow, thoughtful meander into memory, than any torture he might have thought up.

"And we pelted your brother with windfalls for preaching at us so."

"Yes." The misery was pushing the hot tears into the corners of her eyes. She dashed them away with the edge of her sleeve. Devil take her. She would *not* cry. Not in front of Mr. Colyear. No matter the provocation.

It had been *she*—Sally. She had been in the back garden with him, sitting on the high orchard wall with him by her side, lobbing apples at Richard for his mealymouthed prating. They had laughed and laughed, and she had felt special to be allowed within the sacred circle of the young naval men. She had been proud of her arm, as if a young man like Col would notice such a thing in a girl.

And Richard had run away to the house and left them alone in the orchard together, she and Col, that long-ago evening. And she had sworn he might have kissed her, but at the last moment she had shied away, and laughed and thrown more sticks to cover her awkwardness.

The knowledge was there in his eyes. In the dark, uncompromising certainty of his gaze. In the way his mouth flattened into a tense line, the smile banished along with the warmth of the memory.

"Just so. Just as I thought." He nodded briefly, but the warmth faded out of his eyes. He began to shake his head back and forth in maddened disbelief.

"You might have told me, Kent. You might have spared me the—" Something in his voice was off, rusted like a sword left too long in a sheath. The sound of betrayal. "You might have told Captain McAlden. You ought to have. But damn your eyes, you ought not to have done it at all."

But she had. She had done it quite purposefully. And she would do anything to keep it from being undone. "Sir, please." She had to make him understand. "I had no choice. I had to come. I felt as if I should suffocate if I had to spend another day ashore. You have to understand. You of all people—"

"*You* of all people, who was raised by Captain Alexander Kent, ought to understand the seriousness, the utter hell and be-damned gall of what you have done."

He was right. She had known the chance she had taken. But she was a Kent. She had recklessness bred into her bones. Calculating risk came as easily as trimming a sail or riding the crest of a wave into the shore. As easy as breathing. And it had been worth it. The feeling she had gotten this morning, when she had been aloft—she'd never felt so perfectly right, so happy and useful, in her life. She had only to convince him.

"Please. You must understand. I know my duty—"

"There is nothing to *understand*. You have lied to me, from the moment you set foot on this ship. You have lied to me and to your captain. For fuck's sake, Kent. We are an armed naval frigate, at sea, in the middle of a bloody war that has consumed the better part of both of our lifetimes.

What in hell makes you think I don't understand exactly what is at stake here, *Mister* Kent?"

The force of his anger, of his righteousness, bored into her, piercing holes in her audacity.

"Please, sir." She didn't care if she had to beg. She had to try. "I'll do anything. Please. Just tell me what you want me to do."

She grabbed his hand, heedless of his anger, heedless of the eyes that might be watching. Heedless of everything but the need to stop him. She had to convince him, she had to impress upon him the rightness of her cause.

The instant she touched him, she had to let go. Her hand, indeed her whole body now, felt prickly with static electricity.

He, too, drew back from her touch as if he had been scalded. As if she had slapped him, or punched him hard in the chest. The look he gave her was full of ferocious awareness. And anger. At her for putting him in such an abominably untenable position.

And she felt it as well, the seething chaos of her emotions. Another touch of a spark and they would both ignite like a loose powder cartridge scattering destruction across the deck.

Her voice was nothing but ashes. "I'm sorry, sir."

He sucked a deep breath through his teeth to bank the fire of his anger, but his voice was full of fierce, dark heat. "As you bloody well should be, Kent."

"Will you . . ." She couldn't finish her question. There were too many curious ears and curious eyes watching the strange agonizing interplay between them. "What will you do, sir?"

He jammed his cocked hat down upon his dark curls. "What I always do, Mr. Kent. My duty."

Sally stayed at the forecastle rail, quiet and out of the way as long as possible, waiting for the horrible numbness to burn itself out. Waiting for the bo'sun or marine guard to come and put her adventure to an end. Waiting for it to be over. Mr. Colyear would go to the captain now and she would be put off. The best she could hope for was that they might do it quietly, so her family might be spared the scandal.

Sally thought of retiring to the cockpit, or seeking Pinky's advice, but such evasion seemed cowardly. She was a Kent. If she was to be disgraced, she would face her disgrace bravely. No matter what else they might think of her, she wouldn't have it said she was a coward.

And yet, such heroics did not prove necessary. Nothing happened. No one looked her way, or even spoke her name. No marine came to escort her to the captain's cabin. The ship continued to rise and fall beneath her feet and make its way down the Channel without any correction or change of course. Everything around her was calm and easy.

While she was awash in contradictions—wanting to stay on *Audacious* as long as she could, and yet wanting the mortifying and unpleasant experience of her unmasking to be over as quickly as possible. She was no good at it, the waiting—never had been. Everything seemed worse with the sword of discovery poised so precariously over her head. But when the bo'sun piped the men to their dinners, there was nothing for her to do but return to the cockpit.

She trundled her way belowdecks without watching where she was going, still surly with the tension of waiting. Yet the moment Sally pushed open the flimsy bulkhead door to the cockpit, she knew something was wrong from the sudden stillness of the moment, and the curiously silent watchfulness of the other boys. No one met her eyes, or greeted her entrance, already intimidated into silence.

Damien Gamage sat at the far end of the table like a self-satisfied monarch. Seated thusly, he looked decidedly soft in the middle and his eyes had a heavy-lidded, tired look, which, when combined with his full lips, made him appear stupid. His complexion, which was still on the pale side, despite what must have been his years at sea, gave no aid to his appearance. Neither did his hair, which without his hat was a dirty blond that was bleached at the ends by the sun, giving it the aged appearance of ash gray. All in all, the man had all the appearance of a well-fed rat.

But then again, Mr. Gamage could have looked like the blond Apollo himself and she would have found him lacking. As it was his character that she already objected to so strongly, his looks could only serve as further confirmation of her dislike.

His smile, as he waited for her to take note of him, was full of nasty sneering anticipation. She had no intention of giving him the satisfaction. The best way to deal with bullies was to avoid them if possible, and confront them only when unavoidable.

But he had made sure it would be unavoidable. Because there in the corner was her sea chest, with its top wide open. The lock had been broken and the contents ransacked.

Now, when it was already too late, she heartily wished she had taken the time to more closely follow Pinky's instructions, for with some forethought she might have saved herself a great deal of bother and a great many stores. But she wasn't going to dance around the situation. If Mr. Gamage wanted a confrontation, she would give it to him. If she could withstand the stony, detached cool of Mr. Colyear's inspection, she could easily stand up to this soft man. After all, she had nothing to lose. If she was about to be set off at the nearest landfall, then she was going to put paid to whatever bully-boy tactic Mr. Gamage was playing among the midshipmen.

"You must be Mr. Gamage. I see you've broken into my dunnage. People warned me you would, but I had no idea you would do it so soon or so brazenly. I'm Richard Kent."

"I know who you are. But I don't particularly care. You're all the same to me—snotty-nosed children. But you're a boot-licking little brat as well." Gamage said the words with a sort of wearied boredom, a callousness that was devoid of all true emotion. "Shut the door, sit down, and shut up. I've already explained my requirements to these snotty-nosed children and I don't like having to repeat myself."

He sat at the table—which Sally noticed he had all to

himself, while the others perched or slouched atop their sea chests, and not on the benches surrounding the table—and took a long, deliberate sip from a glass of what looked like sherry or tawny port. *Her* sherry, devil take it. Gamage put his near-empty glass down upon the table and a servant boy—this must be Tunney—darted forward to refill it before Gamage spoke again.

"This is *my* berth, do you understand, and you're just visiting here at my sufferance." He didn't even look around to see if there were any challenge to his statement, and indeed no one made the slightest objection.

Sally was disappointed to see Charles Dance, who was both old enough and physically large enough to stand up to Gamage, or at least to help her stand up to him, chose not to do anything. He merely looked pained, but quite resigned to the display. Ian Worth, poor child, was rubbing at his reddened face with his sleeve, as if he'd already had his turn being worked over by the Rat King.

Though she was quaking with indignation in her too-big shoes, Sally refused to be intimidated. Bullies always kept on until someone stood up to them. It was for the good of all the midshipmen that she had to stop Gamage.

"I don't think Captain McAlden would call our presence onboard sufferance." She kept her tone even but firm, to show him she was serious, and that she, for one, wasn't about to be intimidated by such an obvious ploy, senior or no.

"I didn't give you permission to speak." In the dim light of the cockpit, his red-rimmed, hooded gray eyes gave him more and more the appearance of a malignant rodent.

"Don't be absurd, Mr. Gamage. Clearly, you're senior here, and I won't begrudge you an inch of the respect due your experience and seniority, but I'll tell you straight off, I'll not stand for your bullying, or being told what to do in my own berth. And I certainly won't stand for anyone stealing my stores."

Gamage slowly brought his hands up to clap them together in an ironic show of applause.

"Oh, well done, boy, well done. Very brave speech. The

bravest yet." He dropped his hands and leaned back, all sprawling ease. "What are you going to do about it?"

"Exactly what you think I'll do. I will report you to the captain."

"Oh, you will, will you? The captain won't hear of it, if you know what's good for you, Kent. There's a certain code of conduct that one must abide by in the cockpit. A certain rule. But I wouldn't expect you to understand that. It's well-known the Kents are hardly *gentlemen*."

The slur to her family was a low trick, and one intended to provoke her into rash stupidity. And she was more than provoked. She would like nothing more than to plow her fist into his soft skull and pound him insensate. She was a Kent and, girl or no, she knew how to use her fives. But physical fighting, however satisfying, would do her no good. Gamage was easily twice her weight. And he had engineered this scene quite on purpose. She wouldn't be surprised if he had a cosh or some other low fighting trick hidden behind his capacious back. As tempting as it was to show him she had learned more dirty tricks at the knees of her ungentlemanly brothers than his mind could ever comprehend, let along catalogue, she refrained.

She had to do the very thing he did not expect.

And so, she smiled. "That's right, Gamage, I'm no gentleman at all." And then she laughed to show him how patently absurd his threats were.

The laughter caught him off guard. So off guard, he stood up abruptly and promptly lost his balance, thumping directly back down on the bench.

The watching boys erupted into snide laughter at his expense before Gamage shot a murderous look around to silence them into smothering their nervous snickers behind their hands. But she wouldn't be silent.

"I thank you for your dubious advice, Mr. Gamage, but I do know what's good for me. And I won't stand for having my personal property stolen, or being intimidated by the likes of you."

"The likes of me?" Gamage smiled through his teeth.

"And just who in all hell do you think you are, you soft, pretty boy?"

She advanced down the length of the table. "I am Richard Kent, of the Kents of Falmouth, England, and His Majesty's Royal Navy, and—"

Gamage was faster than she ever would have given him credit for. He shot up and caught her face in one of his big hands, dragging her torso across the table and pinching her cheeks together, hard.

She had no choice but to grab his hands to pry them apart to keep his nails from digging into her skin. But she had been pulled off her feet and could get no purchase, dangling from his hands like an ungainly fish on a line.

"Look at you," he said with a strange sort of wonder. "Such a pretty, soft sort of boy." He inspected her face, turning it back and forth with the peculiar detachment of a connoisseur, as if she were an inanimate work of art. Or an animal at a fair. "And it seems Mr. Colyear has discovered he likes pretty, soft boys, for he had you chatting up with him for quite the longest time. Now, what have you and the sly Mr. Colyear been up to?"

It took a very long moment for her to understand Gamage's insidious implication. "You disgusting pig. Whatever Mr. Colyear had to say to me is none of your business," she ground out. "Keep your filthy insinuations to yourself."

Now it was Gamage's turn to laugh at her. "Filthy? What are you suggesting, pretty little Kent? What could the strait-laced Mr. Colyear have said to you to put you in such a pet?"

"Keep your mouth shut, Gamage."

He squeezed her face harder so that she was obliged to put up her hands to pry him off her mouth. "*Mister* Gamage to you, you inconsequential, pretty little brat." He let her go with a shove that pushed her back hard enough to stumble against a sea chest. "Learn some respect for your betters, and perhaps I will keep quiet. Perhaps I can be persuaded to keep from telling the captain what I know about the heretofore impregnable Mr. Colyear. I know how to keep my mouth shut. It only remains to be seen if you know how to keep *your* big, soft, pretty boy's mouth shut."

It was, without a doubt, the most humiliating, ridiculous conundrum in which she had ever found herself. She was being blackmailed into letting an overgrown bully boy steal her stores, by his threat to expose her improper relationship to Mr. Colyear. Whom she was trying to convince to keep her identity from the captain. Who, if, or rather when, he learned her true identity would know that Col was not having an unnatural relationship with her—wasn't even having a natural relationship with her.

What an interesting chat she and the captain would have when he called her to the carpet. It almost gave her a reason to look forward to the interview, if she could rat out the Rat King.

But until that interview came, she owed it to Mr. Colyear to keep his name from being abused with such damaging rumors. She would keep quiet until then.

Gamage's cold-eyed smile gave her the shivers. "Have you figured it out yet, pretty Kent? Have you worked your way 'round to understanding? It's just as I said. This is my berth, Kent. And you are all just here on sufferance."

Chapter Seven

His grandiose, theatrical threat delivered, the Rat King made his exit, scuttling out of the room like the large, ponderous rodent he was, off to find some other bolt-hole.

Well, the man had at least provided her with one reason to look forward to being put off. If she had to face disgrace, devil if she wouldn't take Gamage down and off with her.

But she hadn't been put off yet, and she wasn't going to solve the problem of Gamage by sitting on her arse and feeling hard done by. Her trunk was a mess. Whoever had gone through her things, Gamage, or his "creature" Tunney, had done so in a hurry, with swift, easy predation in mind. Not a thorough job. Not the product of an orderly, efficient brain. She would do well to remember that.

Thankfully, the clever false bottom of her trunk was still intact. Though he'd taken all the food Mrs. Jenkins had preserved in jars, as well as the supply of sherry she'd added for Richard—who never drank anything stronger if he could help it—most of the herbs had been overlooked, hidden in plain sight in their twists of paper. She rummaged around for the other important items. Richard's violin remained untouched, too easily identifiable to be stolen without instant repercussion.

Worth, who was the only one left with her in the cockpit—

Dance seemed to have disappeared—peered over her shoulder. "Did he get everything?"

"Almost." And she had only herself to blame. Pinky had expressly warned her, but she'd been too sure of herself, too sure that such a thing could never happen under a man such as Captain McAlden. But Gamage had proved her wrong. As a result, she would keep his secret just as assuredly as Pinky seemed to be keeping hers.

"What will you do?" Worth's red-rimmed eyes looked huge in his face.

"Make the best of it." She would distribute everything that was left before she had to pack her sea trunk back up. She would have no use for any of it at home in Falmouth, while these poor boys could benefit greatly.

Worth was full of frowning consternation. "Won't you tell?"

"I don't think so," she answered.

When the boy's small, pale face began to crumple with disappointment, Sally tried to explain. "Hear me out, Mr. Worth. My first instinct *was* to report it to the captain, for I have no doubt that he will not tolerate stealing. But I have no actual evidence that Gamage took my foodstuffs, only that it's gone. And Gamage has made sure of that. And he seems too canny, too careful of his own survival, to set himself up to be caught. I doubt he's kept any of it besides my sherry."

"I don't understand." Worth was trying to stave off his tears by swiping his nose on his sleeve. Those white patches on his cuffs would never survive even another fortnight. "Why would he have stolen it if he wasn't going to keep it?"

"He may have the purser, or someone such as a cook's mate, under his power, and they stash it for him. Or he may have hidden it elsewhere, hoping I would raise a fuss and hoping— I say!" She moved toward Ian's sea chest. "See if he's broken into yours."

Ian colored. "It wouldn't be broken into. It's not locked. He had the key from me the first day."

"Devil take him. And Will's as well?"

Ian shrugged, and tried to think of a suitable answer, but his lower lip was wobbling terribly and his eyes were starting to brighten with tears.

"There, now." She found herself pulling him into a brotherly, or actually sisterly, embrace. "It will be all right. I promise."

"It won't be all right. It's awful. I hate it here. I hate it." His tears began to flow freely and his voice was breaking with the frustration and fear.

"Hush, now." Sally took a gentle hold of his hand. "It's just that it's all so new. You'll get used to it."

"I won't. I hate it. And I hate climbing up into the sails the most. And I'm never going to do it again. They can't make me."

Unfortunately, they could. At the business end of a cane, or worse. But she would do her best to see it never came to that. "You'll get used to it, I promise. A few more times and you won't even notice, just the way a young bird gets used to being in the trees. The branches rock and sway but it never bothers him in the least."

"That's because he knows how to fly." But there was at least some laughter accompanying the exasperation in his voice. After another moment, he had recovered enough of his spirits with the hardiness of the young and ignorant to ask, "How do you know so much about everything?"

"I grew up on my father's ships."

"Does your father own ships?"

"No." She laughed. Her brothers, especially Matthew and Dominic, would have been offended to think someone had never heard of her family, much less thought them *merchants*. Sally could just picture their shudders of revulsion at such a thought. "My father and two of my brothers are Royal Navy captains. I come from an old navy family."

"Oh." Worth's face filled with the appropriate amount of awe. "No wonder you had the guts to stand up to Mr. Gamage."

"Fat lot of good it did me," she muttered. "But you're not going to worry about him anymore. I promise. I'll see to it if it's the last thing I do—especially if it's the last thing I do aboard *Audacious*. But in the meantime, Gamage might have thought to hide my stolen goods in your trunk, or Will's, as he'll have noted we're friends."

"Are we friends?"

"Yes," she answered staunchly. "We are going to be the best of friends."

And so Ian let her search through his dunnage to find that while his foodstuffs were also missing, nothing had been added.

But she wasn't about to let Gamage get the best of them, or of her, without a fight. "I tell you what—let's see what else Pinky has to say. He always knows what's going on in a ship."

They found the old salt near the open galley stove on the gun deck, working hand in hand with the captain's steward, Edwards, and two gunroom servants, Moreland and the jovial, and aptly named, Punch, the fiddle player of the morning.

"Well, you were right, Pinky. Mr. Gamage has helped himself to our foodstuffs. But we can still come right," she assured him when he began to shake his head dolefully, showing no pleasure in having been proved right. "He didn't get everything. And I've a few more tricks up my sleeve. What do you think of these?"

She placed her handful of paper twists in his careful, gnarled old hands.

"Fresh spice?"

"As promised." A healthy dose of bold spice made the usually bland and boiled fare available on navy ships more palatable. And Pinky knew well how to use them to best effect, just as he had done when he had served as her father's steward.

The other stewards were peering over Pinky's shoulder to get a glimpse of his treasure. "I also give you leave to barter any of this away as need be—with say Captain McAlden's good man Edwards, for whatever else we might need. Perhaps a bottle of good claret from time to time, in exchange for helping him improve his dishes for the captain? Or better still, for Punch here, perhaps a new violin to while away the evenings in entertainment, in exchange for some gunroom fare?"

Pinky's rosy face glowed with schemes and plans. "Ah, young sir. You leave it to your Pinky. We'll have a fine cruise of it."

"I trust we will. There, you see, Ian? Pinky and I will do our best to keep you from the millers."

"What are millers?"

"Rats, young sir," Pinky supplied helpfully. "So called on account they be dusted in flour from having been getting into the stores."

"You mean we're to eat rats?" Poor Worth was horrified. And growing paler and greener by the second.

"Well." Sally tried to invest as much cheerful nonchalance into her voice as she could. "I never have eaten them before, but I've never been a midshipman before. I expect we shall have a great host of new experiences on this cruise. I daresay Mr. Colyear and even Captain McAlden have eaten their share of millers, and they seem no worse for the wear."

Worth appeared only partially mollified by such hearty sentiments, so Sally changed the subject. "Now, have you somewhere safe, and private," she asked Pinky, "to keep such things away from Mr. Gamage and anyone else in the purser's purvey who might be his creature?"

"I know just the way of it. I'll—"

Sally held up a restraining hand. "Don't tell me. If I don't know, I can't be made to divulge. But there's more." She reached into her waistcoat pocket. "I've a fishing line for you as well, Pinky. Do you care for fish for dinner, Mr. Worth?"

The boy's peaked face lit up with the first stirrings of real pleasure she had seen in him. "I care for anything that will taste better than beef boiled to a pudding!"

"You rest your trust in our Pinky. He'll see to it. And what else?" She turned her eye to the crates forward of the galley. "Do you have the rights to any of that poultry, Pinky? Are there shares of a hen to be found, so we might have eggs?"

Pinky scrunched up his eyes and scratched his bald pate, the very picture of canny calculation. "Might cost a bit, a hen."

"I've a guinea to lay toward her." She held the coin up between her fingers. "But for that money, I'll want a whole hen, not just an egg share."

Pinky caught the golden coin in his palm. "Done, young sir. Done."

"Good man." She threw an encouraging arm around Ian's shoulders. "There, I told you I could make it better. For all of us. Except Mr. Gamage, of course."

Worth's eyes went wide with delighted awe. "You'll share all of that? The food and eggs, and everything?"

"Of course. We're mess mates, Mr. Worth. But beyond that, I told you we're friends. And I hope you'll find I stand by my friends."

"Thank you." After the beginning he had endured in the navy, poor Worth seemed to find it astonishing he might have any friends. "I'm much obliged. But how did you know about the trading and shares of a hen? And a fishing line? I wish I'd thought of that."

"My older brothers have all shipped in the navy before me—and all eaten rats—so I've learned from their advice. But what of you, Ian? From whence do you hail?"

In answer to her query, the boy simply muttered, "Gloucestershire."

Perhaps he came from very low origins, a country parson's or a tradesman's son, if he did not want to be forthcoming. "That's a very beautiful part of the country, I understand."

"I suppose it might be. But it's not very exciting. Nobody in my family is exciting like yours. Nobody ever went in the navy before. Nobody told me what it would be like."

"Everyone in my family goes into the navy. In fact, people in my family have no choice *but* to go into the navy."

And it struck her, as she spoke, for the first time ever, how odd that might seem to others who felt a navy career was impossible. How . . . unfair that might be.

But Ian Worth *was* in the navy and he needed bolstering

up. He needed to figure out that he could make a go of his chosen career despite Mr. Gamage. "Tell me more about Gloucestershire."

He shrugged. "Ciren Castle is said to be very beautiful."

"Is it? Is it famous? I don't even know where that is. I have never been to most places in England. While I have been to any number of foreign ports and exotic locales, I've only ever been to the places between Falmouth and Portsmouth on the south coast. You must know a great deal more about the country than I."

Worth smiled for the first time, a little hiccup of a smile, but a beginning nonetheless. "Really? Fancy me knowing anything more than you."

Pleased her result was taking effect, Sally returned his smile. "There is probably a great deal about which you know more than me. I only know about the sea and sailing and the navy because I was raised with it. You will know a great deal more about however it was you were raised, and all knowledge can eventually be put to good use."

The boy considered that. "I do know some about dogs. My father always kept a very great pack of dogs. And I do know something of farming, and tenants and the upkeep of an estate. Fat lot of good it will do me now."

Sally didn't want to let him slide back into dejection. "An estate? Is your father a landowner?"

"I suppose he must be. He does have a great deal of land. That is to say, he owns Ciren Castle and all the lands of Ciren Park, and the town, I suppose. He is a viscount. Viscount Rainesford. But I'm just his second son."

Such was the lot of the second sons of the world—the spares. Will Jellicoe was another.

While the two younger boys did not have the experience and navy connections the Kents did, clearly they came from families who had enough income to buy them their preferred slots, and enough influence to assist them politically when the time came for advancement.

Perhaps that was why Mr. Gamage, who seemed to have neither patronage, influence, nor friends, should be so very hateful to the boys. "Does anyone else, like Mr Gamage, know about your family?"

Ian shrugged. "I don't know. I suppose Captain McAlden must. My father said he had to buy my berth here."

Sally was sorry to have brought it up when she sensed a renewal of his helplessness. "Yes, we are very lucky to have gotten this berth, Mr. Gamage notwithstanding. Captain McAlden is a very successful frigate captain, and you may be assured that it took a great deal of influence for your father to have gotten you situated here. There are probably a thousand boys who should very much like a chance to earn the kind of prize money Captain McAlden is reputed to have taken."

A thousand boys. But not every boy. Not Richard. Maybe not even poor Ian. Perhaps he had wanted to stay on his father's estate and spend his days working out problems of drainage and irrigation, instead of learning halyards and backstays. Sally hadn't thought much about it before. Not every family raised a flock of sons for the sea. Perhaps there was some wisdom in parceling out one's sons into different lines of work. Perhaps, just perhaps, Richard might not have been so wrong after all.

"Captain McAlden's compliments, Mr. Kent." It was Pinky, come back to find her, looking anxious. "The captain requests you in his cabin. Best come along, young Kent."

So this was it. Sally stood and smoothed down her clothing. It seemed important, important to the dignity of the Kents, that she put in a good appearance. She ought to be thankful that Mr. Colyear seemed to have handled the matter so discreetly. She could only hope that her dismissal would be as private as possible, to spare her family the scandal.

She nodded to Worth, and shook his hand, because it seemed like the right thing to do. "Mr. Worth. A pleasure, sir. Rest your trust safely with Pinky and it will all come right." She turned back to her old friend and did the same. "Thank you, Pinky, for everything. I'll go directly."

The old salt knuckled his shiny forehead and stood back to watch her go. It wasn't a particularly long walk from where she and Worth had been conversing near the foot of the companionway ladders in the waist, but it seemed short, even though she felt as if she were weighed down with shot in her pockets. And despite her best intentions to weather the coming storm with courage and honor, her heart was beating a heavy dirge in her chest.

The marine standing sentry at the captain's door didn't bother himself to look at a lowly midshipman, so Sally had to knock for herself, rapping her knuckles too hard against the canvas and wood door in time with the beating tattoo of her heart.

"Come," the peremptory summons came through the door.

Captain McAlden was alone and seated at a table near the stern gallery, situated so as to take best advantage of the light. But as the vessel was sailing almost due west, the stern gallery was somewhat more dim than the deck had been.

The captain was still engaged in his work and did not immediately look up upon her entry, but continued to labor at whatever paper lay before him.

Sally found the only way to calm, or even hide, the clammy nervousness that was fracturing her pulse and dampening her palms was to let her eyes wander over the cabin, and let the familiarity of memory occupy her mind. The cabin was sparsely but comfortably appointed, with some fine but not delicate furniture. It was smaller than the cabin on her father's ships, and, *Audacious* being a frigate, the space was dominated by the huge twelve-pounders to either side of the hull. A stark reminder of the seriousness of their purpose. The purpose she would soon be without.

"Mr. Kent." Arctic blue eyes probed like an icicle. She waited for the next cold thrust. But instead, Captain McAlden made an impatient economic gesture toward a small table tucked next to the larboard gun. "Your desk is there. May I trust you know the business?"

Fear must have made her stupid. "Sir?"

"Five copies of each order, in a clean, clear hand. Your extra years of schooling will be made useful this evening."

"You need me to act as your clerk?"

"Aye. What did you expect? Though your name is Kent, you are reputed to have the requisite skills for the position."

"Certainly, sir." Her head felt full of cotton wadding. "I thought Mr. Colyear had spoken to you?"

"He did. He recommended you to assist me in place of my clerk, Mr. Pike, who is suffering his usual agonies of *mal de mer* at the beginning of a cruise. Or has Mr. Colyear got it wrong? Have you never played clerk for your father?"

She had, on numerous occasions, writing out letters as he dictated, or doing just as Captain McAlden had bade and making copies of orders and reports for the Admiralty. "Yes, sir. Just so. Demons for paperwork, my father said the Admiralty was." Relief seemed to be making her chatty.

Because all she could hear in her mind, over and over, was, *He didn't tell.*

He didn't tell.

"They still are, Mr. Kent." The captain was agreeing with her and still pointing to the little desk with the feather tip of his quill. "So I suggest you set yourself to it in a timely fashion, if you are to see this work done before your supper."

"Yes, sir." She dove for the desk with such agitated enthusiasm that she knocked the little chair back onto the floor. "I beg your very great pardon, sir."

"Handsomely now, Kent. Test not your zeal on my poor chair. It is the papers you will want to attack."

Sally got to work quickly and quietly, making rapid work of the copies, while all the time her mind kept repeating, *He didn't tell. He didn't tell.*

But then, of course, once she had gotten over the shock, she began to wonder *why*. Why had Mr. Colyear not turned her in? He had every reason to do so. Including the one she had not yet told him—Mr. Gamage's threat. It was only fair that she tell him now. It would be cowardly not to. It would be puny and selfish in the light of his own generous conduct. She could never repay such generosity, such charity, even if she spent the rest of her life trying.

She applied herself to the captain's papers with diligence,

and managed to leave only a blot or two in her wake by the time she was done.

"You've a fine hand, Mr. Kent," the captain said when he reviewed her work.

"Thank you, sir." She stood before his table, and couldn't help but notice a beautiful, small glass-and-gold-encased painting laid out on the desk next to his papers.

"I see you admiring my miniature, Mr. Kent."

"My pardon, sir. It's a lovely portrait," she said sincerely.

"I thank you. It is of Lady Trinity McAlden. My wife."

She might have known. Her father had carried just such a portrait of her mother for years. She had a copy of it at home, in Falmouth. And she'd made sure to pack a third copy for Richard in his sea trunk. "She is very beautiful. And very young."

The captain's smile was bittersweet, as if he had some secret he took pleasure in keeping. "She will be flattered. Although she was young. I had it made for me some eight years ago, upon the occasion of our marriage, but I can say with confidence that she is still the handsomest woman of my acquaintance. And much missed."

"I am sorry, sir. Were you not able to visit with her when *Audacious* was in England?"

"Unfortunately, no. My lady lives not in England, but in the Bahamas, on the island of New Providence." Again the smile. "She prefers the warmer climate."

"Ah." Sally was all agreement. "I don't blame her. It is a most salubrious climate."

The captain chuckled. "You and she are rather singular in thinking it so. But I forget that you must have been to the Bahamas, Mr. Kent."

"Yes, sir. With my father in *Adamant*, in the year '98 or '99. I don't precisely remember." Sally grew conscious that she might be overstaying her welcome, as well as pressing her luck. "Was there anything else, sir?"

"No, Mr. Kent." But the captain seemed inclined for her to linger. He leaned back in his chair and contemplated her from behind the steeples of his fingers. Though she had had some time to become accustomed to it, his icy blue stare still managed to unnerve her. "I'm pleased with you thus far," he began. "I won't scruple to tell you, I had some reservations about you when it took so long for your father to send you to me. I feared you might not be amenable to navy life."

Devil take it. Was there no one aboard *Audacious* who did not know poor Richard's story? Perhaps it was a good thing he had not come aboard, for he never would have been able to overcome such low expectations. "No, sir."

"But you are here now, and you seem to be making the best of it. I commend you on your good sense. Continue on as you've begun, and you'll do well here, Mr. Kent."

"Thank you, sir. Your confidence means a great deal to me, and I will continue to endeavor to earn it."

"Well said, sir. But I hope I may speak to you candidly. I also notice . . . a small but distinct air of antagonism has arisen between you and my first lieutenant."

The blood that had warmed under Captain McAlden's kind attention frosted up her veins. She answered carefully, but with the truth. "Oh, no, sir."

"No?" His tone might have been gentle, but no less probing. "Then is it all on Mr. Colyear's part?"

It took Sally a long moment to realize she was holding her breath. "No." She could not let Mr. Colyear take the blame for his well-justified reaction to her. She owed him that much. "No, sir, it was my fault. I was delayed at the sally port in Portsmouth and Mr. Colyear was obliged to come fetch me at great personal inconvenience. I was not perhaps as appreciative of his sacrifice as I ought to have been."

"Then, for the good of the ship, I would bid you to be."

"I am, sir. Mr. Colyear has been very affable in setting me on the right tack."

"I daresay he has. Mr. Colyear is the most affable first lieutenant I have ever had the pleasure of employing. But don't let that fool you, Mr. Kent. He knows his business, our Mr. Colyear does. He never loses his self-possession, never carries on yelling at the top of his lungs, and still his baritone can be heard quite clearly over the cannons' roar."

"Then that is the measure of an officer I will set for myself."

"You can do no better, Mr. Kent. Mr. Colyear is a man to be emulated, but also a man to trust. I adjure you to trust in him. You, and every man of this crew who applies himself with rigor to his duty, will find in Mr. Colyear an invaluable friend."

"Thank you, sir," she answered, because it seemed to be what the captain wanted to hear her say. But Captain McAlden could have no idea how completely she was forced to rest her trust in Mr. Colyear.

Because the question remained unanswered—if Mr. Colyear hadn't told the captain, just what in the devil did he want in exchange for his silence?

Chapter Eight

Col was waiting, walking quietly across the starboard gangway above, when she came out into the waist. He stilled his pacing—however much he had wanted to disguise it as exercise, it was still pacing—and willed her to come to him.

She did. She brought herself out of the captain's cabin with the same straightforward resignation with which she had gone in. And with the same straightforward manner of speaking. "You'll be disappointed in me, Mr. Colyear."

"Will I?" He was surprised by the edge of challenge in her voice.

"You wanted me to speak to him myself, didn't you?"

Points to her for perception. "Yes. I was hoping you would do the right thing." And spare him the task.

"I didn't." Her tone was more than challenging—it was almost defiant.

Damn, but she was all Kent. And she was not through. "But you didn't tell either, did you, Mr. Colyear? And why is that?"

God help him. Already the tumultuous girl baffled him. "Fuck all if I know."

His blunt exasperation seemed to set her sails back. But it was a small world, a ship, and privacy was a rare commodity.

"Walk with me, Kent." He made himself use her surname. Made himself treat her like any other midshipman under his command. But he still moved upwind, to the lee rail, where the silent wind would blow their conversation away from the ship. "I am supremely conscious that I owe a great deal to your family, and I respect them too much to simply cast you to your fate. But that doesn't make what you're doing right."

"It doesn't make it wrong."

Damn, but she was a tenacious thing. "Kent. I know you know better. Especially with all your talk of knowing your duty."

She let out a gusty, exasperated, boyish sigh. She played the part so well it shouldn't amaze him that no one else was able to see her for who she really was. She displayed no overtly feminine attributes or mannerisms. Or perhaps she did not play a part at all, and the Kent that stood before him was simply who she was—challenging, straightforward, and as useful as a well-honed blade.

The thought was frankly terrifying. Because it was extraordinarily appealing.

"I suppose I do know better. Perhaps I should have spoken to him. Perhaps I should have told him the truth. But I didn't. Devil take me, but I simply didn't want to, Mr. Colyear. I want to stay."

Col could hear the sharp edge of something compelling and deeply felt in her voice. But it was impossible, what she wanted. Although not entirely unheard of. Col recalled reading a pamphlet printed in London of some woman who had served as the captain of the foretop on the *Queen Charlotte* in the prior century. But that woman had been a stranger, a foreigner, with no family to look, or speak, for her. She was not Sally Kent with belligerent brothers and contentious cousins scattered in half the ships of the damn fleet. She was not the only daughter of Captain Alexander Kent. "It's not possible."

He turned away, conscious of not staring at her, of not trying to reconcile remembrance with reality. Of not trying to find the golden girl of the orchard hidden beneath the dark brim of her hat.

She turned as well, and copied his posture as he leaned his forearms across the rail to watch the foam of the bow spray rush along the length of the hull. "He adjured me to trust you."

"Captain McAlden?"

She nodded—a funny little nod where her head tipped back and forth sideways instead of up and down, as if she found the idea just as improbable as he. "Yes. Trust you, he said. He can have little idea of how completely I must trust you to keep my secr—"

"For fuck's sake, Kent." He had almost reached out to stop her mouth, but he thought better of the idea. If he touched her again, he would burst into flame. He already felt as if he were smoldering just standing next to her. And lieutenants did not touch midshipmen in such a way. Not if they wanted to keep their commission.

Not if they wanted to keep their captain's trust. The thought of his disloyalty to his captain was like a rusty blade in his gut, already festering. "I wish to hell you hadn't told me that."

"Well, I am going to trust you. And I promise it will be worth it. I won't let you down. I promise I'm going to be the best midshipman you've ever had. You won't have a lick of bother with me, I swear. If you just let me stay."

He didn't doubt she could be the best midshipman *Audacious* had ever had, if the morning's work was any indication. No, the problem wasn't going to be with her. It was going to be with him. With keeping his wits about him and his mind on his duty, instead of worrying and watching Sally Kent's every move.

She left him to his unquiet thoughts for a long time, turning to look away forward, out over the sea to the west, where the long sunset gilded the rippled surface of the water, before she spoke. "If I am to trust you, then I must also be trustworthy. There is something else you should know. Something I did not want to tell you for fear it would influence you to tell the captain."

Damn their eyes. Wasn't their situation bad enough already? What more could there possibly be to make it worse? "Let me hear it, Kent."

"It's Mr. Gamage, sir. You can't know what he is, although you ought to."

How strange that she was so very much like him. How strange that of all people, she was the one who thought only *she* saw everything. "I am neither blind nor stupid, Kent. I know well what he is."

She pulled back from the rail, her body stiff with indignation. "If Mr. Gamage's character is already known to you, why is he allowed to continue?"

He could only marvel at the picture she presented. Every inch of her face, her being, vibrated with affronted color at the thought of such purposeful wickedness. "Oh, Kent. So very righteous."

"Have I no right to be affronted at Mr. Gamage's tyranny? And petty tyrants the likes of him are always the worst of the lot."

"And so very sure of yourself, and your point. Things aren't always as black-and-white as you are apt to think they are, Kent."

She seemed to lose a small measure of her adamance at the fairness of that remark. Her lovely wide mouth turned down at the corners in wry agreement. But he wasn't looking or thinking about her mouth, damn his wandering eyes.

"No, you are right. It is ofttimes very gray. See what you can make of this murk." She turned to face him and her level gray gaze held nothing but steadfast determination now. "I had an unfortunate encounter with Mr. Gamage, the result of which was that Mr. Gamage accused me of being 'a pretty, soft sort of boy'—exactly the captain's words to me, you understand—and he furthermore insinuated that it might be put about that you, Mr. Colyear, were seen to be liking pretty, soft sorts of boys."

Col let out a vividly descriptive, Anglo-Saxon expletive, the likes of which he had not uttered in all the years since he had learned the wonders of profanity at the feet of an Irish gunner while still an infant midshipman, before he settled for something more mundane. "Damn his insolent eyes. No matter at all that you *are* a pretty, soft sort of boy."

She did not appreciate his rather bleak attempt at humor. "I am not. I'm twice the sailor that Gamage is or ever could be. He is disgusting and vulgar, not to mention a thief. A thief whose influence reaches all the way into the captain's cabin, for how else did he hear those words?" She shook her head, still outraged. "My father never would have stood for such behavior on his ships."

"True. I reckon he should have bent you over a cannon for a proper caning for being so stupid."

"Mr. Colyear!"

It felt good to nettle her. It gave him some semblance of control. God knew he had little enough otherwise. "It is stupid, Kent, for two reasons. One, if you are even half as smart and one quarter the sailor I think you are, you should never have allowed yourself to get into a confrontation with Gamage in the first place. And two, for thinking so little of your commanding officer. Captain McAlden has his reasons for what he chooses to do with his command, and your father would be the first person to remind you of that. It is not our business to question our captain's orders. No matter what sort of petty tyrant Mr. Gamage is—and I will grant you he is—he is also a trained officer. He has more than his share of flaws and his evils, but he's still a useful man. Too useful to put off a ship while we are at war."

She saw the opening, the weak point in his argument, as quick as a gunner sighting down the barrel of a cannon. "Am I not useful enough as well?" She was nothing if not tenacious.

"Damn it, Kent. That's not the point."

"But it *is* the point. Someone has to serve, and it might as well be me. I can do it, I know I can. You know I'm as capable as any boy here and more so than some."

"Bloody hell. That sounds suspiciously like your brother Matthew." Another, more frightening, thought occurred to him. "Did your brothers put you up to this? Or did you conceive of this lunacy on your own? Does your family know you're here, in place of—" He broke off, looked around much as she had done, to make sure they were not being overheard. "They do know, don't they? You will have left some word? Tell me you left word."

She looked acutely conscious and uncomfortable, wincing up one side of her face and tipping her head to try to ameliorate her fault. "No. They know nothing. At least I assume so."

God's balls. The clenched fist in his gut lurched up into his throat. He looked around again for stray ears before he cut his eyes back to her. "Do you mean to tell me that Captain Alexander Kent, the most successful frigate captain of our time, who sees all and hears all, knows nothing of where his only daughter is? How is that possible? Surely such a man would notice when his child went missing."

She shrugged the importance of the suggestion away. "He may not know I am missing at all. By now, he is bound to be at sea, and *I* have not yet written to tell him. I don't imagine"—she hesitated again and looked around—"anyone else would have the nerve to write him, either."

"It occurs to me to ask what became of your . . . missing Kent relation."

She passed a hand over her eyes in the first indication of uncertainty or remorse he had seen in her. "I have no idea."

"Truly?"

"Mr. Colyear, I would not be here if I had had any luck at finding him when he ran away."

"He ran away?"

She nodded with misery, her mouth set tight with distress. "I did not undertake this as a lark, Mr. Colyear, I assure you. I did so for the honor of my family. I could not have it said that he was too"—she lowered her voice to a whisper, embarrassed that she must reveal his stain on her family's honor to Col—"cowardly to do his duty."

"Are you convinced it is cowardice?" Matthew's letters had left Col with the impression that Richard's refusal was, in actuality, conviction. Especially as the boy had gone to such extraordinary lengths to avoid serving. Just as extraordinary as the lengths to which his sister had gone *to* serve.

"Does it matter what *I* think?" she asked. "That is how the world, *our* world, the small world of the navy, will see it, no matter his talk of the church and his affinity for dreary sermons."

Poor girl. She was such a Kent. They could not conceive of a world where any work was preferable to that of the navy. "This life is not for everyone."

"I know." She sighed. But the admission did not seem to afford her any relief or pleasure. "It is certainly not the right life for Mr. Gamage."

He could only agree. "True enough. But after nearly twenty years in the navy there is nothing else he is likely to do. And the navy cannot afford to let a man, even a man with Gamage's reputation, leave the service while there is a war on. We need every man we can get, however flawed."

"And am I not also just such a man, however flawed?" She was quick. Damn quick. And clever.

He disallowed himself the obvious answer—that she was not, and he never could regard her as, a *man*. And he would not allow being a woman to be a flaw. But her sex was definitely a problem. His problem. "Is there no one, besides me, who knows that you're aboard?"

"Jenkins, our manservant at Cliffside, who accompanied"—again the careful hesitation—"us to Portsmouth, and his wife, perhaps. They must have figured it out. But I'm sure my father rejoined his ship at the Nore and set sail before he could receive any communication from them."

"Damnation. Have you no regard for your personal safety? Or their peace of mind?"

She frowned at him in complete consternation. "Why on earth should I have any more regard than Jellicoe, or Worth? Or you? I know what I'm doing. I assure you, I'm safer here than in a bloody ballroom."

"Because—" He bit off the answer he had meant to make. He would not debate natural philosophy with this girl. She would not hear it. She hadn't a drop of dread in her. She was too full of the courage of her convictions and unshakable confidence of youth. She could not conceive of how she might be vulnerable to any injury. Or worse.

But he could conceive of it. He had seen it. More times than he cared to count. And he could also picture what could happen if she should be found out, alone in some private way, by some of the more unscrupulous members of the crew. *Audacious* was a well-run, well-disciplined ship—Captain McAlden's sterling reputation ensured they had no need to fill their muster roll with gallows bait from the prison hulks—but anything was possible in the midst of several hundred men.

"So you will write your father. And that's an order, Kent." Col made his voice firm with command so there would be no misunderstanding. "And then what? It might be months before it reaches him, and months longer still before you may expect a reply."

She looked away, out over the darkening sea. "What else am I to do?"

He could hear the wistfulness in her voice, the yearning for absolute impossibilities. "You could go back and confess all to the captain, and he would see you put off quietly, with no one the wiser, before we leave the loom of the land or are posted elsewhere. Or he might let you stay aboard until some duty recalls us to England. I don't know." Col found himself scraping off his cocked hat and raking his fingers through his hair. "But the point being, it is the captain's decision, not mine. And not yours."

"Or I could just stay and do the work, as I have done." She was as stubborn as the day was long. She was entirely convinced that she was right, and that she could do the job of midshipman without coming to any grief.

"Please, sir." She lowered the tone of her voice to show him she would beg if she had to. "Please."

He could not keep himself from reacting to the soft plea in her voice. It made him look at the wide, apricot flesh of her mouth as she crushed her lower lip beneath her teeth to quell her anxiety. It made him want to do other things with her lips. It made him want to do the unthinkable and keep her with him, no matter the enormous risks. No matter the dangerous cost.

She did not ask him to think of her brothers, or her father. She did not remind him of his debts of gratitude and assistance. She knew her fate and that of her family rested solely in his hands.

"Damn your eyes. You ask too much, Kent."

But she had heard the concession in his voice, because her face lit like a bonfire of hope, dancing brightly against the falling dark. "You won't regret it," she promised, quivering like an eager puppy in her earnestness. "I'll see that you don't."

"Too late, Kent. I already do."

Mr. Colyear did not speak to her again. It was an unspoken agreement between them. He did as she had so cogently advised herself to do when she had come aboard, and kept his stony distance. He endeavored not to speak to her unless absolutely necessary, and Sally answered in the same vein. But she was free to return to her duty in the foretop, with a glee that couldn't be chastened. Not even by Mr. Colyear's dark, adjuring frowns.

She climbed up the shrouds with outright pleasure. There was no one to stop her—no father or servant to scold and lecture. Indeed, it was quite the opposite. If she did not climb the rope ladder like a cat up a tree, she would soon feel the hot end of someone's temper.

Her other enjoyment of the foretop came from her growing acquaintance with Willis, the keen-eyed captain of the foretop. And since Willis had his eyes constantly roving the horizon, Sally could take a few moments to study the deck far below. From the vantage point of the top, one saw entirely different things than one did below. She saw patterns and habits in a different way. Right then, she could see Ian Worth on the quarterdeck, being spoken to by Mr. Charlton, and see Worth start down and across the waist until he stopped abruptly and changed direction, skirting along the larboard rail on his errand.

A glance to starboard found the reason for his hasty re-route. Mr. Gamage was moving in the opposite direction through the starboard waist. Men shied out of his way, mostly the younger ones, or turned their back to purposely avoid his eye.

"Willis, what do you think of Mr. Gamage?"

Willis cut her a look as sharp as broken glass. "I got no opinion whatsoever about officers, Mr. Kent."

"He's not an officer. He's only a 'young gentleman,' like the rest of us, despite his age. Do you know how long he has been with the ship?"

"Longer than I been wif her. An' that's nine years."

"When did he fail the exam for lieutenant?"

Willis lowered his voice though they were quite alone at the masthead, but even at the top of the ship, sound traveled strangely at sea. Willis obviously didn't believe in taking chances. "From what I could see, Mr. Kent, Cap'n never put him up for it. An' it's no wonder. He's not exactly fit for it, is he?"

"No. From what I can see, he's an overgrown, aged school-boy bully. Has he always run the other midshipmen ragged?"

Willis made his answer carefully vague. Until he was sure of her, he would not commit to an opinion. "That's one way o' putting it."

"Does he blame the men in his division unfairly if any-thing goes wrong?"

"He might do." Willis was looking at her now with some-thing less of suspicion and more of camaraderie.

"Does he meddle in other officers' divisions?"

"Only the midshipmen, though that third lieutenant, young Mr. Lawrence, is pretty scared of him. Thought maybe once he passed his lieutenancy he'd be shed of Mr. Gamage, but he's not been so lucky. Just made Gamage meaner to him, seeing Mr. Lawrence pass for lieutenant ahead of him."

"That won't do." Though she still had not figured out

what exactly to do about the problem of Mr. Gamage. Sally's original plan to see *him* put off with her had faded with Mr. Colyear's unexpected decision not to see *her* put off.

Willis's face creased into a crooked smile. "Sound like your brother, you do, when you talk like that. Served under him in *Retribution*."

"That must have been Owen. He's Captain Kent now, in the cutter *Sprite*."

"My 'gratulations to him. Godspeed and good fortune. But it won't be long ere you join 'em in bein' a captain. You Kents know your business."

"Thank you, Willis. I appreciate your faith in me. But I'll only have earned it if I can figure out what to do about the problem of Mr. Gamage."

And she needed to think of something pretty damn soon because below, Gamage had somehow managed to find Ian Worth and was bedeviling him, shoving the boy into the shadow of the quarterdeck, aft below the rail, where Gamage thought no one could see.

Well, she could see, and she was going to do something about it. Devil take him, but Gamage's casual malice made her as angry as a swarm of bees. "Devil take his rat-red eyes."

"Sir?" Willis's voice was full of caution, but she was already sliding hand over gripping hand down a backstay and then striding her way across the deck. She couldn't hear whatever Gamage was saying over the hard beating of her heart and the overloud flap of her big footfalls upon the decking as she neared. She could only feel her throat tighten with the blistering scald of injustice at his treatment of her friend.

"Leave off, Mr. Gamage." She put every ounce of the hostility boiling in her blood into turning her words into a command. "Mr. Worth is needed on the quarterdeck by Mr. Colyear."

Gamage shied a quick glance around as if to assure himself Mr. Colyear's arrival wasn't imminent. "Is he? Sent his pretty little flunky to do his dirty work for him, did *Mister* Colyear? Aren't you supposed to be up in the top, Kent?"

Sally held her ground and reminded herself of her pledge

to Mr. Colyear to keep her unpredictable temper in check. She tried to sound like Mr. Colyear, and to invest her voice with the patient ferocity so particular to the first lieutenant. "Aren't you supposed to act like an officer, Gamage? Leave the boy alone."

It worked. Gamage turned his attention away from Worth—to whom she signaled by a flick of her wrist to make himself scarce—and focused all of his sulky ire on Sally, his voice low and smooth with menace. "Still licking Mr. Colyear's boots, are you, Kent? Are you an ass-licker as well?"

With that shot, he turned around his snide smile.

Sally raised her voice to carry. "At least I'm not a piss-pot bully, *Mister* Gamage."

At her riposte, Gamage swung back on her with his rat-like malicious quickness, and laid a vise-hard hold on her arm. "What did you say?"

Sally wanted to snatch her arm away from his filthy grasp. But she couldn't give him the satisfaction of seeing her squirm. Though her heart was shuddering away in her ears like a loose tiller, she stood perfectly still and met his eyes with an unflinching stare. Devil take him, she was a Kent. She'd eaten colder stares for breakfast.

So she let him tighten his grip on her arm, and waited with only an upraised eyebrow for him to come to his point. Another moment, maybe longer, while he tried to exert even more pressure. Sally looked down at her elbow and then back up at his face. Then she smiled. And batted her eyes. And said in a clear voice, "If you mean to ask me to dance, Mr. Gamage, I'm afraid my card is full."

Gamage dropped her arm as if she were made of fire.

Sally used her freedom to climb calmly up the gangway ladder and into the main chains, safely out of Gamage's reach. "You heard me the first time, Mr. Gamage. I'll wager every-one did. But I'll repeat myself for your benefit. I said you're a piss-pot bully."

Around her she could hear the snickers of the men. An audience was always a good thing. But Gamage had heard the laughter, too, and he'd take out his anger on those below him, who couldn't even defend themselves with their words.

Gamage's face grew gray and brittle with suppressed fury as he quickly looked around, trying to intimidate the men near him with his volatility. But he could find no mark, for they weren't even looking at him. They were looking at her.

Good. After this, she was sure Gamage would focus his malice on her instead of on the other boys.

Gamage finally managed to draw himself together in a pale imitation of an officer's authority. "You'll regret that, Kent. I'll see that you do." His voice was going dry and cracked with humiliation.

"Oh, yes." She began to climb the shrouds, as if she were dismissing him. But she kept her voice carrying. "I'm quite sure you'll take your first opportunity to shove my head into a deck beam or push me down from behind. Isn't that your way?"

"You insult me, Kent," he fumed in impotent fury beneath her, all but stamping on the gangway in a jig of rage. "I *demand* an apology!"

"All right." She was almost directly above him and he had to tip his face up to the sun and shade his eyes to even look at her. "I'm sorry that you're so pathetic a bully you have to pick on boys a third of your age. How's that?"

"You little shite—"

It was at that moment that the full force of Mr. Colyear's displeasure hit her chest like a bomb.

"Silence!"

Chapter Nine

The word was as close to shouting as Col had ever come, and he had no doubt from the reactions of the crew that every man jack of them felt their cods shiver up inside their bodies for shelter.

"I'll have the name of the next man that talks." Col leaned his weight down on the quarterdeck rail and raked the ship with the double-shotted menace in his eyes, just for emphasis. It was a wonder the sharp inhaling of breath didn't suck the wind out of the sails.

Col had observed the near fracas from the vantage of the quarterdeck with amazement at both Kent's daring and her idiocy. The stupid girl was going to wake up with a knife stuck squarely between her ribs, or worse, if she didn't watch out. What had she been thinking to provoke such a man of such proud volatility as Gamage? It was sheer lunacy. Suicidal lunacy.

He was going to go mad trying to figure Kent out. And go mad trying to save her from herself.

If he ever got his hands on her, he would thrash her. And Gamage as well. Never mind that the man was well past the age to be bent over a cannon to kiss the gunner's daughter for punishment. Col would see it done.

As for Kent, if he ever laid hands on her, he would—

He wouldn't. He would make damn sure he never touched her.

But she'd left him one hell of a poxy mess to clean up. Damn her fine gray eyes.

"Back to your work. Move along there, you idlers. Find work or I'll find it for you." The people fell to whatever work was to hand with silent, watchful diligence.

In the starboard chains, Willis dropped down the shrouds as silently as a spider. "Here now, Mr. Kent," he urged quietly. "Best to move back aloft, sir."

Col had other plans. "Mr. Kent. You will join me on the quarterdeck."

The satisfied smirk that cleaved Gamage's poxy excuse for a face told him what was coming, yet Col was a patient man, and let it unfold like a three-penny opera.

As Kent and Willis lowered themselves from the chains onto the gangway, Gamage, unable to resist the temptation of an easy target for his stymied fit of anger, threw a vicious elbow at Kent's passing head. But instead of hitting Kent, Gamage landed the blow on Willis as he stepped between the two officers.

The wiry man withstood it like a gunner, solid and sure in the face of Gamage's misspent rage, but blood spouted instantly from the corner of his mouth, soiling Gamage's sleeve.

Gamage, still spewing ineffective venom, spat, "Mind your betters," at Willis, and Kent, characteristically not knowing when in hell to leave well enough alone, was about to spring herself to her man's defense.

Before she could indict herself any further, Col cracked his voice at them like a whip. "I'll have that man's name!"

The bo'sun, Mr. Robinson, materialized at his elbow. "Mr. Gamage, sir? Or Mr. Kent?"

Col hoped the full weight of his displeasure was settling onto Gamage. "Mr. Gamage. I'll see you as well as Mr. Kent."

He put all the bite he was feeling into the laconic tone, and then turned his back on the whole lot of them, just to show his disdain, and his control. He was surprised to find Captain McAlden had been standing quietly at his back.

"Well. That has put the cat amongst the pigeons. But who is the cat and who is the pigeon, we shall have to see. I'll speak to Kent and Gamage after you're done with them, if you would be so good as to send them to me. Carry on, Mr. Colyear." And with a cordial nod, he wandered away to the lee of the quarter to consult with Mr. Charlton on some point of sailing.

Mr. Charlton looked grave and said whatever was necessary, but he, too, fell silent—as silent as the rest of the ship— when the miscreants gained the quarterdeck.

But Col had no intention of letting the incident become any more of a spectacle than it already was, even for the captain's entertainment. He ignored the midshipmen and left them to stand, stewing in their own bilge.

"Prepare to come about," he ordered before calling to the quartermaster. "Helm about."

There was a general bustle as the men fell to turning the ship into the wind and readjusting all the sails to suit his exacting eye. "Sheet home. Clew down, there. Haul away hard on that jib. *Haul*, I say."

So the rest of the ship was thoroughly engaged with their work when he finally turned to Kent and Gamage.

"I will detain you two"—he stabbed his eyes first at Gamage—"*young*"—and then at Kent—"*gentlemen* for only a moment, before I turn you over to your captain. To whom I will recommend dealing with you as harshly as possible."

Although Col didn't like to envision Kent tied spread-eagled along the weather shrouds in the typical punishment reserved for recalcitrant midshipmen. In such an attitude, too much of her person would be on display to curious eyes, and it might be seen that Mr. Kent was not all he was pretending to be.

But it was out of his hands. The public nature of their set-to had put paid to any discretion Col might have been able to exercise.

His roving eyes found a job for the last few of the men

still trying to provide him with an audience. "Slacken that mizzencourse tack. Mr. Kent, did I see you argue with and insult a fellow officer?"

"You did, sir." The gray eyes that met his were unflinching. No excuses or useless explanations. Col had expected no less, but it was nice to have his faith borne out.

Gamage, however, was another matter altogether.

"And Mr. Gamage, did I see you do the same, and then strike a crew member, a rated man, besides?"

"*He* started it"—he jerked his head to Kent—"the little prick. And the other man ought to know to mind his betters."

Col felt his blood heat by several degrees, and the air in his lungs grew thick and heavy with steam. And yet he made a point of speaking precisely, even methodically. "Shut your filthy mouth, before I shut it for you, Mr. Gamage. You are on the quarterdeck of a frigate of His Majesty's Royal Navy. If I *ever* hear you speak like that again, I will cut out your tongue with a marlinspike and feed it to the sharks. Do I make myself clear?"

Even Gamage had the sense to quake under the sharp blade of the reprimand. He swallowed his surliness. "Aye, aye, sir."

Col took a deep breath to restore his equilibrium without cooling his anger one bit. "As to your choice of language in speaking to the man Willis, what was it our esteemed Admiral Nelson has said to the point? Can't recall, Mr. Gamage? Mr. Kent?"

"'Aft the higher honor,'" Kent quoted instantly, "'but forward the better man.'"

Col could have admired her cleverness if he wasn't so bloody angry. "Thank you, Mr. Kent, yes. Can you conceive of what he meant, Mr. Gamage?"

Gamage shifted his eyes over Col, looking for but not being able to exactly find the hidden trap. He finally answered, "No, sir."

"He meant that the navy only works, and works well, and is able to overcome her enemies and keep her country safe, if each man jack of you, from the officers down to the lowest, unrated boy, treats each other with the utmost respect. Respect, Mr. Gamage, does not mean striking a man for no reason other than to salvage your pride."

And though Col kept Sally's warning about Gamage's insidious allegation in the front of his mind, he strove to be fair, and share the blame. And he was mad enough at her to let fly a few more blasts. "And respect, Mr. Kent, does not mean indulging in a fit of catcalling on my deck, like a bloody *girl*." He leaned into her then with the hard weight of his eyes, if not his body.

And she blanched a little at that, the high color of her indignation leaching away as some of her hopefully better sense returned.

"I will not put up with such behavior from my officers. I will disrate you faster than a lead line can sink and turn you before the mast, seniority, or family, be damned. Now get yourselves below to make your most abject apologies to your captain and pray not to have engendered his displeasure as much as you have mine. Do I make myself perfectly clear?"

Kent was the only one of the two to meet his eye. "Aye, aye, sir."

Sally found, as she marched herself off the quarterdeck and down to the captain's cabin, that half of the crew was watching, and all the midshipmen were waiting for her in the waist. Every one of them from silent Charles Dance down to little Ian Worth.

Will Jellicoe reached out to shake her hand. "Good luck, Richard."

"Good luck, Richard," echoed Ian Worth.

"Thank you, Ian."

She did not need to notice that the courtesy and the encouragement were not extended to Damien Gamage. But for the first time, the other midshipmen held their places as Gamage moved past, and didn't give way for him. It was promising. It might make it all worth it. She wouldn't care how much ire she drew, so long as it stayed firmly away from both Ian and Will, as well as Charles Dance and Marcus Beecham.

The marine sentry at the door banged the butt of his rifle hard against the captain's bulkhead door. "Mr. Kent, sir. And Mr. Gamage."

"Get yourselves in here," Captain McAlden growled. Any hopes Sally had cherished that Captain McAlden would go easy on them were dashed with one look at his face. When they had themselves arrayed at attention in front of his table— for even Gamage knew enough to present his better self to the captain—the man laid in to them with all the chill of his considerable sangfroid. A pick wouldn't have chipped the ice from his eyes.

"Let me make one thing perfectly clear, gentlemen. We are a ship of war. We are at war with an enemy who will not rest until England has been destroyed. It is our job and our duty, personally and professionally, individually and collectively, to prevent that from happening. And it is my duty specifically to make sure that each and every officer under my command is doing his duty to the utmost. And that means there is absolutely *no* time for petty squabbles. I will not have my midshipmen bawling accusations across the deck like Billingsgate fishwives. Do you understand me?"

Sally felt a shiver crawl meekly across her skin. "Yes, sir."

"Tell me the nature of this childish antagonism. Mr. Gamage, you are the senior. Explain yourself."

"I cannot account for it, sir."

"Cannot or will not?" The captain dismissed Gamage's lack of explanation and turned the cold steel of his gaze upon her. "And you, Mr. Kent?"

Sally could give him nothing but the truth, no matter how impolitic. "It is my opinion that Mr. Gamage mistreats the younger midshipmen, bullying them physically and filling them with needless anxiety that interferes with the performance of their duty. And I also have reason to think Mr. Gamage has relieved me of my personal stores."

"Your opinion, is it? Stealing is a very serious accusation, Mr. Kent. Have you proof?"

To Sally's mind, the captain did not seem at all surprised by her accusations, and perhaps—just perhaps—Captain

McAlden sounded hopeful that she would indeed have the proof that he would need to thoroughly punish Gamage. She *hated* to disappoint him.

"None, sir, which is why I did not bring my complaint to you. And the stores found their way into interesting places."

The captain narrowed his eyes. "Explain."

"I understand you enjoyed a bottle of mint sauce with your lamb last night, sir."

She had his full attention now. "Think very carefully about what you imply, Mr. Kent."

"I make no implication, sir. I understand the stewards barter amongst themselves. Fresh food is a valuable commodity, and anyone may try and do the best for his master that he can. The goods stolen from my dunnage have traveled far and wide throughout the ship. As they were meant to, to divert attention from the crime and involve as many people as possible in the blame. As I said, I have no evidence, but I have found it exceedingly strange that the greater part of the midshipmen's mess should be so quickly reduced to millers, with the noticeable, and well-fed, exception of Mr. Gamage."

Sally let her eyes slide sideways over Gamage's soft girth before she raised her glare to Gamage's face. She was obliged by the fact that he did look a trifle green in the gills. He wasn't as confident in his scheme as he wanted everyone to think. He was vulnerable. That was good to know.

Captain McAlden took a long time to mull his decision, turning his back on them to prowl toward the stern gallery. Sally was conscious of working to keep any trace of smugness or expectation from her face, but she was entirely unprepared when the captain turned back and addressed her.

"Mr. Kent. You may report to Mr. Colyear and tell him your punishment is to spend ten of your off-duty hours at the masthead, repenting of your sins."

"My sins, sir?" She thought she might choke on her indignation. She could not conceive of such a miscarriage of justice. She had expected better of Captain McAlden.

"Aye, Mr. Kent." He regarded her coldly. "The sin of not

using the considerable portion of brains with which you were born to better control yourself. There will be no more displays of temper upon my deck. Do you hear me?"

"Yes, sir." She swallowed the hot fist of pride lodging in her throat. She would not cry. She would not embarrass herself and her family by such an unseemly, dispirited display. She jammed her hat down upon her head and made what she could of a dignified exit.

But her self-pity ended the moment she set her sights on her comrades, waiting for her near the companionway.

"Well?" Ian asked.

"Mastheaded."

Charles Dance's face slid into a small smile. "For you, that's no punishment at all."

Sally felt her spirits lighten. She hadn't thought of it that way. And truly, he was right. She was just as comfortable in the tops as she would be in her hammock. Probably more so.

"And Gamage?" Will inquired.

"Still in there. I'm not privy to Captain McAlden's thoughts, but I imagine Gamage is getting more than just a talking-to."

"We'll find out from Pinky," Ian offered. "He might be as deaf as a haddock, but he still has his ears open for all the scuttlebutt talk."

Sally clapped him on the shoulder in triumph. "Listen to you talk, Ian. Why, in just two days, you've become the veriest old salt."

"Thank you, Richard. I'll take that as quite a compliment."

"And so you should."

A shadow eclipsed down them from above. "Move along there, gentlemen." Mr. Colyear's voice was his usual granite drawl. "I'm sure you have duties to see to. And Mr. Kent, I'll see you at the main masthead this instant, sir."

Sally touched her hat and lowered her eyes. Devil take it, but it was eerie, the communication between Mr. Colyear and the captain. How Mr. Colyear could already know the punishment allotted to her by the captain was remarkable, seeing as no message was passed out of the cabin. And judging from his voice, Mr. Colyear was not best pleased at so lenient a sentence.

"Go on, then," Charles Dance advised. "I'll bring you your books."

"Thank you." It was customary for midshipmen to study their navigation while sitting at the masthead. "That's very good of you, Mr. Dance."

"Charles, if you please." Dance held out his hand for her to shake. "I had an egg for breakfast this morning, Mr. Kent, instead of cold mush. And I am sensible to whom I owe my thanks."

Sally felt a welcome smile stretch across her face. Honestly, if such was to be the outcome, she would gladly sit through a hundred hours at the masthead. "You are most welcome." And Dance was right. It was no punishment at all.

The weather held fine and bright, and tucked in between the shrouds and the crosstrees, she was as snug as in any berth, though she was disappointed to see that Gamage was mastheaded for his punishment as well. But in Gamage's case the sentence was made much more severe by his age and girth. It took him the better part of three quarters of an hour to struggle up the shrouds to make the climb to the shorter mizzen masthead, the lowest of the mizzenmast's three tops, and Sally was sure half the crew was secretly hoping he would keel over the side from an apoplexy.

It was a matter of perverse pride for Sally to be seen sitting her punishment far higher than Gamage could manage, in the topgallant crosstrees, because she was conscious of the good opinion of the topmen who worked the trees. And Gamage proved to be sensible to the slur. Across the air dividing them, he gave her a look as mean and unforgiving as a dockyard dog, and drew his thumb across his neck to pantomime his threat.

Sally sent him a mock salute in reply to such impotent intimidation. The sting had been drawn from the wasp by the simple exposure of his ways to *Audacious*'s public. Devil take Gamage, she would meet his challenge, for she had four older brothers, and even with Gamage's supposed superior experience and years, Sally reckoned that altogether, she was privy to about forty years of Kent knowledge, expertise, and dirty tricks. She may not have done it all, but devil take her, she had heard enough to know how to take a man down a peg.

Damien Gamage had no bloody idea of the Kent ways of retribution. He had finally tangled with the wrong man.

With that thought to cheer her, and with hours of idleness in front of her—she had no great need to study "The Requisite Tables," for she already knew them as well as need be since she had no illusions that she would ever actually sit for her lieutenancy exams in front of a board of examination— she had a great deal of time to study Mr. Colyear.

From the vast height of the topgallants, he swam the deck like a sleek leviathan, silent and stealthy, constantly moving forward. He was very near to relentless. Just watching him scan the deck and rigging with the sweep of his eye, and make his judgments with both speed and acuity, made her understand how he was so intimidating to those around him. He held everyone to a high standard, because he held himself to an even higher one. He only seemed exacting because he didn't comprehend that not everyone was as clever and as quick as he was.

But still, he was patient, rarely raising either the volume or the tone of his voice to anger. Methodical, tireless, brilliant. That was Mr. Colyear.

Devil take her for a stupid lubber, but when the afternoon sun cast his shadow upon the deck, bloody Lord God but he was long in the bone. And as handsome as they came. Straight and tall, the most finely made man she had ever had the pleasure to know.

And he did not like her. Not one bit.

So be it. Mr. Colyear's disdain gave her the freedom to deal with Mr. Gamage as she saw fit.

The Kent way.

Chapter Ten

When Sally arrived back at the orlop cockpit at the end of the watch well ahead of Gamage, for he took a much longer time in his ungainly descent from the masthead—no sliding down backstays for him—the confidence and ebullience of her fellow midshipmen had ebbed dangerously.

"Mr. Gamage is going to be twice as mean as he ever was when he gets back, isn't he?" Ian lamented.

"No," Sally countered staunchly. Normally, at least one of the midshipmen was invited to dine with the captain, but it seemed after the earlier set-to that they were all being punished by exclusion. Which had led to the present state of affairs, with all four of the other young gentlemen, Dance, Beecham, Jellicoe, and Worth, awaiting Gamage's return with something close to fearful dread.

It was time for the inmates of the cockpit asylum to revolt, in more ways than mere matters of health and hygiene.

"He isn't going to bother you anymore," she promised Ian. "Even if he's as mad as a hornet, I promise he'll leave you alone. I'll see to it. We'll rid ourselves of him yet."

"The only way we'll ever get rid of him is if he dies, or gets passed for lieutenant," Marcus Beecham muttered.

"Never happen," Charles Dance spoke quietly. "The chances of the French putting a hole through him are greater than him passing for lieutenant, and the Frenchies will never make it out of the blockade."

"There's a better way to be rid of Mr. Gamage." Sally included them all under the umbrella of her smile. "I'm going to poison him."

Only Ian Worth dared venture into the silence that greeted her remark. "And his grog. He likes that well enough. Can you poison that, too?"

"Nothing easier," she assured him.

"You'll get us all in trouble," Charles warned. "Especially Pinkerton. He'll be blamed if there's aught amiss with the food. I don't want any part of that."

"No chance of that. I'll make sure Pinky is quite safe. And I'll not kill him, only teach him a lesson he won't soon forget."

"What do you plan to do?"

Sally held up a cautionary hand. "You leave it to me. The less you know the better, for you can't tell what you don't know, but it should be simple enough with the way Gamage likes to help himself to our food."

She had tried, by arranging with Pinky, to feed them all heartily from their stock of fresh eggs and fish whenever the arrangement of the watches took Gamage away from their mess, but Gamage still managed his predations, simply by reaching over and taking the food off another's plate, or appropriating another's glass of wine.

"Stealing our food and drinking our drink," Ian had groused with his chin in his hands and his elbows propped on the table. "A man shouldn't have to put up with that."

Sally was as fed up with it as the rest of them, and she was more than keen to see Gamage get his due, if only to put some spark and confidence back into her friends. She crossed to her sea chest, and pulled a small twist of paper and a dark bottle out of its depths. "Here we have it, gentlemen. Two small pieces of retribution."

Eight bells rang out, signaling the end of the afternoon watch, and the hands were piped to supper. In another few short minutes Gamage stalked in, and the others, hiding their wary looks behind their hands, slouched out of his path, the way they had gotten used to. Sally did the same, both from the need not to give away her plan with another name-calling set-to, and from her desire to avoid another mastheading from either Captain McAlden or Mr. Colyear.

But there was Pinky, his usual brisk, cheery self, bringing the heavy wooden tray of food to their end of the table— well away from Gamage's spot at the head. He dished up the stew and poured out glasses of slightly watered wine, for with their limited stores, Sally and Pinky had determined on the sacrifice of quality over quantity. The boys fell to the meal, a fragrant, steaming ragout, in their usual omnivorous manner, crouching round their bowls, as if they were in prison and had need to defend themselves.

Sally took her bowl from Pinky and, with a deft turn of her wrist, emptied the twist of heavy spice into one side of the bowl. Once at the table, she uncorked the dark bottle of red wine vinegar and poured its ruby contents into a partially filled glass of watered wine. And then she sat to eat, pretending to eat in the same manner as the other boys, but giving the spice time to dissolve and meld into the ragout. The others all kept their heads down, with the occasional feral look of apprehension at Gamage, but it was nothing out of the ordinary. Even so, Sally made a point of trying not to be caught watching Gamage and give away the game.

Patience, she chided herself, patience. Gamage was a creature of habit, and when presented with an opportunity to act, he would do so predictably. All she needed to do was have patience.

Soon enough, Gamage reached his long arm across the table for Sally's unprotected wine glass.

Sally pretended to try and stop him. "Devil take you, Gamage!" she cried, snatching it away from his reach. "You can't have that!"

But Gamage was Gamage, and was already hooking his finger over the lip of her now undefended stew bowl and drawing it toward him with a sneer of triumph. "I'll take whatever I want."

"Devil take you," she cried again, and stood. "I demand you give that back." But she also left her glass out, enticingly near to Gamage's hand.

Gamage didn't notice, and spooned down her meal with satisfied relish. "Don't tell me what I can," he began around a mouthful of the ragout, "and can't—"

There was a breathtaking silence, as everyone watched Gamage swallow hard and lick his lips, first repeatedly, and then convulsively. He began to gasp for air and grabbed up Sally's goblet of vinegar-laced wine and swilled it immediately down.

And then he exploded.

There was nothing else to call it. He spewed the entire contents of the goblet across the table and grabbed for his throat.

"I've been poisoned! You've poisoned me." And he fell to his knees at the edge of the table, rubbing, almost clawing at his mouth, in some desperate bid to rid himself of whatever poison he thought he had ingested. His face had grown as red as a blister, and water was pouring down from his eyes and nose—he looked to be in the most awful, acute distress.

The midshipmen had all risen to get a better view of their erstwhile tormentor suffering torments, but with the unperturbed curiosity and callous indifference particular to boys, they did nothing to help.

It was Gamage's servant, Tunney, who answered his master's calls of distress. "Mr. Gamage? Mr. Gamage! Help me! Send for the surgeon, quick." He turned from the immobile midshipmen and appealed to Pinky. "Quickly now! Pinkerton, send a boy for the surgeon. Mr. Gamage is poisoned."

"Oh, my! Tha's right terrible, it is. What 'ave you been feedin' 'im?"

"Send for the surgeon!"

"Right away, then. Right away." Pinky's face was polished red with anxiety and he scurried away to the door, calling loudly for Mr. Stephens, the ship's surgeon, to come down from the gunroom.

Sally went to Tunney's aid and helped prop Gamage up. But when the servant tried to give Gamage more wine, he made a spasmodic, gasping sound and flung it away from his lips, dashing what was left in the glass to the floor. Disposing of the vinegared contents, from Sally's point of view, quite neatly.

As amusing as it was to watch Gamage turn alarming colors, their private revenge was turning public. The small space in the cockpit was filling up with people, crowding in to see Mr. Gamage be poisoned.

Mr. Stephens, the surgeon—called from his own supper in the gunroom, if the state of the linen napkin dangling from his waistcoat was any indication—came to the prostrate man, and observed him sweating and weeping from every orifice, and took up his wrist to feel for his pulse.

And in another heartbeat, Mr. Colyear was there, too. The way cleared for him automatically, the sea parting in deference to Moses. Sally looked up from where she crouched on the floor next to Gamage to find his relentless eyes boring into her in unspoken question. She held her countenance and let him look. If he and the captain had decided not to help them deal with the problem that was Gamage, she would not feel the slightest bit guilty for helping herself and her fellow midshipmen.

"What did this man eat?" asked the surgeon.

"Here is the food, sir." Sally stood up, and picked up the offending bowl. "It was my supper, sir, that Mr. Gamage took."

Mr. Colyear turned his slow eye first upon her, and then upon them all in turn, but Sally was astonished to see that not one of the midshipmen so much as blanched or turned coward. They widened their eyes, or looked grave and everything astonished at Mr. Gamage's turn.

"A fit. That's what he's had," said an anonymous voice at the back of the room.

"Nah," muttered another voice she couldn't see. "Divine retribution, that's what that is."

"Silence," Mr. Colyear said quietly, though Sally noticed he did not ask to take the man's name. Nor did he take his eyes from her face.

She stood and willed herself to remain still and untroubled. Gamage was in the wrong. He had taken her food.

In another moment Mr. Stephens rose and said, "Remove him to the sick bay."

Mr. Colyear motioned to Tunney and another man by the door, who carried the writhing Gamage out. But Mr. Colyear also stopped the surgeon when he would have followed.

"Mr. Stephens, if you please." Mr. Colyear reached over and took the bowl from Sally's hands, before he passed it to the surgeon.

Mr. Stephens put up a hand in protest. "I'm a surgeon, not an apothecary. I know nothing of poisons, sir."

So Col held it up to his nose himself and sniffed carefully.

"If you please, sir," Sally spoke quickly to keep him from any further exploration. "It wasn't poisoned. I was eating from it myself, until Mr. Gamage took it from me."

"Is that so?" Mr. Colyear said gravely, proffering the bowl and its remaining food to her. "And would you eat from it again? Now?"

Sally widened her eyes and made a show of swallowing hard, but she took the bowl. "I don't see why not. I was eating it first, same as him." And slowly, she picked up her fork and dished up a piece of the ragout. And slowly, so slowly that Sally was sure every person stuffed into the crowded room leaned forward, she opened her lips, put it in her mouth, and ate.

She chewed the food slowly, as if fearful she might suffer the same fate. But when the first piece was swallowed with no symptom of poison, she took another. And then she sat and consumed the rest of the stew as she had been at the beginning. And then, just as if they wanted to prove their innocence as well, the rest of the boys resumed their suppers, some of them eating where they were standing.

Sally felt as if her face would split in two from the pride

and the love she felt at such loyalty, and from the necessity not to smile at the sheer genius of having pulled it off.

But Mr. Colyear had not been born yesterday, and he knew one way or another how to get the inmates of the cockpit asylum, as he had dubbed them that first day, to fall into line. "That will do, Mr. Kent. But I should nevertheless like a *word* with you." He gestured to the door. "If you'd be so kind."

A glance around the cockpit told her this quiet request had produced the effect that all of Mr. Colyear's stony looks could not. Both Will Jellicoe and Charles Dance stood, and would have stepped forward to confess, she was sure, if she had not made a small, and she hoped, subtle movement of her hand to wave them back.

"Aye, sir." After all, there was no longer any proof. Whatever evidence there might have been had long since been consumed.

But as soon as Mr. Colyear's back was turned to exit through the door, she took a big gulp of Dance's unadulterated wine to mask the smell of pepper on her breath.

Mr. Colyear walked with his usual deliberation from the companionway all the way up to the taffrail at the stern of the vessel. There was only Mr. Horner, who was the officer of the watch, nearby, but he moved forward, to give Mr. Colyear privacy.

Mr. Colyear was not one for speaking abruptly. He was the sort of man who looked, and listened, and thought, and let other people make fools of themselves while they waited for him to speak. It gave weight to his words. The same weight that loaded his brows down with gravitas. It made him a man worth listening to.

She was perfectly happy to wait him out. She could stand as unperturbed as Joan of Arc before the fire, confident that she had done the right thing.

"Do try and look chastened, for God's sake, Mr. Kent," he advised in his sooty, dark tones. "See if you can manage it for my sake, if not for your own."

There was that wry humor, hiding just below the surface of the granite exterior, like the dark shadow of whiskers beneath his skin. "I will do, Mr. Colyear." She transferred her gaze to her toes and wondered if it was humor or the sunset that lit his eyes such a brilliant green.

"Well, Kent. That was interesting." He let another pause lengthen out between them before he asked, "I have to assume that you were the one to orchestrate that extraordinary scene?"

"Actually, Mr. Gamage did, with his predatory ways. Nothing would have happened if he had kept to his own supper."

"So it was perhaps divine retribution," he agreed. "In the form of a Scotch bonnet pepper, if I'm not mistaken. Something you Kents eat as regularly as an Irishman eats his potatoes."

Sally couldn't stop the flush that betrayed her any more than she could stop herself from admiring Mr. Colyear's perspicacity.

"Yes." He nodded as he watched her face heat. "You might want to consider that Matthew Kent didn't come up with all of his own pranks, Kent. He often had help."

And then David St. Vincent Colyear smiled.

The smile was all in his eyes, in the upward cast of the corners and the rare warmth that lit the chalcedony depths, as if that stone had been melted into liquid. When he smiled everything else was forgotten. Everything that seemed stern and forbidding in him metamorphosed into friendship and comfort. It was a smile of such warmth and sly humor she felt a burst of reckless joy break loose inside her.

"Ah. Then I will thank you for the inspiration." She knew she was smiling back at him like a looby. But she didn't care.

"You're welcome." He shot a glance sideways at her. "It was the Scotch bonnet, wasn't it?"

"It may have been. I did have some dried Scotch bonnet pepper spice, before all my stores were stolen, so I can't be too sure. It seems entirely possible that Gamage is the one responsible for poisoning himself."

"Entirely possible," Mr. Colyear conceded with that same wry half-smile. "What a day, divine retribution and all."

He turned and leaned his hips back against the taffrail and crossed his feet. He looked almost . . . casual. Except Mr. Colyear didn't have a casual bone in his body.

But she did. So she turned and leaned her back against the rail next to him.

"Well, Kent. Up until this afternoon, you were doing a pretty fair job of keeping yourself scarce."

She peered up at him, trying to read his expression in the waning light. "I thought I was meant to."

There was a twitch of his lip, a tug at the corner of his mouth, which stood in place for agreement. "You were. You do realize I'm going to have to masthead you again, or be seen as favoring you? You can't go about poisoning people, no matter how much they may deserve it. But I reckon another spate of punishment will only serve to burnish your growing reputation."

"Ah." There didn't seem anything more to add that wouldn't seem vain.

Before them stretched the full length of the ship, and from their vantage point, with the sun setting almost at the point of the bowsprit, with all the symmetry of the hull leading to that one molten point, Sally thought she had never seen anything more beautiful.

"It makes it worth it, a sight like that."

"Does it?" Mr. Colyear did not seem as affected by the sublime poetry of the sight, but still his voice retained its humor. "Worth the risk of attempted poisoning, or the larger risk of coming on board?"

She tried to answer in the same vein. "As it would be pure vanity at this point to take any credit for the first, it will have to be the second."

"Damn your quick eyes, Kent." He spoke on an exhalation, but his tone was gathering heat. "I would think if you felt staying aboard such a great goal, you would take greater care in ensuring you are able to do so. What in hell were you thinking, provoking a fight with Gamage in front of the rest of the crew?"

Trust Mr. Colyear to finally get serious. But she wasn't

feeling the least bit apologetic. Still, she kept her tone light. "I suppose I was thinking he deserved it. And I'd had enough."

"Enough? Enough to make you go home, and quit this godforsaken—" He bit off his words, as if they left the bad taste of too much pepper in his mouth. "Enough to make you do as you ought?"

If it was indignation he wanted, she would match him blow for blow. "No, enough of Gamage's abuse. Poor Worth whimpers in his sleep out of fear of the man. That shouldn't happen to a dog."

"They weren't whimpering tonight, were they?"

"No," she agreed with infinite satisfaction, "they were not."

He drew in a deep breath. "I comprehend your vehemence, Kent, but you do yourself and certainly Worth no good when you engage in a pissing fight like that in front of the people. Those boys need to learn to handle themselves just as well as you do."

She turned to face him, determined to make her case with him, man to man. "Is it too much to hope they might be allowed to learn to handle themselves without having their faces smashed into the walls, or their possessions stolen from them? It seemed too much to hope that you, and Captain McAlden, would give them justice. If you had, I wouldn't have to resort to such . . . skulduggery as occurred this afternoon."

But the heated reply she expected never came. He didn't turn and engage with her in her ire. He remained stretched back, with his elbows upon the rail, looking at her as if she were a curiosity behind a glass case. "Such an intriguing combination of the naïve and the bloodthirsty you are, Kent."

She didn't know how to react to the lightly teasing tone in his voice. She decided upon bluster. "Tell me, Mr. Colyear, would you have tolerated such predations in the gunroom? Would you put up with Lieutenant Rudge, for instance, stealing your belongings?"

"No, I would not tolerate, nor put up with it, and, although you did not ask, yes, I would do something appropriate to the scale of the offense, without unnecessarily involving my captain, or anyone else so wholly unconcerned with it."

She all but threw her hands in the air in frustration. "That *was* what I was doing."

"No." He was all seriousness now. But he sounded, perhaps, a little weary. "What you were doing on deck today was giving way to your feelings, to the impulse of the moment."

"Am I not entitled to my feelings? For they were just." It offended her sense of right and wrong that he could not see it. And it hurt her, as well, to think Mr. Colyear, Col, of all people, couldn't see such injustice.

"I don't dispute the justness of your feelings, Kent. Only your manner of acting so impulsively upon them. You say you want to be an officer, and by God, if you don't have the makings of it. But you've got to think. You can't try to fight every one of those boys' battles for them. They need to test their own mettle, because if they don't overcome their fear of Gamage, God knows how they are to overcome their fear of the French."

He looked out over the ship and she was spared the continued force of those eyes for the moment. But still, he went on. "I know you meant well, Mr. Kent. And no doubt Mr. Gamage deserved his comeuppance. But I would . . . be pleased if you would trust me to know what goes on in my ship. Then, I could trust you as well. As it stands . . ."

All the bluster and argument blew out of her lungs at the simple sincerity of his tone. No one had ever called her trustworthiness into doubt. Indeed, she had long thought of herself as everything trustworthy, everything honest and loyal.

But he was right. She hadn't trusted him, and now he could not trust her. "What a bind I seem to have put us in."

"But you can put us out, Kent. You can pull us out. Just trust me."

She wanted to. She wanted to trust him and rely upon him. She wanted to lay her head down upon his chest and know that it would all be all right, that everything would work out as she hoped. But it wasn't that simple.

"I hope I'm not boasting, but your father would not have recommended me, nor would Captain McAlden have accepted and promoted me if I did not know my business. And although I will admit to a great deal of failure with Gamage, I will find a way to get through to him, to solve all our problems in his regard. I promise you."

"Do you promise you'll look out for the midshipmen? Especially Jellicoe and Worth? I just can't watch Worth be bullied and do nothing."

"They're not babies, Kent. They need to learn to stand on their own two feet."

"Yes, but—"

"Yes, but. We both want the same thing, Kent. We just have different ways, different philosophies, on how to go about it. But until you pass your exams and get yourself promoted first lieutenant, you'll have to learn to accept and obey my orders. Graciously."

Sally drew in a long breath. "Oh, well, *that* may be taking it a bit too far—*graciously.* Could you settle for merely *promptly,* or *skillfully*?"

"Certainly. There is more than one way to splice a line, Kent."

"Do you mean I must work harder to gain the stronger hand on Mr. Gamage?"

The wind carried away the better part of Col's laugh. "I hope you don't mean physically. You're tall, but not even were you to attain your father's height, would I recommend you take Gamage on again. He must outweigh you by something close to eight stone." He scanned her up and down. "You Kents are a lanky, lathy lot. Do have a care, Kent."

He sent another long sideways look her way, and just like that, the deck seemed to shift under her feet and tilt her toward Mr. Colyear. When he looked at her like that—as if he liked what he saw—she felt curiously light and happy. Untethered. She felt warm and melting, like buttered toast ready to be served up to him for breakfast. "I am looking after myself, sir."

"Are you? That certainly didn't look like you're looking

after yourself. It looked to me like you were deliberately courting his ire."

Sally felt the last knot of worry ebbing out of her like the tide. Mr. Colyear not only *saw* everything, he *understood* everything he saw. "Well, I was. I would much rather have Mr. Gamage direct his enmity at me than Ian Worth or Will Jellicoe."

"Ah." He tipped his head up as if he were studying the set of the mizzen royal. Or the rigging. Or anything that wasn't her, so studiously did he not look at her. "I should have realized. Such an intriguing combination of the bloodthirsty and the naïve, the lion and the lamb."

"I'm not completely sure of what you mean, but I'm not entirely bloodthirsty. I was concerned for him this evening—Mr. Gamage—when he wolfed most of the pepper down in one bite. Poor bastard. I did feel a little sorry for him. A very little bit."

She was rewarded for her efforts at levity by the return of his smile. "It does you credit, but you waste your time, Mr. Kent. He certainly wouldn't feel sorry for you."

"I know. He's just not clever enough for the job, is he? He'll never be. No matter what you do to try and help him, he'll never be near as clever and quick and skilled as you are. He can't see things the way you do—you see a frayed line and you know that if it isn't mended a hoist could give way and a spar could fall and people could be injured. You can probably reckon the exact moment when it would give way. Gamage would only see it as an onerous chore to be avoided or as an opportunity to blame trouble on somebody else. He may try, but it just comes out all wrong."

"Are you trying to butter me up, Mr. Kent?" But he smiled again, a wide, full-bodied smile, and she was glad— glad she had done what she did, and taken the risk. Glad down to the toes of her too-big feet that she was the one to put that marvelous smile there, upon his face. Glad that he was happy in her presence. And she knew she would dare just about anything to make him smile at her like that again.

"But it's not idle flattery, Mr. Colyear. You know as well

as I, you're cleverer than any four men put together. That's why you're first, even though you're a decade younger than Mr. Rudge and two decades younger than Mr. Charlton."

"Three," he corrected wryly.

"Three, then." She couldn't keep the smile from splitting her face. She could even hear it in her voice. "It's no wonder no one can keep up with you."

"You seem to manage it."

Something warmer than a blush crept under her skin. "Now you flatter me. I've been mostly at sea since I was a child until the last two years. I have the benefit of a family who talks of nothing but trimming sails and running tides as if it were normal dinner conversation. I've helped at least three of my older brothers study to pass for lieutenant, reading them passage after passage of Robinson's *Elements of Navigation*."

"Then make a study of Gamage, and see if you can figure out the way his tides run. Only do so very carefully."

"Devil take me." There was her solution. A course of study. The idea had merit. It had more than merit. It had possibility. She could see it as plainly as she had once seen that book of navigation before her face. "I shall make a study out of him. If only he will let me."

She turned to Col and put out her hand. "Thank you, Mr. Colyear. You've given me my solution."

"Have I?" His voice was still full of his wry amusement, but he looked at her hand for a very long time before he took it.

His hand entirely covered hers, almost engulfed it, and she felt the span of his bones set against hers. His fingers were strong, and his grip firm, but he did not crush her as he might have done. Instead his hand buoyed hers up, holding it safe and secure.

The press of his palm against hers sent a low heat, a vibration, like the touch of a tuning fork, shaking its way inside her, growing stronger and stronger until she was sure it would rattle her apart. But she didn't want it to end. And she did not let go.

Neither did he. "What am I going to do with you, Kent?"

"I don't know," she said stupidly, because she didn't know what she wanted him to do with her. She didn't have the experience to articulate the hopes and fears careering around inside her. She only knew she wanted more of the melting heat that warmed her from the inside to continue. "Just let me be, I suppose."

"Oh, Kent." He smiled, even as he shook his head. That rueful, begrudging little smile at the corner of his mouth. "Surely your clever little mind has figured out by now, I can't possibly let you be."

Everything else stopped. The ship stopped moving beneath her, and she felt that she was the one tilting, swinging off center, as if she were aloft, and the wind had blown the air clean out of her lungs, and she couldn't draw breath. He was looking at her in that minutely considering way of his, and for the first time in weeks, she felt dirty and disheveled.

Such a ridiculous vanity, when all she really wanted was to serve and to sail. That was what she wanted, wasn't it?

"Mr. Colyear," she said, for want of anything more intelligent to say, and because she simply wanted to say his name.

"One of these days, Kent, I'm going to want to hear you call me Col."

Oh, she wanted to call him Col. Out loud instead of in the privacy of her head. And she was going to tell him so. She was leaning toward him, toward the heat and the certainty of him. Toward the possibilities he brought to mind.

This time, he was the one who stepped back. "But this is neither the time, nor, God help me, the place. Find your berth, Kent. Before I'm tempted to find it for you."

And then he strode away, into the enveloping dark.

Chapter Eleven

For once, Sally did not rise at the very crack of dawn. She had slept in, which for her still meant rising before six bells of the morning watch in the thinning light of the northern hemisphere's autumn.

Firstly, with Gamage removed from the cockpit to the sick bay, there had been a pleasant lack of snoring during the night. Before that, when she had returned to her berth from her unsettling but somehow lovely interview with Mr. Colyear, Gamage's projected absence from the cockpit had eventuated something of a rather raucous victory celebration, during which a vast deal of too much watered wine, and whatever else could be bribed, bartered, or brought to hand, had been consumed.

And secondly, in the course of trying to teach Will Jellicoe how to juggle, she had attempted the feat with wine bottles, but only succeeded in giving herself a stinging bruise along her right cheekbone.

Not to put too fine a point on it, but her head hurt like thunder. She felt as if her skull were being pounded in by a caulking mallet, until the dull throbbing in her temple consumed every other sense. Almost every other sense. The instinct to escape to the air was still as strong as ever.

If Pinky's bemused look and tutting were any indication, her cheek must be purpling up nicely, although her eye didn't appear to be swelled shut, as she could still see. But she wanted fresh air. She couldn't stand still long enough to accept any more of Pinky's ministrations than the cool, brine-soaked rag he pressed carefully to her cheekbone.

"I can't like the looks of that." Pinky's face pruned up in disapproval. "What you need is a good beefsteak on that."

As if there were fresh beefsteak to be had on board. As if the hold carried an icehouse, and as if the closest thing to fresh beefsteak weren't overboiled stew meat, or leathery strips stored dry in barrels. And she didn't need a beefsteak. She needed cool, clean air. She felt as if she would strangle from the lack of air in the cockpit.

"Leave off, Pinky." She shoved herself to her feet. "I'll be fine. Save your breath to cool your porridge," she joked as she left him, still muttering imprecations under his breath.

She kept the rag over her eye as she ascended to the quarterdeck. The sky was overcast, with a flat gray light over the sea. They must be close to the north coast of France for the heat of the land to cause such haze. At the gangway, Sally took a moment to orient herself. They appeared to be tacking southeast by south, close-hauled on the larboard tack with the wind out of the east. She took a sniff of the breeze, to see if she could detect any shore smells, but so close to the deck, her nose was still full of the funk from below. Perhaps when she was in the top she could pinpoint her location more exactly. It was always fun to make a mental guess and then check her calculations from the noon sighting to see if she were right.

Sally climbed to the foretop before the changing of the watch. The smooth familiarity of the ropes beneath her hands, the rhythmic creaks and groans of the arthritic spars, and the quiet chill of the morning air were just what she needed to clear her head. And to think. It had seemed such a simple thing last night to resolve to make a study of Mr. Gamage, but in the harsher light of morning, it was more difficult to sort out how to get around her own feelings of ambivalence to the man, as well as his own antipathy for helping himself.

But that dilemma was too hard. She had much rather keep track of Mr. Colyear, wearing a tattoo on the deck below, and think of more ways to talk to him again. And touch his hand.

Eight bells rang out, signaling the end of the morning watch and the beginning of the next. The topmen who had served through the night went down to find their breakfast as they were relieved by their replacements on the next watch.

"Morning, Mr. Kent." Willis tugged his forelock in greeting when he reached the masthead. "That's a right 'beaut,' as the sporting fancy would have it," he added, pointing to her cheek.

"I believe I'm supposed to say, 'You should see the other fellow,'" she joked.

"Would the other fellow be Mr. Gamage, if you don't mind my askin'?"

"No. I'm sorry, Willis." She had not forgotten Willis's split lip, courtesy of Mr. Gamage, but she was conscious of Mr. Colyear's warning's as well. "But I don't think Mr. Gamage will be giving you any more trouble, so you can put him from your head."

"That's all right then, Mr. Kent. I heard *all* about it."

Oh, devil take her. It was a small world, a ship. Although it did feel good to know she had her division's approval, for however long it lasted. But she couldn't let it go to her head. She had work to do. Work that didn't include gazing stupidly at Mr. Colyear.

So Sally got back to the job at hand, and cast her gaze over the miles and miles of rolling sea. Anywhere but at Mr. Colyear. Anywhere but at the man who loomed so large in every thought from her head and every sigh from her lungs. Anywhere.

But as she was looking anywhere but at Mr. Colyear, her eye was caught by a flash of color passing in the spray racing along the hull of the ship. She looked again, narrowing her eyes against the glare off the water from the white haze of the overcast sky, until she saw it again, a bobbing speck of color. Orange color.

It was an orange peel.

Her heart began kicking hard against her chest, but she kept her eye on the water, moving down onto the futtock shrouds, to get a closer look and try to find another.

"Willis," she called over her shoulder as she descended. "If you would give me leave—" She didn't wait for his answer, but climbed lower still, hanging out off the shrouds, searching the water off the larboard gangway.

"Mr. Kent?"

At the larboard fore chains she saw another peel bobbing along the current, some twenty yards off. "Willis," she called back up. "Do you see that, Willis?"

"Bit of garbage?" he returned. "Orange, is it, sir?"

"Get a glass on it. Search forward for more!"

In another moment the sharp-eyed topman called back. "There, sir. And there. Two points off the bow."

"Well done, by God. Deck!" She turned back, but the contrary wind kept her voice from reaching Mr. Colyear on the quarterdeck.

A large form blocked her passage. "What do you think you're doing, Kent? Get back aloft."

"Mr. Gamage!" He seemed to have made a remarkable recovery from his unfortunate acquaintance with the Jamaican Scotch bonnet pepper powder. And this would make it up to him. "Mr. Gamage, pray be so good as to report to Mr. Colyear that you've sighted garbage floating off the larboard bow. Orange peels! Look."

Gamage looked, but what he could see was entirely different from what Sally saw. "Garbage? What's next? A report that you've sighted a fish?"

"Only if it were a toasted sardine. Gamage, don't you see?"

He didn't. No one saw. Not even Willis, who was staring down at her as if she'd taken leave of every last one of her senses. But Col would see. And understand.

She would bet her soul that her Mr. Colyear would know the significance of those peels in a heartbeat. And she wasn't going to waste any more time trying to help Gamage find his way out of the pit of his stupidity.

But he blocked her way. "Don't think you're going to make a fool of me again, Kent!" he ground from behind his teeth. "We have a score to settle, you and I."

"Mr. Gamage?" It was Mr. Colyear's voice, a piece of bland perfection, as if he were merely taking a turn about the deck for air, supremely uninterested.

"Mr. Kent is away from his duty, sir."

"True, Mr. Gamage. Care to explain, Mr. Kent?" When Gamage stepped out of the way, Mr. Colyear took one look at her and swore magnificently. "Fuck all. What happened to you?"

She waved his concern away impatiently. There were more important things than a bruise, devil take it all. "Compliments of the foretop, Mr. Colyear. Willis and I have seen orange peels—*Valencia* orange peels, I should reckon—floating by on the current west by south off the larboard bow, sir. I thought to get a bucket upon the flotsam to see if there's anything more."

Gamage made a sarcastic scoffing noise. "You've wasted enough of Mr. Colyear's time, Kent."

"If you please, Mr. Gamage." Mr. Colyear's voice regained its usual low, smooth rumble, but Sally could feel his interest, the strange intense ferocity building behind its walls, as he turned those unfairly intelligent eyes to her. "Spanish oranges?"

He understood. Sally let out the breath she didn't know she had been holding. Her words came out in a tumbled rush. "I think it could be smaller, a *tangerine,* from the look of it. I came down to see if I could get it with a net, or a bucket off the side."

Another noise of derision spewed from Gamage before he sneered, "I doubt Mr. Colyear has the time to be interested in fishing for garbage."

"Ah, but I am, Mr. Gamage. And so should you be."

Oh, Gamage felt it now, the careful intensity of Mr. Colyear's regard. The older man stepped back a bit and the tic of his lip proved he was already regretting the fact that he had called that focused regard down upon himself.

"See to it, Mr. Kent," Col instructed.

Sally scrambled for the side, calling to one of the idlers on the forecastle deck, who were no doubt beginning to gather at the prospect of another famous set-to between herself and Gamage, to assist with a rope and bucket.

"Perhaps it might interest you to know, Mr. Gamage," Col continued in that ironically calm tone, "that *tangerines* are winter fruit, grown in North Africa. In Tangiers. Hence the name."

He paused to see if this information would have any effect upon the hearer, before he continued. "They are also grown in *Spain*. Ah, thank you, Mr. Kent," he added as Sally brought the small bit of peel out of the bucket and presented it to him. "It should be well known the dons çarry winter oranges, such as Mr. Kent has offered us, as provisions against disease. So the garbage does interest me, Mr. Gamage, because, as Mr. Kent has no doubt already surmised, it has undoubtedly floated off a Spanish ship somewhere nearby. You will, of course, remember we are actively engaged in a search for just such ships? Mr. Gamage?"

By now Gamage had paled considerably, his face ashen except for two bright patches of high color in his cheeks. Even he must know Mr. Colyear did not say anything lightly and as a result was all the more terrifying for the matter-of-fact manner in which he spoke. There was plenty of irony in his humor, but no hidden meaning. He said what he meant and meant what he said. No wonder his captain valued him. No wonder he unnerved Gamage.

"Good." Col went on in his deep, easy, unbreakable voice. "Perhaps you'll want to think next time before you berate a junior midshipman, Mr. Gamage. Mr. Kent, have you finished those complicated calculations of time and tide and speed of current you are no doubt making in your capacious brain yet?"

Sally swallowed her thrill at having gotten the best of Gamage. Mr. Colyear was doing her a favor, subtly reminding her that finding the enemy was far more important than a temporary triumph over Gamage. "I haven't the gauge of the current, but the tide has already turned and is flowing north-east by north. If the current is anything under five knots, then the dons are somewhere along the coast to the southwest, and likely headed south to the Atlantic coast of France."

"A safe enough assumption, but good. If you please, Mr. Kent, go make your report to the captain. He'll want to know."

She tugged the brim of her hat and did her best to control her smile.

"Honored, sir. Willis has been tracking it, sir. To see if he can get a better idea of the tide. Shall I go back—"

"No. I'll take his report." He canted a look up at the masthead to see Willis scanning the water with his glass. "You report to the captain."

Col was giving her the triumph of telling the captain of her discovery herself. Generous man.

She went directly to the captain's cabin. "Compliments of Mr. Colyear. He and the lookout have sighted garbage from a Spanish ship."

"Which is?"

"Oranges, sir. Willis is endeavoring to track it on the current, sir."

"Excellent. Come with me, Kent." Captain McAlden removed directly to his cabinet from whence he immediately chose a rolled chart, which he opened upon his table.

"The devil of a thing for a Spanish ship to be this far north. But whatever ship these oranges came off, we will find it. If this blasted fog will ever clear away." He scowled out the stern gallery windows at the gray blanket of heaven, as if by sheer force of will he could burn off the offending weather.

And then he was back to the charts, one finger instantly pinpointing their current position, while the other ran west-ward along the inked line of the coast. "He'll be hiding in-land, as close to the coastline as possible to hide the spars and rigging against the dark of the land."

The silhouette of a ship stood out much more starkly and clearly at sea than against the visual backdrop of the land. But he was looking at the flat map, tracing his hand along the chart as if he could see tides and winds and moving water beneath his hands. There was a moment of stillness, and his eyes narrowed at a point she could not see. He had made his decision.

"Thank you, Mr. Kent," he said as he jammed his hat on his head. "And get back to your top."

Sally did not need to be told twice. She held the door for her captain and followed him to the deck, where he gave orders to change course, tacking due south toward the coast of France. "And a guinea to the man who first sights her."

By the time Sally had regained her place at the foremasthead, Willis had already rearranged his sharpest-eyed men to best advantage along the foremast yards, and they followed the trail of garbage long enough to get a sense of the Spanish ship's course. As the forenoon wore on, the wind freshened out of the east, pushing them down Channel, and the sun began to burn off the worst of the fog until they could sight the coast of Brittany off the larboard bow.

Sally could feel the strain, the tension in the air, as if it were a physical thing. Her eyes began to feel gritty and ache. "I'm beginning to see things," she muttered to Willis.

"You may be." Willis kept his eyes moving. "The trick, sir, isn't to look for a ship, but to look for ocean without any ships. If you're looking for what is there, what you expect to be there, your brain will find the thing that's different. I look for the ocean if I want to find a ship."

It was brilliant in its simplicity. "Devil save you, Willis. You could give training to the whole fleet."

"Nothing most of the fleet doesn't already know. Had it from the captain of my top when I first went aloft. Saved my hide a time or two. And made me a fine guinea or two as well."

"I tell you what, Willis. I'll match the captain's guinea if any man of this foremast sights the ship. And I'll split a guinea with the whole division if we sight it before any of the other masts."

"D'you hear that, lads? Look sharp."

"Deck!" came the jubilant cry from a young sailor dangling from the crosstrees above the royals not more than a minute later. "Sail! Northwest by west on the starboard beam."

"What is it?" Willis called up to the lad.

But even as the lad answered, "Dunno. Never seen the like," Sally had the strange speck of a ship in her sights.

"Xebec, fitted as a frigate. Spanish or I'm the queen's uncle. Check the guns, Willis. I'll report." She passed Willis her glass, and swung down the backstay.

"Twelves and eights," he called as she moved deckward. "Twelve and four per battery, and two small carronades, I reckon, as well."

Sally spilled her news as soon as she reached the weather rail where the captain, the master, and Col all had their glasses trained to the southwest.

"Spanish frigate, xebec-rigged. Flying before the wind with studdingsails set. Twenty-four twelve-pounders in the main battery, with a further eight eight-pounders on the quarter. Only two twenty-four-pounder carronades forward." Such a complement of guns gave *Audacious* scant advantage. The English ship had a greater number of guns in their broadside, but of a smaller weight. Their only obvious advantage lay in the greater number of versatile carronades of heavier weight. But she had no idea how to take advantage of such a configuration.

But her captain showed no such hesitation. "By God." McAlden's satisfaction was palpable. "Run me up to his sterncastle, Mr. Colyear, but see if you can keep us in the lee. I want to be between him and the coast. Wear and make all sail."

The orders were flowing out of Col's mouth before the captain had even finished speaking. "Wear ship. All hands to wear and make all sail." Col put everything into his voice to carry above the din of rushing feet and straining canvas.

Kent went pelting forward to return to her division, out of his immediate control. She scrambled back aloft where the topmen were hauling hard to keep up with his relentless orders, as the helm put over and Col worked the men to squeeze every last bit of speed he could from the sails.

"Steady on, Martin. Watch that block doesn't become fouled. Haul away, flying jib. Clew down. Clew down."

And on it went until *Audacious* was flying before the wind, with every available inch of canvas spread and driving the ship forward. With such a strong following wind, the ship leapt forward in great rocking strides, like a huge galloping beast. In the tops they would be hanging on for dear life with fingers and toes. At least he hoped Kent was.

Mr. Charlton had set a course so *Audacious* crept up on the Spaniard from behind, and Col could see the moment when the Spanish ship became aware that they were being stalked. Through the glass, he could observe a sudden flurry of attention to the sails as the Spanish captain tried to spread enough canvas to make his escape and show *Audacious* a clean pair of heels. But it was too late. Col had done his work, and the xebec was being overtaken.

When it became clear that the xebec would not outrun them, Captain McAlden began to smile and rub his hands together in anticipation.

Col knew the feeling. The excitement of the hunt was coursing through his veins. The ship, his ship, was leaping and tossing beneath him like an ambitious racehorse. Under his feet the inanimate combination of wood, rope, and canvas became a living thing, taking on a life force of its own. And he loved it. It was a day for the ages, the kind of high, bright, windy day and fast sail every sailor lived for.

"Well done, Mr. Colyear. We're within an hour of him. You may clear for action."

The praise lodged firm in Col's chest and filled him with pride, but only for a moment. Duty always came before pride. It was the order they had all been waiting for. "Clear for action!"

The call went up and in the next moment the bo'sun's pipes rent the wind with their shrill call. "All hands, all hands to clear for action."

The men sprang to their tasks, the thought and talk of prize money lending urgency, as if they had already counted the money in their pockets and could not allow it to get away. Anything movable was hauled off and stowed away. Furniture was removed and set off in one of the ship's boats swayed efficiently over the side and manned by ship's boys. The canvas and batten walls of the cabins were taken down and every last fire was extinguished.

Above deck, chains were hauled into the rigging to secure the spars from shot, and a full course of net was rigged over the deck to prevent injury from falling spars. The men stripped to the waist and took off their shoes as the decks were sanded down for traction. The change that transformed the ship into a fighting platform took only minutes.

"Ease off, if you please, Mr. Colyear. Just a bit, let him gain back half a cable." The men who were near enough gaped and muttered to each other, but Col had little time to spare for their understanding. They would learn soon enough that their captain was as canny and sharp in the water as a shark. And just as deadly.

When the orders were given and the xebec had worked ahead of the wind, Captain McAlden gave his next order. "Head up a point or two at most. I want him to think we'll try to overtake him on his starboard bow before we hove to and engage."

"Aye, sir." Mr. Charlton gave the command to the helm.

The men may not have understood either order, and may even have wondered if their captain was not up for the fight, but they would be wrong. Col understood. He saw Captain McAlden's eyes alight with a pleasure that was almost hunger for the fight to come. And he knew the man's detailed way of thinking.

Col would lay a guinea against the proposition that the captain was not going to engage the xebec on her rail at all, but fall off and rake her stern, with each gun in the starboard battery paying off as they were brought to bear. So when *Audacious* drew within two cable lengths of the xebec, Col gave the command. "Starboard battery, stand to. The xebec runs high in the water, you'll need to elevate the guns."

As most of the gun crews had gathered at the larboard battery or above on the gangway rail, and could not follow his reasoning, there was much consternation and not a great deal of action. Which was when he realized his mistake—that he had made his order without the captain giving him the command. "Your pardon, sir."

Captain McAlden's lips twisted in amusement. "No need, Mr. Colyear. Your value to me lies not only in carrying out my orders with exemplary diligence, but also in correctly anticipating my orders. You've the right of it. I will want to rake them astern. But don't run out the starboard battery yet. They may have sharp eyes upon us."

Which gave Col ideas of his own. "Here, Redmond. Pass a message up to Mr. Kent to advise me on the lay and manning of their guns. Tell him to report to the deck." If the xebec had eyes, she also had ears. Col didn't want the information trumpeted across the water.

It was only a matter of moments before Kent was sliding hand over fist down a backstay and streaking down the larboard gangway with her particular quick agility. Col had to breathe away the tightness in his chest—the unaccustomed worry.

The report was just an excuse. The simple truth was that he wanted her near. God only knew why. Experience told him the quarterdeck could prove no safer than the foretop, and even if she were near to him, there was nothing he could do to protect her without compromising his duty and thus the safety of every other member of the crew. It could not be done.

And the foretop should be a safe enough place for her. Only the height of the xebec's free board worried him. The height of the Spanish ship in the water meant that her guns would fire high, into *Audacious*'s rigging.

But Kent's agile mind was with the captain's, observing everything and leaping ahead to the correct conclusion.

"They're all to starboard, Mr. Colyear. The xebec's guns on the larboard are still bowsed tight against the port-lid."

She understood the captain's tactics exactly, without being told. She was different from everyone else, even the other officers, as capable as they were—Lieutenant Rudge's face was still flush with consternation at Col's orders. But Kent saw all the possibilities.

The enemy was still frantically making sail, concentrating all their effort on outrunning *Audacious,* and Kent was just like him, already looking up at the sails and back at the xebec, gauging the distance, judging the exact moment for letting the helm fall off. *Audacious* hovered just within range, but in their position off their starboard quarter, the xebec's guns could not be brought to bear.

"Stay." The word was out of him before he understood his intent. "Put." He fished around in the back of his brain for an excuse. There had to be another assignment belowdecks, below the waterline, where she would be safe from all shot. But there was no time.

Because like a shark that could smell blood in the water, Captain McAlden struck. "Cast loose your guns, lads, and load with double shot." And in another half minute, as the guns were loaded and primed, he turned to the helm. "Fall off, Mr. Charlton. Lay me on her stern timbers. Mr. Kent, run up the colors."

Mr. Charlton needed no further instruction to understand his captain's intentions, and swung *Audacious*'s bowsprit smartly across the xebec's exposed stern. Col was instantly at his speaking trumpet, calling for the sails to be trimmed to maintain their speed as they lay onto the larboard tack. But the hours and hours of sail drill were standing him in good stead. His men hardly needed instruction to know what to do.

"Run out and fire as you bear."

The carronades on the forecastle were the first to let go their deadly volley. At such close range—and Col knew the gunners considered anything within three hundred yards as point-blank range—the first shot ripped through the xebec's exposed stern, wreaking havoc the length of her deck. The second smasher obliterated the stern gallery and carried away the taffrail.

The gun crews were on their mettle now. Gun captains touched their golden earrings to sharpen their sight and weigh the roll of the ship before angling the big irons just so, like duelists upon a green.

"Fire as you bear," came the captain's voice, unruffled and confident that his men could do exactly as he had bid them.

The gunner brought two guns at a time to bear, and let go a double-shotted volley careening down the length of the xebec's hull. The third volley worked against the after section of the Spaniard's quarterdeck, dismounting the guns on the starboard quarter, before *Audacious*'s remaining guns sent a crippling blast into the enemy's mizzen.

Just when the xebec's larboard battery might have been brought to bear as *Audacious* crept up her larboard quarter, Captain McAlden ordered the helm put over again.

"Come about," Col was calling at the top of his lungs. With the wind now on the quarter, it was an easy trick for the curtailed sail crew to swing the bow around and lay her large on the starboard tack, and repeat their deadly barrage with the larboard battery.

As the broadside paid off, and the captain was calling down to the waist, "Reload. Double shot," the xebec hauled close on her starboard tack to try and engage.

"Run me under her lee, Mr. Charlton."

"Elevate the guns!" Col barked. With the xebec beginning to heel over as the wind took the sails, her guns would be canted high above *Audacious*'s deck, while their own elevated guns would find their mark in the xebec's hull.

Mr. Charlton ran *Audacious*'s bowsprit straight into the xebec's forecourse.

"Fire!"

The gunners did their captain proud and produced a full broadside that pounded the Spaniard's hull, and shattered the mizzenmast. As the tangle of sails and spars fell to the xebec's lee rail, the captain was shouting, "Get a hook in her. Prepare to board."

The men assigned to boarding parties surged up from the gun crews and crowded the rail.

"She's striking!" Kent was behind the captain. "Sir, the enemy is striking!"

Col wanted to stifle her. He wanted to yell at her to shut up, to stop making herself known and open to the enemy's fire. Yes, they were striking, but they hadn't yet struck and there was still fire— "Hold your fire."

"Lay me alongside her, Mr. Charlton. Get a line into her."

"Boarders, away. Mr. Rudge, take possession of that ship before she sinks, and get off her what you can. Mr. Lawrence," Captain McAlden called to the nearest lieutenant, "assist him. Take a party with the carpenter. Mr. Sanders, see what you can do to keep her afloat. Get across and go below to the cabin, Mr. Kent. Look sharp. Keep them from destroying anything if you can." Captain McAlden handed her his own pistol and shoved her in the direction of the rail.

And Col could do nothing but watch her go.

Chapter Twelve

Sally ratcheted back the hammer of the pistol in her right hand and clambered across the rail in Mr. Rudge's wake, shouting, *"Detener!"* and hoping to God she was using the correct Spanish word for "halt." But the command wasn't much needed, as the portion of the enemy crew that remained uninjured had already abandoned their guns and their stations.

The men from *Audacious* were disarming and crowding the Spaniards forward, but Sally and Rudge turned aft toward the companionway ladder. They burst below into the shattered stern where the captain's cabin would have been, to find the man attempting to light some papers heaped on the deck on fire.

"Avast!" Mr. Rudge cried, and forced the man back at the point of his sword.

Sally sprang forward and grabbed up the candle with her free hand, and attempted to stamp out the licking flames. Pieces of burnt paper floated up and she felt the sharp sting of an ember spending itself against her calf.

"Mr. Kent, take that man's sword."

Sally was unsure of the exact protocol of relieving an officer of his command, and her Spanish was desperately rusty, and she was out of breath. She meant to say "On behalf of Captain Sir Hugh McAlden of His Majesty's Royal Britannic Majesty, I compel your surrender." What she actually said was, *"Para Capitano Don Hugh McAlden yo obligo—* Oh, bother."

She could get the point across even if she could not remember the word for surrender. She brought her arm up and pointed the gun at him point-blank.

The captain arched his haughty eyebrow and looked down his considerable nose at her. *"Para esto me mandan una niña?"*

She shot a glance at Lieutenant Rudge, who asked, "What does he say?"

For this they send a little girl? There was no way she could repeat that to Mr. Rudge. Instead, Sally narrowed her eyes as she looked back at the Spaniard, and simply cocked back the hammer.

The don, thus compelled to promptitude, drew his sword out of the scabbard, and said with ponderous, heavily accented English, "Don Almonso de Talma de Gomez y Viavincencio, of His Most Catholic Majesty's Navy. Whom do I have the minimal pleasure of addressing?"

Mr. Rudge was a gentleman, and ignored the don's subtle slur. "Lieutenant Frederick Rudge, of His Majesty King George's Royal Navy, your excellency." Rudge sheathed his sword and bowed with exquisite politeness. "At your service."

Thus restored to his dignity, the don capitulated with greater grace. "My sword and my command are now yours."

"I accept on behalf of Captain McAlden, and I invite you to join him aboard *Audacious* directly. I am honored to escort you." Lieutenant Rudge swept his arm toward the companionway, even as he nodded to Sally and said quietly, "Keep your sidearm drawn and see what you can do with these papers."

It was no great feat to gather up the charred remains of the Spaniard's orders, and fold them into her waistcoat, before she returned to the deck. With the assistance of a few Spaniards compelled by the guard of the marines, *Audacious*'s people were already hard at work chopping away the fouled rigging of the xebec's fallen mizzen, and clearing away debris.

"Mr. Kent, if you would be so kind." Captain McAlden called her to *Audacious*'s quarterdeck, where he and the don awaited her with cold civility.

"I understand you have Spanish as well as French in your head, Mr. Kent. Such unplumbed depths. If you would do the honors? This fellow seems to think they're necessary."

Sally chanced another glance at the Spaniard who was regarding her with barely veiled impatience, his eyebrow an arabesque of cynical amusement. Devil take the man. He had more than enough English to repeat his earlier observation regarding her sex. But Captain McAlden was beginning to regard her with impatience as well. There was nothing for it but to do it quickly.

"Captain McAlden, I make you known to Don Almonso de Talma de Gomez, of His Catholic Majesty's frigate *Cielo*." Her part done, Sally immediately backed away, to hide herself in the welter of men putting the ship to rights.

"Sir." McAlden inclined his head.

"Capitano Meek-aldain, my sword. I surrender to you *El Cielo*." The don made a no doubt very correct but highly theatrical bow as he handed over his elaborately figured Toledo steel sword.

But Captain McAlden, thank the Lord, wasn't one for pomp. He was all for the prize and was already handing Rudge the sword and then moved to the rail. "Accompany the don to my cabin, Mr. Rudge," he said as he went, "and see to it Edwards makes him comfortable with whatever quantities of sherry are felt necessary, but put a marine on him. Is she serviceable, Mr. Charlton?" the captain asked as the sailing master approached to report on his inspection of the prize.

"Eminently, sir."

"Excellent. Mr. Colyear, put a prize crew on her."

"It'll have to be mostly topmen, sir, with those lateen sails," Mr. Colyear observed. He was always thinking ahead, always two steps before anyone else. "There are over two hundred prisoners, sir, even after the dead. It will take at least twenty of *Audacious*'s men, and a few marines."

"Very good. And to command her?"

"Take Mr. Kent, sir."

Sally froze at the mention of her name, but inside, her startled heart was all but vibrating within her chest. She moved cautiously aft toward the taffrail, feigning nonchalance, until she was close enough to hear the rest of the conversation. With so much activity around her, she was left alone to her eavesdropping.

"Mr. Kent?" the captain repeated, his voice heavy with question.

"He knows these waters between the Lizard and the coast of Brittany like the back of his hand. He's sailed the Channel islands single-handedly on his family's small ketch. He could sail into any English port blindfolded."

She had no time to dwell on the high compliment Mr. Colyear paid her, even as he stabbed her in the back.

"A xebec-rigged frigate of war is not a small ketch." Captain McAlden's tone was matter-of-fact. "Nor is it a midshipman's command, sir. And Mr. Kent is, at present, too useful to me. I collect it was he who spotted the oranges this forenoon? Yes, so I surmised by your sending him to me."

Sally could hear the exasperation in Col's voice. "Did he not tell you that himself, sir?"

"No, Mr. Colyear, he did not. He gave all credit to you."

"I beg your pardon, sir. I had no idea that he would do so. Indeed, I sent him to you on purpose—"

"No apologies, Mr. Colyear. I see it all clearly now." There was a pause before Captain McAlden continued. "But as to the prize, I think it best for Mr. Rudge. He will benefit most from a temporary command. See it done, Mr. Colyear."

Sally listened without hearing as Col called out the rest of his commands, and willed her feet to move. She felt numb, both from relief at having been spared command of the prize, and poleaxed by Col's willingness, even desire, to be rid of her. She had thought they had reached an agreement of sorts, a cordiality. And she had certainly proved her usefulness to him today. What more could he want?

And why did it hurt so much? Why did her throat feel tight with heat?

The answer was hers for the asking when Mr. Colyear found her, after the prize was on its way to the Admiralty, and order had for the most part been restored to *Audacious*. She was at her work with the foretopmen taking down the chains and netting.

He was just there, suddenly, silent and powerful, coming upon her before she knew it. "Two things, Kent."

Sally noticed that he did not ask her to walk away with him, where their conversation might be private, but instead stood firm on the foredeck, where their talk was eminently public. Even so, she was ready with all the arguments she had silently marshaled at the tip of her tongue, but he looked tired, as if the battle had taken every bit of fight out of him. "Are you all right, Mr. Colyear?"

Her question seemed to astonish him. His head tipped slowly back, away from her, as if she had shocked him. As if she had said something damaging and incendiary, instead of inquiring after his health. "You just seem a bit strained."

"I am strained, Kent. It's a first lieutenant's *job* to be strained."

"I'm sorry, sir. I thought you would be having a celebratory bumper of wine with the captain, or the gunroom."

He smiled at that, and said obliquely, "I must teach you to drink brandy, Kent."

"Brandy, sir? Mr. Colyear, sir, are you quite all to rights?"

"No, Kent, I am not. But that is beside the point, which is—I sent you to the captain this forenoon for a reason, Kent."

"Yes, sir. I made my report."

"You did. But imagine my chagrin, Kent, when I found I was to take the lion's share of the captain's admiration for the deed."

"I only saw the orange peels, sir," she hedged. "You were the one to observe what it might mean."

"Don't try my patience or my credulity, Kent. You're as

sharp as a boarding pike and twice as clever. And it is *your* position in this ship that needs to be justified, not mine."

Devil take her. She hadn't thought of that. Only of impressing Mr. Colyear. "My apologies, sir."

"Accepted. Next time, tell the truth about your accomplishment. Saves me the damned trouble of having to set the record straight later."

He was so close, she felt his voice rumble through her chest. Which reminded her that he was *too* close, both for comfort and for appearance's sake. She stepped back. "Was there something else, sir?"

"Aye—three things, actually. Secondly, good work today. Very good."

"Thank you, sir. But if I did do good work, why did you ask to have me put on the prize crew?"

The look he gave her in answer was as hard as flint, and his straight, dark brows rose to show her he thought the answer ought to be obvious. "I thought you should be given a chance to make your way back to Portsmouth, *Mister* Kent. Whereupon you might be able to solve your family dilemma, without anyone else being left the responsibility of it."

She didn't want to admit to his logic. It hurt too much to be logical. "But I'm doing my work, aren't I? I kept myself from a confrontation with Mr. Gamage. I used my head." She didn't like the little flute of desperation playing in her voice. She sounded like a needy child, not a naval officer.

Now he did walk away, leading her along the larboard gangway, where there was less chance of them being overheard.

"Your abilities have never been in question, Kent. You know you do very well. But that is not the point."

She clung to *her* point. "If doing the job well, to the best of one's abilities, and for the good of the king, the country, and the navy, isn't the point, then what is?"

"God Almighty, Kent. You're so bloody vehement. So damned sure. But the only thing I'm sure of is that whatever the point, Kent, it is not mine to make. Nor yours. We serve others. And we serve the rules that govern our behavior. I don't make them, and I don't always have to like them, but by God, I have to obey them. And so do you."

She knew he was right. In principle, she agreed with him. But why should she not be allowed to obey the *same* rules as he? Why was she supposed to have an entirely different set of rules of what was permissible for her conduct? Why should she be able, but not able to serve? And why, oh why, did her throat feel so hot and tight? She ought to be feeling triumph. Instead she felt herself on the verge of tears. "It's just not fair."

"No, Kent. It's not fair. It's not fair at all. But sometimes fair isn't better." He drew himself up and took a straightening pull at his coat. "Which brings me to third thing. Go put on clean linen and wash your face." He nodded his head aft. "Your captain awaits you."

"You've told him, haven't you? That's why you look so depleted."

The hurt, the desperate need in her voice, was like a slick knife in his gut. He wanted to reassure her. He wanted to be able to give her what she wanted and grant her every wish. He wanted, damn his eyes, to touch her and pull her to his chest, and whisper that it would be all right.

But it wasn't going to be all right. And he couldn't make it so.

Because she didn't trust him to.

"Do have a little faith, Kent." And with that he left her, because he couldn't think of everything else he wanted to say.

Col retired momentarily to the blessed sanctuary of his cuddy in the gunroom to wash and change his own linen. But even the gunroom might no longer be a sanctuary, if Captain McAlden's mooted plan to promote Kent to acting lieutenant came to fruition.

Damn his eyes. If he had her to hand, somewhere nearby, within his sphere . . . There were intimacies involved in living with a group of other people day in and day out. There were practicalities to be considered.

There was his sanity to be maintained.

He could see why she might be promoted ahead of boys like Worth and Jellicoe, and even midshipmen with slightly more experience like Dance and Beecham, who were good, but had neither her apparent facility for mathematics, nor her acute eye for telling details. Dance and Beecham reacted, and followed orders. Sally Kent acted, and thought of the orders before they were given.

But God help those boys when Gamage heard of it. To be passed over by Lieutenant Lawrence, who had been in *Audacious* six years almost to the day when he passed for lieutenant, was bad enough, but to be passed over by Kent, who had been with them scant days—hardly a week. It was not to be borne by one such as Gamage.

"Mr. Colyear." The sailing master came out of his private cabin and eased his sinewy frame into a chair in the common area.

Col wasn't in the mood for conversation, so he discouraged it the best way he knew, through politeness and drink. "Brandy?"

"Much obliged. Ah, thank you." Charlton took a deep draught.

"Good day of work," Col offered. The best way to keep himself from having to talk was to encourage others to do so.

"Excellent day of work," Charlton agreed. "And I understand we have the sharp-eyed little Mr. Kent to thank for the prize?"

Col nodded and kept himself quietly occupied with tying a clean stock around his neck.

"He's a Kent, through and through. Though I can see how it wouldn't please you."

That got Col's attention. "Your pardon?"

"Hero worship. Can see it in the way he looks at you. Follows your every move, emulating the way you stand and walk. I've seen it time and time again. It's a natural enough thing, so long as it doesn't get unhealthy. And as long as you don't exploit it."

"Exploit it? In what way?"

"Making him into your creature. Making either a toadie

or a pet of the boy. He's anxious enough to please, and more than capable of doing so. It's a tempting combination."

Unease didn't even begin to describe the sensation crawling under Col's skin. But Mr. Charlton, damn his sharp old eyes, had a point. And Col knew he needed to heed it. "I suppose he is. He reminds me of his brother. Both of his brothers actually—they were both my shipmates. And probably the father as well, though I've never served with him and cannot say."

"Ah. Nor I." Mr. Charlton accepted the explanation. "But it stands to reason."

Charlton sipped his brandy in undisturbed silence for a long time before Col was tempted to break it. He had always appreciated Mr. Charlton's frank opinion. "I understand the captain is thinking of promoting Kent to acting lieutenant in Rudge's absence."

"Makes sense," the sailing master conceded. "He is the most capable midshipman, and the promotion would be a suitable reward for exceptional work. But it will cause collateral damage."

"You refer to Mr. Gamage?"

"I do."

Col was unsure if it was a relief or an added responsibility, to know others worried about the unhealthy amount of antagonism already existing between Kent and Gamage. But no one else knew what was at stake. If their fighting escalated into open conflict, she might be discovered. Or worse. Gamage could be violent and vindictive if not properly managed. "What can be done?"

"Same as we, and you, I note, are doing now. Staying vigilant. Keeping the midshipmen all occupied with work. Keeping them standing opposite watches."

"All of which serve to fuel Gamage's frustration."

"Bound to happen. The man won't cease being frustrated until the moment when he is put to bed with a cannonball. And even then, he will die blaming someone else. Poor bastard."

"That was Kent's summation." At Charlton's look of inquiry, Col elaborated. "Not that he was a bastard—though he is. But that he felt sorry for Gamage. After all Gamage has done to them." Col shook his head. "Hard to fathom."

Charlton took another deep, meditative drink of his brandy. "Older than his years, that boy. Sharper than his years as well. Ah, well. Not to worry. Captain McAlden knows what he's doing. See if he doesn't."

Col could only pray that Mr. Charlton was right. Because Col had no idea of what he was doing, or what he was going to do. And he had no idea on God's green ocean of how he was going to be able to actually live with her, and still conduct himself like both a king's officer and a bloody gentleman.

Sally hardly knew what to think. She climbed to the deck slowly, as if the cannonballs that were being sewn into the shrouds for the dead Spaniards, to weigh them down to the bottom of the sea, were dragging at her feet instead. She understood Col's weariness now. The dread of the coming interview with the captain made her feel tired and old, as if she carried a rock inside her. Each appointment seemed to get harder instead of easier. But it could not be put off any longer.

The carpenter's mate had just finished replacing the door when she arrived.

"Ah, Mr. Kent. We're all here? Good." The captain greeted her cordially. "Do come in."

The captain's day cabin had already been restored to some semblance of order. The walls had been returned, although not all of the furniture had yet made it back aboard. So the group of men who filled the room, commissioned and warranted officers alike, all stood before the stern gallery. Sally was surprised to see that along with the captain were Mr. Charlton and Col, the commander of the marines, Major Lesley, Mr. Stephens, the surgeon, and the third lieutenant, Mr. Horner, as well as the bo'sun and gunner, Mr. Robinson and Mr. Davies.

"Edwards"—the captain was speaking to his steward—"be so kind as to get Mr. Kent a sherry."

"Come, Captain, I insist. A claret at least," Mr. Charlton chided amiably. "What would Dr. Johnson say?"

At the captain's frown, Mr. Colyear quietly supplied the answer. " 'Claret is the liquor for boys; port for men; but he who aspires to be a hero' "—he paused and shot her a glance—" 'must drink brandy.' "

But the captain was having none of it. "Sherry," he insisted. "He's too young for port, or brandy. It would give him the gout."

Edwards hastened to obey.

"Gentlemen," the captain said to the assembly once she had the proffered sherry. "A toast. To our sharp-eyed young midshipman."

They turned. To her. They held up their glasses in her direction, their faces full of pleased expectation. For half a moment she did not know what to say. Her feelings were all tangled up inside her like a knot—hope and elation and dread all mixed up together. But the elation began to win out. They were still looking at her in expectation, so she raised her glass with theirs. "To *Valencia* oranges."

A chorus of assent embraced her. "Here, here."

The captain raised his glass again. "And to our Mr. Colyear. Superior sailing, sir. I don't think old *Audacious* has ever flown as fast as she did today. And Mr. Charlton, by God, sir, I think the don thought you meant to park her on his deck. Well done, sir."

And on he went, happily giving credit where credit was due. "Mr. Davies and Mr. Robinson. Superior gunnery, gentlemen, superior. I hope the Plymouth dockyard can do something with the wreck that you made of the xebec's sterncastle. The gun crews were magnificent."

With that he held up one final toast. "To the men."

"The men," they all repeated solemnly.

It was a perfect moment. If she had conjured such a moment out of her dreams it could not have been any more sublime. She hummed with happiness, like a drowsy, contented bumblebee, drunk on the nectar of her accomplishment.

This is why she had done it. For this feeling of accomplishment and belonging. This feeling of useful fulfillment.

The only thing that could have possibly made the moment better was if her family, her father and brothers, had been there to see her triumph. To share her victory. Yet she could look forward to celebrating with her friends, her new family, her brothers in the orlop cockpit. They would have their own celebration—though perhaps with less juggling.

The mellow contentment spread, leaving her in a satisfied haze. So satisfied and hazy, she had to be recalled to attention.

"Mr. Kent." Mr. Charlton nodded significantly at the captain.

"Yes, sir?"

"Have you ever visited the gunroom, Mr. Kent?" the captain asked.

"Yes, sir. To pass messages for the officers."

They were all looking at her and smiling. All but Mr. Colyear, who looked solemn and grave.

"And how should you like to mess there? I've decided to promote you to acting lieutenant in Mr. Rudge's place." Captain McAlden gave her the news with the same amiable indifference with which he had accepted the Spanish don's sword, pleased, but ready to move on.

But she wanted the moment never to end. It was all she could do to keep from dancing a little hornpipe of happiness right there in Captain McAlden's cabin. She wanted to run down to the gunroom and dance another hornpipe there. She wanted to rush about and shake everyone's hand. She wanted to share her happiness. She wanted to kiss their cheeks, every last one of them. She wanted to throw her arms around Mr. Colyear and—

Oh, Lord. Oh, Lord, oh, Lord, oh, Lord.

She would be living in the gunroom. With him.

Chapter Thirteen

The devil and every last one of his flaming imps take her. The lovely hazy euphoria was certainly checked now.

She couldn't possibly put herself any closer to Mr. Colyear and preserve both her sanity and her secret. But there could be no question of turning the captain down. One didn't refuse a promotion. It simply wasn't done.

The officers were all still looking at her, expecting her to speak.

"I am honored, sir," she managed.

"You've earned it. Acting fourth lieutenant, mind you. And Mr. Horner is promoted to second, and Mr. Lawrence—I hope you will share a bumper with him in the gunroom, since he is still on deck—will be full third. A good day, gentlemen. A good, profitable day."

And so it was done. The party in the captain's cabin broke up. The officers went about their business, and Sally made the trip back to the orlop filled with a different portion of dread making a tangle of her innards. She was glad of the promotion, of course, and the acclaim—who would not be happy to be singled out for such praise? But she would have to take leave of the orlop cockpit—though it was the land of boyish belches and wind—for the more refined air of the gunroom. The thought of the privacy a gunroom cuddy would afford her was a luxury beyond imagining, yet there were her friends, her brother midshipmen, to be considered. How could she leave them just when they had started to achieve their goal? How was she to manage Gamage at such a distance? She hated to lose her friends' company—even the bad juggling.

And how was she to tell them?

But it was a devilish small world, the navy. They already knew.

"Richard." Will Jellicoe greeted her at the cockpit with a hearty handshake. "We've heard your very good news. Congratulations!"

And so were they all anxious to shake her hand and offer their congratulations, even Dance, who actually smiled and said, "Well done, Richard. And well deserved."

Beecham was his usual brash self. "Good piece of luck that."

"A great piece of luck," she agreed. "I wish that we had all been on watch together and so could share in the honor."

"You were on watch with Mr. Gamage, but I didn't notice the captain sharing the honors of finding the xebec with him," Beecham observed.

"No." Though she had tried, she really had, to share the credit with Gamage. If only he hadn't been too stubborn and too stupid to see the opportunity laid out before him. Devil take him. Still she tried to put the best face on it. "I am happy that my removal will give you more room, but I only wish that it was Mr. Gamage who was moving out."

"No chance of that."

Sally turned, as did they all, at the grating sound of Gamage's surly voice. He had scurried in from God only knew what bolt-hole, and was eyeing them all with his jealous distemper.

"Then it's true?" Gamage asked. "The captain's little boot licker has finally achieved his ends?"

"Hardly, Mr. Gamage," she replied, not bothering to rise from where she was seated upon her sea trunk. To do so would only give him greater reason for his aggression. Instead, she dangled her hands over the tops of her knees to show him she was relaxed and calm. To show herself she was relaxed and calm. She could handle him. "My ends would be to see you seized up to a grating for theft, but failing that, to put a stop to your campaign of terror on this berth."

Gamage answered her by tucking his chin and giving her one of his low, nasty, weasel smiles, as he slid his gaze purposefully to Ian Worth. "No chance of that happening with you gone on toward better things, now is there?"

No one believed Gamage would ever move on to better things, least of all him. That was probably why he was so vicious—he was like a caged dog that had given up all hope of getting free but could not stop himself from biting the hand that could open his door. Poor man. If she could set him free, she would, instead of fighting him, of poking him in his cage. She had to at least try.

But no matter what, she wouldn't allow him to single out poor Ian.

"Gentlemen, will you excuse us, for a moment. Mr. Gamage and I have something to discuss."

Gamage looked both deeply amused and curiously wary of Sally's request. His white rat's forehead creased with consternation. On the other side of the berth, Jellicoe and Worth looked adamantly opposed. Beecham opened his mouth, as if to ask if she had lost her mind, while Dance crossed his arms over his chest. Will and Ian looked scared but determined, but they were all, to a man, frowning their faces up tighter than monkey paw knots.

"Richard, I don't think—"

"It's quite all right, Will. Mr. Gamage and I are long overdue for this conversation, and I think it best if it were done in private. So if you would do me the honor of a moment alone with Mr. Gamage?" She indicated the door.

They went. Hemming and hawing and shooting her dark, anxious glances as they shuffled through the door, but they went. Probably only to the other side, where they would listen with their ears pressed to the portal. The thought made her smile.

And she used that smile to face her nemesis. "All right,

Gamage. Now we can talk. No audience, no observers, no interruptions. So we can talk—"

"Fuck talk. All you need to know is you'll pay for making me look the fool today, Kent. You'll pay dearly." Menace dripped off him like cold rainwater. "No one crosses me and gets away with it."

She would not be cowed. And she would not give in to easy hatred.

"You crossed yourself today, Gamage. All you had to do was listen to me and you would have been the smart one. You could have been the one to make the report to Mr. Colyear. You *should* have—I all but begged you to. But you were too busy trying to make my life miserable to improve your own."

Gamage still wasn't listening. He reached out, and quick as a hungry stoat, he had her face pinched hard between the long fingers of his hand. "It will give me great pleasure to hurt you."

"I have no doubt of that." He was already hurting her. Sally tried to answer calmly, though her mouth was all squashed up and the indignation of helplessness made a mash of her insides. She tried to wrest herself from his grip, but Gamage was strong and held fast. He was bigger and stronger, and she had foolishly thought she could handle him. Yet she couldn't just lash back by kneeing him viciously in the cods. She had to think. And get Gamage to think as well. "If you would but think for a moment, Gamage, you could see that I was trying to help you."

"Don't make me laugh, Kent-lick. Why would you want to help me?"

"Because the only way I'm ever going to get rid of you is to kill you, or to pass you for lieutenant."

"You did try to kill me. I know—"

"No, goddamn it, Gamage. Think!" She finally twisted her face out of his grip but made herself stay close. Made herself look him in the eye. "I'm a bloody Kent, Gamage. If I had wanted you killed, you would have been gutted and dumped overboard like a fish carcass and no one would have so much as blinked an eye. I have friends. Real friends.

While you've gone out of your way to make enemies out of nearly everyone. Fear won't watch your back or cover your mistakes—friends will. And you have none. I don't like you and neither does anyone else. You're a mean bastard and you're lucky you were only doused with pepper powder and not an emetic. Or worse."

"So you admit it. I will see *you* seized up to a grating for that."

"Think, Gamage." She was letting her satisfaction at goading him push her off course. She made herself speak like Mr. Colyear, slowly and evenly, so he would get the point. "I don't want you dead. I want to get you what you want."

"And what is it you think I want?" Gamage's face was twisted up with bitter scorn.

"The same thing I want."

Gamage's eyes got strangely wide and almost liquid. As he searched her face he looked . . . frightened. And vulnerable.

"Mr. Kent." Lieutenant Colyear appeared in the doorway, like a beacon from the gloom of the empty companionway. "Is there a problem here?"

"There's your boyfriend now, come to save you," Gamage muttered for her ears alone.

But with his face inches from her own, Sally could see the flicker of fear press white marks into the corner of Gamage's mouth. It gave her strength. "No, Mr. Colyear," she said succinctly. "There is no problem." Sally made her voice confident and answered without letting her own gaze move an inch from Gamage's. "We were just discussing my helping Mr. Gamage with his course of study for his lieutenant's exam."

Over Gamage's shoulder Mr. Colyear's eyebrows rose as slowly as his unperturbable drawl. "Really?"

But Mr. Colyear's astonishment, and his wariness, were nothing compared to Gamage's. The older midshipman drew away from her sharply, as if her very touch might now be poison. "What are you about?"

"I've helped pass four older brothers, Mr. Gamage. I know my way around both the mathematics and the sailing questions you are likely to get. Mr. Colyear can attest to my brothers all having passed."

"That I can." Mr. Colyear looked at her for a very long time in that minutely considering way of his, before he smiled. That same small, one-sided, begrudging smile. "As you don't require any further assistance, Mr. Kent, you will excuse me." Mr. Colyear nodded his head to her, and moved back into the gloom beyond the cockpit door.

Once the first lieutenant was out of sight, and more importantly out of earshot, Gamage came back at her hard, snatching up her coat by the lapels. "If you're thinking to make a fool of me, I'll have your guts—"

Sally fought the urge to tug at the fist gripping her collar. "No joke, Gamage. It's the one thing you want, but you haven't got, isn't it? And I can help you get it."

The slow gears of Gamage's brain ground together to try and figure out what was to his best advantage.

She pressed her advantage. "I can help you, Gamage. I can help you pass. I give you my solemn promise, and I never break my word."

"You'll make me pass for lieutenant or you'll be sorry." His voice was still belligerent and he rattled at her collar for good measure, to show her, or more likely himself, that he was still in charge.

"No." Sally wouldn't blink. She would not give up any of the advantage she had so painstakingly gained. "Kindly leave off your attempts at shredding my uniform. Thank you." But instead of falling back, as he expected, she took a step closer to him, forcing *him* to take a surprised step back. "I'll help you pass for lieutenant—I'll help you study and prepare— only if you behave. Only if you leave off badgering and intimidating the midshipmen. And if you so much as make Ian Worth whimper in his sleep, I'll make it my life's work to see that you *never* get put up for that exam. But as you so cogently observed, I do have a great whopping number of family in the navy. And they do have a great deal of influence. And the three that are already post captains have a great many places for lieutenants. Think about that for a moment."

She let that sink into his thick mind for a long moment while he struggled to weigh his interests against each other.

"If you're at leisure right now, we can start. A Board of Examination can convene in any convenient port, or wherever three post captains can be gathered. It could be at anchor off Brest as easily as Portsmouth, so you need to be prepared as soon as possible. Have you your books? I'll need to take a look at your journals, to see what areas of weakness you may need to work on."

"No." Gamage was walking away from her, turning his back. Hiding. "I haven't bothered to keep a logbook in years."

"Why not?" Even as she asked, the answer whispered at the back of her mind. Matthew had been much the same as a boy. Though she had been younger, she remembered her brother's struggles to read, though he had been, and remained, as clever as they came in other ways—in the actual doing of things. Perhaps Gamage was the same.

Gamage tried to hide behind callous indifference. "Why should I?"

"Because you will be required to produce a book as documentation at your exam. Along with a recommendation from your captain. All right, I can help you with the journal as well. I've a few tricks to make it easier that I learned from my brother Matthew. He wasn't one much for writing and ciphering, either, but he's done very well for himself, so you can, too."

"I haven't said yes." Gamage clearly didn't like this feeling that he wasn't in control.

She wouldn't let him back out. "Then say yes, and get it over with, for God's sake, if not your own. This is your chance, Gamage. I'll not offer again, and the alternative is too depressing to contemplate." Sally went to her own sea chest to rummage around until she found what she was looking for.

"Here, you'd best work from my books instead of your own. I've made copious notes in the margins from my brothers' experiences, especially Matthew's. You can see here, no, here." She turned to an illustrative page, where the margins were filled with her notations. "Some of the questions they were asked at the examination, as well as my own observations when I sailed with my father when I was younger."

When Gamage swiped the book out of her hand, she knew she had him. Even with his attempt to appear casually indifferent as he flipped through the pages, she could see his frightened, almost desperate interest.

"Who the devil is Sarah Kent?"

Oh, the devil surely had already taken her. She had forgotten that it was her own copy of *The Elements of Navigation*—inscribed in her round, childish hand with her proper name, Sarah Alice Kent—that she had packed for Richard in the hopes that it would give him some assistance.

"My mother." She had no idea why on earth that particular lie popped out of her mouth. But there it was. Perhaps, contrary to Mr. Colyear's opinion, she was getting better at lying, at last. "She sailed a great deal with my father when they were first married. Before we were born. She passed it to each one of us in turn."

Sally looked down at her feet in case the lie showed in her face. Gamage was stupid in a great many ways, but he was a cunning fellow and might find her out yet. But instead of giving him any chance to remount his metaphoric guns, she would keep him on the defensive. "Make up your mind, Gamage. That's my offer. Take it or leave it. I won't offer again."

It was terrible, watching him try to decide. Excruciatingly slow. But finally, Damien Gamage held out his hand. "I'll do it. You'll do it. You'll pass me for lieutenant."

She accepted the hand he offered. "So help me, I will."

Or, she suspected, die trying.

Kent blew into the gunroom like a breeze on a bright summer day. The girl—how could anyone who had eyes not see her for a girl, though the bruise on her cheekbone lent her a disreputable, boyish cast—was toting her own sea chest, with ancient Angus Pinkerton, looking as mournful as an old hound, carrying the other end.

She certainly didn't look any worse for wear from her latest set-to with Gamage. She looked to be the same bright, cheerful, neck-or-nothing tumultuous girl she had been before Will Jellicoe and Ian Worth had barged into the gunroom begging for his assistance to keep Gamage from killing her. But she hadn't been killed. Far from it. When Col had arrived to rescue her, she was handling Gamage with a remarkably brilliant solution. Brilliant, but untenable, in Col's opinion, for Gamage was too thick a plank for even her to help.

But that was her way. And her charm. She would rely on her unshakable belief in her abilities, until Gamage came to believe them as well. And then, once he started to believe in her, the possibilities were endless. She was nothing if not entirely full of the power of possibilities.

And she was delectable because of it. Her rosy, gamin face was glowing with satisfaction, exertion, and enthusiasm. He wanted to—

No. Col shut his eyes and turned away. That way lay madness. And the loss of his career. And the loss of his friends. He busied himself for a moment in taking off his coat and settling it carefully over the back of the chair before he let himself take another look.

"You'll be in Mr. Rudge's old cuddy, young Kent," Pinkerton was saying.

"Oughtn't I to get the last room?" She pointed to the cuddy nearest the gunroom's door. "Oughtn't Mr. Horner move up to Mr. Rudge's room?"

If only life followed all the rules. All the rules that kept one safe and secure and from going out of one's mind with undisciplined want.

"No," Lieutenant Horner himself answered. "I asked the captain if I could stay put. All the cuddys are the same size—there are no guns—but I just didn't want to shift my dunnage. And when Mr. Rudge comes back, he'll want his old room back. I hope you don't mind."

Kent had accepted the change without any further comment, though she did venture to dart a quick questioning look Col's way. "That seems eminently logical. Mr. Rudge's room it is."

Col was the only one who minded. The rest of them were impervious to his dilemma. Just as they remained impervious to Kent's identity.

But Col was as impervious as a leaky boat. Now that he knew she would be quartered not less than two feet from his door, something more unruly than alarm hit him deep in his gut every time he looked at her. Everything about her screamed out, *Girl, girl, girl.*

How could they not see it? Even now, as she manhandled her sea trunk into the cuddy, a lock of hair escaped from her short queue and fell across her cheek. That hair, the blazing ginger of the Kents. They all had it—from Captain Alexander Kent down to the boy Richard—that distinctive hair.

She wore it as her brothers had, in an old-fashioned queue, clubbed back with a black ribbon. Col wore his own hair much the same way. They were sailors and were immune to the tyranny of fashion.

But he remembered Sally before, from that summer, when her hair had been long and flowing. She had been too young to put it up, and he recalled a moment of strange, desperate need, when he had surreptitiously touched the long fall of her hair to see if it felt as silky as it had looked. A strange wordless compulsion. He could still recall the slide of the thick, almost lively hair, as it had fallen through his fingers.

Col gripped the back of his chair to stifle the urge to do the same, to test if it still felt like liquid silk. While the other denizens of the gunroom crowded around to welcome Mr. Kent, Col held himself rigidly away, knowing if he did not curb his instincts each and every living and breathing second, he would inadvertently try to touch her.

"The men will be happy tonight with the thought of fresh prize money," Mr. Charlton was saying. "I'll wager they've already taken the measure of that xebec like Admiralty clerks, figuring their shares out to the shilling."

Lieutenant Horner was drawn back into the conversation. "How much do you think it will be, Mr. Charlton?"

"I am not an Admiralty clerk, but I should guess . . ."

The conversation went on around him, but Col did not attend. Every nerve, every sense, every thought was turned to her. Waiting for her.

Even though he did not look, but kept his eyes assiduously turned away from her cuddy, he felt her arrival at the table when she came out at last to take her leisure with the rest of them. The others seated at the long table built into the base of the mizzenmast included the surgeon, Mr. Stephens, and Lieutenant Horner, as well as Mr. Charlton. When Charlton offered Kent a drink, Col found he could no longer keep his shrieking curiosity silent.

"So, Mr. Kent, pray tell us how you fared with Mr. Gamage?"

His fellow officers seemed not to mind his change of conversational direction, for they were all as curious about the confrontation as he was. As Col had so often observed, there were few secrets on a frigate, and far fewer when the midshipmen of the orlop had so publicly and so loudly burst in upon the gunroom to plead for the first lieutenant's assistance.

Her lovely, freckled face flushed a darker shade of coral. "Very well, actually. I'm optimistic."

"About Mr. Midshipman Gamage? You're joking," the surgeon scoffed.

Her confidence remained undaunted. "I am not."

Mr. Charlton spoke. "Forgive us for intruding, Mr. Kent, but that last time you and Mr. Gamange had a 'conversation,' it ended with you being mastheaded for a great many hours."

That made her smile, and Col was almost blinded by the brilliance of her mirth. "I have reason to expect a better outcome this time. I thank you for your concern, but it has all turned out for the best."

"I'll want more explanation, Kent." Col stated it matter-of-factly. Given their history, hers and Gamage's, Col prayed the other officers wouldn't make any more out of it than that.

Jack Horner said flatly, "Only way it would be for the best was if you dumped him over the side."

"No." Her grin got even wider, if such a thing were possible. And she laughed. A full-throated peal of laughter that hit him straight in his gut. How could anyone look at her gamin face and not see her for the delightful girl she was?

"I will say, I'm rather proud of myself. But Mr. Colyear must get the credit, as he told me I'd never get anywhere going up against Gamage the way I was doing. That I needed to learn to read him. And so I have. I have offered to tutor him in his studies so he can pass his exam for lieutenant."

"Impossible." Mr. Charlton was full of not a little professional skepticism. "Mr. Gamage has no mathematical abilities whatsoever."

"That will make it more difficult . . ."

But not impossible. Col could hear the thought even if she had not spoken it out loud. She was nothing if not an eternal optimist. No, it was not just optimism. It was unshakable confidence. She believed she could get Gamage to pass. And if she believed it, she would try, through sheer force of personality and determination, to make Gamage believe it. "How do you plan to accomplish what others could not?"

"I'm not sure," she said candidly. "I fear Mr. Gamage may have some . . . deficiency in his learning." She shook her head. "I don't want to say any more, but suffice it to say, I have some idea of how to help him and will do everything in my power to prepare him for the exam. But even if he only gains the satisfaction of conquering some maths, enough to figure longitude and latitude, then *Audacious* will be a much happier, well-run ship."

"Careful, Kent," Col warned casually. "You'll find yourself mastheaded again for such offhand insults." He only half meant his warning as a joke, but she had to understand the order of things.

She didn't. Or if she did, she ignored it. "The insult, Mr. Colyear, would be in not acknowledging that things need to change."

Her vehemence no longer astounded him. But it did begin to wound him. Because his own passion seemed tepid in comparison. It seemed ambitious instead of loyal, and calculated instead of devoted.

Yet, however vehement, or well meant, her lack of tact

was going to get her in trouble. Although *more* trouble was a more accurate description.

The other officers, especially Mr. Charlton, who did not care for such careless, impetuous talk, and Mr. Horner, who had only a few hours of sleep before he was to go on watch through the dog watches, sought their berths. One by one, the screen doors to the gunroom cuddies shut. One by one, the other inhabitants disappeared, until he and Sally Kent were finally entirely and completely alone.

Chapter Fourteen

"Well, Kent."

"Well, Mr. Colyear." She looked wary and careful, keeping the breadth of the table between them, yet all her chariness couldn't obliterate the lovely, warm flush of her skin. The days in the sun and wind and weather had put roses into her cheeks beneath the freckles, despite the purpling of the rakish bruise high on her cheekbone.

"Are you going to tell me how you got that?" If it had been Gamage he was going to seize the bastard up on a grating and thrash the life out of him with his own hands, and be damned to the consequences.

She tipped her head to the side and brewed up a small bit of the mischievous Kent smile. "Juggling. Wine bottles. Most ill-advised."

He had expected so different an answer that the truth left him bemused. And ill-advisedly intrigued. "I didn't know you juggled."

"Judging from the tenderness of my face, I don't."

He chuckled at her joke, and she smiled back. But only for a moment, before she looked over at the only two cabin doors that remained open, and faltered, the laughter in her gray eyes fading back into solemnness.

She retreated into the safety of formality. "Are you not

going to retire, sir? You've been on deck today longer than anyone, even the captain. You look tired."

He was tired. But the walls that separated the cuddies were nothing but canvas spread over battens. If the fellow next door had a lantern, so he might see to wash, or keep a journal, or read, it shone through the light-colored cloth and cast a shadow of their movements.

To see *her* shadow, to know that nothing but canvas would separate them, to imagine that if he listened very closely, he might hear the cadence of her breathing in sleep, would be nothing less than torture.

He already had an unreasonable fascination for her— there was no need to feed it. He would sleep in the bloody chair if need be.

"I was about to say the same of you, Kent." His voice sounded hoarse to his own ears. Making oneself heard over the guns did that to a man, not the strain of talking to intriguing young women disguised as acting lieutenants. "You look like you've been holystoned."

Her hand rose to touch her cheekbone. "Do I look very bad?"

Her question was devoid of vanity. It held only self-deprecation and astonishment, as if she hadn't thought about it before. "No. You look fine. Like a sailor. Though perhaps more like a prize fighter, fresh from a good milling."

"That's the stuff." The laughing mischief danced back into her eyes. "Perhaps I should keep up the juggling so I'll continue to look the part. It will make a nice change from not bathing."

Damn his eyes. Damn him. Because even if he closed his eyes to the sight of her, he could still vividly imagine the dark shape of her body silhouetted against the backlit canvas wall of his cabin, an erotic shadow, like a mural of an odalisque brought to life. A flesh-and-blood woman, instead of the grime-coated boy she was trying so hard to be.

His mouth ran so dry, all the brandy on board wouldn't be enough to wet it. He opened his eyes and tried to speak normally. "Kent, I should warn you, the screen walls are thin, and light comes through. So when you . . ."—he had to swallow around the word—"wash yourself, you'll want to take care with your lamps. Do you understand?"

"Oh." Her brow pleated up in puzzlement. "Does that mean I oughtn't? Pinky left a ewer of warm water, and I was hoping to finally—"

"No." Damn him for a dog. Clearly her brain didn't function like his. "You just need to be careful. Unless you want Mr. Horner to discover"—he glanced around the empty cabin, but still lowered his voice—"certain things, and to be eaten up with lust and longing, and as hard as a belaying pin, then you had best either make sure he is not in his cabin, or extinguish the lantern before you wash yourself."

"Oh." She drew back, belated understanding steeling her spine. "I understand. But does that mean y—" She stopped, and said no more, but she couldn't stop her eyes from shying down his frame, or keep her face from flaming with a heat that swept downward over her neck like a trail of fire.

But he knew exactly what she had not asked. The hectic heat in his own face was burning away all traces of his pride. Why should he not tell her? She needed to know. To understand. If not for her own sanity, then for his. "Yes, Kent," he informed her quietly. "That is *exactly* what I mean."

Her answer was the barest shred of a whisper. "Eaten up with lust and longing?"

Within her voice, he found a cobweb of hope. "Yes." He kept his eyes on hers, steady and even as his voice. "Consumed."

When she finally spoke, her voice was as small and tight as if she had forgotten to keep breathing. "I'm sorry."

"I'm not."

Her eyes were wide and dark with something other than fright. Something altogether more promising. "I won't light it if you don't want me to."

"You will need the light sometimes. We all do. Just make sure Horner is still on deck."

She nodded, and then brought her head up to look directly at him. "But not you?"

Col held himself very, very still, and willed himself not to react. Not to move. Not to leap across the space that divided them and take her and open her mouth beneath his. Not to so much as move a single muscle. "That, Kent, is entirely up to you."

Her mouth fell open slowly, so slowly and softly he was drawn to it, like a future addict to the first taste of opium. He could do nothing to stifle the instinctive urge to touch the plush fruit of her lips.

It wasn't smart, and it wasn't prudent, and he could lose his commission for misconduct at the very least, if any of the men in the cabins that lined the gunroom walls chose to look out of their doors. But he had known all along that some time he would give in to the craving, to the need to feel her skin beneath his hands. It might as well be now.

His fingers landed lightly along the line of her jaw, even as his thumb brushed the very edge of her bottom lip. Oh, but she was soft and smooth, and altogether alive in a way he had not anticipated. Nothing about this startling girl was what he had anticipated.

Because instead of standing, or telling him he oughtn't, or doing any of the hundred things *she* ought, she stilled, like a wild animal tamed to hand, and simply let him touch her.

Her lip was full, and ripened by wind, and the same rosy pink as the inside of a seashell. He could feel the warm exhalation of her breath on his skin, and it was everything he could do not to lean forward and press himself to her. His hand slid around to cup the back of her neck, to span the slender strength, and explore the soft silk of her hair where the bright tresses whorled upward into her queue. Along the side of her neck a dark freckle beckoned, like a bright copper penny found by chance. It seemed decidedly intimate, his knowledge of that place on her body.

As intimate as touching her face. He skated around the edge of the bruise, tracing the line of unblemished skin, where the rainbow of subdued colors faded into the speckled beauty of her cheek, down along the line of her jaw to the underside of her chin, where he longed to place his lips and taste the ginger spice of her skin.

She turned her face into his hand, almost as if she were blindly seeking the comfort of his touch. He could hear her breathing, shallow and light, and feel the warming of the air between them as he leaned closer to her face. "Kent." He wanted her to look at him, to understand what they were doing. How irrevocable a step they would take if—

He let the rest of the thought die, and brought away his hand. And scraped his chair back. There could be no *ifs*. "Kent."

She came back to herself with the same swift decision she did all things. She stood immediately and stepped away. "My apologies, Mr. Colyear."

"No apologies, Kent."

"Perhaps I should go back to the cockpit, sir."

"Nobody goes *back* to the cockpit, Kent." He tossed his head at Rudge's door. It was all the movement in her direction that he would allow himself. "Go to your cabin. You're safe enough here, and certainly safer than you would be if you stayed in the cockpit. Lock your door. Take care of that burn on your leg. And get some sleep."

God knew he wouldn't. And with that he rose and took himself on deck, where the wind and the night could hide his longing. Perhaps, if there were a merciful God, it would rain.

Sally shut the door and held on to the knob until she could hear the measured pace of Mr. Colyear's footfalls retreat upward to the deck. Only then did she allow herself to breathe, and to collapse slowly down the back of the door. Her legs weren't fit to hold her. Nothing felt fit.

She was as limp and ragged as if she had been hung up in the rigging to dry.

Oh, Col. Col, Col, Col.

She had felt the heavy warmth of his hand all the way from the tight muscles of her shoulder, down to the backs of her knees. An entirely new world of sensation had arisen under the weight of his fingers. She could feel a hundred pinpricks of sensation she had never felt before. Everything was new.

The callus on the inside of his index finger as he casually stroked the newly sensitive skin along the side of her neck. The size of his hand as it spanned the back of her neck. The architecture of her own bones as he moved her to his will. Heat arose from the spot where his finger had alit and washed over her skin, leaving her flushed and flustered.

His long, strong fingers had caressed the back of her neck just as they had caressed the deckhead that very first day. Heat, and something more, something more potent, blossomed under her skin, leaving her breathless and nearly dizzy.

It wouldn't do. Sally tipped her head back and banged it against the door. Hard. So she could knock some sense into her thick skull. So the pain echoing through her head might make her remember who she was, and what she had come aboard to do. The first privacy she'd had in weeks and all she could do was sigh over Mr. Colyear like a moonstruck calf. As if she'd forgotten she was a Kent and not some stupid, swooning girl.

In the corner, a small stand containing a basin and pitcher of warm water had been set up. In her efforts to hide her identity in the cockpit, her ablutions had been minimal and hurried, had never included more than her face, neck, and hands, and had been conducted under the cover of either darkness or a blanket—a soapy swipe under her arms to combat the worst of her dirt. She had not seen her own body in weeks.

Nor had she seen her face. There was a small mirror hanging from the wall—Mr. Rudge's shaving mirror. It must have been inadvertently forgotten in the rush to remove his dunnage to the Spanish prize ship.

The face that filled the small oval was one she hardly recognized, so completely and methodically had she transformed herself into Richard. She hardly knew herself.

She had, once or twice in her life, been referred to as a handsome girl, but she had never been accused of being beautiful. She looked too like her brothers to be considered feminine, with her father's flaming red hair flying like a banner at a masthead, and her gray eyes too sharp and probing to ever be considered warm.

Certainly, she was nothing in looks to Mr. Colyear, who was everything handsome and masculine rolled into one. He was a paragon—as tall and dark and forbidding as any hero of fiction.

While she looked an absolute fright. Sally hung the small lantern on the peg beside the mirror and took a good, hard look. And to think she had thought herself cleaned up enough for the captain's cabin when she had run her fingers through her windblown hair and washed the sulfurous stink of gunpowder off her face. But it was still there, the rime of grime, ringing her face like a high tide mark.

But Mr. Colyear had not seemed to mind. He had touched her anyway and told her she looked just fine. Clearly it had been a merciful lie.

The bruise around her eye made her look like a bailiff's mongrel dog. What could he have been thinking when he touched her face like that?

Sally laid her own finger across her lip to try and understand, to test if she could make the shivery feeling come back. But it wasn't the same. Nothing was the same. When he touched her everything changed.

She had thought that by coming aboard, by becoming Richard, she had finally slipped the leash of ladylike expectations. But when Col had touched her, she felt suddenly feminine beneath the surface of her skin. Under the obscuring cover of her clothes, she became aware of her physicality in an entirely different way than she had while reveling in the athletic glory of climbing the shrouds.

Sally sent up a small prayer that the deck would not suddenly call all hands, or discover a second enemy ship and beat to quarters, and blew out the light. And then, in the low yellow light that leached under the door, for the first time since she came on board, without hiding and gyrating under her linen and blankets, she stripped herself completely of all her clothes and set about giving herself a proper scrubbing off with the flannel square and strong soap she had provided for Richard.

She went after her grime methodically and with vigor, scrubbing until her skin tingled, the way it had when Col had touched her so strangely. And there it was again, the delightful shiver from the slight chill that swept over her damp skin as she soaped and rinsed herself, mingling with the remembrance of Col. Of Col's touch.

Devil tempt her. What she might give for a proper bath, with a copper tub full of hot water and a bar of lemon soap like Mrs. Jenkins made from the fruit grown in the potted trees at home. What might Col think of her if she were really clean, and dressed in something other than a worn-out blue coat? In something fine and pretty?

It was a useless thought. She'd never once in her life looked fine and pretty. She wasn't that kind of girl. Never had been. If Col admired her, at least she was sure he admired her for what she truly was. For understanding oranges and speaking Spanish for the captain, not for useless accomplishments that meant nothing at all in the real world.

She paused for a moment to inhale the strong bracing scent of the marbled castile soap she had purchased for Richard and to shake off the last dregs of dreamy lethargy. It felt so good to inhale fully, to expand her lungs out to the limits of her rib cage, to stretch and move without layers and layers of constricting bands. She felt free in an entirely different manner than she did when she was in the rigging. But free nonetheless.

Once she had changed into fresh linen and clean knee breeches, Sally relit the lantern and carefully examined the small burn on her calf. The ember had expended its energy more on burning her stocking than in the flesh of her calf, but she had an angry red blister the size of a ha'penny to show for the Spaniard's trouble. She dressed it carefully with salve and covered it with a clean bandage. Her father had always been meticulously strict about such things. He used to say that more men were lost to disease and disregard than were ever lost in battle.

But Sally didn't want to think about her father. She wanted to think about Col.

She looked again at her image in the mirror, trying to see what others saw—what Col saw. All she could see was the purplish bruise along the ridge of bone circling her eye, and darker freckles, but other than that, she looked like herself. Without the dirty coating of spent powder and the camouflage of the blue coat, she looked as she always had. Ordinary Sarah Alice Kent who always had plenty of friends and never sat out a rollicking country dance, but never got looked at twice.

But Col had looked twice. More than twice. And touched besides.

And it had felt wonderful. She felt wonderful—warm and awake and drowsy, all at the same time.

Sally blew out the lantern and tipped herself into the swinging cot, a veritable luxury of space and bedlike comfort after the hammock. She stretched out her feet and her back, and turned on her side. Facing the wall separating Mr. Colyear's cabin from hers. Toward him. Toward Col.

She hovered there for a long time, at the edge of sleep, too exhausted and exhilarated to slip the bounds of consciousness, until a shadow crossed the light coming in under her door. In another moment she could hear the quiet sounds of Mr. Colyear letting himself into his cuddy, next door.

The exhaustion dropped away, to be replaced by an avid, almost reckless curiosity. She listened intently, trying to imagine the significance of each small sound as he prepared himself for sleep, until finally she thought she could perceive the creak of ropes that told her he was settling into his hanging cot, and making himself more comfortable. And then she did hear the deep cadence of his breathing, even and controlled, from the other side of the screen wall. She could imagine him, in her mind's eye, lying on his back, with his hands linked behind his head, looking up at the deckbeams above. Thinking. He was always thinking, Col was. Maybe even thinking about her.

Sally inched herself over to the edge of the cot, closer to the wall. There was a little tear in the painted canvas of the wall. "Mr. Colyear?" she whispered at the tear.

His equally hushed answer came back instantly. "Kent. Keep your voice down." His voice was low and soft in that sandy way of his, but she could hear him clearly. He was nearer than she thought.

"I'm sorry." She tried to lower her voice to a hush. "I just wanted to apologize for making things more difficult, when you've been nothing but kind to me, Mr. Colyear. Thank you, for everything you've done."

He took a long, deep breath before he answered. "And everything I haven't done?"

"Yes. That, too."

"You're welcome."

He was quiet for a long time, while something larger and more irrational than butterflies filled her stomach—moths batting around, stupidly flinging themselves at the light that was Mr. Colyear.

"You did well today, Kent. It was one hell of a day."

Relief did make her chatty. "Yes, it was, wasn't it. It was incredible today seeing the oranges, and knowing it meant one of the dons was near. I had gooseflesh all up and down my arms out of sheer excitement. And then finding the ship, and then it being a xebec—so fantastical looking. I'd heard about them and seen drawings but I'd never seen one before, with those exotic, precarious-looking lateen sails."

She drew in a long breath. She was blathering like a looby, but she couldn't seem to help it. And Col didn't seem to mind. He was making encouraging sounds of agreement. "And then chasing the xebec and watching the way you saw everything, and then tacking like that across the don's stern and engaging so entirely at point-blank range. It was brilliant, just brilliant. I don't think there is another captain in the world, or another crew, who could have done it like that today, my father included. You were magnificent."

"Thank you, Kent. That is high praise indeed. It was quite a day." He sounded as if he were smiling. His voice was ashy, but warm, the last smoldering remains of the fire of battle. It was low, and just soft enough to insinuate its way deep inside her. It made her curl up into a tight ball to hug the sound of him close.

"It was the best day ever. And I was so very glad to be a part of it. It was a privilege. Especially as chances are I may not have another like it."

"Won't you? *Audacious* may take more prizes yet. Captain McAlden is an ambitious man. He has plans we none of us know of yet."

"Does he? And am I going to be part of those plans?"

"Who knows," was his noncommittal response.

Sally took another deep breath. "Does that mean you're really not going to tell him? Ever?"

Long silence pressed her into the cot while she waited for Col to speak.

"Ever is a very long time, Kent. And I think we both know it can't be forever."

"No. It can't be forever. But perhaps, just perhaps, it could just be for now?"

She waited in the dark, silent and suspended by her hope. Waiting.

"Yes," he finally answered. "For now."

She didn't need to hear the rest—the *ifs*. She understood him well enough to comprehend it meant *if* she was useful, and *if* she stayed out of trouble, and *if* she could help Gamage with his studies.

"Thank you, Col. Thank you." There was nothing more, nothing substantial enough to say to acknowledge the risk he was taking for her. She would be put ashore, if she were found out, but he could be called before a court-martial, if Captain McAlden or the Admiralty felt that he had put the ship or the crew in jeopardy in order to keep her secret. He could lose everything. Even his good name.

She would have taken his hand to shake, to show him she understood and would honor the chance he was taking on her.

But it was late and they were both abed, and she had to get up in four hours. Yet it felt important, this burgeoning feeling of enormous gratitude within her, and so very carefully, she laid her palm flat against the canvas of the wall. A silent little tribute.

Then, she felt the press of his hand against hers, palm to palm, through the fabric of the canvas. His hand was bigger—the span of his palm was wider, the length of his fingers longer—and heat rose out of his palm in waves. She couldn't draw back. She pressed harder, leaning into the strength and surety of him.

She was not alone. He would help her keep her secret. And she wouldn't let him down. She would protect him and his good name from all harm as well.

Whatever it was, this friendship, this affinity between them, she was not alone. He felt it, too. It only remained to see what they were going to do about it.

Chapter Fifteen

The noon hour saw *Audacious* standing ten miles northwest off the island of Ushant, itself off the west coast of the Department of Finistère, with the city of Brest lying along the Atlantic Coast a further fifteen miles or so to the southeast. And Kent was nowhere to be found.

Only a moment ago, she had been at the rail with all of the other midshipmen—*all* in this case including Mr. Gamage, who, for the first time in recent memory, had appeared with his sextant to take the noon reading. But now neither Kent nor Gamage were anywhere within sight. A wash of apprehension swilled around his gut like a cold swallow of salty seawater.

Col knew he ought to be grateful that she was keeping assiduously out of his way, that she appeared to be applying herself with all diligence to her sworn duty. That he hadn't seen her in days. It had been his objective in rearranging the watchkeeping schedule to keep them apart.

And he couldn't stand it.

"Mr. Worth," he called to the nearest boy. "Pass the word for Mr. Kent."

"If you please, sir. Mr. Kent is in the cockpit, sir, working with Mr. Gamage. If there is anything you require, I'd be happy to do it for you, instead of Mr. Kent."

So she really was doing it—tutoring Mr. Gamage. Or at

least she was trying. And if Mr. Worth's offer was any indication, the rest of the midshipmen would do just about anything to see that she remained trying.

"No need, Mr. Worth. I'll see—" Col had no excuse that wouldn't make him look three ways to foolish. "I'll see to it myself."

Col made his way belowdecks quietly, almost surreptitiously, so he could fetch up outside the cockpit unannounced and unseen. Low light from a lantern shone from under the closed door, and he paused there at the threshold to listen.

"I tell you what." Kent's voice was clear and low. "We'll go over the projection again, but this time, we're going to use different colors of ink for each one of the lines, transects, and arcs. It will make it easier for you to differentiate them, both in your mind and on the paper. So let's make the rhumb line yellow, to stand for the foam in the wake of the ship, because that's the direct line that represents the course you want the ship to hew to. And we'll make the horizon line black, because that's what you see when you look at the horizon . . ."

Amid the clinking of pens and ink bottles, Col let himself into the room as silently as possible so as not to disturb them, or wake Jellicoe and Beecham, who were asleep in their hammocks. Kent and Gamage were seated with their backs to the door, side by side at the table, which had been moved so that it canted across the small room at an angle. The reason for which was soon explained.

"Exactly," Kent was encouraging her pupil. "And remember again that north will be at the head of the paper, and that we've seated ourselves in the same orientation, so that you are drawing your trigonometric projection in the actual direction you will need to calculate, to make it easier to envision."

"And I have to make this basic projection every time? Bloody waste—"

"It's working, isn't it? You've gotten the first two distances right, Damien. Just keep using the framework now, and soon you'll be able to envision it on the paper even if you haven't drawn it out. But for now, until it's in your memory, start with the colored ink and work from there. It will take longer for a while, but soon you'll be fast enough."

Damien? Since when had Gamage become Damien? And Kent was sitting so close to the man that their heads were nearly touching, and her shoulder was rubbing up against his.

"Mr. Kent." He hadn't meant to make his voice so harsh.

She immediately scraped back her chair and rose. "Mr. Colyear, sir, I didn't see you there."

Was that nervous guilt he heard in her voice? Or flustered pleasure? It bothered him that he had no idea. Gamage had risen as well, and now stood looking back and forth between Kent and Col. Now he had to explain himself. "I came to see how you were getting on. You and Mr. Gamage, that is. With your studies."

"Very well, thank you, sir. I was thinking—we were thinking—of asking Mr. Charlton if Mr. Gamage might rejoin the midshipmen in their lessons in the morning, but I realize we need to apply to you, sir, to see if Mr. Gamage might be taken off duty and watchkeeping during the forenoon."

We? The acid scratching through his gut could not possibly be jealousy. He was not jealous of Gamage. He refused to be.

For his part, Gamage seemed content to let Kent do all the talking. But Col didn't like the sharp look in the man's eyes as he kept tacking back and forth between Kent and himself.

"That may be arranged, but Mr. Gamage will have to ask Mr. Charlton's permission himself." Col shifted his focus directly to Gamage so the man had to do the same. "You will have to apply to the sailing master directly for readmittance, and make a case as to why he should do so." Col had not been privy to the dismissal of Gamage from the classroom—it had happened long before he had joined *Audacious*—but he was damn sure that Gamage needed to atone for whatever sins he may have committed personally with Mr. Charlton. And it gave Col a reason to speak to Kent alone.

"Make your case to Mr. Charlton directly, Mr. Gamage. You'll find him in the gunroom at this time of day."

"Aye, sir." Gamage did as Col bid, but still the man kept up that infernal glancing between Kent and Col, as if he had unanswered suspicions. Or maybe Gamage was the one who was jealous.

Col had no further time to contemplate such an unsettling notion, because young Worth clambered through the door. "Compliments of the deck, Mr. Colyear. If you please, you and Mr. Kent are wanted in the captain's cabin as soon as may be."

Col was thankful for the reprieve from his unsettled, inarticulate feelings, and doubly thankful that the summons would afford him more time in her company. "Thank you, Mr. Worth. Come along, Mr. Kent, and get your hat. It's never good to keep your captain waiting."

They parted company with Gamage at the gun deck, and found themselves not more than four minutes later seated in the captain's dining cabin with Captain McAlden and Mr. Charlton, enjoying a dinner of ragout of pork with three removes of good vegetables, pureed potatoes, and cheeses. It was only after the plum duff and the loyal toast that Captain McAlden came to the business at hand.

"Mr. Colyear. I do believe the time has come for your shore sortie."

"My sortie, sir?" Col felt he could hardly think for having been so extravagantly fed.

"I do acknowledge that it is not customary for the first lieutenant to leave the ship, but for what I have in mind, I need a man completely capable of making his own judgments and decisions—of acting independently. And that man, Mr. Colyear, would be you. It only remains for you to inure yourself to the idea of going ashore."

Col had no trouble hearing the amusement in his captain's voice. Captain McAlden knew Col had steadfastly avoided so much as setting a toe ashore since the last time he had landed at Gibraltar, nearly two years earlier. On that occasion, Col had found it so difficult to make his way upon the land without falling that an officer of the constabulary had proclaimed him drunk and clapped him in irons. Col had enjoyed neither the unsettling physical experience, nor the ignominy of being plagued with his supposed misdeeds ever since.

"Perhaps there is someone better suited than I. Mr. Horner—"

"—is young and capable," the captain finished for him, "but I have another role in mind for him. Let me explain my motive, Mr. Colyear. You have done an admirable job as first lieutenant. Most commendable. *Audacious* has taken many prizes, in great part due to your skill managing the men."

"Here, here," said Mr. Charlton.

"But our very success is too much of a deterrent. With the French holed up like mice, safe in their ports, we have no chance to go at them with strength. Therefore, we must use cunning. We shall have to draw them out, by convincing them that their harbor is not the safe haven they have thought it. Blockade duty doesn't give a man very many chances for advancement. However, if we—if you—can occasion the destruction of any number of ships in Brest's harbor, well, that, Mr. Colyear, would be just the sort of thing their Lordships of the Admiralty like to have on a man's record when they see about promotions and giving him a ship of his own."

A ship of his own. Already the words were echoing and magnifying in his head. To have a ship to order as he pleased, to crew and staff with anyone he pleased . . . Col could hardly refuse such inducement, or such an assignment. To do so would be cowardly, as well as ungrateful. "You know I am completely at your disposal, sir, but Brest is nearly impregnable. From my memory, the approach through Le Goulet is exceedingly narrow, and subject to fire from shore. The roadstead is filled with enemy vessels. And the Fortress Brest itself is huge, heavily manned, and more heavily armed. You will forgive me, sir, for saying that to take *Audacious* in such waters would subject her to intolerable risk."

"I salute your memory and your prudence, Mr. Colyear. You may rest easy. What I have in mind is nothing like the trickery employed by Captain Smith's attempt to cozen the French. Nothing so foolhardy or overt. What I have in mind is vastly more subtle."

"You intrigue me, sir."

"Good." The captain favored him with one of his tight, cool smiles. "I hoped I might." He began to unroll the chart of the coast of Finistère handed to him by his clerk, Pike. "What I have in mind is a two-pronged attack. The secondary targets will be two or possibly three of these signal towers and batteries dotting the coast. The area to the northwest of Brest"—he pointed on the map—"is best."

The coast of Britanny was dangerous—rocky and littered with ship-wrecking shoals. The thought of taking a frigate close enough to the coast to effect a landing made Col break out in a cold sweat. "These islands southeast of Ushant are dangerous, sir. Riddled with rocky shallows."

"Yes, I know it of old. I sailed this coast with Captain Smith in '95, and learned it well. The prevailing wind is from the southwest and will push us upon the shore if we are not careful. But we will be careful. We will cruise the approaches to Brest for a few days and make sure we have the feel of it before we attempt to land boats."

Mr. Charlton was nodding along in sage agreement, but it was Kent who already had her fingers upon the chart, already poring over it, as if she were engraving the lines of the map upon her memory.

"I should like to maraud up and down this coast, making surprise attacks on as many of the coastal batteries as possible with landing parties, keeping the French engaged and drawing off troops and materiel, as well as attention, from Brest. Which will all be a diversion for you, Mr. Colyear, whom I will send on to Brest to make what mischief you can there."

"Alone, sir?"

"Take one other man. Anything more and you risk detection. I should like Mr. Horner and Mr. Lawrence to lead the attacks on the batteries, so take a junior warrant officer, or one of the midshipmen."

Col's mind leapt at the chance. To have her alone . . . His heart rattled against the cage of his ribs, pounding his pulse into his ears.

There could only be one choice, but he spoke slowly, as if he were still reckoning it out. "Kent will do, sir. He speaks French. Do you not?" He turned to her.

"*Oui*, Monsieur Colyear," she answered with the appropriate gravity. She didn't show the slightest sign of being affected by runaway emotion. Unlike him.

"Excellent." Captain McAlden confirmed the decision. "Mr. Kent it shall be. Let us assemble the others. Pike, pass the word for Lieutenants Horner and Lawrence, and Mr. Davies as well."

The clerk went to the door to pass the word, while the captain called their attention back to the charts upon the table. "There are two batteries, here and here. As they keep a sharp lookout to sea, I should like to let off boats under cover of darkness, between these islands, and then make our way down the coast. If the ship is noticed at all it will be seen to be continuing down the coast. I should like there to be three parties. First, a party under Lieutenant Horner, and one of the gunner's mates—whom do you suggest, Mr. Colyear?"

"Moffatt, sir. Reliable man. Steady."

"Moffatt then—Mr. Pike, will you also pass word for the gunner's mate Moffatt?—with Mr. Horner, will go to the more northerly tower and destroy, or at least attempt to destroy, it at the same time the party under Mr. Lawrence and Mr. Davies does the same to the southern tower. Both groups will escape back out to sea in boats, and rendezvous on the offshore side of this group of islands known as Les Mulots, here off Beniguet. We will repeat this on successive evenings, sailing up and down the coast and heading inshore only after nightfall, so the French will not know where we mean to strike next."

"And me, sir?"

"You, Mr. Kent, will accompany Mr. Colyear. You will land with the others and then split off, and proceed directly into Brest. When the batteries on the coast are attacked, with luck, the French will be drawn out of the garrison at Brest, either by sea or across land—preferably both. And while they are drawn off, we will engage any that come by sea, while you will create some great mischief, to the port or the arsenal, or a ship—whatever seems best and most expedient. Anything that will disrupt their commerce and hinder their abilities. Any matériel we destroy cannot be put to use for invading England."

"Any, sir?"

"You are to use your own judgment in the matter of how to best effect such disruption and destruction. The arsenal at Brest lies under the cliffs along the Penfeld River, extending for several miles upstream from the fortress. There are a number of possible targets. Take whatever opportunity best presents itself, but I want the port of Brest disrupted so there is the possibility they will be induced to put their fleet out."

Col took a long time to look at the maps to impress the layout of the town and the location of the strong points that were sure to be guarded or fortified. Kent was looking, too, and when he met her eye, a full understanding of the magnitude of the task was reflected in her face. She looked, for the first time since she had come aboard, completely daunted.

It was going to be one hell of a job. "What about the fort itself?"

"I would caution against it. However impressive it might be, such a plan is not practical. Not to mention suicidal. The navy and I have need of all our best officers, Mr. Colyear, and I intend for this to be mischief only, to rattle the French into believing the supposedly impregnable harbor is not so safe, and they had perhaps better take their chances upon the open sea. But the fort itself is too well defended for two men to attack."

"What about the Préfecture de Marine?" It was Kent, with her finger on a spot on the map of the city. "Is not the Préfecture de Marine for all of Finistère in Brest city?"

"How do you come by this information, Mr. Kent?"

"Pinky, sir. Angus Pinkerton, the cockpit servant, was on

the *Danae*, wasn't he? When the ship mutinied and was taken into Brest in the year 1800. And the loyal men were put up in the prison at the castle there. He knows the layout of the town."

"Pinkerton is too old for a shore sortie," Mr. Charlton opined.

"Undoubtedly, but the idea has merit. Mr. Kent, consult with Pinkerton, and get every ounce of useful information out of him before you go ashore."

"Aye, sir."

Captain McAlden sat back from the table. "Are we decided? Good. Let us set sail south to Brest."

Three days of cruising as close inshore as possible, of habituating the islanders to their presence, and navigating the rocky coast and its hazards of small islands and tidal streams, left Captain McAlden confident of his intelligence. The batteries could be taken.

Three days of knowing soon, at any moment, the captain would give the order, and he would be put ashore with Kent. Three days of knowing she would be at his side, his to command, away from all oversight and censure. By that third day, Col thought the vein pounding in his temple would burst, and kill him dead upon the deck where he stood, waiting.

But finally, the night came. The captain chose a beach to the north of the village of Le Conquet because *Audacious* could hove to outside one of the small rocky islands offshore and put off the boats without having them seen from the shore.

Captain McAlden held the deck while the boats were lowered away on the offshore side of the Isle of Quéménès, so even if *Audacious*'s presence was noted, she might show the shore a clean pair of heels before darkness covered the boats' approach. While the presence of an English ship off the coast would not arouse suspicion, for the blockade of France's harbors had continued without interruption for several years now, longboats full of English sailors were sure to be met with both alarm and resistance.

The captain shook Col's hand. "Godspeed, Mr. Colyear.

Do your worst for the French and your best for England, and I shall be very well satisfied."

And they were away.

It would be a long pull of over four miles into shore, threading their way through the rocky islands, staying in the lee of the Isle of Béniguet, until the tide ran high and could help push them the final two miles across to the mainland. They had decided upon three boats. The smallest one could be abandoned if necessary, or hidden along the shore and left as a fail-safe should any of the parties get separated and fail to make their rendezvous.

But he and Kent would be without any other support. It would be too far to come the ten miles back from Brest—a full day's march back overland. As it was, Col was dreading marching so little as one mile. He had not made it one hundred feet off the quay in Gibraltar before the land had started to act strange and unwieldy underfoot. Their best escape would be by sea from the harbor of Brest. If he made it that far. He would have to trust in Providence to see him through.

The night was overcast, and the moonlight shone intermittently on the water. In the inky darkness, the boats moved as stealthily as gulls, winging their silent way across the water toward the low shore on muffled oars. For their landing, Col had chosen a remote promontory north of the village of Le Conquet where a small cove with a quiet sandy beach was hidden from the town by the low-cliffed headland.

Under Col's authority, each of the lieutenants commanded a boat and held the stern tiller steering the boats shoreward. He had positioned Kent in the bow of his own boat, silently swinging the lead line, sounding the depth and searching the water ahead for obstacles. The prevailing winds held steady from the southwest and in a few hours' time of silent exertion—there was never the least chatter from the boat crew as they bent themselves to the arduous task at hand—they made their way through the islands, around the promontory, and onto the beach.

Kent rolled over the gunwale and into the shallow surf like a seal pup, silent, intent, and eager. Any doubt he might have had at putting her name forward vanished as he watched her guide the boat in, hauling it silently upon the shore and into the scrub as if she did it every day.

And thank God. Thank God Kent was as bloody useful as a well-honed pocketknife, sharp and quick. No one else saw things with the same acuity as Kent. And spoke French. He needed her with him, because he wanted to succeed.

The group came together at the edge of the beach where the sand gave way to the low escarpment dividing the sea from the scrub and fields beyond. Lieutenants Horner and Lawrence split up their men, took charge of their groups, and disappeared into the scrub beyond the beach.

Kent was close behind him, her teeth shining white in the night. "Ready, Mr. Colyear?"

"Close your mouth." He said it to cover his own anxiety. But also so he wouldn't be tempted to kiss her on that same wide, lovely mouth. Instead, he handed her one of his pistols. "Do you know how to use it?"

"Ah, yes." Her voice was slightly affronted, slow and droll. "I do, sir."

"Good. Keep it dry." Thus far, he had not felt any of the telltale trouble navigating the land, but it was early days yet—they had only been ashore scant minutes and had only just cleared the beach. He was not out of danger yet. "We'll head southeast, across the fields. Stay alert. Keep your weapon covered, but at the ready. We'll avoid all towns and villages and any persons we can. Stay close. I'm counting on you reading the road signage."

"Sir?"

"You do speak French, Kent, do you not?"

"Aye, sir. But I don't know Breton."

He did not mutter and curse under his breath. He restrained himself. He swore, vilely and at length, only in the comfort and privacy of his brain, where his mistakes didn't expose him to ridicule.

But such restraint did nothing to ease the taut coil knotting up his gut like a fouled line. He had made a horrible mistake. He never should have picked her to accompany him. He never should have agreed to the captain's plan in the first place.

He was behind enemy lines, on shore in Napoleon's France, with his best friend's nineteen-year-old sister, and any moment, he was going to faint like a little girl.

The flatland vertigo began as they made for a thick line of trees marking the edge of a small coastal river. Under cover of the woods, he thought he could balance himself against the tree trunks to ease the sudden, nasty, shifting sensation. He tried to breathe deeply, but his breath began to come in shallow pants, pushing in and out of his chest like a bilge pump. The night felt warm, and inshore, away from the cooling winds of the open Atlantic, the air was denser, heated by the earth below his feet.

And then, just when he thought he would make it, because his boots were wet again with the water of the stream they were crossing, everything tilted, and he went down hard.

So hard, he knocked the breath from his lungs and lay there, with the water soaking into his coat, until Kent, or at least her gigantic feet, appeared in front of him.

"Mr. Colyear!" She was there, hauling him up by the armpits and dragging him to the bank.

Humiliation soaked him as surely as the water. He was, quite literally, staggered, and until such time as the earth ceased rising and falling like the tide, and lay still beneath him, he could go no further.

Kent squatted down before him, peering into his face. A spate of moonlight illuminated her pale face and made her look like an inquisitive owl, blinking at him with the calm wisdom of the ages. "Mr. Colyear? What is it?"

He couldn't hide it any longer. "Sick." He gritted his teeth together. "The land. Makes me sick."

That dusted her back on her heels. Her eyebrows were flying away with her owl face. "Oh. If that doesn't beat all." And she began to help him, unbuttoning his coat and waistcoat as if he were Mr. Worth, a green midshipman and not a goddamn officer of His Majesty's Royal Navy, and her commanding officer to boot. "Of all the people—"

"Shut. Up. Kent."

But she was easing his coat off behind him and loosening the black silk stock at his neck. "It will pass. Hopefully. When was the last time you were ashore? In Portsmouth?"

He would have shaken his head, but even that little exertion made the earth tilt precariously to larboard. So he concentrated on the smooth solidity of the rock on which he was propped, and as he pressed his back into it, the swirling eased. Kent sat herself down comfortably at his feet, checking the compass she unearthed from the depths of her pockets. Prepared, reliable Kent.

"We'll head that way, in a minute or two, when you're able. We have time to sit while you recover yourself." Her face tipped up to the sky. "It's a beautiful night. But not too clear."

So positive and calm. So full of unshakable optimism.

With her so close, he could smell the warm pungency of her castile soap, and see by the dancing light of the sparse moon the myriad colors that made up her ginger hair.

Such beautiful hair.

"Did you cut it? Your hair?" he managed.

The glance she slanted him was watchful, as if she weren't sure if he had been made mad by his infirmity, but at the same time she reached back to draw the messy queue through her fingers self-consciously. "Yes. I made the club, then just cut it off with scissors. I was going to burn it in the grate at the inn, in Portsmouth, but I thought it might smell bad, so I just stuffed it in my valise. Which I left there. I wonder what happened to it." She frowned, turning the corners of her plush mouth down, and pulled the queue over her shoulder to contemplate it. "Why? Does it not look right?"

"No." His answer was gruff. "Fine." It was not fine. It was a crime that anything that alive and beautiful, and full of color, had been in any way curtailed.

"Oh. I just wondered. Gamage has Tunney shave him every morning, although Beecham and Dance do it themselves, and

I just wondered if I was supposed to be trimming it all the time. I mean regularly."

There wasn't much vanity in that, but it bothered him, for not the first time, to think of her living so intimately with other men. Most women only ever saw their own husbands shave themselves, if even that. In the cockpit, and even in the gunroom, she had been in the company of men routinely stripped to their waists. Perhaps even naked in front of her. Every day for weeks.

And what about her?

His curiosity got the best of him. "What did you do? There are no screen walls, no cuddies in the orlop berth. How did you change your clothes or . . ." He let the question trail away, before the words "wash yourself" came traveling out of his mouth with the same speed that images of her doing that very thing traveled into his brain.

What did she look like in the flesh, with her hair down, and her shirt stripped to the waist, running a warm flannel over her skin? Would the water chill it to gooseflesh, and make her nipples contract into tight buds? What color would they be, her nipples? The range of color suggested by her freckles was nearly infinite—everything from soft apricot to dark chocolate brown. The possibilities were endless. And tempting. Always effortlessly tempting.

The air in his lungs heated by several slow degrees. Goddamn his eyes. And his infernal, imagining brain.

She laughed, a low hum that included him, as if he were in on the joke. "Very carefully. And Pinky helps."

The hum strangled to stillness in his chest. "What do you mean, Pinky *helps*?"

She had turned away to scan the tree line—as he should have been doing if he weren't staggered and unable, and also obsessed with her. With this ferociously intelligent girl who was always watching and thinking.

"Oh, somehow he managed to get the hammocks up and down for the watch changes, and I just left—and still do leave—my . . . things in the hammock, and now my cot, and he finds them. And he leaves clean shirts and smallclothes, and the bands I wear around my chest, in my dunnage. It's easier now I've a door, but I'd gotten used to putting on the clean ones while I was under my blankets in the hammock, before I went to sleep."

"So Pinky knows? He knows who you really are?"

"Oh, no." She seemed anxious to keep Pinkerton from any real trouble. "I mean, I suppose he must, though he's never said so. Never said so much as a word. But even though Richard and I do look alike, Pinky was my father's steward. He practically had the raising of us, Richard and I, after my mother died. But he's a good man, Pinky is, and deeply loyal to my father. If he knows, he's kept it entirely to himself."

"I see," Col answered, because there was nothing else for him to say that wouldn't mortify Kent, cause Pinky trouble, or reheat Col's overly active imagination. But just as one worry—of carrying the burden of Kent's identity should something happen to them ashore—was eased, a fresh problem arrived. He had to ask. "You wear bands?"

She nodded, gesticulating about her midsection, as matter-of-fact as if she were discussing the catting of a masthead. "A long, wide strip of linen, under my shirt."

"You mean, wound all around you?"

"Yes, to keep me . . . to fit the coat. Richard was a bit . . . narrower than I."

"Yes, I see." God help him, he could see, in his mind's eye, her pale, freckled body, wrapped in linen. He could imagine her beneath, without the layers of fabric or the obscuring camouflage of waistcoat and coat, being unwrapped. His skin fairly itched with the tormenting prickle of desire under his skin. "Isn't it hot?"

She shrugged and laughed again, quieter. "Depends upon the weather." She darted a quick look sideways at him before she looked back out upon the woods, still alert and watchful.

"Are you hot now?" His coat was folded over her knee, but she had remained fully clothed, despite the still, sticky night air.

"Not much. I'm conscious not to ever take my coat off. No matter what."

"Yes. I see." He let the moment fade away before he suggested, "You can take it off now. I already know your secret."

"Yes, I suppose you do."

She shrugged her way out of the coat, folded it carefully, and set it down beside his. Clad in only the linen of her shirt, her shoulders looked narrow and somehow fragile. Yet she was like a talisman—the compulsion to touch her was so strong.

"Kent." He wanted her to look at him. To see him and understand. For just a moment, no more. "Sally."

He had been longing to say it, her name. It had ridden on the back of his tongue for days, straining to get past the barrier of his good sense. His use of her name was like a lightning rod—she was transfixed, and the moon of her face stilled and turned up to him. A bright streamer of her hair fell across her face, and he pushed it back, hooking it behind her ear.

But that gesture, that touch, led him to the soft, vulnerable skin behind her ear. His hand slipped around to cup the nape of her long, slender neck, where her skin was hidden and warm. His fingers slipped below the surface, into the silken water of her hair.

And he knew. That nothing on this whirling earth was going to stop him from kissing her. Nothing.

Chapter Sixteen

Need unraveled within him like parted hemp. His hand tightened, flexing where it cradled her skull, and her hand crept up to cover and mesh her fingers with his.

"Sally," he said again, because he couldn't think, and because it seemed the right thing to say. And when her name fell from his lips for the second time, her eyes slid shut and her mouth fell open—a gift he meant to take.

The feel of her lips beneath his was new, and extraordinary, and he was conscious of wanting to go slowly, to savor every touch, every taste. Her lips were as chapped and rough as his, but the moment she opened her mouth beneath his, he fell into the inevitable soft sweetness of her.

She kissed the way she lived, with generosity and bright enthusiasm. And with a sureness that left him breathless and racing to catch up. But when he would have taken her face between his hands and lifted her up to him, and followed the dark, twisty path of his desires, she drew back.

For a long moment she looked as disoriented as he, as if the world had shifted beneath *her* feet, but then purpose flowed back into her face. "Are you better now?"

As if the delirious bliss of kissing her had reset his internal barometer, and he was cured. He wanted to laugh at the sheer glorious absurdity of it all.

"Yes." And strangely enough he was. The world had slowly stopped its spinning.

And they were in enemy territory, in the dead of night, and they still had a very long way to go. He needed to have other things on his mind than the exquisite torture of kissing Sally Kent. "Yes." He said it again to convince himself. "Let's push on."

She was there instantly, offering her hand to pull him up, and easing his coat back over his shoulders like a seasoned valet. Or a wife.

He was in the process of trying to banish that particularly ludicrous thought, when she took up his hand, lacing her fingers through his to lead him on, and all thought abruptly ceased again. He ought to have been aware of their direction, of where he was stepping, of the countryside beyond, but every last drop of his sense and feeling was concentrated in his hand. In the chapped texture of her skin, rough around the edges from climbing shrouds and hauling on lines. On the fragile strength of her bones as she kept a firm hold of him, guiding him forward, toward Brest.

Improvise, the captain had told him. *Think on your feet.* How in the hell was he to do that when he couldn't even *stand* on his feet? He knew what to do, what to think and improvise on the deck of a ship, but here on land, he was not so sure. Here, he was depending on the support of a nineteen-year-old girl.

Col was conscious of her at every moment, walking easily at his side. It seemed a natural enough place for her—she fit. He was a tall man, taller than most, and it seemed as if he had spent half his life stooping to move belowdecks, but here he could walk with her tucked in close beside him. She came up to his chin, but their hands met in perfect accord at just the right length.

She was . . . comfortable.

The thought made him smile in spite of himself, despite the still-percolating drip of anxiety that made him move cautiously.

What a ludicrous sight they must make, an officer and a

boy of His Majesty's Royal Navy walking hand in hand down a road deep in France.

For once, he didn't care. From time to time the cool night air would bring him a waft of the scent rising off her body, and his fantasies about the lithe, supple, intriguing body he had never quite seen grew apace, gathering strength like a wave. And under cover of the dark, without anyone to see or censure, he could give in to his impulse, and indulge his senses.

He could run his thumb across the delicate skin on the back of her hand. He could stroke the softness at the inside of her wrist. It seemed little enough, but there was a world of feeling in each and every exploration into the unknown depths that were her.

He took another misstep and even as he gritted his teeth and leaned on her to right himself, and would have forced himself to carry on, she simply sat, pulling him down next to her in the shelter of a hedgerow, and it seemed sensible to sit for a while and get their bearings. They had been moving across the fields unseen and unmolested, until they were past the villages of Lanfeust and Trébabu. The moon came out from behind the clouds at intervals, but in the mostly open farmland of Finistère, the darkness wasn't as impenetrable as it had first seemed under the canopy in the woods.

In the next spate of moonlight, Kent took out her compass to take a reading, and he took advantage of her stillness to exercise his compulsion to touch her, to steady himself with her soft vitality. To depend upon her.

How remarkable. He had prided himself on being a man who never stopped. Who never let down his guard. Who, unless he was dead asleep—and even then he woke up at the slightest provocation—was always watching, seeing, thinking, and planning. Always alert. Always checking his bearings, or the set of his sails.

Just as Kent was doing now. She was the reason he wasn't panicking. He didn't have to fight the nausea tooth and nail because he knew he could rely upon her to see what needed to be seen. He could rely upon her to understand what she saw correctly.

Remarkable.

And all the more reason for him to kiss her again. But at that moment, a dull echo of a huge concussion rumbled across the fields from the north. The sound of the first battery being detonated. Bringing him back to their purpose.

"Come. Let's move on." This time he took her hand, already too accustomed to the pleasure of her intimate company to give it up for the empty triumph of pride.

They kept to the covering shelter of the hedgerows, well away from the roads. They made uneven but steady progress over the course of the next three hours, stopping from time to time as needed.

She gleaned some apples from an orchard as they passed, but when they had quietly skirted a dilapidated inn, at the edge of someplace Kent told him was called Plouzané, Kent touched him lightly on the arm and said, "I'll be right back."

"What are you—" But she had slipped over a stone wall. The thought occurred to him that she might need to answer the call of nature, so he let her go and settled down to wait. They were hidden on a slight hill beyond the inn, and Col could see down into the courtyard.

A flash of movement at the edge of the courtyard caught his eye, but it was Kent, damn her eyes, stealing soundlessly across the deserted stableyard and slipping around the back of the building.

Col nearly stood up. As it was, he drew his pistol and held it at the ready. Ready for he knew not what, but prepared—tense, and hunkered down behind the tumbledown stone wall, waiting for any eventuality. His gut hammered away each second that she was gone, counting out the moments she was out of his sight and inexplicably courting this unnecessary danger.

And then she was flying up the incline toward him, grinning from ear to ear, her imp's face shining with happy mischief. "Here." She handed Col a nearly full wheel of cheese, and a squashed, narrow loaf of peasant's bread that looked more like a cudgel than a loaf.

"Bugger all, Kent. Don't you ever do that again. Don't endanger yourself, or us, or this mission for food. We can do well enough without for one bloody night."

"The food was an afterthought, although you really ought to eat something. I'm sure it would help. I really went for the laundry." Her coat was stuffed with a roll of clothing— dashes of green quilting and red wool. "So perhaps we can move through the city without being noticed overmuch."

With Kent there was always a plan ticking away in that devilish little head. A *bad* plan, by his reckoning, but a plan nonetheless.

"Are you mad?" His words sounded like they had been ground through his teeth, like grist from a mill. But the ebbing of the worry—the sudden fear for her—left him ready to pulverize something, and the only available choice was his words. "Firstly, we are naval officers. We don't take the uniform off. Ever. If we're captured, we will be imprisoned but potentially, eventually, exchanged so we might remain useful to our king and country and Admiralty. But if we are out of uniform, we will undoubtedly be taken for spies and shot out of hand."

The bloody imp was undaunted. She smiled at him. A long, slow smile of mischievous intent, a happy, knowing curve of her plush mouth. "But I'm not a naval officer really, am I? Tonight, I can be just a girl. I can be out of uniform, because I shouldn't be in one at all. Isn't that what you really think?" The blithe mischief shone from her serene owl's face. "You have to admit that it makes better sense."

He did not have to admit to anything. And he wouldn't.

"I know," she said, before he could blast her plan out of the water. "It is a great risk. But a cap and sash can be easily discarded. And they will give you a better chance to get into the city, and to the arsenal and its magazines more easily."

Damn her for being so insightful. "And what's that?" He

pointed to several other items of clothing that were definitely not a cap and a sash.

The mischief in her dimmed, and she looked self-conscious—self-aware and even embarrassed, in a way he'd never thought to see her. "Nothing." Her voice became small. "I helped myself to some clean linen."

"It looks like a petticoat. And a shift."

"A chemise," she corrected.

"Kent?" He put a world of warning into his voice.

Even in the moonlight, she colored such an interesting shade of coral. "I thought . . . I thought perhaps I could move more easily through the streets if I were dressed as a woman. The Préfecture de Marine is in the center of the city, as are the magazines of the arsenal. It will be easier if we don't have to stay out of sight when someone passes. We can still be as quiet and stealthy as you like, but hiding in plain sight. Much more effective. And expedient."

Expediency would have to give way to honor, despite the temptations. "No. I don't like it. I should be embarrassed to have to report such trickery to Captain McAlden."

"Then don't report it. My father used to say the law of the Admiralty is, 'If you succeed, no question will be asked, but if you fail, no explanation will ever be enough.' All we have to do is succeed, and I know we can. I know we will."

Such surety. Such confidence in the rightness of her thoughts. He had to admit the idea was slowly acquiring merit. And the phrase "Tonight, I can be just a girl" echoed in his head, and sent a rush of pleasure so raw, it rumbled through his bones like the thunder of distant cannon fire.

He was tempted. More than tempted. But the embers of his need for her had already been stirred. It would take nothing more than the slightest breeze of a petticoat to fan his desire into flame. "I don't like it," he repeated, more to convince himself than her. But as the captain had told her the first day she had come aboard *Audacious,* he didn't have to like it, he just had to do it.

And the image of her clad in women's clothing had risen like an opium dream in his mind and would not go away, and he began to work out a way to make it possible. "We need to find a place to shelter for the day and stay out of sight."

"Yes," she agreed. "And you can fully recover."

He didn't like to think of himself as an invalid, but whenever he was sure the disorienting movement within his body had finally stopped, the road would rise up to meet him in disagreeable ways. But as always, Kent was there to catch him. And it felt good to sling his arm across her shoulder and snug her up tight. It felt better than good. It felt perfectly right. Thank God she was a strong little thing. Thank God she was as tough and determined as she was useful.

About a mile ahead, across a field to the southeast, at the top of a gentle rise, Col made out the ruins of an old stone barn in the graying light of early dawn. About half of the original building appeared to still be standing—one end was crumbled into disrepair—and it appeared fully abandoned.

"There." He directed her with a gesture of his chin, and together they turned through the hedgerow and up the rise.

They approached the tumbled building cautiously, with their pistols drawn, but it had long ago been abandoned. Weeds grew tall between the cobbles of the yard, and the air held no trace of the scent of animals. Above, the loft was still intact, with an empty window from which they could keep watch over the surrounding countryside and hopefully, when it was light, the harbor, which Col reckoned was near—the breeze brought them the familiar mud-salt smell of the sea.

Kent looked satisfied. "It seems a safe enough place to stay."

The scattered remnants of a pile of hay were strewn in a corner. He slouched against the wall where there was a good prospect down the hill toward the road. "Why don't you see if you can get some sleep?"

She didn't answer, but knelt down on the floor on the opposite side of the window, and unburdened herself of her stolen parcels of clothing and food, setting out the apples, bread, and cheese on a square of fabric. And then she simply looked at him and said, "Col."

Her use of his familiar name resonated through him like a bell, clear and strong.

"You're safe with me," she said. "Just as I've been safe with you."

The truth of her words rose in him slowly, like the tide, inexorable and inescapable.

"You've had a bad night," she went on, "and you need rest more than I do. For a little while, anyway. But you should try to eat first. It will settle your gut and make it easier to sleep." She handed him a wedge of cheese and a slice of apple.

"Is this what you do at home? Order everyone about and tend after them?"

Some of the sureness ebbed from her, leaving her quiet and perhaps a little sad. "No. Not now. There's no one left to tend to. Richard keeps to himself."

"I begin to see why you liked the orlop cockpit so well, even with Gamage's dampening presence."

She smiled. "I do so like those boys. And that's all sorted now, isn't it? Though I do hope nothing goes wrong with Gamage while I'm away. If he tries anything, I shouldn't put it past Will to dose him with Scotch bonnet powder again." A little frown pleated itself between her gingersnap eyebrows, as if she could still solve all the problems at such a distance, if only she concentrated enough.

"So you admit you poisoned him?"

Her smile dawned again over a bite of the apple. "Why not? Though it wasn't poisoning per se—I ate it, too. Although I will admit that the heavy dose of pepper powder did make the ragout, in the immortal words of Ian Worth, 'taste like arse.' "

He smiled, and ate while dawn lightened the sky over the silent fallow fields. The harvest had long since been taken in, and the fields remained empty—Bonaparte's insatiable hunger for soldiers for his Grand Army had likely robbed Finistère of the greater part of its working farmers.

Within minutes he slept, but for only a few hours, his body accustomed to the regular change of four-hour watches. He awoke to find the sun high, and the air still but for the occasional drone of a bee moving through the old farmyard in search of the last of the renegade wildflowers. The sun had warmed the fall crispness out of the day, and heat of its rays pressed warmth into the stone walls.

Kent had fallen asleep as well, drifting off against the wall by the open window, with her head tipped back against the stones and her mouth open with the softness of sleep. Her hand was lax on the handle of the pistol in her lap, and he eased it carefully from her grip.

It was her hair that started it. It shone like dark, spilled honey in the sunlight, glistening and shining, and calling for the touch of his hand—living silk between his fingers. And then, when she did not stir, and he was safe from the truth he would see in her eyes, he turned his hand and let the backs of his fingers graze across the broad speckled planes of her cheekbones, so liberally painted with freckles, vivid and warm dashed across the pale cream of her skin.

Would they be everywhere on her body, in as glorious a profusion as on her face? He imagined again what her skin might look like under the armor of her clothes—pale and painted with the dark landmarks of her freckles. Would they draw him in, the freckles marking her body, and make him want to kiss her, the way the dark spot just on the edge of her pink lip constantly drew his regard?

Just a kiss, he lied to himself. Just one. A moment, no more, while she was here, and they were away from all the eyes, and the ship, and the needy call of duty. While he had the chance to snatch something sweet and forbidden for his own.

He knew he shouldn't. He knew almost everything about his own need to kiss her was wrong—she was a subordinate, they were at war behind enemy lines with a dangerous mission to complete, and she was Matthew Kent's little sister, for God's sake.

But she was Matthew Kent's sister Sally, and he had wanted and waited so very long for her. For years and years. Forever.

And she looked so soft and appealing, attempting to

guard him, asleep in her rumpled clothes. Most of the junior officers were happy to move about the gunroom or the orlop compartment in only their shirtsleeves, but she, who had secrets to protect, kept herself assiduously hidden beneath layers of clothing.

He had kept her secret, but he could no longer keep himself from the soft lure of her honeyed skin. He could no longer resist. And furthermore, he didn't want to.

He kissed the corner of her mouth, where the smooth cream of her cheek gave way to the crushed berry of her lips. Her lips were not exactly soft—they were as chapped and windburned as his own—but they were plush and giving in the relaxation of her sleep.

With his lips upon her, she awoke. Her eyes fluttered open—such an incongruously, deeply feminine movement—and she smiled at him. A smile of such welcoming warmth—sleepy and rumpled, and happy—that all his good intentions were incinerated in an instant.

It was the smile that did him in. A smile steeped in dreams, with her eyes blinking slowly at him in wonderment. Muzzy with sleep. A smile of contentment, and who knew what else, because his brain gave up the need to think for the more immediate gratification of feeling, and he was moving closer to her, bringing her lithe body closer, until he was holding her against him. In response she made a soft sound of pleasure and welcome, and he was lost to the wonder of her warm gray eyes.

It seemed the most natural thing in the world to kiss her again. To taste her again. To let his mouth drift down until her lips were there, beneath his. And she was soft and warm and yielding, and he kissed her slowly, breathing into her, filling her with his resolution.

"Mr. Colyear," she whispered.

He laid his finger across her lips—plush and taut, and sweet, like ripe fruit. "Col," he murmured, as he lowered his head to her lips. "For God's sake, Kent, call me Col when I'm kissing you."

She smiled on an astonished little gust of laughter, and her lips were already open—open and tempting—and he could not resist deepening the kiss.

She tasted tart, like the green apples they had gleaned. Fresh and earthy. A woodland imp come to tempt him into delight.

Her hand found its way along the line of his jaw, and he turned into the sweet chafe of her palm, rubbing the rough texture of his incipient beard against her like an animal trained to her hand. He sounded like an animal, too. The near-howl of low pleasure that wound its way out of his chest was barely civilized.

He pressed closer, letting his gravity settle down into her, importuning her with the weight of his growing arousal. He tried to go slow, to hold the clawing need at bay, so he kissed her carefully, unsure of his welcome, waiting for her to pull back again. To tell him they oughtn't, to put him back onto the road to sanity. But she was kissing him, her mouth rising to meet his, her breath heating and tangling with his. And he was falling, falling into the improbable softness of her being, into the cinnamon-sugar sweetness of her lips. Her arms were around his neck, clinging to him, and then her hands speared into his hair, grasping his skull tightly, brushing and fisting into his queue as she pulled him closer.

He rolled with her in his arms and laid her down, pressing into her. The scent of crushed hay rose around them, wreathing them in the last breath of summer. He nosed his way behind her ear, where her hectic pulse beat under the fragile surface of her skin, where the scent of girl and apple mixed with the light perfume of soap and the heavy base notes of oak and tar on her coat. And he wanted more. He wanted, he wanted, he wanted.

He wanted to taste more than her mouth. He wanted to take her into himself and keep her there. He wanted her to be his in the most basic, primitive way possible. To bind her to him. He wanted to subsume her, to take her into himself and make her a part of him. And he wanted to be a part of her.

He rose up on his elbows to feel the lithe strength of her long body beneath him, to watch as his hands roamed over her of their own accord, searching out every interesting nook and exquisite curve. He kissed her closed eyes, and the soft spot beneath her ear, and the long line of her jaw, and lower, down the endless cascade of her neck, where he plied his teeth along the sensitive tendon, nipping his way to her collarbone. She shivered and sighed and tilted her head, all soft, yielding concession. He followed his lips with his hands, stripping away the knot in her black silk stock, pushing aside the lapels of her jacket, and undoing the long row of buttons down the front of her waistcoat.

And she was helping him, shrugging one arm out of her coat, only to leave off and attack the buttons on his coat as well. She would work three or four loose at a time and then seek his mouth for another intoxicating kiss. He couldn't order his thoughts enough to effectively disrobe either of them, but it didn't matter. One way or another, they would get it done.

"You'd think I'd know how to get breeches unfastened." He kissed her nose, because it was there and it was attached to her. "But I've never gone at it from this angle before."

"Nor I." She was all laughing, tumultuous curiosity, with her beautiful, intelligent gray eyes wide open, watching his every move. He wanted to keep that fiery smile, that impish curiosity on her face. He wanted to extend their stolen moments into hours. He was so glad he was with her, and no other. With Sally Kent. "You're so bloody wonderful. You have no idea how long I've waited for you."

At his words, everything about her, all her sleek, strong edges, softened. She sighed into him and took his lip between hers, nipping and sucking lightly, learning the way of him, until she grew bolder. When she closed her mouth around his, and took his tongue into her mouth, his need became like a current rising in a storm, fast and driven. The taste of her mouth was like water, and he was nothing but a salt bed, parched and dry.

With Sally Kent, there was no coy retreat or astonishment. There was wonder and discovery. Her kiss was as lush

and welcoming as he had dreamed, night after frustrating
night in the hellish confines of his gunroom cuddy.

He speared his big hand into her hair, disrupting the
silken queue, cradling her small skull, holding her still so
he could angle her head to kiss her more deeply. He all but
dove into her, holding her hard against him, pulling her into
him as if he could absorb her essence, her very being.

She spoke, calling his name in little gasping pants of
astonishment. "Col," she said with every kiss, as if she were
trying to convince herself it was real, that he was real, and
that they were truly alone together, with no ship full of
other people or walls between them now. There was nothing to stop them. Nothing but several layers of cotton duck
clothing.

And he wanted it off. He wanted her to himself, completely and irrevocably. He wanted to taste her everywhere.
He wanted to touch her everywhere. He wanted to see her
everywhere. God, how he wanted to know everything there
was to know about her. To leave no part of her body unex-
plored or facet of her mind unexperienced.

He went at her clothes the way he went at everything,
with a single-minded concentration that drove him like a
ship before the wind. For a tall girl, she was light and agile,
and he spread his palm across her back and scooped her up
as easily as if she were made of driftwood, instead of strong
muscled flesh and bone, so he could strip her blue midshipman's coat away. She was as impatient as he, pulling free her
arm and divesting herself of the waistcoat to fling it aside,
already forgotten.

And then she sat up, and lifted her shirt over her head,
and she was halfway to naked. Her bare arms and shoulders
were pale and dusted with golden freckles the color of mar-
malade, and he wanted to lick every last one, but she was not
yet undressed. Around her breasts was the layer of wide cotton strips that wound around her like a shroud. She twisted
to reach the binding.

"Kent. Let me."

He unfurled her slowly, like a spinnaker, set loose to

capture the lightest breeze. But she wasn't a ship or a sail. She was a girl, hidden under all that blue coat, and competence and skill. She was a warm, pink-and-white girl, with small, perfect apricot-tinted breasts.

Col could only look at her, and marvel at the delicate perfection of her, this creature who had dragged him across half of France. It must have been through willpower alone, for she seemed as fragile as a bird. The architecture of her bones was as beautifully perfect and balanced as any ship's spars—trim, nimble, and fast.

He looked and looked at her, drowning in his wonder, until she grew shy under his gaze and reached to cover herself. He could not allow it. He had to see her, to savor the beauty of her body—the wonderous unique strength of her.

He took her hands in his and spread them wide, and after he had decided that her nipples were the exact color of the inside of a tropical seashell, he began to kiss his way toward them. He kissed first the back of one hand, and then the pale pulse at the inside of her wrist on the other, working his way from side to side, from the sensitive joint of her elbow, to the exquisite hollow beneath her collarbone, until she opened her arms and fell back, granting him unlimited access to the treasure of her body. He kissed the soft, scented underside of her breast, and nuzzled his cheek along its sensitive peak, and only when she arched her back, raising herself up to him in silent plea, did he take the tight coral bud of her nipple into his mouth and suck lightly at her breast.

She made a sound of deep pleasure, like the strum of a well-tuned instrument, that vibrated through her and into him. He strummed and stroked her again, playing her to his touch, learning the way of her. And she helped, this responsive, tumultuous girl. Her hands were in his hair, cradling his head, holding and directing him to kiss her breasts and lavish her with pleasure.

It gave him an extraordinary amount of pleasure as well, brewing deep in his bones and surging deep into his soul. The taste and smell and feel of her beneath his hands and tongue only served to heighten his arousal and feed his insatiable hunger. And he wanted more. It was not nearly enough to see only her breasts revealed. He needed to see all of her. He wanted every last inch of male clothing stripped from her long restless body.

But as the last of the buttons on her wide nankeen trousers came free and she raised her hips to shimmy free of them, he had his first glimpse of her vividly colored mons. He all but froze, poleaxed by the splendor of her body as she worked the trousers down off her legs. And there she was.

The freckled skin of her body was like the night sky set on fire—a different sort of Milky Way filled with constellations as yet unmapped.

"Col?" She was looking up at him with eyes pressed wide with concern. "Are you all right? Has everything shifted again?"

Everything had shifted. "Nothing's wrong. You're naked. And you're beautiful."

She tucked her chin down to hide the sweep of pleasure blossoming across her face. "And you're not. Naked."

"By God, I will be." He sat back to pull off his boots and she came to her knees to kneel before him with her hands on her thighs, an erotic, supplicant odalisque, waiting patiently for him to take off his clothes for her.

The sound that tunneled out of his chest was something in the space between a sigh and a groan. It was going to kill him, the wanting her. And his damn boot wouldn't come off.

Kent misinterpreted the sound of his nearly painful frustration. "Col." She reached for his shoulder. "What's wrong?"

"Nothing's wrong," he repeated. "You're naked and you're beautiful, and my boot won't come off."

She reached for his boot then, slapping the back of his heel hard before she slid it off. And he was up and shucking his breeches, and scooping up his coat so he could throw it over the hay, and picking her up and carrying her down, and kissing her. Kissing and kissing her while his body sought out the exquisite torture of her blissful heat.

She felt so bloody, bloody good, so wonderful, he couldn't

think. He could only feel and want. And what he wanted was her. All of her.

He was reaching down to guide himself into her body and pressing himself within. Into her scalding heat.

The rush of ecstasy felt so sharp and so raw he couldn't breathe, and he didn't need to. He didn't need anything but her and the fiercely beautiful friction of her body ever again.

Chapter Seventeen

The pain was a shock—unexpected and abrupt. His occupation of her body knocked the breath from her. Until that moment of intimate possession, it had been like a dream, a deep dream state of incendiary bliss and overwhelming sensation—a delirious suspension of reality and time and consequence. It had felt so good, the extraordinary, blissful rush of pleasure. Until it stopped.

"Are you all right?" His beautiful face was suspended above hers, his forehead creased with a touching mixture of anguish and concern. His eyes, so deep and warm and green—how had she ever thought them hard?—watched her, searching her face for her every reaction. It was remarkable, and utterly overwhelming, to be the object of that singularly focused attention, all that intimate concern.

"I . . . I think so." It wasn't much pain. It was only the slightest burning pinch, and there was something about it—the wonder and bliss that hovered behind it, not entirely gone, but hiding. Although she was uncomfortable, now that they seemed to be done. His long, strong body was heavy upon hers, but heavier still was the pressing tension within. She wanted something else. She wanted that heady rush and tumble of sensations, the pleasure and even the pain, to continue. But mostly, she wanted something else. Something more.

"Do you think, you could . . . say it? My name? Like you did before?"

Would he understand? Would he think her weak or needy—girlish—for asking?

"Sally." He said her name instantly, and then over and over, punctuating each recitation with a kiss. "Sally. I'm sorry. I should have realized—"

He kissed her face, again and again, moving slowly from the corner of her mouth to her nose and then to the surprisingly, achingly sensitive tendons at the side of her neck, where they slid down to meet her collarbone. She turned her head away to grant him access, to give him greater scope for his tender explorations and closed her eyes as heat began to rekindle within, and her body heated with a rush that made her feel feverish and nearly uncomfortable. Little shocks of feeling sparked through her hands, and left her fingers tingling.

Wanting more.

"I want . . ." Except she didn't really know what *more* she wanted.

Col must have heard the embarrassed frustration in her voice.

His smiled faded, and then reappeared, turned upon himself. "God, look at us." Around them, a tangle of clothes was strewn about the loft of a half-destroyed, abandoned barn deep in the French countryside. "We have no bloody idea what we're doing, do we?"

She didn't have time to agree, because he had framed her face with his hands, and was looking at her again, in that focused way, seeing everything she was feeling, every bit of needy, confused yearning, in her face. "It doesn't matter," he assured her. "We'll figure it out. It only matters that we're together. We'll go slowly and figure it out, and you'll tell me what you like."

She reached out to stroke along the long line of his strong jaw, his beautiful face. His handsome, perfect, dear face, made rough and masculine by the shadow of whiskers. He looked dark and dangerous, and so very far from her restrained, controlled lieutenant. "I like you," she answered. "Very much."

His smile came on slowly, growing and spreading, like a sunset, until it was nearly blinding in its beauty. "That's a very good place to start, Sally Kent, because I like you, too. I like you very much. This much."

He began to kiss her again, taking her mouth in slow, exaggerated nips. His tongue advanced into her mouth by degrees, seeking her out, asking without words for her to join him. To taste him. To feel him in every way that she could.

His lips were firm and almost rough, made taut by the sun and wind, and she was taken by the need to catch his lower lip between her teeth to nip and play, to appease the inappeasable yearning that grew from something deep inside, a ravenous hunger for more of him that she could no longer control.

"Yes," his whisper encouraged her. His body began to move in time with his mouth, undulating into her, pulsing burgeoning heat and delicious friction through her veins.

"Oh." The word was something close to a moan. "I'm getting some idea now."

"As am I, my Sally girl. As am I." His smile widened across his face, wry and deeply amused, crinkling up the corners of those hot green eyes focused so powerfully on her. "All sorts of ideas."

She began to move with him and a drop of pleasure fell from some great height inside her, and spread in rippling waves, growing and unfurling within until it was lapping at the very edges of her being. It was beautiful and fierce, this bliss building within her, pushing her apart, breaking her into a thousand different pieces of desire. She held on to him, anchoring herself to his strength. She held on to Col, her rock, her salvation.

Her hands were on the curved muscles of his arms, flexing and sculpted, strong where they lifted the small of her back, arching her into him, urging her to join him. So she did, because with each surge of his body into hers, the landscape of what was possible shifted, opening up unmapped continents of experience, uncharted oceans of desire.

Everything was new and intriguing. The feel and taste of his warm skin beneath her hands and mouth. The sight of his naked, muscled splendor. The sound of his pleasure as she stroked her fingers across his flesh. She wanted more of the tang of his mouth, more of the firm tantalizing pressure of his lips slanting across her mouth, opening her to his pleasure. And the more he pressed, the more she enjoyed, and the more she enjoyed, the more she wanted. The more they kissed, the more she felt his kisses elsewhere, and not just on her lips, or on the side of her neck as he made his way down to her collar. The heated sensations were spreading, winding in a serpentine path throughout her body, spiraling into her chest, turning and coiling deep within her very core.

"Col." She said his name, over and over, because it seemed the only thing she could say, the only thing she needed to say. He was all she wanted, all she needed. His hands stroking her body, his lips kissing her mouth, his body pulsing deep within hers.

She grappled her arm around his neck and pulled herself flush against him, glorying in the long strength of him and the delicious friction of his chest against hers, as she wrapped her legs around him. She slid her fingers into his glossy, dark hair, fisting up the black curls, holding him to her so she could fill her desperate longing for the taste and feel of his lips on hers, pressing into her, hard and deliberate.

There was nothing of subtlety or finesse in him. Or in her. She was ungovernable in this hungry need that rose up inside her. She gloried in the firm grasp of his hands against her bottom guiding her to him. She dug her own hands into the sure strength of his shoulders, holding on to him as wave after wave of drowning pleasure crashed over her.

Above her, Col looked as if the bliss would consume him. His head was thrown back and he was gulping in air, as if he had to shut his eyes to keep it all contained within him. But still he smiled.

This was her Col. This was the memory she had carried

within for six long years, this man who laughed and loved and learned everything with such dedication. With such beauty and power and strength. The movement of his body grew stronger, more emphatic, and so did the tantalizing pleasure. Everything—every feeling, every thought, every need—intensified, and left her greedy and grasping at each riotous burst of sensation, each tempting pulse of blissful delight, straining to reach some greater portion of bliss.

"Sally. My God, Sally." Her name on his lips was all she needed to urge her on forward down the river of her desire, to propel her over some unseen edge.

She was drenched in bliss, drowning, sinking until she was fighting the dark undertow of need, straining and kicking her way to the surface. And then everything changed, and ended, and began. Bliss detonated within her and she was floating at last, warm and sated, and free.

She might have dozed; so strong was the feeling of languor that she felt as if her very bones had melted in the heat of their conflagration. Col had rolled off her slightly, to relieve her of his weight and let her breathe, but still he held her close. One arm was wrapped around her middle and the other was tangled in her hair, tethering her to his warm side.

He needn't hold on so tight—she wasn't going anywhere. Indeed, with long hours of daylight stretching ahead, there was no place else she would rather be than naked in his equally naked arms. She wanted to make the delicious intimacy, the heady feeling of being enclosed by his strong protective arms, last as long as possible.

She nestled closer, rolling so she could rest her head on his chest, and hear the solid cadence of his heart thudding slowly back to normal beneath her. Except that it accelerated slightly the moment she let her hands play across the smooth skin of his chest. Curiosity, and perhaps some small vestige of feminine instinct hidden deep within, urged her to trail her fingers around the circumference of his flat nipples. Just the thought of how she had felt, of the exquisite sensations that had cascaded through her own breasts when he had done exactly that same thing to her, sent a spasm of want spiraling deep into her belly.

"Playing with fire, are we?" His voice rumbled through his chest and directly into her ear.

"Yes." She smiled against the smooth curve of his chest. "My fingers are already singed, and I don't have any butter, so I've got to find a way to ease them somehow."

"Umm." He turned her away from him and gathered her back against his chest, rolling them to their sides. His arm encircled her waist from below and his leg was thrown over her hip, enveloping her in his warmth. "A well-known cure for burns. But I think I may know just where to get some butter. And honey."

His fingers opened to splay and press into her belly, urging her back against his growing arousal, and Sally felt every muscle tauten and tense with anticipation, as his mouth nuzzled against her nape.

"Do you?" She could hear the needy gratification in her voice, the edge of breathlessness wondering for what was to come.

"Oh, yes." His voice echoed quietly from just behind her ear, as he slowly loosened the fist from her hair, and skated his palm down, across her collarbone and through the valley of her breasts, over the flat plane of her belly and lower, until his fingers teased the rim of her navel.

Sally wanted to stretch and curl up all at the same time, but he held her fast, so the quivers shook themselves deeper under her skin.

"You like that, do you?" She could feel the teasing smile in his voice.

"Almost as much as I like you."

"Almost?" His hand trailed lower, sliding into the curls at the apex of her tightly clenched thighs. "Perhaps I can do something about that. Perhaps . . ."

His clever articulate fingers slid into her folds and Sally could feel the slick moisture of her body rise to his touch, easing his passage.

"Col." His name was both benediction and prayerful plea.

"Yes," he murmured in answer, and speared another finger into her along with the first, filling her with need, cupping and holding her at the threshold of yearning.

"Col," she said again, because she had nothing else to say, no words to encourage or plead with him to continue, to help fill the aching void that opened within her at his slightest touch. The void that only he could fill with his body.

But somehow, he understood. Or perhaps he was deviled by the same hungry demons, by the same yawning need. He withdrew his fingers from her heat in order to ease her thighs apart, his hand gentle but insistent on the inside of her knee.

In another breath Sally felt the velvet probe of his body against her entrance, and she arched her head back as pleasure pulsed across the surface of her skin and he slid deep into her body.

Her exhalation was a gasp, of gratified shock and wanton delight. She had known that such a thing—such a position—was possible. Indeed, it had been impossible to grow up in her world, with its dockyard whores and 'tween deck doxies, not to understand that human congress could take such a shape. But she had no earthly idea of how it would *feel* to be so utterly and entirely possessed by him. To be so surrounded and subsumed by him, the smell and taste and texture of him, that she felt the very air she drew into her lungs had come from him.

It was fierce and primitive and undeniably arousing to feel such possession. To feel a part of him. To feel, as her need pushed her over the brink, that at long last, they had become as one.

Col made love to Sally Kent until the dusk began to settle over them, and the ebbing rush of their breath echoed from the stone walls of the loft and made him aware, once more, of where they were. And what they were supposed to be doing. Of what they had just done.

God Almighty. What *had* he done?

They had been at it for what felt like hours and his breeches were still tangled around his ankles. His shirt and waistcoat were nowhere within sight, he had flung them off with such abandon. His coat he didn't even remember removing. And his heart was still hammering away like a carpenter in his chest. He was completely done in.

And he had never been so glad.

"You have straw in your hair." Her voice was nothing more than a wisp of sound, but he could hear the gentle warmth and the sweet intimacy. He turned to regard her beneath him, all vivid beauty and honeyed warmth.

He didn't have the heart to rush. After what they had done, another moment or two hardly mattered. And once they left, they would have no further chance at this lovely closeness, this glorious, naked intimacy. He rolled onto his side and reached for her. To keep her near. "Shows what you know. It's hay. And it's in your hair, too."

"Is it?" She exhaled another smile and reached up to comb her fingers through her gorgeous, blazing mane to find the offending pieces.

"Here, let me." It was just an excuse to run his fingers through the vibrant waterfall, and let the rough silk slide through his fingers.

When had he become such a sensualist?

The moment Sally Kent had climbed aboard, and his life and everything else—self-discipline and restraint—seemed to have gone over the rail. But now it would be easier. They had it out of their systems. They could concentrate on the tasks at hand, now that they had put paid to this infernal attraction once and for all.

Speaking of which. "I'm sorry to say this, Sally love, but we need to press on."

"Of course." She began reaching for discarded items of clothing.

He rolled onto his back and began to hitch his breeches on over his hips and button up the fall. She smiled at him over her shoulder and she looked so appealing, so sweet and soft, it was everything he could do to keep putting on his shirt instead of pulling her back beneath him and taking her again.

Goddamn his eyes. What had he been thinking? He had just tupped Sally Kent, the sister of his oldest and closest friends, on the floor of a barn, and he had barely gotten his boots off.

And he wanted to do it again.

The heat washing his torso ought to be shame. He ought to feel scorched by it. He ought to be rehearsing his apologies. He, who had never been rash and impetuous, had been just that, making love to this tumultuous, irresistible girl without any thought as to where they were and where they had to go. No thought at all as to the consequences.

"Kent. Sally," he corrected. "I— Are you all right?"

"I'm fine." She smiled and turned away, and began to collect the rest of her scattered clothes, rising to walk across the room in all her naked glory, completely unaware of her effect. Or her effect on him.

If he didn't know better, he wouldn't think it her first time. She was handling this business of being ruined with far greater aplomb than he appeared to be. By all rights, the virgin daughter of such a man as Captain Alexander Kent ought to be tearfully expecting a proposal.

The thought of fathers in general, and that father in particular, chilled the breath in his lungs. "I'm sorry. We shouldn't—I shouldn't. I should have known better." He ran his hand through his hair. "I regret—"

"Don't." Her voice was low and soft, but decisive, and Col had been in the senior service long enough to know an order when he heard it. "Please." She smiled, but he could see the sheen of tears at the corners of those wide gray eyes. "I can stand anything but regret. I know it was a mistake. But it was a glorious one. And I don't ever want to regret it. Ever."

Col knew he ought to say something to comfort her, to reassure her that he felt no regret, but Kent wasn't the kind of person who wanted empty assurances. She would see through them in less time than it took him to spout them. Especially now, with the impossibility and danger of their assignment looming before them, with their very lives in mortal danger. It did not seem to be the most propitious time for a proposal.

Yet there were other dangers. "What about the consequences? What if—"

"You needn't worry, Col. I know my duty. And we both know that our duty comes first."

She hadn't understood his meaning, but he was glad she understood that nothing could change between them at present. They still had an enormous task to do. "Yes. It does." Was that relief, the cool feeling washing through his gut? "I'm glad you understand."

"I've always understood that, Col. Now what have you got planned?"

It *was* a relief to move back to the solid ground of duty. "I've been thinking about the captain's desire for us to make the French put to sea. I don't like the idea generally, but I'm convinced what will do the most damage is a fireship."

"Why don't you like it?"

He waved her question away. It would take too long to explain his almost irrational, visceral dislike of the destruction of a ship by fire, when he was only too happy to destroy any number of French ships by blasting them to pieces at point-blank range. "The problem is that we'll need two ships, one for the fire and the other as a prize, to get us back to *Audacious*. Not to mention a boat to get us out to the ships in the first place."

"Three vessels then. But for the last, something like a ketch or a sloop, that can sail close to the wind and make it out through the narrows of Le Goulet into the teeth of these devilish prevailing westerlies?"

"Exactly."

Col moved toward the open window, where the daylight proved that the rise did indeed provide a view to the south, all the way across the expansive roadstead of the bay, and east toward the city of Brest. From their vantage point, they could count the number of sail at anchor, and observe the movements and manning of the enemy vessels. He turned to retrieve his satchel, only to find Kent handing him his telescopic glass.

He didn't even have to explain. He could rely on her. He

had been relying on her all night to get him across the countryside. God only knew what he would have done had he been on his own, or with someone less clever than Kent. "Tell me what you see."

She was already focusing her glass on the harbor, counting with minute nods of her head. "Twenty . . . one sail of the line. Lord, what a fleet. Four three-deckers, four frigates, two corvettes, two brigs, and one cutter. The ships of the line seem to be anchored close in to one another. But we'll have to find a fairly large ship to fire in order to put the cat amongst the pigeons." She swept the glass to the east side of the bay.

Col followed suit, focusing on a worn-out-looking ketch apart from the others. "Do you see her, the *Belle Ile*? She should do to set afire. Doesn't look like much crew, if any." His gaze swung back to rake the beach front, taking note of the activity, which in the heat of the day wasn't much. Some of the French people's ardor for the Grand Empire seemed to have worn off in the waning days of the autumn.

"What about the *St. Etienne*? Off the west side of the city, the part they call Recouvrance? A *chaloupe* rigged for coastal trade. You could use her to take another vessel."

Col swung his glass back. "Call it a sloop, damn you." But he hoped there was warmth in his voice, as he only meant to tease her. "She will do well. Let us pray she remains there tonight. But if we draw enough people off the beach, or at least into the city, we should have our pick."

"How do you plan we do that?"

"We'll do to the city what we will do to the harbor—fire it. We'll set fires as we go."

"We'll have to make it through the gates first, with our satchels and weapons. That will only work with the clothes." She gestured to the neat pile of purloined clothing.

"We'll never make it through the gates, even in purloined clothing. Not with your red hair."

She was nothing if not stubborn. "These Breton are Celts. There may be redheads among them."

"Too chancy. I'd rather see if we can get a boat upstream

and ride it inconspicuously downriver into the city. But you are right. The uniforms must go."

The smile she gifted him with was his reward for being perceptive. She pulled some clothes out of the bundle. "Here. These might do for you, if you'll have them."

It was a tightly knitted jersey of faded blue-gray and a pair of equally faded, wide, dark trousers—what any fisherman or sailor of this coast might wear. He felt a right idiot in clothes other than his own, and it occurred to him that for the past twelve years he had never worn anything but his uniform. But evidently, the time had come.

The jersey fit, mostly because it stretched, but the wide trousers were going to be too broad and short by half. But if he used his sword belt to cinch them up, they would serve. Or at least keep him from being spotted for a British officer. "I feel naked without my uniform. Like a knight without his armor."

"Lord. What a pair we make." Behind him, Kent's voice sounded quiet, subdued somehow. "I—I'm not sure what I can do with my sword. Or the gun. I didn't think of that, when—"

"My God." He hadn't meant to say anything, but it just came out. He might have felt naked—she all but was.

She looked the same, and yet remarkably different. She looked, without the uniform that had turned her into one of a set of six midshipmen, unique and decidedly feminine. The neckline of the bodice was scooped, and for the first time, he saw the long elegant line of her neck slide down to her shoulders. The delicate knobs of her collarbone framed the speckled swath of skin above the rounded rise of her breasts, and he wanted to touch her there, along the fragile ridge of her shoulder, and let his fingers sweep down to dip beneath the edge of the bodice.

Her hair was tumbled over her shoulders and her mouth was open, ever so slightly, in an unspoken question, and her lower lip looked plush and soft, and it made him wonder how anyone could not see what was to him so obvious.

"What's wrong?" Her forehead was pleated with concern, as if she thought him still weak and unsteady.

He shook his head to negate such a thought, all the while letting his eyes wander down her form, over the worn cotton shift and faded bodice of indeterminate color and undoubted antiquity, to the shabby quilted cotton petticoats and apron that did remarkably little to hide the fact that she was an enormously attractive, well-formed girl.

It wasn't jealousy that licked its greedy flames at his gut this time, but something stronger. Something that made him want to wrap her up in the obscuring folds of his sea cloak rather than let any other man see what he ogled so voraciously.

It was possessiveness, pure and raw and anything but simple.

"Everything is wrong. We'll never pass unnoticed with you looking like that. The damned Frenchmen will be all over you like musket fire."

She did not mistake his meaning. She wasn't coy, his Kent. Only the fact that her wide, happy smile was all for him appeased him. "But you'll be my Frenchman. And you'll keep their eyes from me."

"I may be able to keep their hands off, but I'll never be able to do anything about their eyes. We've got to make you more unattractive."

She took him seriously. "Some dirt should suffice. But I'm sure the long walk to the river north of here will get us hot and sweaty enough to look rumpled. And from a small boat, in the dark, it shouldn't matter. We'll put the weapons in the bottom, along with the clothes." She spoke slowly, as if she were reckoning it out as she went. "I should row, so you can look ahead, with you—how can we disguise your intent? The wine bottle perhaps, so you'll appear drunk. Yes, drunk and singing, and lolling about the stern, letting me do all the work. Yes! Can you not see it?"

He could, damn her clever eyes. Her enthusiasm was potent and her logic hard to resist. Everything about her, especially dressed like this earthy French girl, made her hard to resist.

He should have been sated. He should have been so replete with satisfaction that thoughts of the pleasure he had received from her body ought not even cross his mind. He ought to have been self-disciplined enough to haul such thoughts back into line.

But when she poured the greater part of the stolen bottle down the front of his jersey, and advised him to gargle with the rest—"So you'll smell like stale wine"—he gave in to his lesser instincts.

"You'd better kiss me before I do. For good luck."

He meant it to be brief and easy—a quick smacking kiss. But she was sweet and solemn when she walked to him, and touched his face, and rose on her tiptoes to kiss him. The moment her lips met his, he became hungry for her again, for more of the drugging softness, more of the pleasure that streamed through his veins like an opiate.

God help him or the devil take him, if he could bottle her, he would, so he might take a taste of her every day for the rest of his life. Because they didn't have the luxury of time. Their future was as precarious as a jury-rigged sloop.

"Kent, we shouldn't."

"I know, but I want to anyway. Is that very bad?"

"Very. But I'll tell you what, Kent. Help me burn down Brest, or blow a ship up, and I'll make love with you for a very, very long time as a reward."

She laughed with all the glee only she could feel at the thought of such wanton destruction. "Done."

Col helped her gather up the weapons. "I hope to hell I don't regret this."

Chapter Eighteen

It had sounded so simple in the shelter of the barn. Their improvised plan began well enough, though she was as tense as a racehorse, heading down the river with her load of ridiculously grumpy-for-no-particular-reason lieutenant. He was only meant to *act* drunk and ornery.

She was meant to look as old and worn as an ill-used donkey, so she kept her head down and rowed, letting the flow of the water push them downriver as dusk began to darken the sky, while she reviewed their tentative plan—to stop wherever the quays were deserted and set opportunistic fires nearby as a diversion, before they found a ship to fire and send at the French fleet.

"Remember," Col repeated Captain McAlden's words, as they rounded the last bend in the river and approached the ramparts denoting the heart of the city, "anything to cause confusion."

The plan was like Col, sound and effective. But at the moment he looked neither.

He was arrayed in a drunken sprawl in the stern, humming away like the sot he was meant to be, though he kept a careful watch on the river at her back as she rowed.

"Pull a little bit harder for the west bank. If I look hard enough, I can see your breasts through your bodice."

"Chut." She tried to make a French sound of dismissal,

before she lowered her voice. "You're meant to be too drunk to notice such things."

"A man is never too drunk to notice such things." His green eyes were bright and shining with something sharper than simple lust. "It only helps a little that you're as dirty as a coal barge."

"*Merci, mon coeur.* Now, *chut,*" she hissed. Over her shoulder the ramparts of the city walls loomed over the river. She began to mutter to herself in French, in hopeful imitation of Gallic invective. "*Cochon.* Pig. *Peste.*"

There were two guards stationed on the ramparts' water gate, leaning against the wall and talking to each other. She was trying to keep well out of the pockets of illumination from the great torches set into the side of the battlements, but Col spoke low and urgent.

"Handsomely now, Kent. Let them see you. Slow down and act tired. You have nothing to hide. Except, of course, your breasts." Though he did casually kick the bundle of their uniforms deeper under the stern sheets.

Sally did as he bid, kept her shoulders hunched and her head down.

"*Alors, ma belle,*" a suggestive hail came from somewhere above, high on the walls. "*Votre homme—il est mort?*"

"He wants to know if you're dead," Sally translated quietly for Col. "And at the moment I'm tempted to oblige." In answer to the hail, she shifted her shoulders theatrically, in hopes of achieving the casually callous indifference that was the Gallic shrug. "*Mort de vin,*" she slurred as sourly as possible, before she shot a look at Col. "Dead drunk," she whispered. And kept on rowing.

Low hoots of laughter followed them, but they were past. As night settled low and dark into the fortified city, she followed Col's instruction to steer them alongside a quay on the west bank. She would have tied the boat off but Col whispered, "Don't make the painter fast. Just hold it steady and be at the ready to shove off."

He made a show of heaving himself up onto the quayside, and made his misguided way across the open space with the unsteady, rolling pace peculiar to drunken sailors the world over, and turned down an alley, presumably to answer the call of nature.

Sally was torn between wanting to watch for him, and keeping herself as inconspicuous as possible, slouching low against the quayside to avoid the gaze of both the soldiers on the rampart beyond and anyone passing by. But as the first few minutes passed with no sign of Col, her nerves began to get the better of her. A bell from a nearby church began to toll the hour, and by the time twelve full strokes had rung out over the city, Sally's heart was pounding in time with every clang.

Col finally appeared, wandering seemingly aimlessly back out across the open space, walking in an unhurried, uneven fashion toward Sally and the boat, even though she could see the licking flames of fire beginning in the alley behind.

But still he came slowly, until she thought she would scream, before he finally dropped into his posture of drunken relaxation in the stern of the boat. "Pull hard downstream."

Sally bent to the oars for all she was worth, until she was nearly out of breath from the combination of fear and excitement, and the strange exhilaration of watching Col tackle both his role and his duty with such daring élan. Yet, she could only see behind, and she was transfixed as the eerie orange glow grew brighter, leaping from one thatched or tiled rooftop to another until it seemed to consume even the massive city ramparts.

"Au feu!" The cry of fire went up, and a bell began to peal out the alarm.

Sally felt the terror of the greedy flames as only a sea person could. She paused at the oars to stare as the fire grew larger, and the townspeople began to be silhouetted against the orange glow of the flames.

"Steady on, Kent," Col told her. "And for fuck's sake, keep rowing."

Three stops on the west bank—near the monastery of the Capuchin monks, near the buildings of the more heavily guarded arsenal, and lower still, across from the buildings of the fortress itself—three fires, all growing slowly to light up the night.

And as they went, the alarm bells followed, clanging out from church steeples and bell towers, until it seemed half the city must be awake. And still, on they went.

She stayed in the boat, because he ordered her to, and because in the beginning, it seemed like a smart plan. But she was no good at waiting. And when he instructed her to pull up to the east quay, just upriver from the fortress, she could no longer hold her tongue.

"Col, I'm coming with you."

"No." Both his face and his voice were grim and determined, as if he had already battened himself down to withstand her.

It was beyond ridiculous. "Why are you deliberately trying to stop me from helping you? I could—"

"No. You're helping me by staying in the boat."

"The boat is fine on its own. It doesn't need me to defend it. I could be so much more useful if you would let me—"

"No." He hit the bottom of his voice. Bedrock with no further leeway.

"Why not?"

"Because I said no." Sally could practically see the frustration and exasperation coming off him in waves. "Because I'm still your commanding officer, Kent. Just because we fucked doesn't give you the right to challenge my authority."

Sally had never been slapped before, but she reckoned this was what it must feel like—scalding heat scorching her face and a topsy-turvy feeling wringing up her innards, as if she were being churned up in a wave.

But she was a Kent, and she would damn well give as good as she got. She made her words hit back. "You may be my commanding officer, *Mister* Colyear, but that doesn't make you any less of a *cad*. And just because we *fucked*"—it hurt to even say the word—"is no reason for you to start treating me as if I hadn't a brain in my head, or an ounce of usefulness in my fingers."

"Jesus, Kent. I don't have time—"

"Sally." She made her voice firm and positive, even though she felt anything but. The knot of doubt sitting at the bottom of her stomach like day-old porridge wouldn't go away. She'd thought it all such an adventure. She'd thought it was worth it for the beautiful experience of being loved by Col that afternoon. She'd thought nothing but Col mattered. But now everything had changed. But the devil could take her before she'd let him ruin it without a fight. "It's *Sally,* Col, Sally, until the minute we get back on board *Audacious* and I have to act like you don't exist. But until that moment, I do exist, and you"—she jabbed a finger at his chest—"need me."

"I can do this better alone." Col was as immovable as a granite boulder, solid and hard. And just as wrong.

"You couldn't have done *any* of this"—she threw her arms wide—"if you'd been alone. You would probably still be facedown in a stream, not a mile from the coast, if you'd been *alone.*"

"Damn you, Kent. Damn your fine gray eyes." His voice broke, cracked open like a spilled yolk. "Don't you understand?" He grabbed up a fistful of her bodice and hauled her flush against his chest. "I can't protect you if you don't stay in the damn boat. If you don't stay in the goddamn boat, and something happens to me—if I'm shot or taken—the only thing that will keep me sane, the only thing, is knowing that you can get away. That you are so capable, you will find a way to steal a damned ketch all by your bloody self and sail it all the way through Le Goulet and back to bloody fucking Falmouth. You don't fucking understand."

The anguish in his voice lashed at her, punishing her for her intransigence. But she was a Kent, devil take her, and she had come too far, and done and said too much to back down now. He had to understand as well. "*Ask* me. Nicely."

The wind went out of his sails for a moment. But only a moment, before he took a deep breath and *asked*. "Please. Please, Sally Kent. Will you please stay with the goddamn boat, so I can—"

"Yes, thank you, I will. So go."

He kissed her, hard, as if he could press his will upon her.

And then went away at a run, and Sally had to swallow the cold heat of her own fears and misgivings, and wait. The bells from the church towers were still tolling out their warnings, and it seemed to Sally as if there could not possibly be a person left in the city who did not know they were under some sort of an attack. Who would not be looking out for just such a person as David Colyear, skulking in their shadows and lighting their world on fire?

And while she was postulating dire predictions, Col came back at a run, low and fast, all but jumping into the boat.

"Pull," he ordered, his breath full of strain. "Hard and fast." He looked back up the street as she yanked the painter free and pushed them off.

"Who is after you?"

"Just row, damn it. Or let me." He moved to take the oars from her.

"No." She shook him off as the heavy tramp of boots echoed down the street and across the water. "Not even you can row that fast. I've got a better plan." It wasn't a plan really, just a crazy idea, born of fear and desperation, and the thought that people only ever see what they are looking for, unless they see something else. She pushed him to the bottom of the boat. "Lie down."

Col's long, lean body took up nearly the full length of the boat, and barely fit beneath the thwart, but he did as she directed.

Sally pulled hard on her starboard oar, and sent the boat whirling sideways, so they were drifting in lazy circles toward the middle of the stream of the river. Then she slid off the thwart seat, climbed atop Col, and pulled the top of her bodice loose. She all but shoved her bosom into his face. "You wanted to see my breasts? Well, try and look happy, Mr. Colyear, sir. As if you like fucking your midshipmen."

"Kent?" His voice was brimming with warning. "If I may be so imprudent as to say so, you don't look anything like a bloody midshipmen now. You look—"

"*Chut,*" she hissed. And with that she began to pantomime what she hoped looked like a bout of noisy, acrobatic peasant sex. *"C'est ca! Encore, mon brave, encore."*

"God Almighty, Kent." Col was laughing against her breasts, as if the same insane desperation had infected him. "You're going to get us killed. But at least I'm going to die happy."

"We're not going to die," she insisted. But she pulled the highly identifiable red wool cap Col had been wearing when he went off to light the fire off his head, and hid it beneath her skirts before she laced her fingers through his lovely dark hair. And then rammed his skull hard against the thwart. "Pretend, Col," she instructed quietly through her teeth. *"Pre-tend."*

"I don't have to pretend this." His big hands came around to clasp her bottom and press her down against the hard length of his body.

Sally clamped her hand directly over Col's mouth. Soldiers with guns at the ready had burst out onto the quay, their burning faggots held high in search, the red whorl of torchlight dancing on the surface of the water. "Stay down," she instructed Col, as she began to move above him with greater enthusiasm, swaying back and forth, as if she were on a rocking horse. *"Ooh. Là, mon brave, là!"*

Across the water, one of the soldiers called out. *"Au bateau. Arrêtez!"*

She ignored the directive, and kept on pantomiming, rocking herself against Col's laughing, supine form, watching all the while, reckoning the time and distance until they would be out of range of their guns. The boat had already drifted half a hundred yards from the shore.

"Arrêtez!" they called again. *"Retournez au quai!"*

Sally tossed up her hair as if she hadn't noticed them until that moment. *"Moi?"* she asked breathlessly, before she sent them a lazy smile. *"Peut-être le plus tot possible, eh?"* she answered. "Now, pull me down," she instructed out of the other side of her mouth.

Col reached up to tangle his hand in her hair and yank

her back down into the boat against him. "What else did you say?"

"Maybe later."

"Damn your eyes, Sally Kent," he swore into her ear, but his voice was full of bemused laughter. "I always knew you were a game girl, but this beats all."

Sally wasn't sure if that was a good thing, but Col was holding her tight against him, and that did seem to be a good thing. They stayed there in the bottom of the boat, holding on to each other, ears straining and waiting in the dark of the river, until they could see above them that they were drifting under the rampart of the fortress.

Col pushed himself up to cautiously take a bead on their position. "They've gone." He promptly set her aside and took the oars. "Cover yourself. Not that I'm not appreciative, but don't ever do that again."

His voice was light, but strained, as if he were making an effort to be . . . nice, so Sally tried to reciprocate with the same. "Rest assured, I hope to *never* have to do that again."

A quick smile was all the response she got. Col rowed as swiftly as possible the rest of the way downriver, passing under the big guns of the Fort of Brest and out into the harbor by riding the midstream current out onto the outgoing tide.

The anchorage where the many ships of the French navy were moored lay primarily to the south of the city, just below two smaller islands of the estuary of the Élorn River. They would have to establish the fireship farther across the bay to the west, so the wind would push the vessel straight into the fleet where they stood clustered together in the lee of the land.

The ketch Col had picked out, a worn-out coastal trader in ill repair, still rode at anchor a cable length and a half from the shore to the west of the city. But the sloop he had chosen to take them out of the harbor was no longer at her mooring.

"The *St. Etienne* is gone."

"Damn their eyes." Col paused and looked over his

shoulder, scanning the inky darkness for a suitable replacement. "What about that? It looks American. And fast."

Sally was pleased to note that he had asked her opinion. The vessel in question was a sharp-built schooner anchored close in to the beachhead, where she must have been unloading stores after eluding the offshore blockade. "She'd make a valuable prize. She'll likely go like stink, as the Americans are fond of saying."

Because nothing traveled as fast as stink—the truth of which was borne out by the heavy smell of ash and smoke coming from the city, even though they were to windward of the conflagration. Half the city was awake with the toll of bells, and just as they had hoped, in the French fleet, boats were being lowered away to send crewmen on shore to fight the fires. Leaving the warships vulnerably undermanned.

"The big ketch first." Col turned the boat in the direction of their potential fireship, while Sally dug their weapons out from their hiding places beneath the stern sheets. She looped the canvas belt for her short sword over her shoulder and took up a pistol. Unlike the last time, when she had boarded the xebec dangerously unprepared, she now knew enough to keep the gun in her left hand.

As they came within a quarter of a cable length to the ship, she felt the penetration of Col's regard.

He nodded at her. "That's it. All ready? Silent as we go."

The vessel appeared deserted as they approached—the eighty feet of deck remained empty, and at the stern, the wheel was lashed fast. Col brought the boat under the starboard bows, and Sally tied off the painter before she took up her weapon.

But Col said, "Stay here until I give the all clear."

Sally bit back the argument gathering behind her teeth and nodded her understanding, but the moment he had disappeared down the aft hatch, she followed him over the rail. She was no bloody good at waiting. And besides, she could better stand ready on the deck than she could in the boat.

To prove her point, she could start on a few simple, useful tasks while Col checked the lay of the deserted vessel. She began by casting off the bow anchor cable, so the ship would swing around in the wind onto its stern anchor and be headed in the right direction.

The cable was thick, and she had to put the gun down to use two hands to hack her way through the hemp rope and then feed it through the cathead, so it made no splash going over the side. She had just finished and was contemplating her next move when a heavy crash sounded from below.

She instinctively dropped to the deck in a crouch to listen, but when no other sound was forthcoming—no further noise or cry of alarm—she cursed herself for being so skittish. Col was probably only breaking up the furniture to start the pyre for their fire.

The ketch was rigged like an old-fashioned mortar ship, with square sails before the main, so her next job was to go aloft to unfurl the main course from its yard, so the ketch could be pushed easily across the bay, before the westerly wind. She climbed the narrow shrouds slowly, hampered by her skirts flapping against her legs and getting in her way. Once she had gained the stability of the masthead, she had to take the time to tie off her skirts between her legs, before she could ease herself carefully along the yard and cast loose the mainsail. That done to her satisfaction, she headed higher, to unfurl the small square topsail.

She had loosed all but the last point when the unmistakable reverberation of a gunshot blasted through the hull.

Sally immediately scrambled down a backstay as quickly as her cumbersome skirts would allow, but she had dropped to the deck before she recognized the metallic clang of steel blades meeting at killing force.

She followed the sound as it grew stronger. At the foot of the mainmast, a tarpaulin covered the central hatch. She hacked away the lashing and threw back the tarpaulin to reveal two figures, their blades illuminated by the dim light of a lamp that had been knocked to the floor of the hold. Col, his jersey crimson with blood, was fighting at close quarters with a heavier man.

The sinister, metallic clash and scrape of the blades

echoed up from the enclosed space, and she could hear the grunts and pants of exertion as the two men battled for their lives.

Devil take her—she had left her bloody pistol near the cathead at the bow. She could try to retrieve it, but—

She didn't have that moment to waste. Col was already hurt. It would only take that moment for Col to weaken, or slip, for the Frenchman to find another opening and run Col through.

She would have to brazen it out. She could only tighten her suddenly damp grip on her short sword and launch herself onto the deck below with a roaring shout.

She landed hard, with an ungainly tangle of skirts, and rolled to her feet, but the diversion gave Col exactly the opening he needed. When the Frenchman whirled to face this new threat, Col was the one to see his chance, and thrust his sword home.

Over the pounding of her heart, she heard the slick, sick sound of the blade running through flesh, and the agonized grunt of pain as the Frenchman fell to the deck, his life's blood spilling to pool silently at his feet. Yet, she was still knocked back onto her knees by the ferocious mixture of satisfaction and relief that roared through her.

A man lay dying, but it so easily could have been Col. It nearly *had* been.

"Col, are you all right? How badly are you hurt?" She turned to find the lamp, already teasing out scenarios in her head. They had caused enough destruction in the city to satisfy Captain McAlden without further endangering Col. If he needed a surgeon, they would abandon the rest of the plan, and simply cut the stern anchor and run out Le Goulet to meet with *Audacious*.

"Not as badly as the Frenchman." Col's voice was wrung out, almost bitter with exertion, and he was bent over, resting his hands on his knees to catch his breath, his bloody sword still clenched tight in his hand. The gash across his left arm continued to bleed sluggishly, and his trousers were soaked in blood.

Sally held the lamp closer to examine the wound, which proved not to be a saber gash, but a bullet torn across the thick of the muscle of his left arm. Both the jersey and his skin were charred with the dark burn of powder. "He must have shot you at point-blank range."

Col shook away her concern. "He missed. It just grazed me. Let's get back to the job at hand. Load and prime the bow guns. There's a small powder locker forward. Then we'll see to the sails. Lively now. Someone will have heard that shot."

"First, let me bind that, then I'll load your guns. I've already loosed the sails." She pulled up her skirts to find the cleanest portion of the petticoat to rip away for a bandage.

"Did you?" He looked up at the luffing canvas to find his own answer. "You're not very good at taking orders."

"I am when they're good orders, sir." She met his eyes directly, almost boldly, as she wrapped the linen strip tight around his arm. Let him try to tell her she hadn't been needed, and she might be tempted to put another ball in him herself.

But he was already past the point of arguing, moving on and thinking ahead. "That'll do, Sal. Thank you. I'm going to knock out the windows in the stern cabin for a greater draft of air, and then see if we can find more canvas and furniture to start a pile here."

"What about him?" Sally's eyes were drawn to the prone body of the Frenchman. "Ought we to do something for him?"

Col spared him only a glance. "He's dead. There's nothing to do. Get to work. We don't have much time. That shot will have aroused attention."

But Sally found she couldn't be as cold-blooded as she had thought. She had seen a dead body before—it was hard not to in their world—but never one so . . . freshly dead. Never one in whose death she had had a direct hand. Never one she had watched die.

It occurred to her then to turn and search the shadows of the ketch's hold. "He was alone?"

"Near as I can tell." Col straightened and sheathed his sword. "There were no signs of any other crew. I think maybe he had been hiding out here, squatting, if you will, to escape service elsewhere." He jerked his thumb in the direction of the French fleet. "Or the army. Either way. Do yourself a kindness, Kent—don't spare him another thought."

She didn't need Col to remind her it could have been him. She didn't need to look at his arm to know it almost *was* him. And the night was still far from over.

But still, she couldn't stop the strange painful heat within, like a tear along her heart.

"It's not a game anymore, is it, Kent?"

She looked up to find Col's eyes upon her, that hard meticulous attention. "It never was. I'm not soft, Col. Only human."

He nodded and blew out his breath. "Then perhaps you'll understand why I needed you to stay in the damn boat."

His twisted logic made her smile. And apply some twisted logic of her own. "Of course. For the same reason that I needed to get out of it. Now, shall we get to work?"

"By all means."

Neither of them had conceded anything, and yet they seemed to be in accord—they worked better as a team than they did alone.

Another thirty minutes of work piling up rotten canvas and old furniture, spilling out powder and lamp oil, and they were almost ready to get under way. It only remained for them to hoist the spanker sail at the mizzen and cut the stern anchor, before Col took the wheel and steered directly for the largest ship of the line, a seventy-four-gun warship, standing at the head of the French fleet's anchorage.

They had to time it just right, to set the fire with enough time to engage the whole vessel, to gauge the wind and set the helm so that it would carry the fireship into the fleet, and to be able to abandon the ship with enough distance to escape themselves. There was almost no margin for error.

"Ready, Kent?"

"Aye, sir."

Col's eyes were everywhere—checking the fill of the sails, gauging the closing distance to the fleet, calculating their progress over the water. "Light it."

Sally threw the lantern down through the main hatch and watched as the flames caught hold immediately. Heat built in no time, and she backed away from amidships, retreating toward the helm, as the flames licked over the combing of the hatchway.

This time, when Col ordered her into the safety of the boat now tailed off the stern, she was glad to go, though she was less glad to again wait for Col, and worry for his safety. Every moment brought another chance for a misstep. The ship was becoming enveloped in fire. The drifting smoke stung her eyes and the heat of the flames built so she could feel it through the hull of the ketch. Above her head, the fire climbed into the rigging, and the canvas of the mainsail began to dance with flame, while the draft from the conflagration below pushed hot air into the topsails and propelled the ketch onward. And still Col steered the vessel closer and closer to the anchored fleet.

"Col?"

She had just run out of all patience when he came sailing over the taffrail above her head to cleave the water with a nearly silent dive. He bobbed to the surface a dozen yards away, calmly treading water as he waited for her to cast off and row out to him.

"Devil take it, Col. Did you catch fire?"

"I may have done," he said as he grappled his way into the boat. "I didn't stick around to find out." He paused, dripping cold water and trying to catch his breath. "Pull hard away."

She did so, putting her back into it and concentrating on moving as fast as she could at an oblique angle from the fireship, so they could hide among the other vessels dotting the bay and not be seen by the sharp eyes of the fleet behind.

In the stern sheets, Col looked exhausted and drawn. Combined with the pain of the wound and the blood loss, the strenuous preparations to launch the fireship had taken it out of him. And still there was the American schooner to take.

"How's your arm?" The saltwater of the bay had washed away the worst of the blood, but there wasn't light enough to see if the bleeding had stopped entirely.

"I'll live." But his voice was growing thin and streaked with pain.

Behind them, the alarm had finally gone up in the fleet. Bo'sun's whistles calling for all hands pierced the night, and crewmen appeared with pikes and oars to try to fend the fireship off. But the flames had almost entirely engulfed the ketch, moving higher and higher in the rigging until at last the topsails had caught fire, and the tongues of flame all but leapt from spar to spar and ship to ship.

They had done it. Together they had put the French to rout. They had accomplished what they had set out to do.

But they themselves were still in danger. She didn't like to think what still might happen if they tried to take the American schooner. Especially when there were other alternatives to hand.

"Compliments of the oars, Mr. Colyear, I thought you might like to know the French fleet is on fire."

He didn't want to smile, but as he looked over his shoulder at the scene, and then back at her, the corners of his mouth stove in. Just enough to encourage her, and give her heart. It was a begrudging smile, but a smile nonetheless. "Thank you for that report, Mr. Kent."

"Pleasure, sir. But if I may?"

"Yes, Kent?"

"Compliments of the oars, sir, but seeing as you're still leaking blood like a bleeding pin cushion, might I make a suggestion?"

His answer was as wry as it was weary. "You will anyway."

"If I had taken one on my fin, I shouldn't want to tangle with any Americans. Nasty, those Yankees are. Stubborn and particularly possessive about their ships."

"Are they?"

"They are, sir." She made a slight correction with her larboard oar to take them in the direction she had in mind. "If I were shot to pieces and leaking blood like bilge water, I would steal that rich man's yacht, there, instead of trying to tangle with and outwit Americans."

Col pivoted slowly to regard the vessel she had indicated with a toss of her chin. "That one?"

"That one," she confirmed. It was a sleek yacht of about sixty feet of keel, dark and battened down. A pleasure craft, a rich man's toy, left to sit and gather barnacles during the long days of war. "You could sail all the way to the Bahamas in that one, like a French grandee."

Nothing could stop his smile now. It was so broad, they both could have sailed away on it. "Well, then, Kent. It's a good thing I've always wanted to be a grandee."

Chapter Nineteen

It was a relatively simple thing to steal a rich man's sloop. The state of its cables and lines, and the stiffness of the canvas sails, told Col that the vessel had been riding unattended at its mooring for a very long time—in a time of war, men could spare no thought for leisure.

Yet, however long it had been out of trim, the sloop could still sail—at least long enough to get them offshore to meet up with *Audacious*. With no crew aboard with which to fight, they had only to slip the mooring and sail away.

Col gritted his teeth against the stinging ache in his arm, and hauled up the mainsail, but he was glad enough to take the wheel when Kent told him she could manage the jib on her own.

In such a hampered state, he was content to set only the few sails necessary to propel them forward. The fore and aft rig of the sloop meant they could sail nimbly against the wind, and through the narrows of the Goulet passage with only the jib and main.

There was no need for any kind of subterfuge, as around them other vessels were slipping out as well. Fisherfolk and traders alike were willing to chance the enemy's offshore blockade in a effort to save their livelihoods from being consumed by the conflagration that seemed to have spread to the harbor. Col eased out the main sheet and fell in behind a swift, lug-rigged *chasse-marée.*

Sally Kent came aft to where he stood at the wheel, looking for all the world like a hardworking fishwife and not the languid, kept lady of a grandee. She was constantly working, trimming the set of a sail, or coiling lines as she came, her eyes no doubt cataloguing every peculiarity of the *chasse-marée*'s unusual rig.

"Have you never seen a *chasse-marée* before?" He still kept his voice low—sound traveled strangely over water, and there was no need to court any further danger through carelessness. He'd had more than his fill for one day.

"Oh, yes," she answered. "A smuggler, I reckon, since he doesn't stink of fish."

"We'll be chasing him down in *Audacious* come tomorrow."

Sally gave him a quick little smile in appreciation of life's strange little ironies. "Shall we cut out the wait and simply go after him now?"

He smiled back. "I think we've done enough for one night. We'll sail northwest toward Ushant and hope to meet up with *Audacious,* or another British ship, by daybreak."

She took a place just abaft him as they cleared the land and parted ways with the other vessels—a moonlit specter of a lieutenant, dutifully awaiting his orders. But now that all the activity and exertion of passing through the narrows was behind them and they had reached the open roads of the sea, he could no longer hold off the aching exhaustion. The burning pain in his arm where the Frenchman's ball had ripped a raw strip from his skin intensified, until his whole left side felt as if it were still on fire.

As if she could read his thoughts, Sally indicated his arm with a quick toss of her chin. "You need to get out of those wet clothes. And that needs to be attended to."

"It'll do till we get back to *Audacious.* But I won't say no to getting dry."

"I stowed your clothes below." She indicated the small cabin just forward. "I'll take the wheel while you change.

Although for my part, I'll be glad to be rid of these skirts. I had a devil of a time in the rigging of that ketch. It's half a wonder that I didn't come to grief then and there."

He was glad he hadn't known. Glad he had thought her safe, in the boat. God knows how he would have faced the Frenchman if he had thought her in danger. "That is why I ordered you to stay in the boat, Sally."

She looked at him sharply, as if she were ready to argue, but instead, she lowered the pugnacious angle of her chin and chose her words carefully. "And now you know why I will be so happy to change back into a boy." Her tone was determinedly light, as if she were trying not to antagonize him by a return to their previous argument. "It was nice enough being a girl, but you didn't seem to mind me being useful as much when I was in my uniform and wearing trousers."

Nice enough? That stung, though he hardly thought she meant it to. "Well, I must admit I was wrong. You were useful enough wearing skirts when you sat atop me and all but bared yourself for those soldiers, weren't you, Kent?"

Embarrassment flamed across her face before she turned away and ran her hand roughly through her hair, in a rather masculine gesture of mortified frustration. But as he watched the long strands slide through her fingers, he found he didn't want to tease her anymore. He was sorry he had let his damned fear get the better of him, because now he wanted nothing more than to pull her to him, and touch her, and simply be with her in whatever little time remained to them.

But she had moved away, just out of his reach. Her voice was tight and quiet. "It was the best I could think of at the spur of the moment. And it worked, didn't it? And they were a very long distance away. They couldn't see anything, not really." She covered her mortification by reaching over and poking at his wound. Viciously. "You need to put a dry bandage on that."

"Have a care, Kent. If it will make you feel any happier, you can put those damned skirts to use now, by ripping them to shreds for bandages."

"I think I will do." She fished under the quilted skirts, and in a moment the petticoats dropped into a puddle at her feet. She flipped them into the air with a neat kick and caught them handily, before she sat on the deck next to him and commenced rending the fabric into long strips. A sharp little nod of her chin was all her concession. "You'll have to take the jersey off." Then her eyes shot up to meet his briefly before she added, "It's not as if I enjoyed it."

Oh, but Col had. He was almost ashamed of the base lust that had filled his gut at the sight of her poised above him in the little boat. Almost. But he was furious with himself for having been so furious at her. He had no idea of what such a display must have cost her. "I know, Sally. I'm just sorry I got us in a situation where you felt you had to do it."

His apology seemed to hone some of the bristles off her anger, and she busied herself with the bandages while he gritted his teeth and pulled the jersey carefully over his head.

She sucked in a breath at the sight, but began wrapping fresh—or at least as fresh as could be expected given the day they'd had—lengths of cotton fabric around his arm. "Look at you," she chided. "How ever are you going to keep your promise now?"

"My promise?"

"Exactly." Her voice fell to a very small whisper. But he heard every word. "You *promised* me that if I helped you burn down the town you would make love to me. I can still see the glow of the city from here."

Blind need slid under his skin more effectively than the bullet had. He clamped his jaw together to keep from making a low, inarticulate sound of want.

She looked so incongruously prim, sitting there by his side in the moonlight, daring him to use up all the unspent lust inside him. Daring him to allow her to do the same. But he had nothing left in him of tenderness.

"Not done playing with fire, are we?" He took up the nearest length of rope, pointed the bow straight out to sea, and lashed the helm on course. And then he turned to her. "I'm already halfway there, but you'll need to take those off before you choose the softest plank."

He could see the shock of excitement pass through her. Her mouth fell open, and her breath began to come in shallow, fast gasps of air. Above the scoop of her bodice, her breasts began to rise and fall with increasing urgency.

But she didn't hesitate. Her hands went immediately to the tapes at her waist, instead of the neckline, and she stepped away from him and then simply let her skirts drop.

And she was completely naked from the waist down. Just as he had known she was when she had sat atop him in the skiff. Just as he had been thinking all the way down the river, and across the bay, and for every single instant since.

But now he didn't have to imagine. He could see her long, bare, naked legs, and the flame of ginger hair at the apex of her thighs. And then in a show of supreme defiance, she peeled off her bodice, ripping the laces apart, and threw it into the pile of her skirts. And then, with one fell swoop, she kicked the whole of her women's clothing overboard.

By the time the costume hit the water, he had shucked his trousers and was on her, picking her up in his arms and carrying her down to the deck.

She was as bold as he needed her to be. She didn't shy away from the contact, his Sally Kent. She wrapped her legs around him, clinging to him like a vine, strong and tensile. When he had her on her back, she was already open to him, and all he had to do was bury himself inside her scalding heat.

Col had to shut his eyes to blunt the force of the sensation, the excruciating pleasure of being inside her, of having her beneath him.

The easy camaraderie of their first encounter was gone, and in its place was something hot and furious and needy. Something carnal. Something that made her hook her ankles together behind his back, and pull him into her with a force that left them both breathless.

It was all the unspent fear and anger and frustration of the night. It was physical excitement and emotional exhaustion.

If he kissed her, over and over, his mouth delving deep into her, he would not have to think. He would not have to feel the jangling fear that had twisted his gut into a vicious knot. He would not have to confront how important, how dear, Sally Kent had become to him. How necessary.

So he gave himself over to the lust that rose like a gale within him. He let her fist up his hair and pull his mouth down upon hers. He welcomed the unabashed hunger that had her pulling at his lips with her teeth and digging her hands into his shoulders.

He kissed her back with the same ferocious animal need, sweeping his tongue into her open mouth to plunder and twine with hers.

There was nothing more of slow surprise or delicate wonder. There was only heat and friction and open, greedy need. The skin over his bones felt hot and tight and his lips felt as if they would blister from the scald of her kisses. But still he wanted more.

He wanted to obliterate the gaping hole of fear within him. He wanted to go back to the way it was before, and at the same time stay right where he was, tangling his body with hers. He wanted to see her, to use what little time was left to them basking in the glory of her vibrancy.

He rolled onto his back and set her on top of him, so he could spread her hair out and let it run through his fingers. It fell like a russet curtain of silk, stained with the dark, dangerous scent of fire and ash.

Need clawed its greedy hands higher and he tangled his hands in her hair, to pull her mouth to his, as if he could press his ferocious hunger upon her. As if with his kiss he could obliterate the worry. Because if he didn't, it would eat him alive.

Sally pushed away from the almost bruising pressure of his mouth. She was gasping for breath, and grasping at the frayed edges of her sanity. The irrational hunger and need crowded out all thought, until she was nothing but raw, undiluted, unrefined feeling. Until she felt the edges of her very self blur and bleed into his, and she couldn't tell where he started and she left off.

But sitting up brought her no distance, emotional or physical. Instead, it brought a jolt of pleasure so strong it ripped through her. A bolt of bliss so fierce and so needy, she could not contain the cry that broke from her mouth. She grabbed his shoulders to steady herself, even as she ground down against him, feeding the flame of greedy friction that grew stronger with each movement at the joining of their bodies.

"God, look at you," he muttered, and she had to close her eyes against the sharp force of the bursts of saturated pleasure sparking under her skin.

"Please," she begged. Her voice held nothing but want and greed, and though she knew what she wanted, she didn't know what she asked of him. She only knew that she couldn't control the intensity of the need coursing through her like flood tide. She didn't know how to tame the wild instinct to push herself against him where their bodies were joined, and at the same time kiss him and touch him and feel the heat and strength of his body wrapped around hers.

But he wanted it, too, for he rose up as well, lifting her knees and holding her to his bare chest, so they were face-to-face. She wrapped her arms around his neck and buried herself in the exquisite friction of her nipples brushing against the heat of his chest. In the rasp of his whiskers against her cheek as she rubbed herself against the side of his neck. In the pleasure coiling ever higher in her belly every time she rocked into him. In the salty taste of his skin on her lips.

And then there was nothing but the feel of his strong hands on her hips, urging her against him, over and over, higher and higher, until at last the bliss exploded under her skin and she was gone, flying and floating above on the weightless tide of her love.

She came back to herself reluctantly—almost resentfully—watching with a sort of remote detachment as he carefully disengaged their bodies, and lay back upon the deck and pulled her into his arms.

They floated along for a very long time, content in their silence, their still-naked bodies wrapped together under the velvet blanket of the night sky.

But as much as she wanted the interlude to continue, to stay suspended in time and space, she knew they couldn't stay that way forever. And so did Col.

"Sally. I have to ask you. If I took the boat and let you take the sloop, would you go?"

"To England?" she asked slowly, unsure if he was giving her any choice. "No. Don't make me go, Col. Please. I don't want to go."

Col blew out a long breath. "But surely you can see— We can't go on, not like this. If you went, I could tell them Richard had died, or been captured, since he is presumably alive, somewhere in England. But it will solve all our problems."

However much she hated to be described as a "problem," Sally could admit to the soundness of the plan. She could in all probability leave Col safe—there was irony in that word—in the boat, still tailed off the stern, and sail the sloop back to England on her own. She could even sail to the very mouth of Falmouth Bay and anchor in the Channel in front of Cliff House, and slip home and go back to being Sally Kent with no one the wiser. She could see it clearly.

But she simply didn't want to. She didn't want to be Sally Kent, sitting at Falmouth with nothing to do, and no one to be but herself. She didn't want to sit and wait and wonder at what Col, or even Ian or Will or Damien, might be doing so far away from her, across the sea. She wanted to continue to watch Col do it in person, to stand by his side and sail with him.

She didn't want to give him an answer.

"What more do you have to prove, Kent?" he prodded. "You've proven yourself as a sailor—the equal to any of your brothers at their age, I'll daresay. But it's only going to get harder from here on. It's only going to get more complicated. More dangerous. You know we *can't*—" He began to repeat his warning, as if he needed to remind himself as much as her. "I can't afford to worry about you. I can't afford to let my concerns about you overshadow or take away from the hundred other things about which I'm meant to be vigilant."

"I can look out for myself. And I can look out for you as well. I can," she insisted. "If you'll let me. I can work, Col. We can work together. Please. Don't make me go back. There's nothing there for me to go back to."

He said nothing else, just pulled her close and held her against his chest where she could feel the slow, sure beating of his heart counting out the minutes of their time together. Nothing, not even their hearts, could stand still. They would have to move on.

They didn't speak of it again. Sally re-dressed herself in Richard's uniform and became a midshipman once more. Col put on his lieutenancy along with his coat and brought the sloop alongside *Audacious* just as the dawn was lighting the sky in the east, bringing them a sunrise colored with a cloak of smoke and ash.

Captain McAlden greeted them on the quarterdeck. "Mr. Colyear, you are very welcome back aboard. Come and tell me what you accomplished in Brest. We could see fires from five miles out to sea. Well done, sir."

"Thank you, sir." Col was quick to acknowledge her assistance. "Mr. Kent was of inestimable value."

"Just as I thought he would be." The captain included her in his congratulations. "Well done, indeed. You must come and tell me all about it over a breakfast. No doubt you are hungry. But first—" The captain had moved to the lee rail to inspect their prize. "Let us dispose of the yacht quickly. We have new orders to rejoin the fleet as part of the inshore squadron off Cadiz. An unarmed yacht is a midshipman's command. I will leave it to you to choose, Mr. Colyear."

"Send Kent, sir."

The moment the captain had made his request of Col, she had expected it—knew he would feel compelled to do it. But still, his ready suggestion of her name cut her to the quick.

Yet this time, Captain McAlden did not accede to Col's wishes. He looked at Col sharply, but if the captain was recalling the last time Col had suggested something similar when the xebec was the prize to be disposed of, he did not say. "Did you not say Mr. Kent was of inestimable help?"

"Yes, sir." Col was quick to agree, but he said no more in defense of his suggestion, and he continued not to meet her eyes. "There is alternatively Mr. Gamage, sir, but I will leave it for your decision, sir."

Col was trying to remind her. Trying to let her remember she served—they both served—something far larger than themselves.

She nodded to him briefly—a quick tuck of her chin, no more. But Col saw it, and, she hoped, understood.

Nothing could be the way it was ashore. Or even before, when they had been becoming friends. They had been away only two nights, but already it felt as if it had been a lifetime.

Now, she could be nothing but Richard Kent, midshipman. And he was indisputably back to being Mr. Colyear, her superior officer.

"No." The captain was shaking his head. "I am sorry to disappoint you, Mr. Kent, but it will have to be Mr. Gamage. He's the most senior, and he's made enough progress, Mr. Charlton has been telling me, that he should be able to navigate the sloop back to England successfully. And if he doesn't"—he lowered his voice—"well, he's the most expendable, though it gives me no pleasure to say it, despite the progress in mind and improvement in temperament."

And yet Sally felt no relief, no easing of the cat's-paw scratching up her stomach.

"And passage to England in the sloop may afford him the opportunity to sit for his exam. Yes." Captain McAlden was moving back to the quarterdeck rail, searching out Gamage, impatient to be gone, his mind already engaged in the challenge of finding and rejoining Admiral Nelson's Atlantic fleet somewhere off the coast of Spain. "Mr. Gamage?" The captain set his voice to carry across to the waist of the ship. "You're being given command of this prize. Sail her to the first port you can make in England. Mr. Pike will write you your orders—here is Mr. Pike now. Get aboard her directly. Take three men."

"Tunney, Marsan, and Griggs." Col had the names at the ready.

"Mr. Pike, make it so. Take the sloop in to Plymouth," he ordered Gamage. "You'll get a better award for such a ship there, though some damn south-coast smuggler will undoubtedly buy her. But still, the men will get their money, and be happy."

And it would also take longer to rejoin any ship that might bring Gamage back to them, Sally thought. But whatever the captain's reasons, he did not share them with her, or voice them aloud. He merely shook Gamage's hand. "Good luck to you, Mr. Gamage, and godspeed."

Sally was sorrier than she might have thought to be only five days ago to see Gamage go, especially when both Will Jellicoe and Ian Worth came to the rail to shake his hand and see him off. It spoke well of the change in them all. But there were more changes yet to come.

And it was for the best. Best for the ship. Best for the midshipmen. And best for her and Col. Gamage could no longer hold his threat over them. They would be free to ignore each other in peace, now.

And so Mr. Gamage, who had given *Audacious* such trouble, for so long, was at long last gone. It was a new day. And they were bound for Spain.

Chapter Twenty

The land off the Spanish coast looked blue and low in the morning light, and it faded away into stretched dunes of sand to the south and the Cape Trafalgar. Nearer to the port of Cadiz, where the combined Spanish and French fleets had made their bolt-hole, the coast was rocky, and rose in sheer walls against which the waves ended abruptly.

That morning, they were again cruising the entrance to the Cadiz harbor, running south along the coast on the larboard tack in very light, easterly winds. The larger ships of the line, sailing with the main body of the fleet somewhere to the southwest, would have heavy work on such a day, but *Audacious* could still make good speed, sailing two points large with the wind on the larboard beam.

Captain McAlden—or perhaps it was Col who was feeling so reckless, or bored—had taken them nearer in than any other ship of the inshore squadron. With the wind off the land, they could sail so close to the shore that Sally could smell the distinct fragrances of sea lavender and honeysuckle that wafted out to her now and again over the briny stench from the salt flats, and could see the ripple of the tidemarks on the sands of the beach below the town.

In the blue-tinged morning light, the houses of Cadiz looked like sugar cubes stacked up upon each other—a crumbling, blazing white castle of a city, punctuated here and there by the spires of churches, and focused upon the elegantly tall lighthouse near the harbor mouth.

Indeed, Sally could well imagine her opposite number in the Spanish fleet stood atop the lighthouse just as she was, training his glass upon *Audacious,* and sending reports down to his superior on the number of sail offshore, and the rising swell.

Because while the surface of the sea was as calm and still as the mill pond upland of Falmouth, Sally didn't like the long cadence of slowly rising swells that were pushing toward them from out of the west. It boded for a gale to be brewing somewhere out there in the deep Atlantic. Which meant the combined fleet of the bloody French and Spanish would undoubtedly continue to stay holed up safe and sound within Cadiz harbor, while the British frigate squadron would be left to claw their way off the bite of the lee shore.

Despite the favorable easterly wind, there would be no action today.

They would instead spend another day in drilling. Mr. Colyear would undoubtedly give them plenty of sail work, tacking back and forth across the harbor mouth, but it would be another few hours before the forenoon watch was to be called and the orders given to clear the ship for gun drill. And Cadiz, for all its spun-sugar picturesqueness, was not, after a long month of blockade, that interesting.

Sally lowered her glass, and let her eyes slide aft along the weather rail to where Col stood, as firm and steady as ever, canvassing the set of the sails, and trying to eke out another half-knot of speed from the ship. It was a strange thing to feel so connected to him, even at such a distance. As if the backstay ran directly from him to her heart. Even if he did not always wish it to be so.

With both Gamage and Mr. Rudge gone off on prizes, Col was shorthanded, and the remaining officers often had to stand watch on watch to keep *Audacious* to rights. Such a disposition of time rarely left them any time together, and alone, not at all.

Or perhaps that was how he wished it. Perhaps the result

of their last rather cataclysmic joining was this polite estrangement, this chilly acquaintance. At least her work in *Audacious* kept her too busy for retreating into solitude. It was almost a pleasure to work so hard there was no time to think, no time to brood. No time to do anything more than collapse into her cot at the end of one watch, and drag herself out at the beginning of another.

Sally let the sigh trapped within her out, hoping Willis would merely think her bored beyond thought, instead of stupidly lovelorn.

"By God."

The strange disbelieving excitement in Willis's voice had Sally turning to find him all but hanging off the larboard shrouds, staring hard at the port. She didn't waste time asking, but yanked open her glass and followed the direction of his gaze.

"Topsails, sir," he explained before she could focus her eye. "More than one ship."

"How many do you make?" she asked out of one side of her mouth, while she half turned her head to bawl at the top of her lungs, "Deck!"

The urgency of her voice sent a ripple of instant alarm through the ship.

"Four now. One after the other." Willis's tone was filled with solemn awe. "Jesus God, I think they're finally coming out."

And there they were, in the pinprick that was her glass's view of the harbor. The forest of bare treetops that were the hidden fleet were blossoming with sail.

"Mr. Kent?" Colyear's voice could be heard clearly without his speaking trumpet.

"Topsail yards being set. One ship of the line and four, no, six, lesser. The enemy are coming out." Sally tried to shout the words clearly, but her voice was a scrawl of frantic excitement.

Captain McAlden materialized out of nowhere and was at the rail with a glass in his hand, confirming her report even as Willis called out higher numbers, as from his higher vantage point he could see more and more of the fleet set their sails.

"Two seventy-fours, moving, and at least five third rates."

Seconds ticked by as McAlden kept the glass at his eye, and then he turned calmly and snapped it shut. He took in the sail, the sea, the weather, and the rolling swell. "Lay us on the starboard tack, Mr. Colyear."

Everything else was drowned out as the orders to tack into the wind had the men springing to the sheets and braces, but in another few minutes Sally saw the signal *"Enemy have topsail yards hoisted"* flutter up the mizzen backstay to spread the news to the rest of the inshore squadron.

Good God Almighty. Were the enemy fleets really coming out at long last? She never would have picked such a day. There was a gale brewing. Did they think so highly of their sailing abilities—they who had holed up in port for months, with no sail or gun drill—that they thought to outrun or evade the entire British fleet? Did they not understand how hungry the British navy was for their ships, and their very lives? And in a gale that anyone who had weather eyes could see coming? Devil take every last one of them. Such obvious, irredeemable folly was inconceivable to Sally.

She kept her glass trained on the harbor and the slowly moving sets of sails blossoming toward the harbor mouth. As *Audacious* came about into the wind, there was a long moment of greater vision as the sails were hauled to the starboard tack.

"Lord, I make fifteen under way, Willis."

"I make another twelve still making sail."

Nearly every ship within the harbor had stirred. The entire fleet was putting to sea. "Deck! Twenty-seven ships making sail or under way!" she screamed, just as confirming calls from the mizzen, who had the clearest vision of the port laid out behind them as the ship came about, reached her ears.

Another set of signal flags soon flew at the mizzen. *"Enemy ships coming out of port."*

"Six more of the line. And maybe five frigates. All French, that lot, from the look of their sails."

Sally swiveled her glass out to sea to sight the British frigate fleet commander's ship, the *Euryalus*. Long moments passed as the other ship, some few miles out to sea, worked to read the flags hanging listlessly in the light breeze. And then finally, *Euryalus* ran up the flag in confirmation.

"Keep at it, Willis." She slid down the backstay like a crazed monkey to make her report to the quarterdeck. "*Euryalus* is in receipt of our signal, sir. And Willis has the count at thirty-three of the line and five frigates. All French, the frigates."

McAlden nodded in grim satisfaction. "Captain Blackwood will signal the admiral. In the meantime, keep track of each and every sail. Back to the tops, Mr. Kent. I want each and every ship of that fleet identified and assessed."

"Aye, aye, sir." Sally scrambled to comply. "Names and ratings, lads," she called to the lookouts.

The names rolled off her tongue like incantations. In the van was *Formidable,* and *Rayo.* In the center, *Santissima Trinidad*, *Bucentaure*, and *Santa Ana.* Willis fed her the ratings—French 74, Spanish 112.

Sally's head was full of calculations and comparisons to try and remember or guess which ships were still in Admiral Nelson's fleet and how the number of guns would match up. Heady, terrifying work. Her voice was growing hoarse and raw from calling down to the deck in a voice loud and clear enough to be heard.

The rail below was filled with men taking a long look at the enemy they had tracked, and searched for, and awaited for so long. They watched with practiced, assessing eyes as the individual enemy ships maneuvered, and they made experienced judgments about the prowess of the enemy allies' sailors and captains based on the set of their sails.

"Stand off," Captain McAlden ordered, and Col was already moving to position the ship farther out, sailing upwind and giving the enemy searoom to lumber out of port and make sail to the northwest, while the signal flags relayed their information to Captain Blackwood in the *Euryalus*, who was in charge of the frigate fleet.

"Wear ship."

"Fall off," Mr. Charlton ordered the helm.

"Where are those frigates, Mr. Kent? I—" the captain was asking from the deck, but in the cacophony of orders and sails working, whatever else he had meant to say was lost.

"They're wearing ship, sir." Willis's sharp eyes never left the enemy fleet.

"Deck!" she cried.

And then, even as Willis was still searching and counting sails and spars, Captain McAlden shucked his blue coat, handed it to the master, and swung out into the starboard chains. He climbed up the ratlines in his waistcoat and shirt-sleeves to have his own look at the disposition of the enemy fleet. He was perhaps not as smooth as the younger and more agile topmen, due to the grave injury he had received some years earlier at Acre, but the devil and all his grinning imps, he was no laggard.

"Willis, prepare yourself for a visitor."

The foretopman gaped. "Jesus God. Now I've seen it all."

As soon as the captain made the foretop, Sally handed him her glass. "The frigates remain in their lee, sir, showing no indication of joining with us."

"No," the captain agreed. "For they think—quite wrongly— that we will take to our heels if they come out." Captain McAlden closed the glass with a crack and Sally saw something she had never seen before—a full smile winding its way around the captain's normally straight lips. It was a bit unholy, that smile, hooking off one side of his face and lighting his eyes like the glint of sun off snow.

It was altogether frightening. And undeniably exciting. The enemy fleet had come out, and sooner, rather than later, they were going to have one unholy hell of a battle.

Captain McAlden spoke as if he had heard her thoughts. "We will have no fight yet, Mr. Kent, but we will stay with them, and track them until they bring it to us, or Admiral Nelson's fleet arrives to meet with them. Whichever comes first. In the meantime, Mr. Kent, I would be obliged if you would assist your colleague Mr. Jellicoe with the signals, as we will have more than a number of them today, as soon as we wear ship." And then he was gone, down the backstay like a midshipman, calling out his orders to the deck. "Mr. Charlton, wear ship."

Willis set his lads scrambling for the royals even before they heard the mixed voices of Mr. Charlton putting the helm over once more, and Col ordering the sails hauled over hard, to fall off the wind and carry the ship's momentum back southward. Sally was suddenly glad for the seemingly tedious hours of sail drill they had endured in the Channel as *Audacious* came about into the wind as smartly and swiftly as Col could have desired.

It was a long day of watching the enemy, and signaling all their information to the line of English frigates waiting for just such purpose to the southwest. Captain McAlden was a cool one, staying with the enemy fleet as close as could be as they made their ponderous way down the coast, swooping in close to gauge the strength and numbers of each ship, and then easily sailing closer to the wind to westward so he might relay his reports by signal to the *Euryalus,* and therefore to Admiral Nelson.

Sally didn't think she had ever worked as hard as she did with Will Jellicoe, sending a constant stream of information as Captain McAlden thought necessary. Even knowing the codes well, she was still forced to constantly flip through the code book and work the signals out on a slate before they could find the necessary flags, set them out in order, tie them on, and haul them up. And then the reverse, hauling down and untying, and especially refurling and storing correctly so they might be found again easily. It was laborious, mind-stretching work, and it lasted until the last instant of daylight, when the dark of the coming night finally allowed them respite.

The French, and especially the Spanish, did nothing to disguise themselves through the night, though Captain McAlden took all precautions and had all the lights put out on *Audacious,* allowing him to sail well within the enemy's range. He was not through any mischance going to let himself lose them.

In anticipation of the battle, which to them seemed entirely inevitable, but which the Spanish and French seemed to think they could avoid, the captain asked Mr. Colyear to arrange the watches so more men could have a long stretch of uninterrupted sleep in order to be well rested for the grueling day to come.

Which meant that Col and Sally were finally in the gunroom at the same time.

Yet the brief look he gave her—fierce but somehow bleak, all dark scowling brow—did not encourage her to seek him out. She went instead into her own cuddy to attend to other equally important matters.

She must finally write to her family. She must write them all and explain herself. She hardly knew where to start, except at the beginning when she had first thought of taking Richard's place, but at this point, after so long, and with uncertainty looming, her reasons at the beginning no longer seemed important. What was important was that they know she loved them, and that she hoped she had honored them, and that they would honor her for that.

It was difficult, but once she had made an honest start, the words poured off her pen. More than anything else, she wanted them to know she had been happy aboard *Audacious*. As happy as she had ever been in her life. But she could not bring herself to tell them the chief reason why she had been so happy. Or with whom.

She could not tell them about Col, other than to say Mr. Colyear had been everything an officer ought. Everything in a friend. Everything to her.

Everything that she no longer wanted to ignore. He was too close, too important. "Col?"

"Kent." His voice came through the dividing wall, gravelly with strain. "What are you doing?"

"Writing. I've finally written my father."

"Finally?" He swore vehemently under his breath. "Damn your eyes, Kent."

"I know." She took a deep breath. "I've told him all—"

"All?" This time his voice was sharp with something closer to alarm than frustrated disbelief.

"All my reasons for joining, and coming on *Audacious*. And my hopes that my conduct will speak for itself." She took another deep, fortifying breath. "Will you see to it he gets it?"

"Me? Why not Captain McAlden, or even Angus Pinkerton?"

"Because I know I can trust you. And it just seems right that I should ask you."

"I can't promise what I can't deliver, Kent. You make a very great assumption that I will survive while you will not."

"You will," she stated simply. "Of course you shall survive. I cannot conceive of any other outcome. You're . . . essential to this ship. To this world."

"Your confidence in me is startling, and humbling, but I assure you I am as mortal as any other man."

"And so am I," she insisted. "And you must promise me one further thing. If I am hit, you must promise not to let them take me below."

"Are you afraid?"

"I'm not afraid of doing my duty. I'm not afraid." But she was. She was afraid of what her life might be if he were not in it. Of the loneliness that would result from their inevitable, final separation. She could only pray that she was the one to fall, and not he. "If I'm hit, you must let me die."

"Damn your eyes, Kent." He swore again, violently and vehemently, under his breath. "You ask too much."

"Think of yourself, if I should be discovered. Think of my family. It would be better if I were to die with dignity and honor than to have my family shamed."

"You should have thought of your family before you entered into this harebrained scheme."

"I was thinking of my family. I thought of nothing else."

"Come now, Kent." He wouldn't let her get away with such willful self-deception. "We both know that's a lie. No one who takes to this life the way you did does it solely for someone else. You did this as much to please yourself as to save your family's name."

"I didn't do it to *please* myself." She could hear the distress in her voice, and feel the heat building at the back of her throat. "That seems so tepid, so insipid. I did it because this life—the navy—is the one thing in the world I'm good at. Because it's the one thing in the world that makes me feel alive. Because it's the thing I dreamed of, night after night, when I was made to go home to Falmouth and sit and wait. I'm no bloody good at waiting."

She felt taut and picked apart, as if the tangled skein of her lies was unraveling her. As dizzy as if she had been spun across the deck. And somehow the tears, which through months of trial and tribulation she had not allowed herself to shed, now were coursing down her cheeks. She dashed them away with the back of her sleeve, but this was the truth at last, the truth she had not even dared to put in the letter to her father that lay sealed atop her sea chest. It felt good to finally say it, and to share it at long last with Col. "But you probably already knew that."

"About how bad you are at waiting?"

"That, too."

"Yes, Kent. I knew. And what I didn't know I guessed. But I am glad. Very glad."

It was all the declaration she could hope for. She went to her door. Mercifully, the gunroom was empty, and Col had not taken the precaution of locking his small cabin door.

She was through and standing in front of him before he could do or say anything to stop her. "I am glad as well. Even if I die, I've no regrets."

"No regrets," he affirmed. And reached for her.

Just as she was reaching for him. She went to him without hesitation. Her hands were in his hair and she was pulling his mouth to hers just as he was fanning his thumbs along her jaw and angling her head to bring her closer.

His lips were firm and his mouth met hers in quiet desperation. She dove into him, into his strength and his rightness and his fierce, fierce tenderness. He broke off the kiss, leaving her feeling empty and wanting for only a moment, to step away, drape a shirt over the keyhole, and douse the lantern before he returned.

The dark pressed into them, impelling them into each other's arms. There was no way to see, to look at each other, so they could only feel. They made no sound at all, as their lips and hands explored the shifting boundaries between them. She pressed herself into his warmth, into the surprising softness of his hair, and the rough rasp of his face against hers. She wanted to feel him, and taste him, and know everything about him, explore every aspect of his being, discover every facet of his character as thoroughly as he had uncovered hers.

"Kent. Sally." He eased back enough to breathe, and then, when he couldn't stay separated even that small distance, he rested his forehead against hers. "I'm glad you came. All I could think was my only regret would be that I was going to die without having kissed you one last time."

She didn't want to hear any more of death and dying. She didn't want to think of it. She wanted to think of life and love. She wanted to feel alive. In his arms.

She silenced his words with her lips. She wanted to taste the salt of his skin and navigate the byways of his muscles and tendons where they curved over the frame of his bones, and gave him breadth and substance.

His hands were streaming through her hair, pulling it from its queue, tugging it away from her scalp as he ran his fingers down its length. "Ah, Kent. You have no idea how long I've waited to do that."

"How long?" The skin along the side of his neck was sensitive. She could feel the pulse of his heart under the surface, and hear the way his breathing changed when she kissed and nipped along the strong tendon than ran down to his shoulder.

"Forever," he breathed into her hair as he reciprocated, kissing along the line of her collarbone. The heretofore unremarkable surface of her skin lit up with searing sensation

and previously unknown satisfaction. Everything felt more—
more important, more intense. More inevitable.

She wanted to take off his shirt so she could map the
uncharted territory of his skin. Her hands were at the knot
of his cravat, unraveling him, and giving her a taste for more.
For more of his warm, glowing skin, more of the luminous
power of his body. She unwrapped him like a present to herself, kissing down the line of his throat and across his chest
until his head arched back.

He made a wordless sound of both anguish and encouragement, and she kissed it away. "Hush. Let me."

"Kent. We can't. We'll be heard."

"We can. We'll be quiet. Silent as the gr—" No, she would
not even think it. "We will be quiet. You'll see." She punctuated each whisper with a kiss until she reached the hollow at
the base of his throat. "Please. Don't make me beg."

He swallowed and closed his eyes, so she decided to beg
anyway, because when she moved her mouth lower across
his flat brown nipple, he tipped his head back and made an
appreciative sound deep in his throat.

"Please, Col. Please let me kiss you." She suited word to
action and pressed her lips to his chest. "Please let me touch
you." She ran her hands across the warm wonder that was
the wall of his torso. "Please let me undress you."

And her hand skimmed down to address the buttons on
the fall of his breeches.

He made another sound that might have evolved into
a protest, but she stopped it with her lips and whispered,
"Hush. You have to be quiet."

"Kent." He was the one begging now.

"Hush," she repeated her whisper, even as she smiled
against his lips. "Why don't you see if you can occupy your
lips on something other than talking."

"Oh, Kent. Be careful what you wish for."

His passive acceptance of her ministrations was at an
end. He backed her into the only wall that wasn't made of
board and batten, and began to divest her of her clothes.
While he worked with his hands to peel away the layers of

her fabric armor, he kept his lips on hers. She held him to her, urging him on with her enthusiastic compliance. She let her tongue seek out and then tangle with his, and as soon as that remarkably sinuous slide began, she was compelled to move her body as well, arching and stretching against him.

She needed to be naked. She needed the feel of her skin sliding along his with the same intimacy as her tongue danced with his. She reached down and lifted her shirt over her head, and then went straight to work on her bands, pulling them loose and pushing them down to her hips in a messy tangle, rather than wait to neatly unwind them.

His hands were at the buttons of her nankeen trousers, pulling away the loose bands now wreathing her hips. But the deep darkness itself pressed like velvet against her skin and she grew achy and unsatisfied without the reassurance and warmth of his body against hers.

"Col, kiss me," she begged in a low voice.

"Oh, Kent." She felt the vibration of his answer hum through her. "I do believe I will."

But he clearly did not mean her mouth, for she could hear him drop to the floor, and she felt him put his wide, strong hands against her hips, urging her to lean against the wall as he pushed her trousers, and then her smallclothes, down to pool around her feet.

His hands circled her ankles and lifted them up, one at a time, to step her out of the pool of fabric at her feet. She toed her clumsy shoes off, and when he peeled her cotton stockings down, she was left naked before him. Her breath began to draw short—small, noisy gulps of air. She put her hand over her mouth to stifle the sound, but she felt loose, unmoored and adrift, without his anchoring weight against her.

And then he said, "I want to see you. But I can't. So I'll taste you instead."

She felt a soft press of air and he blew his breath against her mons, but nothing prepared her for the gentle probe of his tongue along her most intimate flesh. She made a very small sound of shock and surprise, but not dismay. Only of discovery and subsequent delight as he explored the folds of her sex. Sensation, heat, and need blossomed under her skin, and she felt full of wonder and strength, and she wanted more.

She angled her hips to appease the breathless, hungry craving that came from deep within. And then it began, in wave after tiny wave, growing, spreading out from her center, radiating from the place where he touched her, so carefully and so precisely; she felt as if she couldn't breathe and didn't want to, didn't need to. She had no need of air, she needed only him and the feeling building until she felt she would do anything to appease the want.

If his hands had not been at her hips, holding her up, she would have slid down the wall. She would have lain splayed on the gun deck, open and unresisting. Anything for him to continue, anything for this feeling of incipient pleasure.

And then he turned his head and set his teeth delicately against her. Heat and tight bliss burst under her skin and she was spinning, unraveling like a line cut free of entanglements. Free and flying away within herself. And with him. Still with him.

His hand was on her, moving within her, as he stood and gathered her to him, spent and unprotesting. She felt the blunt velvet probe of his body against hers, and then he was within her, and the emptiness she hadn't even felt was banished anew in a fresh resurgence of pleasure as he rocked into her. The pleasure was still pulsing through her body in small waves that lapped at the very edges of her being, but with each surge of his body into hers the waves grew stronger, until they were crashing and breaking across her skin.

And he held her tight against him and begged against her ear, "Don't let go," and light burst inside her at the same moment as his climax roared through his body and into her.

And she didn't let go. She couldn't. And she never would.

Chapter Twenty-one

Col fell asleep sitting on his cabin floor, slumped against the side of the hull, with Sally Kent still wrapped tightly in his arms. And he continued to hold her, continued to breathe in her scent, and continued to marvel at his insane good fortune in loving her, until the last possible moment. Until they had no choice but to separate, slowly, poignantly, and carefully, and get on with the coming day. And the coming battle.

Dawn brought Admiral Nelson's battle fleet hard upon the horizon to the southwest, making all sail to bear down upon the enemy, who sailed on steadily to the south before *Audacious*. The wind had moved up a point to west by north, but was still light. At the current rate of speed, it would be hours yet before the fleets made contact.

And still his arms ached with the loss of her.

She came on deck before the watch was called, and he could do nothing but look at her. Look at the barely veiled warmth in her fine gray eyes. Look at the spiced cream of her skin and the full perfection of her bitten, chapped lips. Marvel at the vivid ginger of her beautiful hair.

Look but not touch. And perhaps never again touch.

He forced himself to speak evenly, though his chest felt tight, as if one of his ribs were already broken. "I've assigned you to work with Jellicoe at the signals again, as both the squadron leader Captain Blackwood and the admiral are prodigious signal makers, and will expect timely responses and confirmations from Captain McAlden. So you'll have your hands full."

But mostly, he assigned her to work on the quarterdeck simply because he wanted her near.

She frowned at the signal locker, as if she knew, just as she had that first evening she had come aboard, that the task he assigned her was nothing more than busywork, designed to keep her safe and out of harm's way. "Mr. Colyear, I assure you"—she lowered her voice to speak privately—"that I can take care of myself. I know what I'm doing—"

"Kent." Col lowered his voice as well, the better to convey his urgency. "You have *no* idea. This battle is going to be beyond all notions of care and skill. This battle will be nothing short of chaos. This will be two entire fleets of the biggest warships in the entire world hammering each other into utter oblivion."

He forced himself to look away from her gamin face. Forced himself to check the weather gauge and the set of his sails. "Nothing but fate will decide what happens today. Nothing but fate will decide who lives and who dies. If you're in such a bleeding hurry to go to your death, let me assure you, a ball can find you as easily on the quarterdeck as in the foretop."

But on the quarterdeck, she would be closer to him, and he could do as she asked last night. On the quarterdeck, he could keep her from the surgeon and from discovery.

She seemed to understand. She nodded, and said, "Yes, sir," and moved to her station, immediately setting to work, reading the first signal of the morning, which had been relayed down the line of frigates stretching from the enemy to the British.

"Signal from the *Euryalus,* sir." She was reciting off signal numbers to Jellicoe, who jotted them down on the slate.

Captain McAlden appeared as if summoned, and took her report. "Mr. Kent?"

"Frigates join north of battle fleet."

The captain took a long moment to study the disposition

of the enemy fleet, strung out in a long line moving slowly along the coast, the speed of the wind, the slow descent of the British fleet, and the readiness of his ship before he made his decision.

"We'll clear the ship for action, after we've piped the hammocks up, and the men down to breakfast, Mr. Colyear. But handsomely, quietly, as we move offshore to join the squadron. We'll keep our gunports closed. I don't want to alarm the enemy in any way that might induce them to run."

Col gave the necessary orders, and the routine of the ship continued uninterrupted. But for him, every minute of every hour stretched out abominably.

He knew his place. He knew his job. The ship was his to sail, his to maneuver, his to make right so Captain McAlden and the gunners could blast the French to splinters. He couldn't look at the guns, or the destruction. He needed to keep his eyes on the topmen, and keep them working until they were needed elsewhere. The tasks at his hand demanded a single-minded focus that left no room for doubts. Or searching out the masthead for her form. Or worrying about her.

Despite his strong words to Kent, doubts assailed him. Was he wrong to keep her on deck? Might she be better off aloft?

The answer that whispered across his brain was that the French liked to aim high, to dismast their enemy's ships in the hope that they could no longer sail. Such a tactic might work on the open sea, in a battle between a corvette and frigate, but this battle would be unlike any that had gone before.

The Nelson Touch, their admiral called it. What it would be was an out-and-out brawl, with each ship engaging the enemy on their own, firing at will, not a neat line of battle in which the two fleets would keep their distances and lob cannon fire across the intervening sea.

There would be no distance. There would be no safety. It would not matter where in the ship one stood. All would be in harm's way, under enemy fire. It would be utter, unmitigated carnage.

"All right, Mr. Colyear." The captain was eager to join

the fight. "Give me all the speed you can from the set of your sails. Let us join up with the fleet."

Col was at the trumpet calmly giving orders in the same steady voice he used every day, willing the men to put their faith in their superior skills and trust that those skills would out.

They set a course southwest by south, but Col was forced to lessen his rate of speed so he didn't outstrip the enemy fleet and give them a chance to turn their heels back for Cadiz. Yet he was glad of the necessary distraction of keeping their rate of speed through the water low. It gave him a challenge, and the men work to fill the long hours of anticipation.

Which clearly the captain felt as well. He was pacing along the weather rail, studying the enemy fleet and no doubt thinking up his strategy for each and every scenario that entered his mind. From time to time he would look over *Audacious* as if he could see what he wanted done in the way of preparations.

"Captain, sir? I'd like to get started—"

"Excellent, Mr. Colyear. You may clear for action."

Col turned to the waist and called to the men, "Clear for action, gentlemen."

A wave of excitement, just like the rolling swell beneath the decks, lifted the people. A grim, manic industry gripped them all, and the men, especially the younger men, flew to their duty.

The ship became a new place. The whole of the deck, from one end of the bows to the other, had been cleared of every obstacle save the huge guns, and the gunports of both sides of the hull were open in the flat morning light. All the bulkheads and screen walls were removed and stowed, as well as all the furniture and belongings of both the men and the officers. What furniture that could not be stowed below the waterline was normally put off in the ship's boats, but Col could envision the confused melee of disabled ships and potential prizes, and wanted to have every boat they could man available if the need should arise, so he ordered the dunnage stowed as tightly as possible.

"Make it so," he told the flustered stewards when they objected. "Find the damned room somewhere else, if you don't want to have to pitch them overboard. The boats will not be put off."

Col hoped his own emotions were more tempered. It was not his first battle, and it was the duty of every officer to set a steady, confident example for the men. He had long since learned to channel the strange mixture of dread and euphoria into something useful, something as hard and precise as a blade, cutting away everything that was not important. But he had never had to think of anyone but himself—he had never been tempted to *allow* himself to think of anyone else.

But there she was, close to hand on the deck, all but dancing with excitement and anticipation as she strove for patience in the tedious working of the signals with Jellicoe. He took pity on her.

"Mr. Kent. Get chains up to brace the yards on all the tops and then rig up the netting."

"Aye, aye, sir." She fell to her tasks with alacrity, gathering the topmen of her division to shift lengths of chain out of the lockers where they were stowed belowdecks, and haul them aloft, where they were placed to secure the yardarms and prevent them from falling should the rigging that tied them to the mast be shot away in the fighting.

Below the yards, they rigged slack netting, both as an obstacle to potential enemy boarders and to prevent anything shot away from above, spar, rigging, or men, from falling on the men working the guns. Col could see she also had the foresight to chain rig most of the netting, too. He could just hear her explanation.

"For what good would it be if it were shot away as well?"

When that was done, she made for the flag locker on the quarterdeck to pull out more British flags. "May I rig a few more flags, sir? My father always made sure to have several flying, lashed to different masts during a battle, so that if one spar should fall, it could not be said that he had struck his colors."

"Well done, Kent. See that they're hung fore and aft as

well. The smoke from the guns will be thick and we'll want to be as easily identifiable as possible. I have no fear of the French, but I should hate to have an English broadside shot into us by accident."

She smiled, as he hoped she would. But he did not have time to dwell in the warmth of that admiration. They were coming up to the squadron of five frigates running just north of the weather column of the admiral's fleet, which was arrayed in two long columns, like two arrows poised to fly straight for the heart of the enemy's fleet.

It was difficult for both Captain McAlden and Col to ease themselves into a position behind Captain Blackwood's *Euryalus,* but not because *Audacious* was a poor sailor. Rather because she was such a fine sailor, they had to lessen their rate of speed, and ease the trim of their sails to let others have pride of place.

But second in the small line of frigates or not, *Audacious* would be ready.

"Stand to your guns. Load and run out."

There was a strange hush, a grim, ferocious quiet, as the men complied. Behind him, Col heard Kent let out what sounded like an oath.

"Mr. Kent?"

"Signal from *Euryalus,* sir. Frigates are not to engage." She kept her eye to the glass. "New signal going up. Attend line of battle ships to assist as needed."

They both looked to Captain McAlden to gauge his reaction. But he was too cool a man to let himself be seen to cavil at any order, no matter how repugnant. "Stand to."

The relief that flooded Col's chest was not cowardice. He would not allow it to be. It was something else. Something deeper and more important. Something that had everything to do with his feelings for Sally Kent.

"If you please, sir." Will Jellicoe was pointing south to the weather column of the battle fleet. "Signal from the the admiral as well."

Col and Kent shifted their glasses to the *Victory,* leading the northernmost column steadily toward the French line.

"'England expects every man will do his duty,'" Kent read.

Captain McAlden, perhaps because his reaction to the last signal was fresh in his heart, was nonplussed. "I had expected something rather more stirring from Nelson. But let us call the men to hear it. Have the people gather in the waist."

Col called out the order and the bo'sun's pipes roused the men to gather. The topmen hung down from the yards, their focus for the instant on the deck rather than on the gathered fleets. In the waist the gun crews were, almost to a man, stripped to the waist, with handkerchiefs tied either about their loins or around their heads and over their ears to buffer the coming cannon roar, with brawny arms folded over their chests, looking pale and stern, and mortal. The very best of England.

Captain McAlden stood at the foremost edge of the quarterdeck. "Your admiral sends the following message: 'England expects every man will do his duty.'"

There were some stirring cheers, but more typical of *Audacious* was the bo'sun, Mr. Robinson's, growl.

"Lay us alongside any of 'em, sir, and we'll give 'em a double shot of our duty."

"Thank you, Mr. Robinson. For your benefit, I propose to do exactly that. We will be more than dutiful. We will be *Audacious*."

"Huzzah!" The raucous cry was taken up and repeated three times.

"Another signal," Will Jellicoe called. "Number sixteen."

"Close action, sir." Kent passed the order to Captain McAlden.

McAlden acknowledged the signal with a grim smile.

"Close action, lads. Back to your stations," the captain ordered. But as he did so, across the bow the enemy fleet was falling into disarray. "Glass."

Kent immediately handed him hers, and she was forced to wait, all but twitching with eager nerves to find out what was going on. Col's own glass revealed to him that the whole strung-out line of the combined allied fleet was wearing ship, turning slowly away from the wind to change direction.

Even without a glass it soon became apparent the enemy was now, when it was too late, attempting to run back to the shelter of Cadiz. "What the devil does the French admiral think he's doing?" Kent breathed in wonder.

"He's sealing their fate, Mr. Kent," Col answered. "He's trying to run, and he will dishearten his men in doing so. And they are not sailors enough to make it work. Look, their line is already breaking as a result. Our admiral will know just how to take advantage of such confusion."

Indeed, the fight began before the enemy had had time to reorganize themselves into their long line-of-battle formation. Under Admiral Nelson's signaled commands, the two columns of the British fleet seemed to dive into the gaps that had opened up, aiming their ships into the midst of the enemy fleet without even bothering to answer their ranging shots.

But even without superior gunnery, the French and Spanish began to learn how to make their shots pay off. The enemy began pouring fire into Admiral Collingwood's ship *Royal Sovereign,* as his lee column of ships was the first to breach the enemy line.

It was another full half hour before Admiral Nelson's *Victory* did the same with the weather column. Captain McAlden was flinty with a rigid self-discipline Col was having difficulty emulating.

He felt each echo of cannon fire as if it pounded directly into his chest. It was hell—living, breathing hell—to watch and do nothing as his brother sailors in other ships were subjected to such withering fire. "I don't know how to do it, sir. It kills me to watch and to think we could be doing something for those poor devils."

"Patience, Mr. Colyear. We will. We will. But we are not yet commanded to fight. But as the other frigates all stand in attendance on Admiral Nelson's weather column, let us advance so we can be more useful to the lee."

Col was grimly glad of the employment and spread all

canvas before the wind to cut *Audacious* across the divide between the advancing columns, to stand to Admiral Collingwood's assistance. His *Royal Sovereign,* as well as *Belleisle* and *Tonnant,* had been the first ships to break the enemy line, and, in drawing the brunt of the enemy's fire, were taking a savage beating.

Together, Col and Mr. Charlton did exactly as their captain had bid, and sailed *Audacious* directly into the teeth of the fight.

"Take me after that bloody Spaniard," the captain growled as he pointed off the larboard bow, where the *Santa Ana* was locked with *Royal Sovereign.* The air around them filled with the deafening roar of cannon fire and the acrid stench of billowing gunsmoke.

"Cross her bow. Fire as you bear!"

"Fire!"

And the gunners were raking away, sending double- and treble-shotted broadsides slamming down the length of the *Santa Ana's* deck, before the captain ordered the helm about, and set to doing the same to *Indomitable's* stern, trying to draw the French frigate *Cornelle,* which hovered beyond the sulfuric cloud of the action, into the fight.

"Hard about!"

Col tried to close his mind to everything but the handling of the ship. "Hawkins, haul away. Get a line on that tack. Brace over hard." He lifted his speaking trumpet and directed his men calmly.

But he could not rid his peripheral vision of Kent. And he could not keep himself from moving her to the lee side of the firing, to take her away from the hail of bullets from the musketry and grenades that rained down upon them from the damned frog ships' mastheads. "Kent, see to that loose sheet. Look lively."

He tried to shut his mind to everything but the yards, and ignore all thoughts of the topmen, scrambling and dodging above. He tried to focus only on sheets and tacks, and keeping the wind enough in his sails to do exactly what his captain ordered. He had to stop thinking, and let himself rely upon his experience, upon his years of work and his instincts, to see what needed to be done and to do it. He tried to close his ears to the deafening din and hear only Captain McAlden. Anything else would drive him utterly and completely mad.

Sally had never in her life heard, or felt, such a deafening roar. It was just as Col had said it would be—chaos. Sixty-odd ships, and hundreds and hundreds of cannon were blazing away, battering each other to pieces. She had told herself she had the heart of oak of every true British sailor, but at that moment, she wished she had a heart of stone.

Yet, the press of the noise and the confusion of the smoke in the fleet brought her a clarity that seemed impossibly wide. She was acutely aware of things before she understood them. The first heart-pounding rush of fire through her blood passed, but the opiate of battle, the state of heightened awareness, clung to her, throttling her to action.

The entire mizzenmast of one of the French ships—she could see by the painted markings that it wasn't British—fell to tangle on *Audacious*'s larboard quarter. Sally's heart was hammering double time at the top of her throat, but she could see what needed to be done, and without conscious thought or waiting for orders, she sprang up with the quarterdeck carronade gun crews, taking up a boarding axe and swinging into the chains to cut away the wreckage.

"Have a care there, Kent."

She could barely hear Col's warning over the deafening roar. She had just begun to hack away at the tangle of ropes holding the fallen spar to their rail, when *Audacious* heaved up beneath her with the recoil of the main barrage. Sally had to grapple onto the chains to keep her balance and hold on as the tremendous shock wave from the broadside concussed her, but still she managed to hang on with one hand. Blood began to seep from her nose, and she soon felt a trickle of warm blood drip from her deafened ears and slide down her neck. She spit the blood out of her mouth, and swiped away the rest with her forearm. The sleeve of her coat came away with a gory smear of grimy blood, sweat, and gunpowder.

In the heat of battle, it became more and more difficult to hear orders, or even see the disposition of the ships around them. Smoke obscured the deck, and the din from every corner was so loud, she could no longer hear Col, only twenty feet away from her, trying to keep a check on her and order her out of harm's way. But she was never unaware of him, tall and straight, holding the deck, standing firm like a talisman.

On and on she worked, moving wherever she was needed—righting a dismounted gun, clearing a fouled line, keeping the deck clear for ammunition to be brought up to the carronades. She lost track of all sense of time, until slowly, she became aware that around them, the guns of the ships of the line had finally begun to fall silent, and the heat of battle began to ebb.

Sally was deaf and numb and exhausted and enervated all at the same time. At first, all she could do was look to Col. To simply look and know he was there was enough. She could think of nothing more.

But though the din and concussion of the guns ceased to assault her ringing ears, the battle was far from over for *Audacious*. Indeed, the fact that *Audacious* had only served as an ancillary to the larger ships during the heat of the battle left her intact and functioning where the ships of the line were not.

"Clew down that line, Hawkins."

First Col's voice and then the captain's began to be discernible.

"Hoist out the boats, Mr. Robinson," the captain was ordering. "Mr. Lawrence, sweep the water for men. Mr. Horner, get across to *Royal Sovereign* and see what assistance we may proffer. See if we need to take her in tow."

Sally could now appreciate Col's seemingly unexplainable decision to keep all the ship's boats on board, for they had never had more need of them.

"Mr. Colyear, take control of that *Swiftsure* prize. That'll teach the damn French to make over our boats. Mr. Charlton, as soon as the boats are away, move us on in support of *Collosus*."

"Kent," Col called.

Sally gave up trying to decide whether he called her because he could rely upon her, or because he wanted to keep trying to protect her. She simply jumped down into the boat and set about organizing the marines to board the two-decker.

"Swords at the ready. Take prisoners as you go."

The strange numbness was gone. Her heart again began to thump against her chest, but she still felt that strange sense of tunnel vision, of the world narrowing to the next oar stroke, or the next step, the next move.

They went up the French two-decker's side and over the rail, swarming as quickly as possible up the batten ladder and with grappled ropes. Sally was breathless from the climb and her strange inability to breathe and think all at the same time.

Only to be met with no resistance. The deck of *Swiftsure* was a messy welter of dismounted guns, fallen rigging, and the bodies of the dead.

She followed Col as he strode forward across the deck with his sword drawn, looking for resistance. He passed the abandoned helm and began scaling the quarterdeck. "Put a man on the wheel. See if the helm responds or if it's been shot away." On he went, across the quarterdeck, with her following, past a fallen French officer until he was at the taffrail and hauling down the French colors.

It happened so quickly and so nonsensically that Sally had little time to think, only to react.

The officer was only an ensign, and little more than a boy to her eyes—fourteen or fifteen at best. Richard's age, her mind was telling her, as it filled with pity for the poor boy whose chest was a ghastly mess of blood.

And even as she was thinking the Frenchman had not much longer to live, the lad found the strength to raise up with one last surge of strength and sweep his sword in a mortal blow aimed at Col's head.

She should have used her pistol—Col's pistol that he had handed her as she joined the boarding party. She should have shouted to warn Col to mind his back, to take care, to bring up his sword arm as he turned. And perhaps she may have. She didn't know.

It all happened so fast, and at the same time so shockingly slowly, that everything happened as if she were watching it from the end of her telescope. Time elongated even as her vision narrowed. She simply threw herself in the French boy's way, reaching out the hand with the pistol and hoping to deflect the blade's deadly arc away from Col. Of all things away from Col.

But she mistimed her lunge. The sword skipped off the barrel of the pistol and she felt the icy-hot sting as the edge of the blade sliced into the side of her face.

Chapter Twenty-two

And then Col was there, striking the dying man down with a vicious cuff from the butt of his pistol. As the Frenchman fell, Col addressed him from the long end of his sword.

"Give way!" he roared. "Haul your blasted colors."

Blood was filling her eyes and pouring out of her face, but all she felt was the hot sting where the blade had struck her.

It was only a cut, not a mortal blow, and only bleeding so because that was what head wounds did. It was no worse than the gush from her nose had been earlier. Combined with the blood from her nose and ears, she must be an absolute mess.

Sally wiped the blood from her eye and winced at the stinging pain, but as it settled into a hot burning throb, she strove to think no more on it. It was a small injury after such a day. She was alive, where so many around her, especially on the deck of *Swiftsure,* were not.

Col was in front of her, offering her a miraculously white handkerchief from somewhere deep in his coat, and pressing it to her cheek. "Hold that there." His face was grim and tight.

She held the cloth over her eye. Better. For a moment. The stinging heat intensified, but she strove to carry on. "It's nothing. Just a superficial cut. I'm fine."

God knew it was nothing compared to the poor French lad, or the rest of the carnage under her feet. The mutilated, torn carcasses of men littered the deck. The destruction on the deck of the *Swiftsure* had been terrible, and unlike the British, the French weren't wont to toss their fallen comrades, or parts of comrades, overboard with the same grim fatalism and professional determination to keep the deck and guns clear, as were the English.

Col wasn't nearly as sanguine about her injury as she was. "You need to go back to *Audacious* and have Mr. Stephens see to you."

"When we're through," she insisted. "It's only superficial. Mr. Stephens has better things to do at the moment aboard *Tonnant*. And I'll not have my face sewn up by one of his loblolly boys."

Even as she said it, she wobbled sideways. She felt lightheaded, drunk almost, only the sensation wasn't pleasant or euphoric. She felt as if the hot pain were pushing her off her feet.

Col seized her up, with one hand at her elbow and another taking her hand, steadying her. Just as he would have done for anyone. Any one of the midshipmen. But he might have let go of one of the other midshipmen. He held on to her.

Will Jellicoe came up across the deck to them, his trousers still impossibly white in the midst of such incredible destruction.

What a strange thing for her to notice. She must be losing quite a deal of blood to be so light-headed.

"Compliments of Captain McAlden, Mr. Colyear, sir," Will was saying, "but you're wanted to go aboard another prize. You're to bring back the French captain, if he's still alive, and Mr. Kent is to stay in command—God," he exclaimed when he saw her. "What happened to you?" His eyes were wide and dark in his sooty face.

"Saber cut," Col bit off. "Go back with Mr. Jellicoe," he said to her. His eyes were pouring worry over her. "My compliments to the captain, Mr. Jellicoe, but you may tell him Mr. Kent—"

Sally wouldn't let him finish. "I'm fine, sir. Just a touch light-headed. But I'll manage. There's no need for me to leave *Swiftsure*. I'm not likely to get another chance to command a third rate again. And you're needed elsewhere."

"This is not a discussion, Mr. Kent." Col held firm. "You are, to use a colorful phrase, leaking blood like bilge water, so you will obey my orders, which at the moment are to sit down and recover yourself." He propped her against the rail. "Compliments of *Swiftsure,* Mr. Jellicoe, tell the boat Mr. Kent is injured, I am staying to secure the prize, and that I have need of you as well. That is all. Now, who is in command of this vessel?" Col demanded of no one in particular.

When no answers were forthcoming, Sally addressed the wreck of the ensign who was still slowly bleeding his life away into the deck. *"Monsieur. Où est votre capitaine?"*

"En bas." The poor boy's answer was thin with despair. *"Blessé. Il n'y a personne d'autre."*

"Below, he says, wounded. And that there are no others."

"Christ. No wonder they couldn't even strike their colors." Col's relentless gaze swept the deck. "Well, tell him the ship is ours. Moffatt, strike that flag and put up our colors."

"Aye, aye, sir."

Col turned back to her, his eyes still hard and devoid of compromise. "No one else, he says? Not even a surgeon?"

But in the intervening moments while he had been speaking to Moffatt, the last agonized breath of life had eked out of the poor Frenchman. "He's gone, sir."

And because the well of her pity had not yet been wrung dry, she found herself rising, wanting to stand on her own two feet. Wanting to move, needing to prove she was still alive by living through the sharpening pain. "With your permission, sir, I'll go below and venture to find out."

But Col was clearly a dog with a bone he meant to chew on for a while longer. "You should stay put."

What had he once told her? *There's more than one way to splice a line.* "All right. I can see what needs doing from here. I'm worried that the weather will worsen. Are there anchors still remaining under all that mess?"

The diversion worked. Col's all-seeing gaze swept forward, over the welter of spars and rigging littering the foredeck, cataloguing the debris that would have to be cleared before he could even assess the state of *Swiftsure*'s anchors. His mind leapt to the problem, and he began to move away, forward. Over his shoulder, he growled, "Stay put," with the frustration of a man who knew full well she would disobey him. "Mr. Jellicoe, set a man clearing this rigging away, and then see what still needs plugging below the waterline. Here, is the French carpenter alive and working? You there—"

"*Marin*," she supplied helpfully, both so the dazed French sailor standing nearby would know he was being addressed, and to remind Col that she was eminently more useful working instead of sitting. "I'll look for both the carpenter and the surgeon, and put an eye to what needs repairing below, shall I? I'll never be able to climb, so Mr. Jellicoe can see to a jury rig for the foremast. *Marin*," she called again to the French sailor, without waiting for Col's answer. "*Venez avec moi.* Come with me."

It was too sensible and useful a suggestion for him to pass up. Col nodded grimly and turned back to his own work. "Moffatt, get the towline worked from *Audacious*. We'll want at least two anchors at the ready at the bow, and another kedge at the stern."

As the companionway near the waist had been shattered beyond safe use, Sally was forced to pick her way forward to find a ladder below. By the time she found the surgery deep in the hold, the captain of *Swiftsure* had already expired of his wounds, but the quantity of French wounded meant that the surgeon, Dupuis, and his assistant, were still employed ceaselessly in caring for the injured and dying.

But there was one officer, besides the surgeon. Ensign Gravois proved to be the French equivalent of Ian Worth—small, inexperienced, and absolutely astonished to find himself still alive.

"I was charged by my *capitaine* to make the surrender of his ship to you, monsieur," he said with formal gravity, and made her a beautifully correct bow. Sally thought he would have handed her the captain's sword, except her hands were too busy to accept it—she was still holding Col's handkerchief to her hot face with one, while gripping a nearby post to keep her upright with the other.

"I thank you, monsieur, but it is not I who am in command. And I think, under the circumstances, the formalities can be dispensed with. Come, is there a carpenter or a mate? And I will need you to organize anyone who is hale enough to work the pumps. It's going to be the devil of a thing to keep this shattered ship afloat."

Even in the short time she had been belowdecks, the motion of the ship was becoming more violently pronounced. The long swell out of the west she had noticed two mornings ago when the enemy fleet had come out of Cadiz was racing toward them with a vengeance.

Sally kept Gravois with her, using him to translate and convince the dispirited remains of the French crew to work to save themselves from the oncoming gale with the same élan they had fought the British. Hours passed in a feverish haze of toil as they worked endlessly to man the pumps to keep the vessel afloat through the course of the fiercest gale Sally had ever had the displeasure of witnessing or experiencing.

She left Ensign Gravois to continue to chide and shame his men into action, and took a smaller party of men onto the deck to report and see what help they might be there.

Audacious had taken the big, lumbering wreck of *Swiftsure* in tow, but as the gale howled out of the Atlantic onto them, the wind tore at them from the west, pushing them relentlessly onto the shallow coast.

Just as Sally had feared, *Swiftsure* was endangering *Audacious,* pulling the smaller frigate onto the lee shore. Before Sally could even open her mouth to voice her concerns, Col was headed down the deck.

"We'll have to cut the towline," he yelled over the shriek of the wind. "Put two men to cut the line, and take another party to the kedge. The rest, come with me."

The strain on the cable was so great, it took Moffatt only

a single blow to hew through the line, which went sailing over the rail with the strength of a lash.

Col and his men immediately dropped the anchors at the bow, while Sally saw to the kedge astern.

As the gale wore on into the night, many of the English ships in tow, as well as the French and Spanish ships around them, had to be cut free or abandoned. Thanks to Col's foresight, *Swiftsure*'s anchors held firm, although the relentless working of the sea against the battered frames of the hull caused the weakened joints to work loose, and the seams to open with regularity.

Moffatt proved himself to be an anvil of a man. While Col kept the watch on deck, the mate came below to work tirelessly with Sally, hammering iron spikes to shore up loose timbers and plugging leaks with every bung they could find or fashion.

But anvil or not, even Moffatt had his weaknesses. "I don't like the lay of this Frenchie, sir," Moffatt fretted. "She's like to work apart like a poxy French tart."

"Nonsense, Moffatt." Sally tried to bolster his flagging spirits. "This ship is as British as you, built with English oak by the Wells brothers at Depford yard. She'll hold together still, despite the drumming we gave her. Poor old girl didn't deserve such rough treatment from her own brethren, but we can keep her shored up, if we stay at it."

A stout-built ship she may have been, but they still had to man the pumps constantly, and it was everything Sally could do to keep a steady rotation of men at the heavy, exhausting work in order to keep the sea from overtaking them.

There was little opportunity for rest, and absolutely none for sleep. Sally prowled the distressed hull, always finding more work to be done. No matter the pounding blaze in her head, she could not rest. As long as Col worked so tirelessly above, she would work below, keeping the men working in rotation so none of them stayed on deck too long. Not even Col.

When Will Jellicoe brought her a mug of dark aromatic

coffee that he, or perhaps Ensign Gravois, had conjured out of God only knew where, she said, "Take one up to Mr. Colyear, Will. He'll have greater need of the fortification."

"No need," Col said as he came down the companionway, slapping his sopping hat against a post. "I'm already here. For the moment, anyway. Thank you."

He took the proffered cup, and over its steam, he narrowed his eyes at her. "Why haven't you seen to that? There's a damn French surgeon, so fetch him now."

"He's been busy—" she began to explain.

"Fetch him now, Mr. Jellicoe, if you please. Sit down, Kent, before you fall down." He took her arm, as if he would steer her someplace more suited to his purpose.

"Where?" she joked with bleak humor. She had been spelling the men at the pumps with easier though necessary jobs, such as restoring the batten walls and securing all the openings the British cannon had blasted in the ship, but there was no furniture, even in the captain's cabin, or in the wardroom where they stood. There, the stern gallery had been obliterated in the fight, and rain and seawater were blowing sideways through the opening, dousing them in a chilly mist. "I was about to see if we could rig up a tarpaulin to keep out the worst of the weather, and keep us from taking on any more unnecessary water."

"After you've seen the surgeon." He steered her out of the wardroom and sat her on a companionway stair. "Has the surgeon even had a look at you?"

Sally gave up trying to convince him her injury was superficial, and as such, too low on both her and the surgeon's list of priorities. "As you like it, Mr. Colyear."

"Nothing is as I'd like it, especially not this, but it's the way it will be."

Before Sally could puzzle out that cryptic statement, Dupuis arrived.

"See to it," Col directed him with more belligerence than Sally thought was warranted. "Make a clean job of it, damn your eyes."

"It's clean enough." The surgeon sniffed as he peeled off the handkerchief and peered at her forehead. "Bathed in its own blood."

Sally didn't think she had a nerve ending left after the numbing exhaustion of the battle and now the gale, but she was wrong. The pain, which had settled into a dull, omnipresent throb, flared anew into a searing heat. She felt as if her face were on fire, with pinpricks of flame licking across her skin as he lashed her face together.

She was glad Col stayed the entire time. He crouched next to her, holding the lantern high so Dupuis would have adequate light, and his knee pushed up hard against the outside of her thigh, solid and reassuring. Sally had to clench her hands into the fabric of her trousers to keep from reaching for his hand with every stitch, every sharp burn of the needle and thread.

To keep from crying like a girl.

She clenched her eyes shut and concentrated on breathing without twitching.

"*Calme-toi*," Dupuis kept adjuring her. "Stay still."

And, thanks to Col, she did. With his help, it was over soon enough, and she was anxious to return to the diversion of working to keep the damn boat afloat.

The moment Col was summoned back on deck, she was up and back at it, hauling spare spars and canvas up from the depth of the hold, using every bit of stored timber that could be found, to continue with the endless round of repairs. She kept the entire crew busy—no one could be spared, not even the wounded. Injured men were put to work reworking and splicing lines into usable cordage, or picking apart what could not be saved into loose hemp to stuff into leaking seams.

But by the third—or was it fourth?— day the pain was sapping the last of her strength. The heat in her face wouldn't abate. Her skin felt scalded, and the constant fight to save the ship began to seem to Sally like a scene from Dante's *Inferno*—a vain struggle without any end. It seemed as if *Swiftsure* began to take on a sort of hellish slant, a dreamscape of sullen dripping gray, and strange yellow lamplight.

She wanted to be on deck, where the blessed dark and the chill night air could cool the heat within her.

Col's voice sounded in her ear. "Kent, I don't like the way you look. Get below and rest."

"I'll rest when this bloody hurricane is over. When the gale starts to abate. Is it abating, do you think?" She turned her face up to the blessed cool of the rain, letting it wash over her, and douse the fire in her face and in her throat.

Devil take her, but what she would give at that moment for a nice sip of British tea.

And that was when the night closed in upon her and went completely black.

It was almost three more days before the hurricane did finally begin to abate. In all, it had been seven days of unending work and ceaseless toil. Seven days of incessant worry. Seven days of watching Sally Kent's condition go from bad to worse.

Seven days of self-recrimination, of mentally retracing his steps, of wishing he had done things differently.

He could have prevented it. It never should have happened. It never would have happened if he had ceased trying to order fate, and had left her aboard *Audacious*. He should never have ordered her to take part in the boarding. He should have left well enough alone. But he hadn't.

He'd had seven days of being afraid. More afraid than he'd ever been in his life. Afraid she was slowly dying as he watched.

So at the first sign of lightening skies on the seventh day, Col was on deck. "Sway out those boats, Moffatt, and get a line to *Audacious*. I want to get this damn ship back under tow."

Oh, damn his eyes. What was he doing, taking his frustration out on Moffatt, who had been exemplary, as had everyone of the small band under his command? They had all worked until they dropped. After seven days, even Moffatt had begun to look as beat up and exhausted as if he had been flogged around the fleet.

Everyone in the bloody fleet must feel the same. Those who were still alive, anyway. Col looked out over the anchorage. Around them, every ship was in disarray, and he could see that more than one ship—English, Spanish, and French alike—had gone to the bottom in the howling gale. Fate was a strange, fickle, unstoppable thing. He wouldn't be surprised if the weather hadn't ended up killing more men than the cannonballs.

But Col would be goddamned to hell if he would let Sally Kent become one of the casualties.

He had done for her everything he could—kept her dry and saw to it she rested—but it was little enough. The fever that gripped her was beyond his limited powers. And he'd had too much to do, too many other lives to save by keeping them from going to the bottom, to do anything more than scoop her up from where she had fallen to the deck and keep her below, checking on her from time to time.

The moment *Swiftsure* was back under *Audacious*'s tow, Col had Sally bundled into the skiff and home where Mr. Stephens could have a proper look at her. Col didn't trust the poxy French bastard, Dupuis, with his sneering, shifty eyes, to see to her anymore. After all, it was under his auspices that she had taken ill. She'd been in a feverish haze, half in and half out of her senses, for days, despite his care.

When they reached *Audacious*, Captain McAlden frowned down from the height of the quarterdeck as Col passed Kent's inert body up over the rail.

"What goes on here, Mr. Colyear?"

"Kent has been injured, sir."

"How?"

"In the boarding, sir. Before the storm." Col climbed aboard quickly and then found he had to restrain himself from reaching to take Sally out of the bo'sun's arms. "With your permission, sir, I'll take Mr. Kent to Mr. Stephens now."

"Mr. Stephens remains aboard *Tonnant*. Is it urgent?" But then the captain seemed to think better of having this conversation in front of the men. "See Mr. Kent to his berth in the gunroom, Mr. Colyear, and then attend me in my cabin. We are ordered to Gibraltar and there is a great deal to be done. And a great deal to be discussed."

Normally, Col would have been proud to note that *Audacious* was in remarkable shape after the gale. The hull and rigging had been set to rights, and every wall and batten, sea chest and chair, in the gunroom had been restored to its correct place.

Col left Sally, pale and listless, in Pinkerton's meticulous care and repaired immediately to the captain's stern cabin, which seemed luxurious in its spartan accommodations after the bare wreck of *Swiftsure*. Col became suddenly aware of his dirt. He had not spared the time to change out of the soiled uniform he'd worn ever since the battle. He may have reeked of more than saltwater and saltpeter, but he was in no mood to waste time on the niceties.

"Captain McAlden?" he said directly. "I need to speak to you, sir."

"Come in, Mr. Colyear. Whom did you leave in command of *Swiftsure*?"

"Mr. Jellicoe, sir, assisted by Moffatt, but they need to be spelled if you can spare men. But it's about Mr. Kent, sir."

"I'm sending over Mr. Horner." The captain nodded to his clerk. "See to it, Mr. Pike. Now, Mr. Colyear, go on."

"As I said, sir, Kent was injured in the boarding."

"How badly?"

"A saber cut. Not deep but serious enough. But there was no time to allow the surgeon to attend to him."

"What? Was there no French surgeon in *Swiftsure*?"

"Yes, but it took some time before Mr. Kent could be or would allow himself to be attended to. The wound was to the face, sir." Col unknowingly fingered a line curving from his temple midway down the side of his cheek in illustration.

"Ah." The captain drew still.

"Yes, sir. But what you need to know—" Col's voice stumbled in his haste to speak the secret that felt as if it were eating him alive. "He is not Richard Kent."

McAlden froze for a very long moment and then pushed slowly away from his table, and sat back in his chair. "I am aware that—"

"No, sir. I beg you would listen to me. The boy is not Richard Kent—"

"But Sarah Alice Kent. Sally," McAlden finished quietly, "his sister. I know."

"You know?" Of all things, Col never expected this. "Captain Kent—he wrote to you?"

"No." Captain McAlden shook his head. "I have waited in expectation of just such a letter, these past months. But as yet, I have not had the pleasure of correspondence with Captain Kent. For all I know, Alexander Kent may yet be unaware that I have his only daughter on board."

"Then, how did you—" Col let the question slide away. He was all too aware that by asking others, he would have to answer the same questions for himself.

"It may surprise you to find that I have known from the first. Since the first day you brought her aboard my ship, Mr. Colyear."

Damn him for a fool. All this time. All this time he had strangled the guilt that was eating him alive. And all this time, she had never really even had a secret to keep. "How?"

The captain's face lit with that same strange, small smile, as if he had his own secrets to keep. "Intuition. Experience with highly imaginative, active girls. I am not sure I will care at all for your answer, Mr. Colyear," the captain continued, "but I find I must ask, when did *you* first discover the secret of Miss Kent's sex?"

With that word, Col felt himself heat and burn to a cinder. "I beg your pardon, sir?" he stammered.

"I assume you discovered her during her recent illness?"

Here was the perfect, ready-made excuse. Here was the perfect circumstance to excuse himself from responsibility. And culpability. But he was an honest man—and he wanted to be rid of the burden of his guilt. He owed Captain McAlden, not to mention the Kents, the whole truth.

"No, sir. I've known since we weighed anchor."

If Captain McAlden was surprised, he made no show of it beyond a slow lifting of his eyebrows. "I see. Who else knows?"

"No one, sir. I've told no one."

"I'm sure you haven't." Captain McAlden smiled. "I have always admired your frankness of character, your steadfast loyalty, and your unimpeachable honesty, Mr. Colyear."

The captain may have meant his words as compliments, but Col felt each one like a blow. "But she's been living on a ship with two hundred and sixty-odd men," the captain continued. "Someone else knows. Someone else always knows."

"Perhaps old Pinkerton, sir, the orlop berth servant."

"Ah. Of course. And Mr. Gamage as well. Strangely perceptive man for a blockhead, Mr. Gamage. He came to me with his suspicions some time ago. And for his honesty was rewarded with the command of your sloop, Mr. Colyear, thereby keeping Kent's secret. I rather like the touch of ironic justice in that. But I had much rather you had come to me with your news sooner, Mr. Colyear."

There was nothing Col might say to acquit himself. Nothing he would allow himself to say in his defense.

"It seems we've all been keeping secrets on *Audacious*," the captain said philosophically. "I hope it may give Captain Alexander Kent some relief to know so many people have been looking after his unorthodox, but highly useful, recruit."

Col needed no reminder to think of her father—to think of all of them. His friends. Her family. "Will you write him now, sir?"

Captain McAlden took a long time before he answered. "I think not. At least not yet. Not until we know how she fares, one way or the other. The next few days will, I'm sure, tell."

And there it was, the truth he had been keeping, even from himself. For the first time, the mortal possibility leached into his chest like acid, turning his heart to cold, aching stone. But he nodded. "I'll see to her, sir."

"And I am sorry that I cannot allow you that luxury, Mr. Colyear."

"Sir?"

"In days such as these, Mr. Colyear, the navy has need of all its intelligent, able-bodied, and even abler-minded young men. Mr. Lawrence has been promoted to first, while Mr. Horner I have just now sent to command *Swiftsure*. And you, Mr. Colyear, are to report immediately, before the morning watch has ended, aboard *Tonnant*. *Tonnant* is too large to take in tow, so you will be left to bring her into repair while the main body of the fleet makes sail for Gibraltar. When possible, you will follow with all haste. Are your orders clear?"

Col swallowed his feelings down like hot shrapnel. "Yes, sir. I thank you."

"You are most welcome to the command. Good luck and godspeed, Mr. Colyear."

There was nothing for it but to go, though he felt as if his boots were weighted down with lead shot. He should have had some notice, some greater amount of time to prepare. To say good-bye.

When he reached the gunroom, Angus Pinkerton was just coming out of Kent's cuddy.

"How is she?"

"Quiet, sir. But weak. Too weak." He shook his head. "I reckoned I'd make a posset to see if I can strengthen young Kent up."

"Yes, you do that, Pinkerton."

"Thank you, sir, I will. But . . ." The old man hesitated. "Seeing how things is, I don't rightly know what I ought to do with this."

Pinkerton brought out from the fold of his coat a creased and sealed missive, and passed it carefully to Col. It was the letter Sally had written to her father before the battle. The one that she had asked him to see delivered.

If he had to go, if he had to leave her to the care of this ancient, grizzled mariner, not knowing what her fate might be, he would do her one last service.

"Are you a praying man, Pinky?"

"Of course." The old tar smiled. "Me 'n Saint Peter been on speaking terms these fifty years."

"Then I will ask you to do me the favor of interceding for her, Pinky."

"I can do that, sir, if you'll be so good as to safeguard that"—he pointed to the letter—"for me."

"Consider it done, Pinky. I know just what I need to do."

Chapter Twenty-three

Sally awoke and knew somehow she was in Gibraltar. She knew she had come to this place—this lovely airy room with fresh, clean linen on a wide bed—some days ago. And they had been kind, and called her Miss Kent, and given her tea, and bade her to sleep.

What happened before that was lost in a haze that was half dream and half memory. She remembered Col being gruff and unhappy, and ordering her about in that low, vehement tone of his. And Pinky tutting and fussing and making her drink the foulest concoctions. But she had been tired. So very, very tired.

And, she found, she was still as weak as a torn sail. Even rising up in the bed was exhausting.

"Good morning, miss." A cheerfully plump woman bustled into the room with a vase of fresh wildflowers. "I didn't know you was up. Why, you look a hundred times better today."

Did she? Without a mirror, Sally had no idea what she looked like. But she said, "Thank you, ma'am," because it was only polite, and she needed to be polite considering she hadn't the devil of an idea to whom she was speaking. Or for how long she'd been imposing upon their hospitality.

"They'll want to know you're awake," the cheerful woman

assured her as she headed for the door. "And I'll warrant you'll be hungry."

"And thirsty." Sally's throat felt as if it had been holy-stoned. "I thank you, yes."

She fell back onto her pillows, stretched her achy muscles, and was trying to reckon out just where she could be when Captain McAlden walked into the room.

"Ah. *Miss* Kent. Good to see you improving."

"Captain McAlden, sir," she stammered, entirely unprepared to meet with her captain while in bed. And wearing a nightshirt.

Oh, devil take her now. She could feel her whole face flush with embarrassment. She hitched herself up to sitting.

"Please." He held up a polite hand. "No need to rise, Miss Kent, though you can't know how it pleases me to see you awake and lucid."

Miss Kent. Clearly, she was found out. It only remained to know if she was disgraced as well. "I take it," she began cautiously, "we are in Gibraltar."

Captain McAlden nodded. "*Audacious* made port three days ago, and I made free to have you brought here, to the home of a friend, Mr. Harvey, and his family. You may stay as long as you like, until you are recovered. They are happy to have you, and quite discreet. You needn't worry that there will be any awkward questions."

"Thank you, sir. But then I'm afraid I'll have to be the one with the awkward questions. What's to become of me? What *has* become of me as Richard Kent?"

"Sensible of you to ask. The world knows that Richard Kent was grievously injured in the Battle at Trafalgar, and, as a lifelong friend to your father—as is Mr. Harvey, in whose house we are guests—I thought it best to bring you here, to recover."

Her gloomy outlook brightened. "So I am still Richard, and I may become Richard again, when I am recovered?"

"No, Miss Kent. I fear that would be impossible. As a

friend to your father, I simply can't allow it any longer." He tried to put paid to her ambitions, but his last admission was telling.

"Any longer?"

"It may surprise you to know, as it did your friend Mr. Colyear, that I make it my business to know exactly what goes on in my ships. At all times. From the moment a new crew member comes aboard, Miss Kent, and speaks warmly of her family traditions."

Devil take her. She didn't think her face could get any hotter, but still it heated by several degrees until she was sure she was as bright as a winter orange. "I see."

"Yes, well." Her captain was none too comfortable himself, tugging at his cravat as if his steward had tied it too tight. "I wish to the devil that I had seen things as clearly at the start. At the time, I didn't see the harm. You were eager and spectacularly able. I had need of you. To put you off would have put me in arrears of my schedule. And quite frankly, I wasn't sure if your father was playing a joke on me, or I on him. Either way, I regret it. I will admit that my ambitions got the better of me. You cannot know how deeply I regret it. I should have put you off from the first."

She wouldn't hear of it. "I don't regret it. Not in the least."

"Do you not? I think, dear Miss Kent, your injury has been rather more grievous than you imagine."

The quiet pity in his voice strangled the air from her lungs. A feeling too much like dread—an acid combination of fear and helplessness—crawled its way under her skin. She couldn't speak. She was too busy trying to swallow back the hot scald of fear. And there was nothing left to say anyway.

Captain McAlden filled the charged silence. "You have done well, Miss Kent, very well. No one could have done better. I wish to hell you were Richard Kent, for I'd know very well what to do with you then. I wish I had a dozen of your kind of Richard Kent with me every day. If you were Richard Kent, I'd ship you back into the gunroom post-haste and take pride and pleasure in watching your inevitably rapid advancement. You were good for my ship, Miss Kent."

"I *can* go back. If you let me. I can be Richard, you'll see—"

"No. No." He said it emphatically. "I owe it to your father. I can do nothing less than send you home to him."

"He's not there, sir, but on the West Indies Station. And madder than a hornet, I'll reckon, when he hears what he missed at Trafalgar."

"You're going home, Miss Kent." He said it quietly and kindly, but there was no mistaking that Captain McAlden had given her an order.

It would do no good to tell him it wasn't home. That it was just an empty, rambling house high on the cliffs without her family there with her. She beat back the heat in her throat and made herself speak clearly. "I understand, sir. I thank you for your kind attention."

"I hope I do not overstep, but if you should find it . . . difficult being ashore, perhaps, with your father on the West Indies Station, you might try a voyage to the Bahamas. I recall you saying you particularly liked the climate."

"Yes, sir." She nodded her head, grateful for the diversion. "Yes, I did. It is kind of you to remember."

"If I may, let me also recommend Lady McAlden as a friend to you. I know she would deem it an honor to have you visit, and would very much like to be your friend. As I hope I have been."

Sally felt the hot press of tears fill her eyes. She dashed her wrist across them. She didn't want to cry. Not now. Not after everything. But there was nothing for it. Her cheeks were already wet.

But her captain did not censure her lack of control. He was kind enough to turn and walk to the window, and remain there for a long moment, admiring the view. "You remind me of her, you know. When I met Lady McAlden, she was a young woman equally resourceful and adventurous, not to mention ambitious. I am confident you will become fast friends."

"Thank you, sir. You are very kind. That means a great deal to me." She knuckled her achy forehead. "It has been an honor to serve you and *Audacious,* sir."

Captain McAlden made her an elegant bow, and then took her hand. "The honor has been mine. Good-bye, Miss Kent. And godspeed."

"Thank you, sir. Godspeed to you and *Audacious* as well."

Captain McAlden made his solemn way to the door, but then paused at the threshold. "Ah. I see that before I go, I fear I must ask you the favor of temporarily becoming Richard Kent once more. I see a visitor below, who has requested to see you."

The impetuous words were out of her mouth before she could stop them, though she strove belatedly for just the right amount of casual curiosity. "Is Mr. Colyear here as well, sir?"

"Alas, no. Acting Commander Colyear is helping to oversee the repair and readiness of *Tonnant* off Cape Trafalgar, and is also, I understand, helping the commander of that squadron in fending off challenges from the Spanish who have tried to retake the vessels."

Which was all a fancy, calm way of saying that Col was still out there fighting. Still in harm's way. And most assuredly not come to see her. She swallowed down another bitter dose of disappointment.

"Your visitor is young Mr. Jellicoe."

Sally could feel the corners of her mouth curve upward at such welcome news. If she couldn't have Col, she was more than glad to have Will.

In another moment she could hear her friend's bounding footsteps on the stairs.

"Richard," he said as he burst into the room, bringing all his sunny energy. "How do you go on?" He came over immediately and crawled right up, to sit on the bed. "Well, you're coming along nicely."

"Thank you." She laughed. "It's very good to see you, too. Though I must say, I'm so very sorry to have let you down, Will, and left you shorthanded with *Swiftsure.*"

"It's all right. You'd been clouted on the head, hadn't you? It was a hell of a thing. Lord, but it bled right proper, didn't it," he added with his characteristic affinity and fascination for gore. "I was amazed you lasted as long as you did. Moffatt was, too. And both he and I slept for a day when we got back to *Audacious*. At least I did."

"I have to thank you for everything you did for me, Will. You were a true friend."

"You're welcome, Richard." He shook her hand happily. "So when are they going to let you come back to *Audacious*? It's been brilliant with so many people gone. Marcus, Ian, and I have all been promoted to acting lieutenants!"

"Congratulations. I am very pleased for you. But I shan't be coming back, Will." She looked her friend in the eye. "I'm being sent home."

"For a clout on the head? I mean, I know it's bad—I can see *that*—but for that they're sending you home? Half the lieutenants on *Tonnant* and *Royal Sovereign* have lost arms and whatnot, and they're not sending them home. At least, I think not. Though they do have to send the *sailors* home who've lost arms, since they can't haul or work anymore. But *officers* are different. Admiral Nelson went about for years with only one arm. But I suppose you heard that he's dead. Died in the battle."

"Yes, I knew. I'd heard before I got 'clouted on the head.'"

"Oh, right. I remember. But I'm sure if you ask Captain McAlden, he'll let you stay."

"No. They're sending me home for another reason, Will." Sally decided not to dance around the topic any longer. Because Will Jellicoe had been her friend, and she wanted him to know. "Because they've discovered I'm a girl."

Will looked at her, his mouth open in astonishment, before he burst out laughing. "You're not," he stated with all the confident conviction of a twelve-year-old who cannot imagine the world to be such a strange, disordered place.

And when she only smiled at him patiently, waiting for him to see the truth and understand, he blustered, "But you're one of us."

"I am, aren't I? Thank you, Will. You have no idea what that means to me. I will treasure your opinion always."

He slid off the bed, away from her, but Sally was glad to note, he went no farther than the bedpost. He draped his arm around it, and stood with one foot leaning against his shin, nonplussed but not really taken aback. "It's not just my opinion. Everyone feels that way, I'll wager. Especially Mr. Colyear and Moffatt. He'd not let anyone say a word against you, I'll warrant, girl or no. He really liked how you called him an anvil of a man."

"Did he?" But the endorsement did make her smile again. She'd no idea she had called the mate "an anvil" out loud. Must have been when she was too exhausted to remember. "And what did Mr. Colyear say?"

"Oh, nothing. He's already gone. He was given command of a prize, *Tonnant,* and left *Audacious* to take command of it."

"Ah, yes, Captain McAlden told me that."

"Mr. Lawrence has taken his place, as first, and Ian and I are both third, though I've laid him a groat I'll make second before him."

"Have you forgotten Captain McAlden doesn't approve of gambling?"

"No, but without Mr. Colyear there to see to things . . . Well, things are different now. Though I will say, it's not the same without him. Too much work for one thing." He looked up at her again, searching her face as if he could find the fault that showed her to have been a female. "Are you sure you can't come back? We could use the help. And girl or no, it won't be the same without you, either. None of the rest of us ever would have had the bollocks— Oh, I beg your pardon. But, well, you know—to take on and poison Mr. Gamage like that."

"It wasn't really poison. But thank you, Will. I might try, but at the moment, until I'm strong enough to get out of bed, I can't promise anything."

"You should come back. Because if you are a girl, it's going to be a lot harder to live with that face than it will be to live with us."

He could not have doused her any more effectively if he had pitched her headfirst into a cold bucket of seawater.

Whatever else Will had to say, and whatever fond fare-wells she made herself say, passed without any further notice. Because the casual, unthinking cruelty of his words had awakened in her a dreadful suspicion that could not be allayed until he had finally left, and Sally was alone, and could ease herself out of bed and make her slow, shaky way first to the bedpost and then across the few steps to the corner, where there was a mirror.

And then, as her face slowly came into view past the edge of the frame, she saw what they had been talking about. She saw the swelling and the purple bruising that seeped across half of her face. She stared at the long sweep of stitches that itched and bristled from her face like hedgehog spines.

And she finally understood.

She was completely and utterly ruined in the one way that she had never, ever envisioned or even thought possible.

The real trouble began the moment she had to return to Sarah Alice Kent and leave Mr. Midshipman Kent behind.

Her period of recovery in the home of the sherry merchant, Mr. Harvey, passed without incident, and her voyage back to Falmouth went as well as she could have hoped because, as her sea chest held no clothes other than her uniforms, and she had no inclination to get suitable replacements, she chose to continue to be Richard. As Mr. Kent, she was shipped back to England in the more spacious comfort of a three-decker, with a number of other officers also being invalided out, who did not look or stare at her face, just as she did not stare at their missing limbs. As Mr. Kent, she traveled easily by post along the wet winter roads. As Mr. Kent, she knew what to do.

Every day, she thought about how she was to effect the change back to Sally, and every day, she managed to come up with a fresh excuse as to why she need not.

Because as a veteran of Trafalgar and therefore a hero, she was given the utmost respect and deference. As Richard,

her wound gave pause—the bandage could not be hidden—
but it was a pause followed by the proffering of ale or claret,
depending on the class of the beholder, and the promise of
the best rooms. As Richard, she was patted on the back and
thanked, and had her health and good fortune drunk to.

But once through the doors of the imposing Queen Anne–
style house on Cliff Road, everything changed. Almost
everything.

The house was exactly the same. The same key let her in
the door, and the same umbrella stood poised against the
wall of the entryway, exactly where she had left it the day
she and Richard had departed. The entry hall still smelled
vaguely of dune roses, and the drawing room fireplace was
still laid with alder logs, and the house still echoed with the
emptiness of a family that was gone.

Everything was the same. Only she had changed.

"Mr. Matthew?" Mrs. Jenkins waddled up the corridor
from the kitchens. "Or is that you, Mr. Richard?"

"No, Mrs. Jenkins. It's Sally. Sally Kent."

"Oh, Miss Sally! Oh, Miss Sally, what happened to you?"
Mrs. Jenkins greeted her sudden return with tears of sorrow
and despair. "Oh, when I look at you, I can only think of
what your dear mother, God rest her soul, would say, and I
don't think we'll ever forgive ourselves. Isn't that right, Jenkins?"

"Oh, aye. It's a terrible thing what you had to do, Miss
Sally, go off like that, though I know why you'd done it. The
country's full of nothing but talk of the fearful battle. I only
hope your brother appreciates it as he ought."

"Thank you, but it's not so very terrible, Jenkins. Many
men lost their lives that day. I rather considered myself for-
tunate to come away with so little lost but my vanity."

But Mrs. Jenkins could not be consoled out of her tears,
for she had nursed the secret of Sally's disappearance like a
viper to her bosom. "We ne'er could tell a soul. And not
knowing . . . Oh, you never did have enough vanity for your
own good. And now, what are you to do, living out your

days a spinster in your father's house, hiding your face from the world."

It was a shock—a nasty, cold, breath-stealing shock—to hear her own fears articulated so baldly. The specter of such a future sent spiders of chill crawling up and down her skin. "Surely it's not that bad, Mrs. Jenkins. Surely I'm made up of more than a scar."

But she couldn't even convince herself. And with every passing day, every day that she looked in the mirror and saw the same vivid cobweb of dark red lines snaking their way around her temple, she feared it was more and more true. And she grew more and more fearful.

It was a new sort of fear. The kind that followed her from room to empty room. That accompanied her about the garden. The kind that crept up to her in the middle of the night and kept her from sleep.

Not that she was getting much of that. She still awoke on watch time, after only four hours of sleep, to hover on the edge of consciousness, waiting for the sound of the bell, or the shrill of the pipe to call her to duty, before she would remember and give in to the despair.

She hadn't been afraid of dying. But she was afraid of exactly what confronted her now. Of living like a ghost in her own life. Of living on, alone. Of living without him.

Col didn't write. Each day brought the horrible moment when the post would come. At first, she would go to it eagerly, sure that by now he would have heard, that he would have kept her as fresh in his thoughts as he was in hers, and written. Others wrote, but he did not. November came and waned into December, and still nothing came. She took to walking out, longer and longer tramps along the cliffs, to prevent herself from waiting, hating the fresh stab of hurt at each successive daily disappointment.

The others who wrote included her brothers, on various stations, and her father in the West Indies, still oblivious to her former absence from the house, and the changes that the time apart had wrought.

The navy itself even wrote to inform her that the Courts of Admiralty had adjudicated the prizes owed to *Audacious* and that Richard Kent could collect his monies from them. But of course, she was no longer Richard Kent, and she could summon no authority, moral or otherwise, within herself to impersonate him again. The devil could take it all, for the devil was most assuredly in the details.

Of Richard, she knew little and heard less, only that he had written to the Jenkinses in the autumn, asking that his clothing and books be forwarded to an address in Cambridgeshire, which proved to be, when Jenkins had gone to deliver the cart himself, a coffeehouse whose proprietor could provide him no further information.

She was alone. She ate alone. She walked alone. She slept alone. She lived almost entirely in the lonely privacy of her own head, curled up for hours in the safe harbor of the deep, shuttered, padded window seats in the drawing room, from which she could watch the early winter rains lash the garden.

She didn't even hear the commotion in the hall above the nattering patter of the rain.

"Ahoy," a stentorian voice rang out across the house. "Is there no one here?"

"Owen?"

"Sal! Get you out here, I've someone I want you to meet."

Sally sprang up, and ran into the entry hall, only to find it deserted, and the door wide open to the dripping rain. She took up an umbrella, and called back to the kitchens, "Mrs. Jenkins, Owen is home! And he's . . ."

Out the door and across the gravel of the drive, the most elegant carriage she'd ever seen was disgorging the single most elegant female Sally had ever had occasion to see. Her brother Owen, whose shock of vividly orange hair contrasted superbly with his uniform coat—complete with epaulettes!— was handing out the most beautiful, most glamorously dressed woman ever to grace Cliff House. Every inch of her petite frame was covered in fashionable sky blue silk and lace, from her pale oval face and perfectly coiffed, mahogany hair to the tips of her jewel-encrusted shoes. She was exquisite. A tiny china doll of a young woman.

Sally skidded her gangly, oversized frame to a noisy halt in the gravel and handed her brother the umbrella. And said the only thing she could think of. "Owen, you've been made post."

"I have," he agreed cheerfully, as he took the umbrella. "But let me get my darling out of the rain, and inside before I'm overcome with congratulations."

He held the umbrella high over the doll and her exquisite face that had silently watched the exchange, and swept "his darling" into the house.

Sally followed, but at a slower pace, feeling as if her pockets were weighted with stone.

Because the look that had slipped into the young lady's eyes at the sight of Sally was enough to set her well back on her heels. It was enough to make her want to run howling to the quiet of her bedchamber and smother herself to death with one of the pillows. It had been nothing more than a momentary widening of the corners of the girl's eyes and a shocked tightness around her mouth before it was masked behind manners as fine as the Madeira lace dripping from her silken sleeves. But still, the rejection stung like an entire hive full of hornets.

Owen, being a Kent, and singularly obtuse, saw nothing. "Sally! You naughty dog!" he chastised her as she crossed the threshold. "I've been sent to take you in hand. Give your brother a kiss, there's a good girl."

"I'm hardly a girl anymore, Owen," Sally muttered even as she complied, for there was nothing else to say that wouldn't make her seem the veriest shrew in front of the extraordinary, beautiful young woman who regarded her from behind impossibly thick, dark lashes. And she had so, so missed the camaraderie and noisy comfort of her brothers.

"Welcome home, Owen." She hugged him until he set her back down on the flagstones, though her insides felt as if they were being pulled as tight as a backstay, and her throat felt suspiciously dry and hot. *Taken in hand.* Devil take Owen. And his *darling.*

"Lord, what a scare you gave us, Sal. I had no idea it was you, and not Richard, in *Audacious,* the whole time. I would have seen *you* before, or sent word or some such, or at least visited at Gibraltar, except that I was already gone, back to England with the news of the battle."

"You were there? At Trafalgar?"

"In *Pickle.* Fast cutter. Left immediately with Collingwood's dispatches for the Admiralty. I understand you had quite a blow."

She had in more ways than one. Leave it to Owen to so typically understate a hurricane as to call it a blow. And all that time. All that time her family had been so close at hand and she didn't know. "But how did you hear about me?"

"Had a letter from Pater. All spelled out. Well, most of it, anyway—I'm still all-fire to find out what the hell happened to Richard."

"I'm afraid I don't know." And that still didn't tell her how her father had found out.

"Oh, well, Pater will be home soon and put it all to rights."

"Father is coming home? When? When, Owen?"

"Soon I should think, and the others as well, as I'm sure he wrote to them, same as me. And it's just as well. For they can all come home to celebrate and wish me happy for getting married."

"Married?" she echoed stupidly, too astonished to absorb any more of his blows. But he wasn't done yet.

"That's right. I've brought you a new sister." Owen gestured happily to the elegant young lady standing so quietly and patiently by his side. "To live with you, and keep you company, and keep you from getting old and lonely."

He meant to be his usual, blustery, brotherly self, but every word stung, every intended kindness brought fresh pain, as if her brother had given his swarm of hornets pikes and knives. There was nothing she could do to protect herself. And Owen, damn his leathery hide, just sailed on despite a desperate shushing noise from his wife.

"Oh, she doesn't need to be cozened, do you, Sally? The truth is that Pater sent me to have a good look at you, and let him know what's what. So let me see." He took up Sally's chin in the ruthlessly frank grip only a brother could, and had a good long stare at her, as if she were a rudder gudgeon he was considering replacing.

"Not that bad," was his assessment.

It was too much, however, for Sally.

She did what only a younger sister of delicate sensibility could do. She swore violently, smashed her boot into her brother's shin, and fled.

Chapter Twenty-four

Her new sister-in-law found Sally at her breakfast the next morning. A glance at the tall case clock by the door told her it was seven o'clock in the morning. Devil take the girl. It was too early for such an exquisite creature to even be awake, let alone looking like she had just walked off the pages of a fashion plate.

Sally had quite purposely hidden herself at the back of the house, in the many-windowed garden room her mother had loved so much. But still the girl found her, tracking her down like a well-groomed scent hound.

"Good morning," the silken creature said with the breezy certainty of a woman who is quite sure the world will do its utmost to please her. "What a lovely room. This is a charming home. From Owen's description, I thought it should be a dark, poky old house with no comfort or taste. But I can see that he's too influenced by what he's used to aboard ship to take any notice of the finer aspects of decoration. This is absolutely lovely. I'd like to join you, if I may. We didn't have an opportunity to be introduced last afternoon. I'm Grace. Lady Grace Burroughs, as was. Lady Grace Kent now, I suppose, wife of Captain Kent."

The creature had hardly drawn a breath, letting her words tumble merrily out, like a little tinkling brook. And her smile was full of her own pleasure at her newest incarnation of her title, as if she had spent days wasting ink in the margin of her schoolbook—for she looked to Sally no more than sixteen—trying out variations of her married name.

"How do you do?" Sally rose, mostly because Lady Grace had remained standing through her breathless speech, and seemed to expect that sort of courtesy. And it made it devilishly easy to look down upon her from Sally's height.

Lady Grace, however, was not intimidated. She rewarded Sally's feeble attempt at politeness with a bright smile. "Very well, I thank you. But please, you must sit. And may I join you?"

"Of course," Sally answered, because she did not know what else to say that would not be either rude or ridiculous.

But when Grace sat, and gave Sally a smile of sunny expectancy—all bright eyes and delicately arched brows—Sally felt she had no choice but to fill the awkward silence. "I must apologize for my behavior yesterday. I don't want you to think I don't wish you very happy, or that you're not welcome here. You are. Most welcome."

Sally hated her awkwardness and resentment. She knew how to act in a gunroom upon a ship. Devil take her, she had mastered trigonometric navigation and dealt with—even poisoned—Mr. Gamage. Why should it be so hard for her to speak easily to this silly creature? "I hope Mrs. Jenkins saw to your needs and made you comfortable."

"Oh, yes, very. Though I have my own maid with me as well." Lady Grace gestured to the girl who at that moment entered the room with a well-laden breakfast tray. "I'm sure you will think me a silly thing to elope with my maid, but—"

"Elope!" Sally couldn't hope to hide her surprise and shock.

"Well," Grace hedged, with a smile of delighted, twinkling mischief, as she waited for the maid to leave. "Thank you, Dawkins. Not really eloped, as my Captain Kent made sure we were married by special license. We were married in London, at the home of Sir Charles Middleton—do you know him?" But Lady Grace did not wait to hear if her question was to be answered, and went on with her happy tale.

"My parents had no objections. Indeed, they were quite pleased with Captain Kent. And they are a great deal older and quite used to letting me have my way."

The nasty twinge twisting up Sally's innards went beyond resentment. It was most assuredly jealousy. For the first time in her life, Sally could almost want to change places with this girl—the kind of girl she had always dismissed as shallow and pampered, and far too insulated from the real world for her own good.

But what would it be like, just for once, to feel the world at one's feet? To be *used* to having one's way?

"I suppose it only felt like an elopement," Grace continued, "because we came away so suddenly. But we were coming to see you, just as we ought." She turned her candle-bright smile back on Sally. "To make sure you were quite well."

Sally bridled at being so patronized. "As you see."

Grace was not put off by her cool tone. "Yes, and I am glad. Though I am sorry he was so . . . rough with you yesterday. I do know my dear captain can seem hard, almost too brusque and decisive for some people, but I will tell you, from the moment he received that letter, he thought of almost nothing else but you."

It was strange, and certainly off-putting, to be the focus of such well-meaning pity.

"I am sure you mean to be kind." She spoke firmly and quietly, just like Col would have, never raising his voice. "But I know my brother of old, and if he thought of nothing but me on the first days of his honeymoon, then I think perhaps something may be wrong with *him*."

Instead of taking offense, Grace laughed, the kind of sparkling, delightful laugh that reminded listeners of little silver bells. Sally did not know how she could hate her any more.

"I said *almost* nothing. Of course, he has been everything attentive. I don't mind telling you that the moment I made up my mind that we should come and see you, your brother put all his energy into making it so."

"Does he always do exactly what you want?"

"Nearly always. Shouldn't he?"

Sally put down her teacup with a clatter. "Are you very spoiled?"

"Oh, terribly! It is my very finest accomplishment and skill," Grace said, wide-eyed with all possible frankness, "to make people do what I want."

Despite herself, Sally was amused. And impressed. She had not thought it possible for the creature to be so honestly self-aware. "Can you teach me?"

If Grace's smile had been wide and bright before, it now became blinding. "Oh, most assuredly. I should like nothing more! But I will warn you, in the process, I shall be trying to get what I want from you."

"From me? What could you possibly want from me?"

"I want to live here with you."

No. It was the first word into her brain, and Sally actually put her hand across her lips to prevent it from leaking out of her mouth. "Are you in your right mind? Here? In this old house? With me? This is practically the end of the world, and I hope you won't mind my saying so, since we're being frank, but you hardly seem the kind of woman who can exist apart from a place like London. I mean, look at you. I'm sure you're best viewed in candlelight."

"Actually, morning light is best, as it brings out the contrast of my complexion and my hair. But that's not important. The thing of it is, when my darling Owen goes back to sea—for I am quite convinced he will get a ship in no time—I will be desperately lonely. Desperately. I've waited all my life to find the one man whom I could love enough to make my husband. And I have done so. But he's to go away, out to sea, and no one else in London will understand that loss. They will want me to go to parties and be gay, and not care about how he's gone. They won't understand. But Owen says you do. He says that you're as used to it as anyone could be, from your family all going away all the time. So I thought I should like to be here with you."

Devil take Owen. Devil take them both. The problem was she *wasn't* used to it, no matter how often they had gone away. She didn't think she would *ever* get used to it.

And what a cat's-paw that would be, with two lovelorn females—and possibly the two most unalike females in the entire country—moping about the house all day long. Sally was already heartily sick of herself. It would be insupportable to add another.

"It may be a longer while yet, before Owen is given a ship. Just because he's been made post doesn't mean he'll be quickly given a command."

"Will he not? But he is a hero of Trafalgar, just like you. And he is brilliant. Everyone tells me it is so, and I know it from my own experience of him. And of course my father, Lord Burroughs, will use all of his not inconsiderable influence on his behalf. That, combined with your own father Captain Kent's excellent reputation in the navy, will assuredly gain him all the influence and patronage he needs."

She was probably right. But her speech brought up another problem. "*I* am not a hero of Trafalgar, Grace. *Richard* is. I don't know what Owen has told you—"

"Oh, he has told me all, for he does not believe there should be secrets between a man and his wife, even family secrets. He told me you took Richard's place for the sake of family honor when Richard refused to go. Oh, and that is another thing—Owen also says that we need to find Richard, and see him, and tell him everything as well, so he will know what to say to people when they speak to him of Trafalgar, as they will. For he doesn't know a thing, does he? Owen says he's been hiding somewhere in Cambridgeshire, learning to make sermons the whole time."

Sally was not going to go galloping about the country trying to fix Richard's problems. Doing so was what got her into so much trouble from the start. "Frankly, I had much rather not. And I fancy Richard does not want to be found."

"Oh, that's nothing. I'm famous for making people do what they think they don't want to do. You'll see."

"Yes, I think I already do," Sally admitted with a strange wonder. "For you've already made me like you."

"Have I?" Grace cried with delight, before she bounded up to alight upon Sally with a well-scented embrace. "Oh, I am so glad. I should like to be your friend of all things. I think you the most intrepid young woman I've ever heard of, with all your exciting exploits. I quite envy you your adventures, and I'm beyond thrilled that you're to be my sister. I never had a sister, but if I got to pick one out, she would be exactly like you!"

"Would she? A great galumphing thing like me? Aren't you afraid I'll try to grind your bones to make my bread? One of my feet is bigger than your entire body. I could snap you in two, like a precious porcelain doll."

Grace laughed again, just like Christmas bells, merry and bright. "Stuff and nonsense. I won't hear of any galumphing, whatever that is. You, my dear new sister, are above all that. You are a goddess, brave, burning, and statuesque. And besides," she said, digging into her meal, "I'm not so very fragile. I may look dainty, but I could eat girls like you for breakfast." She paused and smiled up at Sally. "But I had rather not. I had much rather love you, and live with you, instead."

There was nothing Sally could do to defend herself against such a ridiculously charming, heartfelt appeal. She had been lonely, for far too long. And it just might be interesting to try something new for a change, and have a sister.

"Do you know what I should like above all things?" Grace asked from the window seat in Sally's bedroom, where they had repaired after their walk.

After a fortnight, Sally had gotten used to Grace's outrageously scattered style of talk. It kept her vastly entertained. Far too entertained to brood. Or mope about.

"A ship to sail, a star to set her by?" Sally joked. "No, that would be me. For you, how about either a chocolate *gâteau* or a house full of babies?"

"Babies?" Grace was so surprised at the suggestion that she rolled off the window seat and sat up. "What on earth would I do with babies? I would much rather have a chocolate *gâteau*."

"You would love them, of course," Sally said simply, and then asked, "How old *are* you?"

"I am one and twenty."

"As old as that?" Sally had missed the mark by almost six years. And never in a hundred years would she have thought Grace to be the elder of the two.

"It's only that I'm so petite," Grace explained as if she could tell what Sally was thinking. "People think me younger. And that I'm so spoiled."

Sally smiled at her sister's frank assessment. Whatever Grace might be, she was not deluded. She knew her own strengths and she used them ruthlessly. It was something Sally would do well to remember. And emulate.

"Well, I should like it of all things if you had babies. It would please me to no end. And I think you should like it, too. Especially if you're planning to live all the way out here with me, after Owen is gone. If you had a baby, you would have a little piece of him left behind, for you to mind, and love and spoil, all in your own turn, when he is gone."

"Oh. Well, I hadn't thought of that."

"Had you not? Dear Grace, you do know where babies come from, do you not? Or are you just counting on God giving you your way, and handing you the appropriate baby when you want one?"

"Oh, Sally, how you can make me laugh. Of course I do know. Owen was very good in explaining it to me, but at that point, you know, I already had a fair idea of the way of things."

"I imagine you did." But Sally had much rather not hear about the particulars of it. If she had to listen to Grace praising Owen in this, as she did in all other things—well, Sally didn't think the bounds of siblinghood could withstand the assault of such information. She did not want to know about the process, only about the result.

"So it's decided, then; you're to have the babies, and make

me an aunt, so I will have nieces and nephews to spoil and ruin."

"Shall you? What a droll person you shall be." Grace's smile showed she was becoming enamored of this version of their future.

"Oh, yes. I will be useful and funny, and I will take all my nieces and nephews—I think it fair to say yours will only be the first—on all the marvelous adventures their careful mothers will not allow. Especially my nieces. I will take them sailing in Falmouth Bay and teach them all the wonderful, useful, enjoyable things no one else would teach them. Like how to whistle like a sailor. Every boy should know that, but so should every girl."

"Will you teach me?"

"Of course. Especially as Owen will hate it. He likes to think you're delicate and soft. It should be fun to disabuse him of his ideas."

"Oh, Sally. How I do love you already. You will make a most treasured, favorite aunt. You know everything. And I have ever so many questions that Owen will only laugh at and never answer."

"Questions?"

"Yes!" Grace sat down on the bed. "I should like to know what it was like. What your life was like aboard ship. With all those men. And of course, what dear Owen's life will be like once he receives his ship."

"Well, a captain's life is very different from what mine was like as a midshipman." For one thing, her brothers never had to hide and lie about who they were. Although they may have anyway.

"Owen says midshipmen are all blockheads and must eat rats," Grace said with an avidity bright enough to rival Will Jellicoe's. "But I can't imagine you were ever a blockhead."

"Thank you, Grace. But I'm a blockhead enough about some things." Many things. All the things that included Col. "Maybe not about naval things, like navigation and watches

and eating rats—they're called millers, just so you know—
but about everything else. All the things that you do so well.
Going out in the world and making it like you."

"Millers," Grace repeated solemnly. "But why should
you think the world does not like you? You have only to
smile! I know you have a smile that quite lights up a room,
when you try to. And even when you don't. You have that
special something your brothers have—a gleam in your eye
that entrances."

"That is only a sister's kindness. Ask Owen. He will be
glad to tell you tales of his tall, awkward sister."

"Stuff and nonsense. I know in your current state you
may not be in the way of seeing yourself as kindly as perhaps you will again, when you are fully recovered."

Here, at last, was the heart of the discussion. Grace had
been tactful, and even subtle about her scar, and didn't bela-
bor her point, but every day, she managed to bring their conversation around. But Sally had to admit, she didn't mind. It
did her good to talk about it, and not be forever walking on
eggshells, tiptoeing around the topic of her ruined face.

"Grace, I am not going to recover. There is no cure for
this particular evil. I will always have this horrible scar."

"My dear sister." Grace clasped Sally's hand. "The scar
will fade. They always do. And it is only superficial. When
people look at me, all they can see is my little doll face, and
would treat me like a doll, but I will not allow mere appearance to be the measure of who I am. And neither should you.
And really, Owen was right. Your scar is not that bad."

"*That* bad being . . . ? A deep powder burn? A missing
eye? An amputated limb?"

"Oh, Sally! It is only because the scar is still somewhat
new and pink. In time, it will fade. And I haven't even
broached the possibilities of *maquillage*. I'm a positive wonder with face powders. How do you think I manage to make
myself look so flawless?" Typically, Grace paused only long
enough to draw breath. "But honestly, anyone who knows
you, and loves you, does not even see it. Now that I know
and love you, I see *you*, not your scar. Your brother sees you,

the same sister he has always adored. He cannot see that there is any difference."

"But there is a difference."

"Only because you say there is one." And then, after a long moment, Grace narrowed her eyes at Sally. "Goodness, if I did not know better, I would say what you are truly suffering from is not a saber cut but a broken heart."

Sally's sad, broken heart made a little hiccup of protest in her chest, but she ignored it, just as she had taught herself, and moved on. "Don't be ridiculous. You know perfectly well I'm a tall, frightening ogre who has no heart. And you have got me off topic, which is you making me those nieces and nephews. And you can best do that alone, without my help, so off you go."

"Ahoy, there." Owen's voice spiraled up the staircase. "Sally? Grace, my love? Where have you gotten to?"

"There is my brother now." Sally made a little shooing motion at Grace. "Off you go. This is your chance."

"Sally!" Grace slapped playfully at Sally's knee as she sprang to the door. "I'm up here with Sally. But don't come up here unless you've wiped your great dirty boots."

"Yes, I've wiped my great dirty boots," Owen replied from the doorway with his usual cheerful bluster. "I've brought the post."

Sally steeled her heart against the sharp shard of expectation that wedged itself into her chest.

"What news?" Grace asked.

"Father has written," Owen replied, "although from his letter, I cannot reckon how he did not outrace the post."

All of the trepidation Sally had managed to carefully stow away inside her over the past two weeks began to unfurl within her chest.

"But what does it say?" insisted Grace.

"In the wake of Trafalgar, he writes, the Admiralty have been generous with leave, and he expects to be home no later than—"

"When, Owen, when?" Grace was all but hopping up and down.

"Well, if that frigate I've been watching enter the Carrick Roads is any indication, I would say this afternoon—"

Sally didn't wait to hear the rest. She tore up to the top of the house, to the balcony surrounding the gabled roof, as fast as her pounding heart allowed. There, in her glass, a frigate was just passing out of sight along Pendennis neck.

"Happy sight, is it not, Sal? And the others are coming, too. There's letters from Dominic—"

"Matthew?" Sally's voice was rising on the high tide of her excitement.

"And Matthew, and even Daniel. Damn his eyes, I haven't seen Daniel in years. Well, there you have it, Sal. It seems we are all come home, to see you."

She wasn't going to cry. She wasn't. She was going to face them all with all the happiness such an event—to have her brothers home at once—could occasion.

Almost all. It had not escaped her notice that Richard still remained quite conspicuously absent.

"And coming to see me as well, I hope." Grace's teasing smile showed she was not in the least bit put out by Owen's omission. And it was a comfort to Sally to know that her delightfully outgoing sister-in-law would be more than happy to make herself the center of attention, if only to spare Sally.

"You may count upon it, Grace. They will be wild with delight at a new sister," Sally assured her. "And we will have a wonderful homecoming. Just in time to celebrate Christmas together. Does Father say how long he may stay?"

"No, but you may ask him yourself this very evening."

Not even her apprehension at seeing her father—and more importantly him seeing her—could dim the happiness blossoming in her heart at the prospect. "Let's go warn Mrs. Jenkins to prepare herself for guests."

"Yes, let's," agreed Grace, and led the way to the stairs. "Oh!"

She stopped halfway down, and turned up to Sally. "Now I remember what I was going to say." Grace clapped her hands together in delight. "Of all things, I should like a ball."

Chapter Twenty-five

Of course, they held a Christmas ball. A very little ball, by Grace's estimation, but a ball nonetheless. And the first ball Cliff House had ever hosted, at least within Sally's memory.

From the moment they left the rooftop, Grace could think and talk of nothing else. As far as she was concerned, Sally's father and brothers had done the equivalent of moving heaven and earth—in the form of the very recalcitrant Lords of the Admiralty—to get themselves home to see her, and Sally owed it to them to celebrate.

"There is such an abundance of good news," Grace enthused. "Captain Sir Alexander Kent's baronetcy, our marriage, your brothers' safe returns, and the navy's thrilling victory at Trafalgar."

She would have included Sally's recovery, but one look from Sally—her own version of that low-browed bit of silent thunder Col had perfected—was enough to stop Grace in her tracks.

Everything was as right with her world as Sally could hope. Her father had come home, and the last of her trepidation, which had eased under Grace's cheerful onslaught, survived only until the moment he stepped across the threshold, and grabbed her up in a crushing embrace.

"There she is. There's my girl. Home safe." He all but

squeezed the breath from her, just as he had when she was little.

Captain Alexander Kent ignored the hubub of greetings swirling about them and smiled down at Sally as he cradled her face. "Now, what's all this?"

The worry and fear inside her spilled the heat gathering behind her eyes at his gruff tenderness.

He brushed her tears carefully away with his thumbs. "Why, you're right as rain. A little frayed at your seams, perhaps, but right as rain. The devil take me, my Sally, but it does me good to look at you. You do remind me so of your mother."

"Papa. I am so glad you are home." Sally smiled away her tears.

"So am I, my girl, so am I. Glad you are home as well. You gave me quite a fright."

"I didn't mean to."

"Oh, I think you did. You meant to show me the error of my ways." He patted her cheek gently.

"No, truly. I only meant to preserve the Kent family honor and good name."

"Oh, I'm sure you did," he agreed as he let her take his sea cloak. "I have your letter."

Sally could hardly recognize the folded missive he pulled from the inside of his coat, so worn and battered it had grown. But it was her own letter that she had written at Trafalgar. Pinky must have given it to Captain McAlden.

"But I also think you meant to show me you were suited for other things than staying put in this house," her father went on.

Sally had no desire to lie to her father. She'd seemed to have worn that impulse out with Col. "You're right. And I am sorry for the pains that letter must have given you, because if you read it you must have thought I was dead. I hope Captain McAlden also wrote immediately from Gibraltar to tell you I was recovered?"

"Oh, I have had any number of interesting correspondents, including Captain McAlden, who did write to me from

Gibraltar, just as you suggest. And also Angus Pinkerton, who scratched out a few lines to tell me he was looking after my young Kent, whom I did not realize at that point was you. Yes, many interesting correspondents, with the notable exception of you. And this letter."

"I am sorry, Papa."

"As you should be. But now that I can see you are fine, I am not exactly sorry. I learned a great many things about you, and about myself, that I never would have learned otherwise. And it all came right in the end." He looked around him at his house, and drew Sally in to his shoulder. "Such adventures you have had. And there are more to come, for I understand we are to have a Christmas ball."

For the ball, Sally let Grace have free rein—to be honest, there was no other choice. Her sister-in-law was as swift and decisive as Nelson himself in bringing the affair about, and taking every one of them in hand. All Sally could do was to put herself in Grace and her maid's powers, and submit herself to be powdered.

"Sit still, Sally, before you give poor Dawkins fits."

"I don't have fits, my lady," Dawkins disagreed pleasantly. "I simply endure."

Grace laughed at her maid's dry sarcasm. "You are so droll, Dawkins. That is why I love you so."

"The only reason I love you," the maid attempted to grouse, "is because you pay me so well. And you do justice to my handiwork. Just as Miss Sally here will, if she would kindly stop twitching like a choirboy with a sneeze up his nose."

"That's because I *have* got a sneeze up my nose," Sally countered. "I'm going to—"

"Don't you dare," cried Grace, as she shoved a huge linen handkerchief into Sally's face. "You'll ruin it, and there isn't time to start again."

"Almost done." Dawkins stepped back, and stared at Sally with the same meticulous appraisal Col had used aboard *Audacious*. "Just a dab more— What do you think, my lady?"

Grace joined Dawkins in staring down at her, like an artist in front of a canvas "Just a bit more pink, right there, for warmth. Just a touch— No more! There." Grace smiled as she inhaled. "Well done, Dawkins, well done."

"I thank you, my lady. If you do the honors"—Dawkins handed Grace a small mirror—"I'll get the dress."

"Have a look at yourself, Sally, and see what you think."

Sally could not help but think of the last time she had taken a good look at herself in a mirror, and took a deep, steadying breath. But instead of plummeting, her spirits began a cautious soar.

Somehow, some way, they had made her look as soft and fresh as a newborn cygnet.

"How do you like it?" Grace was nearly hopping from one foot to the next. "We've subdued your freckles only a little bit. So they're still the focus. But up here, on your temples—"

"You made it almost go away." Sally pulled the mirror nearer, to examine her reflection. "It's hardly noticeable."

"You see! I told you the powder would take some of the most obvious redness away. Will you trust me now that you can finally see yourself?"

On close inspection, the lattice of lines was just visible under the dusting of powder. It was her own self, only better. Much better. In all her life she had never looked like this. "I trust you, Grace. But you are wrong. I can't see myself at all. I see someone much better."

"Ha and la. Not better, but perhaps prettier. Or at least, more aware of your own prettiness. Just as you should. Now, there will be some curiosity to see you, as people do know you've been away, but so will they want to see your father and brothers. And me. There is nothing odd in all you Kents coming and going and always being away. So, if people do see your scar, you must let them look, and soon they'll find there is nothing to see. And now the dress. Put your hands up, *handsomely* now—I know you will like that navy talk— for it's already pinned together, and it needs to go over your head in one piece."

Fabric settled over her and Sally carefully pushed her arms through the lace-edged sleeves. "Orange?"

"It is *not* orange. It's apricot. Apricot silk gazar, with threads shot through with a hundred different variations on the color to make it spark. Don't touch."

"How am I to wear it if I can't touch?" Sally grumbled, just for form's sake. She couldn't always let Grace have her way—there'd be no living with her if she did. "I will look like a tall winter orange. I will lay you a groat my brothers will immediately pounce upon the words 'tall tangerine.'"

"They will not, if they know what's good for them, and I mean to make sure they find out. You do not look like an orange." She took Sally's hands in her own and spread them out wide. "You look like a deep drop of sunshine. Or a tall, flickering candle flame. Oh, yes, I like that. So much more dramatic and suitable. Perhaps a more dramatic look—some darkening around her lids?" Grace consulted with Dawkins.

"Nope. None of it." Dawkins held firm. "Needs to be all coltish and fresh first time out of the gate. You mark my words. You're a go, Miss Sally, just as you is."

"Thank you, Dawkins. And you, Grace. Thank you." She laughed to dispel the little jangle of excited nerves. "I feel ridiculously like a ship, about to be launched. Perhaps one of you ought to shout 'well away.'"

"Well away!" Grace and Dawkins chimed.

And so she was. Except that the first person she met at the bottom of the back stairs was her missing youngest brother.

"Richard!" Sally had no inkling that he would be there. She ran down the stairs to greet him.

But Richard, already dressed in the somber black of the clergy—though at fifteen there was no way he could yet have taken holy orders—stepped away from her intended embrace and bowed to her with a solemn dignity and enough condescension to get her back up.

Damn pup, playing at charity. And the juxtaposition of his blazing red hair with the light-eating black of his garments was nearly ridiculous—as if the devil himself were masquerading as a preacher. But he was her brother, and she had missed him so very much. And she had so much to ask.

But Richard was not yet ready for reconciliation. "I don't see how you could have hoped to get away with it."

Devil take him. He'd come up to speed awfully fast. But whatever Richard's greeting lacked in familial warmth, it certainly made up for in familial candor. And it prompted her to answer in kind.

"Hoped?" Sally blew out a long breath and strove to keep a humorous, albeit slightly sarcastic, tone. "I did get away with it, Richard. Though little good it did me. For all the world knows, Richard Kent and not his sister, Sally, is now late of His Majesty's Navy. So you'll have to learn to take pride in your exemplary record, Richard. You're a hero."

There was undoubtedly more teeth in her tone than was nice, and Richard felt bitten. "So my brothers have already informed me."

Ah. That accounted for a great deal of the petulance. "I don't doubt they have, for they can be bully boy bastards at times. But they're our bully boy bastards, Richard. And it's very good to see you." She hugged him anyway, even though he held himself stiffly.

"I didn't ask you to do that for me, Sally." Frustration, and perhaps embarrassment, colored his voice. "You always try to do that. Solve everything. I was perfectly happy to defy Pater on my own. You needn't have gone off like that. Like . . ."

Sally found she wasn't as prepared to forgive and forget as she had thought. Certainly she didn't like being condescended to by Richard, any more than she had liked it from Grace. Thank God they were in the back corridor and not in the drawing room, so they could simply have it out. "Like what, Richard? A man who knows what is due to his family? Or at least thinks he does?"

"You don't understand." For all his attempt at playing the preacher, he still sounded like a sullen fifteen-year-old boy.

It made her feel older, and perhaps a touch more charitable. And it was ridiculous to continue to rehash the same argument they'd been having for years. "No. I don't suppose I did."

He straightened at her calm, conciliatory tone. "Well, you could hardly be expected to, with your education as it has been."

"Careful, Richard." She used Col's voice on him, that low, softly adamant tone. "Don't come the preacher with me. Because no matter what you wanted to do, you violated trust. You violated Father's trust, and the trust of the service as well. Doesn't that mean anything to you?"

"No. I never said I would go. Quite the opposite. But you implied it, all of you, because it was what you wanted to hear. But the only trust I have ever striven to keep is God's. It's God first and duty second, and not the other way round."

His tone was more than sincere—it was passionate. And that was something she did understand. Sally thought again of Ian Worth, and his inexperienced misery aboard the ship. Richard would have been even more miserable, despite all his family experience. Perhaps more so, because of it. "And is that what you've been doing all these months, your duty to God?"

"I am trying to do so. I found a teacher who consented to take me as a pupil. Though I hope, now that Father has come home, to convince him to let me study at Cambridge. My teacher says— But no matter. I can't go to Cambridge without money. I had hoped that after what has happened, and with this baronetcy, he might be more amenable to giving me enough funds."

And there was her answer. She had to smile at the strange irony of it all. "Well, Richard, it turns out you already have the money. Your prize money from *Audacious* is waiting to be collected from the Court of Admiralty. As Sally Kent, I can't touch it, so you might as well have it, to put to good use. Perhaps it shall be your recompense for letting me use your good name."

Richard was nearly speechless to have the object of his long desires so easily and so unexpectedly given to him. "Really? Are you quite sure?"

"Absolutely. It can be paid out only to you, Richard Kent, and I am clearly no longer he."

"Thank you. That's . . . very thoughtful and generous of you. I—" He shook his head and sat down in the chair next to the garden door where she changed her boots, and then looked at her, perhaps differently. "You always work something out, don't you? I suppose that's why I was so mad, before. Because for once, you couldn't, or wouldn't, work something out with Father to keep me from having to go. So I thought I would try and do it on my own. That's why I disappeared. You'd never have let up otherwise."

"Yes." Sally sat herself down on the bottom stair, disregarding Grace's potential outrage for her abuse of the dress. "I do see now, you had to do it on your own, Richard. I didn't understand. And I was wrong not to help you. I should have. But I was mad, too, you see, because I *did* want to go. So I took it into my own hands, and solved the problem my own way as well. A fine pair we are."

"But why did you do it, Sally? How did you even think to try?"

Sally shrugged. How could she possibly explain? "The sea possessed me. It always has and it always will. And perhaps I shall go back, perhaps even while Owen is still ashore. With the French off the water, it seems the perfect time. I want to visit a . . . friend in the Bahamas. I begin to find myself very much *de trop* at the moment here, with Grace and Owen so in love. Entirely unnecessary. So I'll go off and try to find my own way in the world, just as you have done."

"But on the sea, anything may happen. And the Bahamas . . . The heat and the diseases—"

"I'm not worried," she assured him. "I find I'm rather hard to kill."

"Oh, Sally, you joke, but you're not invincible. And you are not unnecessary. But you *are* irreplaceable. Lord help me, I could never forgive myself if something had happened to you."

"Something did happen, Richard. Life is like that."

He had the grace to flush, but it only made him look more

earnest as he peered at her face, trying to see her scar. "Yes. So I see."

She tried to sit quietly, the way Grace had told her. *Let them look and soon they'll find there is nothing to see.* But Sally couldn't keep still. She was just no good at waiting. "Please don't stare." She tried to joke. "It's a bad habit in a clergyman."

"I'm sorry. I didn't mean to stare," he went on in his quiet, determined way. "But after what Matthew and Owen said, I had expected much worse. Though I shouldn't have thought you, of all people, would really mind. You never gave a fig for looks or vanity. I thought you would take it as a badge of honor."

Sally found herself smiling at her brother, for once in perfect accord. "I rather think I do. I was all for Grace— have you met Grace yet? Be careful, she's a force of nature— covering the bloody thing up with powder, but now that it's hidden, I feel a bit—" She shook her head. "You will shake your head and chastise me for my language, but I feel a bit naked without it." She reached up and brushed away some of the powder with her fingertips.

"Yes, I can see it better now. Do you know, it rather suits you. Makes you look rakish."

"Thank you." Sally knew she needed to be conciliatory as well. "Just as your black suits you."

He looked down at his coat, and then back at her. "I'm sorry I'm not the man you, or any of my brothers, wanted me to be, Sally, but I'm not in the least bit sorry, or ashamed, of the man I am."

"Oh, Richard. You shouldn't be. And I am sorry I ever tried to make you feel that way. I am sorry I tried to make you be for the sea. If there is anything that I've learned from my experience, it is that the life of the sea is not for everyone."

"But it was for you."

Sally scrunched up her nose, trying not to smile. "I fear you're right."

"You always did like it."

"No, I didn't like it. I loved it, Richard. I absolutely loved it."

"And you missed it, the sea?" He was genuinely trying to understand.

Devil take her. She did miss it. "Like a dead friend."

Her sincerity, or perhaps her choice of words, set him back on his heels for a long moment. But then he nodded. "And you're finding it hard to live without it. Without doing the thing you feel you were born to do."

"Yes." She could only agree. "I'm finding it very hard."

For the first time in a long time, Richard's smile was genuine and unguarded. "Then perhaps we're not so different after all."

"No." Sally took his hand in hers. "Not so very different after all."

But tonight she was going to be different. She was going to be her new self. This person who had conquered trigonometric navigation, found a xebec using oranges, poisoned Mr. Gamage, and faced down the guns of Trafalgar was going to do something she never thought possible—conquer a drawing room.

But while the evening was only a ball and not a battle the likes of Trafalgar, she still needed a strategy. She needed to find a safe anchorage, and gather her strength before she ran out her guns.

She would start with the solidly reassuring presence of her brothers. Matthew and Dominic stood to one side of the room, talking and laughing together as they greeted guests with nods and smiles. She squared her shoulders and walked quietly—but she hoped confidently—into the drawing room that had been emptied for the dancing, making her way directly for the safe mooring between the bulwark of her brothers.

"Oh, Sal, there you are," Dominic greeted her. "Good. Owen's wife was just about to send me in search. Lord, look at you." Dom ran his gaze down the length of the shimmering gown, from neck to hem, before he lifted his mischievous eyes to hers. "You almost look civilized."

The old ease with her brothers was still there, as strong as ever. And with sibling ease came sibling contempt, leaving Sally free to give as good as she got. "As do you, Dom, as do you. Almost."

He swept her a teasing bow. "I thank you. However, you may not like me so well when I tell you Grace has instructed me that I'm to partner you for the first dance."

"Don't be absurd, Dom. I'm not dancing."

"Sal," he began with his version of a stern-cabin voice, "Grace says—"

"No." In this matter, if nothing else, Sally was determined to have her own way. It had done no good to tell Grace she had never learned how to dance properly in the first place. "I'm too fond of leading, if you must know. So I will only dance with you once you're too drunk to object."

"There's our girl." Matthew nodded in satisfaction at her humor. "It really ain't that bad, Sal. In this light, you don't even see your scar."

Sally was glad her brothers could be counted on not to treat her like a china teacup. "Thank you. One of the benefits, Grace tells me, of candlelight. But do you know what? I've decided I don't mind if people see it. I never did care what people would think, so it's really far too late for me to come all missish now."

"Thank God," Dom said with hearty relief. "I thought that Grace was going to totally make you over into . . . well, you know. One of them. One of *those* girls."

"And here I thought I was doing such a good job of it. Now I definitely won't dance with either one of you. And just to even the score, I am going to make you dance with one of *those* girls. Georgiana Howe will be perfect for the job. I fancy she's been sadly infatuated with you for years, the poor dear. She's there—the beautiful little blonde. Smile, you lucky jackass, she's looking."

Georgiana Howe had always been the kind of girl Sally had known but dismissed—just as she had originally tried to dismiss Grace. Georgiana was kind, considerate of others, and unfailingly polite. And by the delicate, flushed look of her face as she glanced surreptitiously in the direction of Sally's brother, she was still hopelessly in love with Dominic. But it was time for Sally to make new friends and look beyond the surface appearance of things. She only hoped Georgiana was prepared to do the same.

Sally smiled at Georgiana, and waved. Which set Dom off nicely.

He hauled her arm down like a loose jib. "Don't wave, for God's sake, Sal. One doesn't wave in a bloody ballroom." But the bite faded out of his words as he looked, and then *really* looked, at the girl.

"How would you know? And it's too late. She's already coming over." Despite her lighthearted tone, Sally braced herself for the encounter, even as she adjured herself that she looked fine. It was one thing to say she didn't care, and another thing to keep her silly nerves from making a soup of her insides. But even a lovely girl like Georgiana might prove unequal to the task of gazing dispassionately at Sally, who was finding she had more of vanity than she had ever thought.

Let them look and soon they will find there is nothing to see.

But Georgiana didn't look unequal. She looked as sweet, and beautiful, and breathless as a butterfly as she neared their group.

"Georgiana, how nice to see you." Sally was thankful her voice was cheerfully steady. And Matthew, God bless him for being the least obtuse of her brothers, gave her hand a quick, reassuring squeeze.

"Sally." Georgiana leaned in as if she might kiss Sally on the cheek like an intimate. There was an awful, almost imperceptible moment of hesitation, and Sally froze, but Georgiana merely tilted her head the other way so her sisterly kiss landed on Sally's unblemished cheek. "What a pleasure. I may still call you Sally, may I not? Or have we all grown so old and formal over the years?" Her smile was genuine, but determined—the kind of smile that was called putting one's best face forward.

Georgiana appeared as nervous and ill at ease as she, but if the girl kept her gaze riveted on Sally's face, Sally reckoned it was only to keep from peeping up at Dominic. Though what the poor girl saw in her brother, Sally would never understand. There was no accounting for taste, but such generous graciousness ought to be rewarded.

"Heavens, no." Sally laughed. "I've never answered to Sarah, so it's no use trying to start now, especially among old friends."

"Yes. And good friends, I hope." Georgiana's laugh was a breathless flutter as her gaze swung inevitably toward Dominic, as if she were a flower following his sun.

"Yes, thank you," Sally returned automatically, but realized as she said it that she meant it. How silly she had been not to realize that she had had friends for the making here in Falmouth all along.

But while Sally was busy with her wistful pondering, their little group had lapsed into an awkward silence. But there was her salvation. Grace was approaching with Owen on her arm.

"Georgiana, may I have the pleasure of introducing you to my brother Captain Owen Kent and his wife, Lady Grace Kent, whose recent marriage we celebrate this evening. Miss Georgiana Howe."

Georgiana and Grace were both everything polite, and elegant, and gracious. Grace began by exclaiming sweetly on the beauty of Georgiana's gown. "What a beautifully delicate shade of pink. It is quite perfect on you."

Grace turned to Sally, and with a smile and a single raised eyebrow, prompted her to join the conversation.

"Oh, yes. I agree," Sally chimed in. "You look very lovely tonight, Georgiana. Doesn't she, Dominic? May I also introduce my brother Dominic, Commander Kent? I realize you may know him of old, but I think it has been quite some time. Dominic, I'm sure you remember my friend Georgiana, Miss Howe?"

Georgiana turned and curtsied, and made a shy present of her smile to Dominic. A smile that held the soft luminescence of dawn, of hope and promise. And trust. Georgiana gave Dominic a smile of such infinite trust, it was as if she simply *offered* him her heart, because she trusted he would keep it safe forever.

Not even hardheaded, and even harder-hearted, Dominic could withstand such an appeal. "Miss Howe." Dominic bowed very correctly, but the stunned expression never left his face, as if his internal barometer were already swinging to the high that was Georgiana.

Completely done in. In the space of five seconds, Sally reckoned, Georgiana's sweet smile had shot him through, as cleanly as an arrow from Cupid's own bow.

"Georgiana, Dominic is lately back from the East Indies and in dire need of civilized company. Won't you take pity on him and introduce him around?"

Dominic came out of his momentary trance with alacrity. "If it would not trouble you to do so, Miss Howe, I would be most appreciative."

Devil take the poor man—he was definitely smitten.

As was the lady. "Not at all, Commander Kent. I should be most happy."

Dom bent Georgiana an arm, and they were gone. A brief pang of what must be loneliness dashed across Sally's heart at the sight, but she swatted it hastily away. Life, and *her* life, as imperfect as it was, must go on.

"Neatly done, Sal. Cut out at his mooring." Matthew chuckled. "Should I ask whom you have in mind for me?"

"No one would have you. And I reckon you're not fit to be housebroken yet."

"Ha! Nor are you, dear sister, nor are you. We shall have to stick together, we two inveterate tars."

Another pang. But a good pang. A companionable pang. Or perhaps it was only the stiff whalebone support of her stays, pushing against her chest, making her feel as squashed up as a tinned sardine. But the stays could not be helped— without them, Grace had insisted, the dress wouldn't hang right. What she needed was air—clean air, not the stifling mixture of heat and clashing perfumes.

Perhaps now that she had made an appearance, and seen to it that Georgiana might have her chance to enchant Dominic, she could retreat to the safer harbor of the garden for a proper lungful of cold night air.

"By God, this *is* going to be a good evening." Matthew's abrupt exclamation called her back to the present. "There's Colyear."

The floor seemed to move under her feet, shifting violently, as if she were suddenly on a rolling, pitching deck, and not a solid, immovable drawing room floor. As if her moment of final reckoning had come, and she was, at long last, going down with her own ship.

Chapter Twenty-six

Sally followed Matthew's smile of happy anticipation across the room, and there he was. Col. Not more than twenty feet away. Here, entering her home. Walking into her drawing room. Looking for all the world like a prince.

Oh, devil take him. He was magnificent. Magnificent. There was no other word that would do him justice. This evening, there was nothing, absolutely nothing, casual or disheveled about him. Not a seam or pin was worn or out of place. His long, dark hair had been cropped to buckish town standards, but he had lost none of the ruddy tan that marked him as a seagoing man. The lovely, dark caramel of his skin was enhanced by the contrast of the blindingly white starched shirt, collar, and cravat, over which he wore a coat so black it absorbed the light, while his pale, golden waistcoat shimmered in the candlelight. The effect was severely, heartbreakingly elegant.

Without his rugged, well-worn uniform—his armor against the world, as he had called it—he should have looked effete. A macaroni, a man to be dismissed. But he didn't. He appeared grave, and stoic, and handsome, and very, very much in control.

Unlike her. The time she had spent recovering, both in body and in spirit, fell away, until she felt as exposed and alone as she had that morning in Gibraltar, staring at the mirror, feeling her heart rend irreversibly, watching all her hopes and dreams bleed away. Learning to be afraid.

And Col did not smile. He did nothing to reassure her.

His chalcedony green gaze was the same—grave and direct, almost severe—and leveled entirely at her, as if he had only been waiting for her to see him. He came across the threshold toward her without excusing himself to her father, who broke off his conversation to watch Col's measured, determined progress across the widening width of the room.

She could not do it. She could not stand and be raked broadside by his gaze. She tried to duck behind Matthew, to turn away and hide, but in another instant her brother's hand was at her elbow in a grip that would have done a gunner proud.

"Matthew, please!" she whispered.

"No, Sally." His voice was soft but implacable. "You don't need to cut and run. We're safe with Colyear."

Her brother could not possibly understand. She was *not* safe.

"Sally? What's amiss?" Grace's question was a whisper at her ear, as she took up Sally's other arm. "Are you all right? You look faint."

No, she should say. *No.* She was not all right. She *should* faint, and let herself be carried off to safety, but that was a coward's way out, and she had come too far, and done too much, to let cowardice have its way with her now. And she had never in her life done anything so foolishly maidenly as succumb to a swoon.

Matthew was striding forward to greet Col. "Colyear. Good to see you, man." They shook hands as old friends— Matthew reaching his left hand out to grip Col's shoulder. "No longer a lieutenant of His Majesty's Navy, I understand?"

The deck beneath her tipped back, tossing her the other way, as she grappled for equilibrium. Col leave the navy? How could he? He was brilliant at his career. Simply brilliant. No one else could hold a compass to him.

Why would he do such a thing. Why?

"Kent." His large, browned hand, with his beautiful, articulate fingers, clasped Matthew's.

The startling effect Col was having upon her sensibilities was even more pronounced close up. The sight and scent of his skin, the warmth and power radiating off his body drew her to him like a lodestone. His sheer size made her feel small and insignificant. But she wanted to feel small and insignificant. She wanted to be invisible.

"May I introduce you to my wife?"

No.

Anything but that. She could not face meeting his wife, some beautiful, accomplished, whole—

"I would be honored."

Col's voice, low and steady, was the one that answered.

Oh, God. God and the devil and Saint Elmo all at once. Of course, it was Owen who had spoken of his wife. But the clockwork of her heart was already irretrievably broken, smashed now into small bits that would never fit back together. Sally covered her confusion and fear and impotent rage by keeping her face turned resolutely to the floor, holding herself in tense readiness for the moment when Grace would have to let go of her arm to greet Col. Willing the shattered timepiece of her heart to somehow mend itself and resume beating correctly.

"Lady Kent. Your servant, ma'am. May I offer my congratulations?"

"You may." Grace was everything charming and happy. "I have heard so much about you."

Col sliced the sharp blade of his gaze toward Sally. She shrank back, away from him, away from the cutting pain of that nearly merciless look.

But Sally's jerking movements reminded Grace of her presence. "Mr. Colyear, have you been introduced to my husband's sister, Miss Sarah Kent?"

Grace meant to be helpful, but her voice held a soft warning, an instruction-to-be-kind tone, that made Sally pray for a hole to open up in the floor. A hole filled with a raging, spinning vortex of water, so she might jump into it, and drown the hideous rush of shame, and grief, and loss his mere presence occasioned. How did one dark look from him reduce her so effectively? How did all the inhibitions and worries she thought she had banished come flooding back to swamp her the moment he appeared?

"Miss Kent," Col responded in his deep, quiet, solid voice, as he bowed over the hand she hadn't thought to offer. "It is an honor."

"Mr. Colyear." Her own words came from somewhere at the bottom of her throat, thick and stupid, as if she had never spoken before, as if she had not yet even learned how to move her mouth to speak. She shut her mouth, and shut her eyes, clenching her eyelids tight, so she would not have to see him look at her.

Let them look and soon they will find there is nothing to see.

But she was no bloody, earthly good at waiting. And the silence—the awful, roaring silence of all the words she could not speak—defeated her, and she had to look. He could not be in her world, in her presence, and she not look at him. He had been water and air and sunlight. And he still was. He was everything. Everything she could not have.

Col was acknowledging her words with a slow nod of his head, as he continued to regard her in that grave, solemn manner. Three short, sharp, vertical lines pressed upward between his brows. Oh, God. Even his scowl was so dear it hurt.

Under the heavy weight of his gaze, she could find nothing placid or safe to say, nothing to fill the aching, growing void. She could only watch him look at her, in a silence so deep and so profound, they might have been anywhere else in the empty world, and not two feet away from each other in a too-crowded drawing room.

But she could not find any words.

"Miss Kent." It was Col who broke the locked silence. "*That,* if I may say so, is an extraordinary scar."

She did not even gasp, the way the others around her did. She did not raise her hand to hide her face, as Grace did in instinctive sympathy. She did not let heat gather in her eyes. She absorbed the blow in silence, without flinching, because numbing pain was leaking from her chest, filling the emptiness of her lungs until she was drowning.

Even as all around her protest erupted, hot and withering. Even as from the dim edges of her vision, Sally could see her brothers rise up together, like a dike before the ocean, to block any further inundation of grief. Even as they spoke.

"Damn your eyes, Col—" Matthew began, but he melted away into the periphery of her vision, his threat left unfinished.

Grace's outrage, too, had been unmistakable. "Now you see here, sir, there's no need for that sort of—"

But Owen said, "Grace. Come away." And they faded to the fringes of her awareness as well.

Because Sally saw something the others had not. She saw how carefully Col was holding himself. How watchfully.

She could see that Col was poised on the very same knife's edge as she.

It gave Sally, if not exactly hope or ease, then at least . . . curiosity. If he was not there to wound or expose her—and she was sure he was not—then why the devil was he there?

There was nothing and no one but Col as he stepped close, and closer still. Until he was too close, and she had to look up, up to see the hard lines etched into the corners of his face. He was scowling at her, fierce and insistent, but the effect was strangely blunted by the reassuring, homey scent of starch from his linen.

He raised his right hand, and gently traced the long pink outline across her temple with the tip of his finger. His touch along the angry length of the scar was electric, an uncomfortable rush of vibrating heat.

"It reminds me," he said, his voice gentled into roughness, "of a saber cut, taken in hand-to-hand action by a courageous colleague, someone who saved my life. Someone who is very, very dear to me." His expression did not change. He did not smile to reassure her, but only looked, and looked at her unflinchingly. Willing her to do the same.

"I wonder, Miss Kent," he continued, oblivious to the scene he was creating, "if I might persuade you to do me the honor of taking a turn about the room, so you can tell me just how you acquired such an injury."

And he was already turning, tucking her arm over his, and leading her away.

Sally wasn't sure how she moved, how she put one shaky leg in front of the other without falling down. She hardly knew what to think, or do, or where to look. All she could do was feel—the solid strength of the arm beneath her hand, the heat radiating off his person, the reassuring shelter of his tall form as he steered them through the assembly.

People were staring, not least her own family. A glance revealed Grace white-faced with concern, though Owen was whispering into her ear. Near the door her father stood with a look as still as coming thunder, pent-up and watchful.

And she did not know how to reassure him. She did not know how to reassure herself. Yet she let herself be towed along in Col's wake, promenaded across the room while Falmouth society wondered what on earth such a handsome man was doing with coltish Sally Kent.

Sally willed words into her mouth. "I think, sir, that we are making a scandal."

"I think, Miss Kent," he answered quietly, "that you did that months ago. In fact, I've come all this way to make sure of it."

Was that humor, or censure in his voice?

Sally turned sharply for the arched entry to the drawing room, and from there hurried them down the central corridor toward the relative quiet at the very back of the house, where the old part of the building spilled into the gardens.

But having already vented his cryptic lure, Col chose to keep both his unhurried pace, and his hold upon her arm. "Handsomely now, Kent. What I have to say will keep, at least for a few minutes more."

"Stop it," she whispered out of the side of her mouth. "Stop all this calm assurance. You don't know what you're doing any better than I."

"Don't I?" One dark eyebrow taunted her. "Perhaps I've learned."

Something that had to have been a spurt of jealousy speared its poison through her heart and she nearly stumbled, but his hand was there, at her wrist, and his arm had found its way around her waist, buoying *her* up this time.

She tried to hurry out of his embrace, not yet ready to so easily forgive the hurt his absence, and now his presence, brought her. Sally led them into the dimness of the garden room. Two small lamps had been lit on the tables, well away from the windows, so visitors could admire the view of the lantern-lit garden beyond. When she stepped through the doorway, the moist, pungent fragrance of the indoor garden of potted plants filled her lungs. It wasn't the oak and tar of a tall ship, but it was real and familiar enough to steady her.

She was on her home ground. And no longer his subordinate. She could treat him as an equal. She had a right to protect herself. "You can let me go now, Mr. Colyear. I'm not going to run away."

"I never thought you would, Kent. Running away isn't your style at all, is it?"

"No. So you can let me go."

"I think not," he said carefully. "I think I mean never to let you go again."

The broken pounding of her heart was hammering away, pulsing heat into her veins. Eroding the carefully cultivated veneer of numbness. "Co— Mr. Colyear. Don't say things you don't mean, or will regret."

"Kent. You ought to know me well enough to know I never say things I don't mean."

"Well, you needn't. I could see by your ferocious scowl when you entered that you came to salve your conscience. They don't know." She gestured back at the drawing room as a stand-in for her family. "I never told them. I mean, they know that I served under you, and of course Captain McAlden, in *Audacious,* but they don't know that I was . . . that we . . ." She stumbled over the words, because with the memory of *exactly* what she had done in his arms came the icy heat of remembrance and awareness prickling across her skin. "No one knows. No one will ever know."

"*I* know." He stepped in front of her, the seemingly solid wall of his chest fencing her in, keeping her from evading him. "And what about you? Do you know? Do you remember? I sure as hell do. I remember every detail. Every night. Over and over again. I can't get you out of my mind. I can't think of anything, or anyone else, but you."

"Of course I remember. Of course, but . . . It's not the same. I'm not the same." The fear she had tried so hard to keep at bay was escaping, making her voice ragged around the edges, coming out of her mouth in shreds. But she had to do it. She moved closer to the table and its lamp. "Look at me. Really look at me."

Let them look and soon they will find there is nothing to see.

But Col was different. He saw what others did not. He saw everything.

His gaze was as dark, solemn, and level as ever, cataloguing every nuance of her ruined face. Reading her the way he used to read the sea, like a book open before him, all its secrets manifest to him.

She was the one to turn away—she was no good at waiting—but his hand came up to stop her, and retrace the uneven line that knitted across her temple and down the side of her cheek. This time, the touch of his bare finger over her skin was a mixture of pleasure and pain so heady, she felt upended, as if she were being churned up by a wave upon the shore.

"Do you know what I see when I look at this scar?"

She wouldn't answer him. She couldn't. All she could see in her own mind's eye was the bristle of stitches as black as hedgehog spines in the mirror at Gibraltar and the ugliness of the now pink, uneven lines cobwebbing her skin.

But not Col. "I see loyalty. And devotion. I see what someone, what *you,* were willing to sacrifice for me. I see love. Only love could leave such a lasting mark. How could I not be moved by that?"

"I don't want your pity." She broke away and gave him her back, too ashamed of the hot tears stinging the back of her eyes. She didn't want him to see how hard this was for her. She wanted to be strong. She wanted to be Kent. But in the time she had been away from him, she had grown too used to being Sally. And even his profession of love hurt so bad she could not draw breath.

"It's only a scar, Kent. And I see it. It's like a map of my failures. But it's not all I see." His hands were on her shoulders, turning her to face him. "Stand still and let me see."

She closed her eyes against the sheer intensity of his voice. "Please, Col. Don't."

"I can't seem to help it. Are you . . . Are you wearing face powder?"

He sounded as incredulous as if he'd found her wearing a knife. Which, of course, she was, in her garter. Why should she not? And why should she not wear face powder if she so chose? "It's not as if it's a sign of the apocalypse."

His smile was quiet and slow. Not exactly begrudging, but perhaps rusty from lack of use. "I've already seen the apocalypse, Kent. And so have you. But I never thought to see you like this."

"Devil take you, Col. I might say I don't want your pity, but for God's sake, don't think that gives you leave to level me so completely, like—"

"No." The quiet, but insistent, sincerity in his voice stopped her. "Like a woman. I never imagined you looking so very, very much like a woman. No. Like a *lady*."

Sally held herself very, very still, as something too fragile to be hope tried to blossom in her chest. And in that moment, he stepped close, so close she could feel the warmth of his breath against her skin and the strength that emanated from his tall, powerful body.

"Ah, speechless at last. This would be my opening, then." And he lowered his head toward hers.

Sally watched spellbound as his mouth came closer and his eyes fell shut at the first trembling contact of their lips. It was the barest of touches, so light and so bittersweet it was almost unbearable.

And then his lips firmed and softened all at the same time, and he covered her mouth, pressing heat and wonder into her.

It was too hard. It was too soon. If she opened to him and gave in to the opiate of her hope, she would never be able to come back.

But he couldn't hear the words in her head, and his mouth was covering hers so she could not speak them. He pressed in, leaning into her, licking at her lower lip, teasing and worrying at it until she was kissing him back, inching the tip of her tongue forward to touch his. And then he was in her mouth, and it was bliss, and deliverance, and redemption and everything it could be. He was everything he could be, and everything she wanted.

She let her hands rise up, to run and fist his dark, glorious hair between her fingers, and press—

"Sally?" The warning voice came only a moment before the door swung open.

It was only Grace, thank God, and not her father. Or worse, her brothers. The moment it took for Grace's eyes to adjust to the dim light gave Sally the time to spring away from Col and set herself to rights.

"My dear," Grace said as she came in, reaching her hands out to Sally. "Are you quite all right?" Her glance darted between the two of them. "Oh!"

Sally felt the heat of a blush rush across her cheeks as awareness flared in Grace's eyes. She shot a glance at Col, who had drawn himself into his usual attitude of stony indifference, though there was a flush of high color under the tan of his skin.

Grace took another step forward before she came to an abrupt stop. "Oh, I beg your pardon." Her hand rose to her mouth to cover her shock. "I never imagined, but I should have seen. Of course. You're in love."

She grasped Sally's hands and kissed her on the cheek

before she began to back toward the door. "I'll . . . I'll see to it you won't be disturbed. For a few minutes longer only, mind you. I'll put the others off."

And she hurried out to shut the door behind her.

Sally stood where she was, poised on that knife's edge, between the past and the future. And for the first time in her life, she was too afraid to do anything, or even speak.

But Col wasn't afraid. "It would seem, Sally Kent, that your real secret is at last out."

Chapter Twenty-seven

She hadn't smiled at him. Not once.

Col's own smile had been knocked off his face by the sight of her, across the room, as he had entered her father's house. He had not expected what he saw—a beautiful young woman laughing amongst her friends and family. Hadn't she told him she was no good in a ballroom? Hadn't that been why he'd come?

He had expected the girl he had left in the gunroom of *Audacious,* wounded and grinding her teeth to hold in the pain. He had expected the atrocious scar, which at the time he left her had waved its banner of black silk across her temple and cheek. He had expected her to be seated quietly by the side of the room, attended occasionally by her family.

He had expected, quite frankly, to save her.

But she didn't need saving. She'd somehow already saved herself.

The situation made him feel the way he did when he had first put in at Plymouth, determined to come to her. The way he always felt on land—unbalanced and unsure. A fish very much out of water.

She hadn't smiled at him. But she had kissed him.

It was promising. And it gave him a place to start. "Your secret is out, Sally Kent. Everyone knows you love me. Everyone but you."

Her mouth, her lovely apricot-marmalade mouth, slid open in astonishment. She stood as if transfixed, suspended between two wants, holding herself back, as if she were both afraid of him and afraid he would leave.

Col decided to leave her in no doubt. He stepped close, and gathered her to him, sliding his hands around the small span of her waist. She had lost weight, which was scarcely possible, given how much better Cliff House's kitchen was bound to be than any gunroom cookery.

And there were other, more subtle, changes as well. The breasts that he had spent so much time imagining were pushed high and round by the incredible gown. He wanted to tell her that with breasts like these, she needn't worry about her scar. No man in his right mind would look at her face when there was such a glorious alternative.

But he had learned better than to tell such things to Kent. She would get indignant, and he would be told off and banished before he could use any of his better persuasions. And he had much better persuasions.

"When I close my eyes, I can scarcely recognize you at all. You feel different. And you don't smell like a sailor anymore. You smell sweet and clean and—"

"Are you telling me I stank before? Are you saying—"

He stopped her mouth with a kiss. "Shut up, Kent. You smelled no better and no worse than any twenty boys living on a crowded orlop could do. No," he contradicted himself. "You smelled of *castile* soap. But now you smell as you look—entirely of woman. Of something—" Words began to fail him. "Fresh and new."

"It is only soap now. It's nothing special, or magical." She was shaking her head, preparing her arguments.

He refused to let her. He had come all this way, and endured so much, for one purpose. For her. He would not be deterred now. "No, it is only *you*. And it is unique."

In response, she crushed her lip between her teeth, still trying desperately to hold back. He wouldn't let her. He wanted to kiss her again, and bend her over his arms as he took her mouth, but she was stiff and unyielding—everything about her posture still warned him off.

He changed tack, shifting to windward. "And what about me? Do I not smell nice? Do I not look nice? I rigged myself up like this for you. Are you not pleased to see me? Have you not thought about me? Thought about how on earth I might be getting along without you on board to help me, and to see all the things that only you and I could see? Have you not worried about me, even a little?"

"Don't be ridiculous. Of course I wanted to know. Of course I thought of you often. And you look just fine. Very fine, if you must know. But you do know, for you have a mirror and a brain, so you must know how uncommonly handsome you are turned out."

"Thank you. It does me no end of good to know you find me handsome." He grasped her hands, cold and white within his brown clasp. "You must know I've done it all for you, Sally Kent. To impress you. To remind you. To tell you. That I love you."

Col could feel his pulse, his heart, slamming against the inside of his chest. He was open and exposed, luffing in the breeze, until she would decide which way to steer.

She was frowning, and shaking her head. "I think you love the person I was. If you love anyone, it's Kent, not Sally. But I'm not Kent anymore. I've changed. Everything has changed."

"How?" His voice was nothing but gravel. "To me your scar changes nothing. Damn my eyes, but I can barely see it."

"No," she said carefully, as if she were thinking her way through. "The scar is just superficial, and I will not allow it to be the measure of who I am as a person. But neither can I now allow my usefulness, or my seaworthiness—for lack of a better term—to be the sole measure of my worth, either."

"Sally Kent, do you think I only value you for your *seaworthiness*? That I liked you—that I love you—because you're useful?"

"Of course." This time she was frowning at him. "Don't try to deny it, because you know it's true."

"My darling Kent, you daft girl. I like Moffatt. I find him useful and highly seaworthy, but I've never thought of kissing him."

"Well, that's because he's a man."

"True. What about Long Peg? She was useful—eminently useful, according to many—and she's certainly seaworthy."

"Col, that's not the point."

"Which is that I like you because you are all those things and more. But mostly because you are simply you. You could do anything, or nothing. You could sit around and drink tea all day long from this day forward—although I would be very surprised if you did—being nothing but decorative instead of useful, and I would still love you. And I would still want to marry you."

"Col. You can't mean it?"

"Why not?" He kissed her to prove it.

He had told himself he would learn restraint with her. He told himself he would be gentle and loving, but everything about her tested his restraint. He kissed her like a man too long at sea who has forgotten the taste of freshwater. He dove into the softness and welcome of her mouth.

"Sally," he began, reaching for the blazing splendor of her hair, all bound up in ladylike precision. He wanted to see it down. He wanted to let it slide through his fingers and see it fan out across a pillow. "Let me kiss you. Let me be with you. Let me take care of you and make you mine. Because whether you realize it or not, I am already yours."

"I don't need you to take care of me."

"Kent. Haven't you been listening? I need you to take care of *me*. To watch my back. No one else can possibly do it. No one else ever has. Only you. We can take care of one another. Please, Sally."

He could see the change in her the moment she started to consider the possibility. Her face began to clear. The warm colors, hidden beneath layers of rice powder, began to fill back into her face, like a painting taking shape before his eyes.

"Oh, Col." She smiled at him slowly. That impish, mischievous, gamin smile that spread like the rising dawn across her face. "For God's sake, call me Kent while you're kissing me."

He grabbed her up in her arms. "I'll take that as a yes."

They were married within the solid stone walls of the Church of King Charles the Martyr, as generations of Kents had done before, on a day so very much like the first— streaming down with rain—that Sally took it as a propitious sign.

Grace had found another perfect dress—a blue watered silk that made Sally feel elegant and strong, and did not prompt her brothers to make unflattering alliterations.

Col surprised her entirely by wearing a blazingly new uniform of a post captain, his gold epaulettes shining in the watery light streaming through the stained-glass windows.

She did not even wait until she and her father had reached the altar. "Col! You've made post!"

In answer, he gave her one of his slow, unfurling smiles, and spread his arms wide. "As you see."

"But I thought—"

"Dearly beloved," the rector began.

"Why did you not tell me?" Sally asked over the prayer.

"It was meant to be a surprise. A wedding present."

"It cannot be a wedding present if there is no wedding," her father reminded her.

Sally was not in the least chastened. She may not have eaten millers, but she'd eaten colder stares for breakfast. She kept her eyes on Col. "Do you have a ship?"

"Miss Kent," the rector intoned severely. "If you would please postpone your inquiries—"

"I think not. Grace tells me there are to be no secrets between a husband and wife, so I think I ought to know exactly what my bridegroom's prospects are before I marry him."

"You'll be happy to find I'm quite rich," Col offered. "I've earned a very respectable fortune from some very nice prizes. You would be very pleased to know that a xebec frigate pays out well, but not nearly as well as a French 74. We got a very high share of that one. And then there was a very fine yacht that I have fond memories of."

"Fond?" But she wouldn't be sidetracked even if her skin was heating inside the fine silk of the dress. "What about a ship?"

"A ship? Yes. Did you know *Swiftsure* has been taken back into the fleet? You will be happy to know our Captain McAlden has been gifted with the command of her."

That did indeed make her very happy. "How wonderful. She was a wonderfully stout-built ship. Perhaps he will be posted to the West Indies so he might see his Lady McAlden more often. She must be missing him."

"Yes, but you must attend to me, Kent, or you'll never get your answers or your wedding."

"Sir!" the rector interjected.

But Col sailed on. "Now, where was I?"

"You were speaking of *Swiftsure* being taken back into the fleet."

"Clever girl. Yes, as the Admiralty had already commissioned a new *Swiftsure* while she was with the French, he's had to rename her. Do you want to know what he's christened her?"

"By all means, if it will get you to your point."

"*Irresistible*. I thought he had named it after you, but apparently he was thinking of *his* wife."

"Col." She gave him her happiest smile.

But he was Captain Colyear, and he was standing at the altar, so he continued on in his wryly grave, straightforward way. "And don't you want to know who has command of *Audacious*?"

"You can't mean— Col!"

"I can. How soon do you think you'd like to go aboard, Mrs. Colyear?"

Sally did not know how she could be any more happy,

like that honeybee buzzing with the nectar of happiness.
"Very soon. But we had best attend to the business of making me Mrs. Colyear first."

"Thank God," the rector and her father said together.

"Although"—her smile was still all for Col—"now that I think on it, perhaps I would prefer to make a scandal."

"Too late." Col smiled back. "You've had your chance at that. And when I take you aboard *Audacious* this time, I mean it to be for good."

And it was.

Read on for an excerpt from the next book by
ELIZABETH ESSEX

A BREATH OF SCANDAL

Coming soon from St. Martin's Paperbacks

Commander William Arthur Jellicoe missed the sea. He missed the clean salt tang of the air, he missed the steady rise and fall of the deck beneath his feet, and most of all, he missed the deep sense of purpose in fulfilling his duty. As far as he could tell, the land offered nothing but inactivity, pretense, and at this particular moment, another silken slave market his mother had all but press-ganged him into attending.

Not that she would have characterized the evening's entertainment in those words. No, his mama, the Countess Sanderson, had decreed Lady Barrington's ball—held at her enormous country house for the purpose of launching off her protégé, a Miss Preston—a glittering affair, an event not to be missed, even though the London "season" had not yet started. The ballroom fairly glowed from the warm light of hundreds of candles, and the air was thick with the smell of beeswax and the heavy scent of too much French perfume.

William thought he would choke.

Ten years at sea in the exclusive company of men had left him feeling ill-prepared for the hidden agendas and managing matrons of even country ballrooms. His sister Claire, on whom he had thought he might depend for companionship and amusement, had disappeared after the second set with a bevy of friends. There had been that promising moment earlier—a bit of a set-to in the second dance—but it had been hushed up and passed over almost as soon as it had begun. He had been there less than an hour and was already contemplating something neither he, nor any of his previous naval commanders had ever considered—a hasty retreat.

Good God. This was what he had come to—uselessly propping up the walls of country drawing rooms.

He needed a drink.

A real drink, not the lukewarm champagne being passed out on trays. The damned starched cravat was strangling him, and the form-fitting evening coat he had been made to borrow from his slightly smaller, older brother felt as hot and tight as a shroud. Why he could not have been allowed to appear in his own comfortable, albeit worn, uniform was beyond him, but so were most of society's strictures. Like the strictures that said a crowded ball was a worthwhile way to pass one's evenings. If it were already this bad his first week back on land, before the family had repaired to London for the season, the coming months would be nothing short of torture.

William shoved himself away from his post against the wall, and ducked down a corridor, steadfastly avoiding the eyes of any female, whom it seemed, always wanted to dance. He had agreed only to escort his mother and sister—he drew the line at dancing with every wallflower in the place. Young ladies' minds were full of desperate agility—they made the mental jump from dance partner to wife in one graceful leap.

And William was not in the market for a wife. Definitely not. That was his older brother's job, to get himself a wife, an heir, and a spare. But without active employment, Will was adrift, out of his element, restless and dissatisfied having been turned ashore at the prime age of two and twenty, but he was determined to while away the time as pleasantly as possible until a ship should come ready and he might be called back into service. Yet, with Napoleon exiled to the island of Elba, it was proving to be a long, thirsty wait. And not one he wanted to pass in the company of giggling, marriage-minded chits and their managing mamas. Or his own managing mama.

He thought of the card room, but while he was in the mood for something to pass the interminable time, his brother had thoughtfully warned him that Lord Barrington's guests played notoriously deep, and he wasn't about to waste his hard-earned fortune or use up his luck on something so foolish as card games.

So William prowled down the dimly lit hallways looking for a more likely place to moor up. There had to be a suitably masculine room—one that contained a drinks tray—along one of these damned endless corridors. His long-legged stride took him around another corner, where the low, orange light shining from beneath a door led him to the perfect haven—a private library, its walls covered in bookshelves and its tall windows mercifully cracked open to the bracing, damp night air.

The room looked to be a wood-paneled sanctuary—a safe, snug harbor where he could while away the evening until he was called to escort his mother and sister home. If there were a just God, the room would house a decanter of brandy.

He shut the door behind him and made for the tray beside a couple of deep armchairs near the low-burning hearth, when a small noise—the faint clinking of glass—made him swivel toward the bookshelves.

William stopped as soon as he saw her. Damn his eyes—a female, looking like a cat at a dog fight, half-crouched behind a table, her eyes wide and dark and still in the firelight. For the longest moment they both just stood there, dead in the water, each hoping the other would be the first to blink.

So bloody much for sanctuary.

William recovered his gentlemanly instincts, and began to back toward the door. "I beg your pardon."

She seemed to recover just as quickly from her start. "Oh," she favored him with an almost imperceptible, dismissive toss of her head. "It's you."

"Is it?" William stopped to take a second look. God's balls. Did he *know* her?

She made him no answer, but turned her back, and without another word, bent back down to peer into a cabinet.

Which treated William to an absolutely spectacular view of the young woman's backside. In the current fashion-of-the-moment, she was clothed in a soft, high-waisted gown of some indeterminate, virginal color, which ought to have appeared demure, but which flowed over her body in a foamy, liquid wave. He tried not to stare, but her lean curves appeared very nice indeed, especially the way they seemed to dissolve into a pair of very long legs.

This was a sight for which the land seemed admirably suited, and one which he had not had the pleasure of viewing for quite some time.

William's curiosity, as well as another, less cerebral part of his anatomy, was piqued.

It took him a moment to drag his brain, and his voice, back up into his throat. "Well, if it *must* be me, may I be of some assistance to you?" It seemed only polite to ask while he stood there perusing her lovely derrière.

"I doubt it." She didn't even spare him a second glance, but continued to rattle through the cabinets.

"What are you doing?" Not that he didn't mind the view.

"Getting a decent drink," she said with some asperity. With that she stood and turned, bottle in hand, having excavated one of Lord Barrington's finer French cognacs from the dark recesses of the cabinet. In the low light, the strong architecture of her almost plain face was thrown into relief. She looked as ardent as a ship's figurehead, long and slender in her flowing gown, with her chin tossed up, daring him to gainsay her.

It was *she*—the girl from the dance floor. The one who had knocked Gerry Stubbs-Haye down with a carronade of a right. In the half-dark of the firelight, she looked much less the brawny Amazon than she had standing over old Stubby's prone form. At this distance, her chin, though tipped up defiantly, had a definite wobble.

And, if the dark, liquid shine in her eyes was any indication, she looked near tears.

Oh, fuck all. William had a definite weak spot for young women in distress. Half the whores on Gibraltar knew that all they had to do to earn a coin was gift him with a tear and a tale of woe. But if there were to be tears and tales of woe, a decent drink was an absolute necessity.

With that thirsty thought in mind, William said, "Well done," and turned to cross the dark, patterned carpet to the tray, from which he produced two crystal glasses. "I hope you don't mind if I join you?"

Her surprise was evident in the look she gave him—all chary, narrow suspicion, with her lips pressing together and her eyes creasing ever so slightly at the corners. But it forestalled the tears. "You're not going to fuss?"

He shook his head even as he smiled. "No. Should I?"

One straight brow bowed up and away, telling him she knew just as well as he that young ladies ought not drink anything stronger than punch, or perhaps wine at dinner. And certainly not clandestine cognac. "Or tattle?"

As long as she didn't cry, or giggle, he didn't give a cold damn what she drank. But she certainly didn't look like a giggler. She looked a bit plain, but somehow interesting in a very direct way. And she had the bottle.

Will raised his hand in solemn pledge. "I am an officer of His Majesty's Royal Navy. I do not 'tattle.' I assure you, you can trust me."

She made a sound that was very nearly a sneer. "Trust. I don't trust anyone."

"Then you are smart. And I like clever girls. I like girls who have cognac even better."

"Do you?" Her eyes flicked over him, up and down—a quick appraisal.

He gave her his best version of a charming grin. "Yes. I consider your intention most refreshing."

"Really?" She tried to look down her pert nose at him. "It was meant to be appalling."

William could feel a laugh build in his chest. She certainly was a saucy little piece of brightwork, and just the sort of wayward girl he liked. Which was to say, she appeared to be unlike every other insipid miss lining the country's ball-rooms, with their simpers and mealy-mouthed smiles.

"You'll have to do better than that, if you hope to appall me. Because you're holding a bottle of very fine, aged French cognac, and I very much hope I can persuade you to share it." He held out the glasses in supplication.

"Said the spider to the fly." Her look was unflinchingly direct. "Don't think I'm not watching you. Try anything and I'll knock your daylights out, too."

"How delightfully bloodthirsty of you to offer, but as fond as I am of a good mill, this evening I am in search only of a decent drink. I'm a sailor you see. We're a notoriously thirsty lot."

His ridiculous pronouncement took her sails aback, and knocked the last of the wobble out of her chin. "Who *are* you?" she breathed.

"Well, I thought you knew. You said, 'It's you,' and I assumed we'd met." William waited for her response before he said more. Who knew what sort of plan she might be engineering behind those innocuous, deep blue eyes? One mention of his family name and she might turn into one of the female fortune hunters.

But the light of avarice didn't appear to be shining in her eyes. The bright sheen of wounded defiance was. It was a look he knew all too well. He'd been a defiant young midshipman once himself.

"No," she admitted. "We haven't been introduced. I only recognized you from the ballroom. You were the only one who—" She shrugged the rest of the sentence away, perhaps still trying to stave off those tears with an attitude of indifference.

"The only one who was impressed?" he offered cordially. "Surely not."

Her eyes slid up to meet his, dubious but curious. "Were you? Impressed?"

"Yes. And amused. I'm Will Jellicoe. Formerly Commander William Jellicoe, of His Majesty's Royal Navy, but at the moment I'm just another half-pay sailor with a power-ful thirst."

Her chary suspicion didn't ease, but she nodded, as if she were storing that little piece of information away in her brain. "If you're in the navy, why aren't you in uniform?"

"Against the rules. Especially for relatively junior, half-pay officers. Especially when my mother commands me otherwise. And my brother, who is apparently an arbiter of male fashion, said it was too shoddy. In fact, he said the damn thing still reeked of tar and black powder. For myself, I hadn't noticed."

The girl looked at him for a long moment, her gaze hold-ing steady with his, as if she were weighing him out. Decid-ing if he really was trustworthy. Then she slid a glance toward the door. "Did you lock it?"

Well, damn his eyes. Perhaps *she* was an heiress wary of fortune hunters. Or perhaps, she was something else entirely.

While that possibility was vastly intriguing, it was also dangerous. Will might have been the second son, but he was not on the market for a rich wife—nor any wife for that matter. And he had absolutely no intention of getting himself in an untenable position by locking himself in a room with a young miss. "No, I assure you, I have no intention of . . ."

But she was walking away from his disclaimer, crossing to the door to try the handle. Yet she didn't open the door, as he had expected, and as propriety demanded. Instead, she dragged a chair up and jammed the back securely under the door handle so it couldn't be depressed. "There," she said as she stepped back. "Now you're safe."

He was *safe*? Locked in a darkened room with a wayward, pugilistic young female who seemed quite experienced at jamming chairs under doors to prevent unannounced entry? Holy hell. His cravat hitched itself tighter. He'd felt safer at Trafalgar.

But damn his eyes, not half as intrigued.

And he was certainly intrigued now, as well as thirsty. And then the wayward girl cemented her appeal by returning directly to uncork the bottle, and pour him a very generous portion of Barrington's finest, before she took the other glass from him, and retreated a safe distance to fill her own.

And while she did so, her surreptitious gaze took a long, meandering trip from the tip of his polished boots to the top of his sandy head.

William decided to sit back in the deep leather chair and let her look. He hadn't any idea what game she was playing, but he was interested enough to see the hand out. She seemed prudently wary of him, keeping her distance, but there were ways around that—patience and charm.

He raised his glass in a toast. "To appalling acquaintances."

And everything changed. She smiled, a slow, secret grin that spread full across her face, and made dimples appear deep in her cheeks. In the low glow of the firelight, the deliciously impish grin made her look pretty and devilishly sweet. The kind of sweet he wanted to taste.

The impulse caught him out of the blue, but when she smiled, she didn't seem so plain, or ordinary. Her drawn, defiant face came alive with warm color and humor, and she became much more of a fey, mischievous woodland creature—all sleek, dark auburn hair and twinkling, knowing eyes the color of the Atlantic on a fine day.

Eyes which raised to his, as she took a seat in the opposite chair. She held up her own glass in reciprocal toast. "Yes. To appalling acquaintances."